IMPERIAL
NIGHT

Ashes of Empire #3

WE SHALL PREVAIL

ERIC THOMSON

Published in Canada
By Sanddiver Books Inc.
ISBN: 978-1-989314-25-8

Sanddiver
Books

PART I – INTO DARKNESS

—1—

A random psychic signal, faint but unmistakable, pierced the veil of Sister Katarin's evening meditation and shattered her serenity. An SOS beacon here? The Void Ships had not rescued any Brethren in well over ten years.

When *Dawn Hunter* passed through the Yotai system five months earlier, headed for the Wyvern Sector on a mission to recover technology that survived the empire's collapse, she hadn't picked up anything. It was, without a doubt, newly activated. But the signal seemed more than slightly incoherent, in a manner Katarin couldn't quite explain. Perhaps the mind powering it didn't belong to a trained member of the Order. Wild talents weren't unusual. In fact, they were appearing more often than before, as if birthed by the apocalyptic end of humanity's first interstellar empire.

But a wild talent in possession of a Void beacon? Only sisters and those few friars with a strong enough talent carried the amulet-like brain wave amplifiers. She opened her eyes and glanced at the tiny cabin's display, where a countdown timer showed the minutes left until *Dawn Hunter* jumped to hyperspace on a course for Wormhole Yotai Four, the first of six wormhole transits still separating them from home. Twenty-five minutes. She reached out and touched the communicator pinned to her black, loose, single-piece garment.

"Katarin to the captain."

A few seconds later, a male voice replied.

"Kuusisten here, Sister. What's up?"

"I'm receiving a Void rescue beacon signal from Yotai."

Lieutenant Commander Alwin Kuusisten didn't immediately reply. When he spoke, it was to ask, "Are you sure?"

"The signal is not particularly intelligible, which makes me believe someone probably found a beacon without knowing what it was, but it's real. And since none of the off-world habitats survived the Retribution Fleet's scouring, it can only originate from the planet."

"Are you telling me we should visit Yotai instead of jumping directly for Wormhole Four?"

Katarin released her legs from the lotus position and stood in a fluid movement that belied her years. Like most Sisters of the Void with a powerful talent, what the more mystical among them called an open third eye, she seemed ageless. The coppery red hair framing her round face remained untouched by gray, though the deepening laugh lines on either side of her snub nose and the crow's feet radiating from the corners of her green eyes marked the passage of time.

Over two decades had passed since she first stepped aboard the former imperial starship *Vanquish* at Captain Jonas Morane's invitation after she and the other survivors of the Yotai Abbey massacre joined his crusade to save a spark of advanced civilization on a distant human colony.

"If you consider the risk acceptable."

Katarin was *Dawn Hunter*'s chaplain and counselor, making her the senior member of the Order aboard. She and three other sisters were auxiliaries holding temporary naval warrants and worked alongside a crew drawn from the Lyonesse Navy. As such, she could only recommend, not issue orders.

Originally owned by the Order of the Void, which used them for commerce, transport, and during the empire's collapse, rescue, *Dawn Hunter* and the rest of the Galactic Dawn fleet now served as reconnaissance and salvage vessels in the Lyonesse Navy. The republic's handful of irreplaceable warships rarely left the Lyonesse wormhole branch nowadays since their sole mission was protecting the planet and its irreplaceable Knowledge Vault.

"Yotai hasn't been a risky proposition in over twenty years, Sister, and we're in no big hurry. I'll ask navigation to update the plot. We should reach its hyperlimit in twelve to fourteen hours. If you're still getting the signal once we come out of FTL, I'll see that we pinpoint its location and send a shuttle."

"Thank you, Captain. The Almighty wouldn't place this across our path without reason. I'd rather investigate than spend the rest of my life wondering whether we left one of ours behind."

"You and me both. Was there anything else?"

"No."

"Kuusisten, out."

Katarin embarked on her usual post-meditation yoga exercises — stretching muscles, loosening joints, and probing her body for signs of weakness or developing health problems. A challenge in her small cabin, but she used the lack of space as an inspiration for unorthodox movements.

Besides, going through the daily routine helped calm a mind seeking plausible answers for the sudden appearance of a Void beacon on Yotai where there was none five months earlier. *Dawn Seeker* had rescued the last beacon holder on that benighted planet shortly before the Retribution Fleet ended Grand Duke Custis' dreams of a second empire with a devastating orbital strike.

If they found a member of the Order, or even a wild talent strong enough to activate the beacon, this voyage would end on a high note after an otherwise unremarkable cruise that had taken them within four wormhole transits of the former imperial capital, Wyvern. They'd recovered some manufacturing machinery, though whether the engineers on Lyonesse could put it to use expanding the star system's industrial base was questionable.

Almost a quarter-century after the last imperial strike groups ravaged rebellious planets, much of the advanced infrastructure in star systems beyond the surviving core around Wyvern had crumbled or simply vanished. Lyonesse wasn't the only world with starships on the hunt for salvage. However, it was probably the only one intent on building an industrial base advanced enough to support thirty-sixth-century technology.

Katarin was working through the last exercise of her routine when her cabin door chimed.

"You may enter," she said without interrupting her motions.

The door slid aside to reveal a young woman clad in the same type of loose, black one-piece garment as Katarin. In her early thirties, with bobbed blonde hair, elfin features and intense blue eyes, Sister Amelia was a graduate of the abbey's training program on her first Void Ship cruise. She politely bowed her head without crossing the threshold, in deference to her superior's tiny personal space.

"I felt a strange sensation moments ago, Sister. It reminded me of the Order's rescue beacon we were taught to identify, but also seemed quite different."

"Well done, Amelia. Yes, that was a beacon. Faint, rather incoherent, but unmistakable. Did Cory and Milene pick it up?" Katarin finished the movement, joined her hands in front of her face, and bowed to end the exercise period.

"No, Sister."

Her answer didn't surprise Katarin. Amelia was one of the stronger talents and trained by Sister Marta, who opened her third eye, while her two cabin mates were older, with less sensitivity, though she couldn't fault their abilities as healers. At this distance, the beacon wouldn't register with them.

"Captain Kuusisten is taking the ship to Yotai so we may investigate and perhaps save one of ours, trained or not."

"Why did we not sense the signal when we came through on our way out?"

"A good question. We won't know until we meet the person presently holding that beacon, but there are many plausible answers. Give me examples, Amelia." Though the young woman's formal training period ended well before *Dawn Hunter* left Lyonesse, Katarin never missed a chance to further her education. Amelia was a crew member for this voyage as part of her ongoing development before she chose a path among the many open to someone with her abilities.

"A ship carrying one of us, Brethren or wild talent, arrived on Yotai in the last five months." Katarin gave her an encouraging nod. "Or someone with the talent, either trained or wild, found a beacon that escaped the Yotai Abbey's destruction while scavenging through the ruins of Lena. It is unlikely any Brethren survived both Admiral Zahar's purge and the Retribution Fleet only to stay in hiding for so long."

Though Amelia was born on Lyonesse within weeks of Grand Duke Custis' rebellion against Empress Dendera and this was her first venture into the wider galaxy, she'd been taught the Order's history, especially the bloody parts. She knew about Pendrick Zahar, now long dead, proscribing the Void and ordering the murder of every sister and friar in the Coalsack Sector. Katarin was among the few who escaped.

They'd been heading for the Order's motherhouse on Lindisfarne aboard *Dawn Trader* when Captain Morane saved them from pirates. Once Morane convinced them their chances of reaching the distant planet via warring star systems was virtually nil, they'd joined his crusade.

"Any more examples?"

Amelia thought for a moment, then shook her head.

"No, Sister. Those cover the possibilities."

"Very well. Please inform Cory and Milene. When *Dawn Hunter* emerges at Yotai's hyperlimit tomorrow, and we get a better sense of the one transmitting, we will continue this conversation."

"Yes, Sister."

"You may go."

Shortly after the ship went FTL, Katarin made her way to the mess compartment for the evening meal. Although *Dawn Hunter* was a naval vessel, rather than refit her to build separate messes for the officers, non-commissioned officers and ratings, the Navy decided everyone would eat together.

Considering the size of a Void Ship's complement, it struck most as a sensible decision at the time. Now, over two decades later, no one questioned the arrangements, although many of those transferring from warship duty to one of the Void Ships found the contrast in atmosphere a tad startling.

As was her habit, Katarin sat with whoever was present after picking up a tray of food from the buffet. Tonight, it was the turn of *Dawn Hunter*'s ordinary and able spacers from the beta watch, currently off duty. Those on the alpha watch would come in one-by-one, eat, and return to their posts while the gamma watch crew members were fast asleep in their bunks.

"Hey, Sister. We understand you picked up a signal from Yotai," Able Spacer Barrand said by way of greeting as Katarin put down her tray and dropped into the single vacant chair surrounding that table.

"It could be someone belonging to our Order, Arils," she replied in a pleasant tone, smiling at him. "Captain Kuusisten is taking the ship past Yotai for a closer look-see. If I'm right, we might take on a passenger."

"Been a long time since any Void Ship picked up a sister or friar," Ordinary Spacer Yera Carp said. "It's strange you should hear a beacon now."

"The Almighty moves in mysterious ways."

Barrand chuckled. "Don't we know it?"

Katarin took a bite of the chicken curry — reconstituted, after this long in space — and chewed on it while a pensive expression crossed her face. The crew members, who recognized her moods by now, steered the conversation in a different direction. She was grateful for their attempt at distracting her, but the nagging sense of strangeness she'd first felt about the beacon grew with each passing hour, and her night proved to be less than restful.

The next morning, a subdued Katarin joined Captain Kuusisten in *Dawn Trader*'s bridge a few minutes before they were due to drop out of hyperspace and silently took a seat at an unoccupied console.

"Sister." Kuusisten glanced at her over his shoulder. "I trust you're well."

"As always, Captain. But I confess to trepidation at finally discovering who is holding an Order of the Void rescue beacon in her hands after this long."

"You and me both."

The first officer's voice over the public address system cut off her reply.

"All hands prepare for transition to normal space in one minute."

A klaxon blaring three times followed the announcement sixty seconds later. Then, Katarin's innards tried to escape while the colors of the rainbow twisted into psychedelic shapes before her eyes. After a few heartbeats, the emergence nausea dissipated, and she heard Kuusisten interrogate the sensor technician.

But before her brain could interpret the petty officer's words, she picked up the signal again. This time it was much stronger. Almost too strong, considering they were still several hundred thousand kilometers from Yotai, and in a flash, she understood why the mind behind it seemed virtually incoherent.

"Captain, we must find whoever has that beacon," Katarin said in a gentle tone.

"Is it a Sister of the Void?"

"No. A wild talent, but not one who can become a sister."

—2—

"Well, well, well. Look who finally stopped by for a visit." Lieutenant General (retired) Brigid DeCarde, the Lyonesse Defense Secretary, dropped into a chair across from Jonas Morane.

The latter, who'd been staring into a half-full beer mug, raised his seamed, angular face and smiled at her.

"Emma's attending one of those endless academic cocktail parties I studiously avoid, and I figured it was time I showed my face in the only place where I'm not automatically fawned over by obsequious ass kissers." He made a hand gesture as if to indicate the main room of the Lannion Base Officer's Mess. "You're the first soul brave enough to approach me uninvited."

DeCarde, a tall, fit, square-faced woman in her early sixties with deep blue eyes and short sandy hair, snorted.

"That's because I know you're only human, like the rest of us, and not a god come down from the heavens so he could save humanity. Why Emma remains active in academic circles years after resigning as Education Secretary is beyond me."

Morane ran splayed fingers through his stiff, silver-tinged black hair, as he often did while thinking, then shrugged.

"I can't figure it out either. But Emma has enough energy for both of us and still terrifies the university's board of trustees and most of the deans, which helps keep their worst instincts in check. Are you staying for supper?"

She nodded. "I'm meeting Adrienne so we can discuss a few matters where the walls don't sprout ears the moment we look secretive. By the way, where are your bodyguards? Don't tell me you ditched them."

"That would be impossible, even for me." Morane nodded toward a taciturn, square-jawed man with short dark hair and a muscular build a few tables over. "Warrant Officer Madden is taking one for the team. The others are next door in the Sergeants' and Petty Officers' Mess, eating their evening meal. It's only because we're deep inside Lannion Base that they're leaving me under Madden's sole protection. You know how those Pathfinders can be."

"Good. Otherwise, I'd be ordering Adrienne to convene a court-martial for dereliction of duty." Movement by the door caught her eye. "And there she is. How about you join us? We can always use the wisdom of Lyonesse's foremost statesman."

"I'd rather not intrude on a conversation between my Defense Secretary and the Chief of the Defense Staff. I'm sure I can find a few old shipmates with whom to break bread."

"Nonsense, Jonas. Adrienne will insist. Having you among us informally is a genuine treat. Let's ask her."

A slender, olive-skinned woman, also in her early sixties, wearing a black Lyonesse Ground Forces uniform with the three stars of a lieutenant general on her collar, took a chair at Morane's table. She studied him with watchful dark eyes for a few seconds.

"Glad you're in the mess enjoying life as a mere mortal for a change, sir." Lieutenant General Adrienne Barca possessed an almost hypnotic, low-pitched, husky voice. "And what did you wish to ask me?"

"Jonas is avoiding one of Emma's cocktail parties and decided he would hang out with the unwashed masses he once led instead of sitting alone in that mansion he calls home, waiting for one of us to beg for his wisdom, permission, or signature."

Barca chuckled.

"Some things never change. Brigid and I were planning on supper in the private lounge so we can discuss a few things where the bureaucrats won't overhear. Please join us. It's been too long since we last enjoyed each other's company in an informal setting."

"I don't want to impose myself. A good leader knows he shouldn't get involved when his people are working out novel ways of keeping him under control."

"Impose yourself? Perish the thought. I insist."

"In that case, I accept, but as I've asked you before, please call me Jonas. When I'm here, I'm nothing more than a long-retired veteran with a life membership in the Lannion Base Officer's Mess."

"My apologies." Barca sounded anything but contrite. "Force of habit. You were my military commander and president for too long."

One of the mess staff, a woman in a crisp white tunic and black trousers, approached their table. She nodded politely at each of them in turn.

"Good evening and welcome. The private dining room is ready, General."

"Thank you, Sarah. Could you please add a table setting and warn the kitchen? President Morane will join us."

The latter gave Barca a sharp glance.

"At once, General."

"And a chair outside the door for his bodyguard."

After Sarah walked away, DeCarde turned her eyes on the republic's head of state and raised a restraining hand.

"Don't get mad at Adri. The staff would be shocked if we called you 'Admiral Morane' or just 'Jonas.' After all, you hold the highest office in this star system. Not that your casual attire reflects that exalted status."

A frown creased Morane's forehead.

"What do you mean casual? This is one of my best business suits. I know better than visiting the mess while looking like a bag of hammers."

DeCarde smirked at him.

"Your suits look better with the accouterments of office."

"I can't always be a fashion plate like you, Madame Secretary."

Barca shook her head in mock despair before climbing to her feet.

"Shall we?"

Morane drained his mug and nodded at Warrant Officer Madden, who stood with the energy of a compressed spring. DeCarde noticed his loose, unbuttoned jacket sported a familiar bulge under the left arm.

"I see Madden is carrying his sidearm even in the mess. Excellent."

"Are you looking for faults in the guard detail, Brigid?"

"No. Just making sure my old regiment is upholding its lofty standards."

As they headed for the corridor leading to the private rooms, Barca said, "Sarah can bring you a fresh pint of ale, if you like, but I've ordered a bottle of the Dereux Grand Cru."

He grinned at her.

"Forget the ale. Only a fool refuses that particular nectar."

"And did you wish to visit the Knowledge Vault afterward? I'll be happy to make arrangements with the duty officer."

"So I can gaze upon endless ranks of hermetically closed starship-grade alloy cabinets?" Morane shrugged. "Thanks for the offer, but I'll pass. The vault's safekeeping is now your responsibility."

"But it is your brainchild," DeCarde pointed out.

The low buzz of two dozen conversations died away the moment they left the main room and entered a softly lit passage paneled in pale wood and decorated with paintings depicting Lyonesse landscapes. Barca led them into what was unofficially dubbed the defense chief's private lounge back when Morane put up the twin stars of a rear admiral and became the first head of the newly independent republic's military establishment. Neither the furniture nor the ambiance had changed since then. It remained a cozy rather than a luxurious space, albeit one without windows since it was set deep inside the granite cliff that housed Lannion Base's primary facilities.

Three settings were carefully laid out on one end of a dark, gleaming wooden table capable of accommodating twenty guests with ease. Wine glasses sat beside each while a dark green bottle held pride of place in the center of the small grouping.

Barca indicated the head of the table where the Chief of the Defense Staff usually presided over private functions.

"Would you like to sit in your old chair?"

"I'd rather you did. That seat is for the admiral or general in command, not the president. I'm merely a last-minute guest."

Barca and DeCarde exchanged glances. At the latter's silent urging, Barca inclined her head.

"As you wish."

Once they were seated, Barca reached out to pick up the wine bottle and served her guests before filling her glass. After placing the bottle back in its spot, she raised the glass and said, "To your health."

"And yours," Morane replied before taking a sip. He nodded approvingly after swirling the wine around his tongue and swallowing. "Excellent vintage. You keep a fine cellar."

"I'm keeping faith with the example you set for us when you were Chief of the Defense Staff." Barca carefully placed her glass on the table. "Ah, here's our first course."

After the server left, Barca said, "I'm meeting with Brigid where I know we won't be overheard because of strange news reported by our intelligence people. I figured if Brigid thought it might be something worrisome, she'd bend your ear. But now that I can tell you directly…"

Morane's eyes lit up with interest. He had created a security unit, initially at company strength, shortly after taking command of the Lyonesse Defense Force to give himself eyes and ears across the settlement area, as well as a military police capability. Those eyes and ears mainly belonged to part-time soldiers, members of the Ground Forces' reserve units who lived and worked or studied within the civilian community. Over the years, Morane and his successors had used the intelligence gathered by this eclectic group to head off many problems before they became political firestorms.

"We're listening," DeCarde said.

"Have you ever heard of a faction within the Order of the Void calling themselves the Lindisfarne Brethren?"

"No." Morane and DeCarde shook their heads in unison.

"Isn't Lindisfarne the Order's homeworld?" The latter asked before taking a bite of her appetizer, smoked fish.

Morane nodded.

"Indeed. That's where *Dawn Trader* was heading when we saved them from those rogue frigates on our way here, remember?"

"Sure. It's on the other side of the empire from Lyonesse, or rather the former empire, right? I wonder whether the Order's motherhouse still stands."

"Chances aren't particularly good. If memory serves, it has several wormhole termini with connections to what were frontier star systems a generation ago." Morane speared a piece of fish with his fork.

DeCarde watched him enjoy the delicate flavors. "They liked living dangerously."

"They preferred living as far from Wyvern and the imperial throne as possible. This is delicious, Adri. But you were saying?"

"Several of my reservists, university students, heard whispers of these Lindisfarne Brethren while interning at the abbey and the outlying priories. Strangely enough, those whispers come mainly from friars and not sisters."

"Did your spies find out what this new faction represents?"

A grimace spread across Barca's face.

"Not directly, but my intelligence analysts examined the Order's activities over the last few years and think the Lindisfarne Brethren want Lyonesse to become the Void's new motherhouse."

"So?" DeCarde asked. "If the Lyonesse Abbey is the only one left, then it becomes the de facto motherhouse."

"Perhaps, but there could be a wholly secular political component. Our records show the Order ran Lindisfarne as a colonial fief. The head of the Order acted as governor in all but name, while the planetary administration was, at least at the higher levels, entirely staffed with Brethren, mostly friars."

Morane cocked a skeptical eyebrow at Barca.

"And you think this Lindisfarne Brethren faction wants control of Lyonesse?"

"Do you still see Sister Gwenneth from time to time? You two were co-conspirators back in the day."

"Sure. She visits Emma and me every few weeks for a day or two of rest and relaxation away from the abbey. We keep it quiet, so the news nets don't pry."

"Did she ever mention the Lindisfarne Brethren or discuss her abbey proclaiming itself the Order's motherhouse?"

"No. We stay away from politics, both the secular and the theological kind, as much as possible. When I'm home, I'd rather talk of anything but those."

Barca took a sip of wine, ate a bite, then asked, "If this were merely a push to re-designate her abbey as Lindisfarne's replacement, don't you think she would have mentioned it? Then there's the apparent secrecy. Again, if it were simply a matter of proclaiming Lyonesse as the home of the Order's motherhouse, why the whispering?"

"Adri could be on to something." DeCarde pointed her fork at Barca. "It's no secret many within the Order think they should be the guardians of the Knowledge Vault instead of the military. Control of the planet's administration would give them their wish."

Morane let out an exasperated sigh.

"I thought we solved that question long ago when I asked Friar Whatshisname, the loudmouth who is the Order's designated boor — pardon me, chief administrator — how many divisions the Almighty could field to protect the vault from barbarians and unscrupulous politicians."

"Friar Loxias. We believe he's one of the driving forces behind these Lindisfarne Brethren."

"Oh." Morane, now wearing a thoughtful expression, finished his appetizer, then sat back and took a sip of wine. "Assuming this faction wants the Order to control Lyonesse and set up a theocracy of sorts, how can they believe the people would stand for it? The planet's original colonists and most immigrants before the empire's fall were fleeing tyranny. They'd never let the Void sweep aside our republic's institutions."

"That is the puzzling part," Barca admitted. "We can spin theories all night long, but short of suborning a sister or a friar and spying on the Lindisfarne Brethren from within, I can't see a way we might determine whether this movement is benign or malign. I was hoping Brigid might ask that you sound Gwenneth out when you next meet. If we can settle the matter while not alarming anyone in the administration, especially the vice president, so much the better. With elections coming up in just under two years, she's more skittish than usual since she fancies herself as your potential successor."

An ironic grin briefly twisted Morane's weathered features.

"Agreed."

DeCarde chuckled at his expression.

"Don't be shy, Jonas. Tell us what you really think of your vice president."

"Charis is a talented administrator, a decent human being, and has Lyonesse's best interests at heart. The fact I'm not a fan of her style is neither here nor there. I made sure the constitution required the senate to choose the president and vice president separately from each other. That means I can't complain if they gave me someone with whom I don't enjoy the same sort of easy relationship as I have with you two. But she's appointed a lot of the right people."

This time, DeCarde scrunched up her face as if she'd caught a whiff of rot.

"Not all of her appointments are what you might consider the right people."

"If you'll recall, I nominated a few duds as well during my first term. Sometimes, you're stuck with folks who aren't your picks because of political considerations. The president serves the people, and the people's various constituencies deserve broad representation at the highest levels."

"How did we turn into politicians? Before landing on Lyonesse, I was nothing more than an honest Pathfinder battalion commander and you a starship captain."

"Someone needed to step up once we decided the empire was finished for good. I'll speak with Gwenneth and find out what's going on in her flock."

— 3 —

Lieutenant Commander Kuusisten, a stocky, muscular forty-five-year-old with close-cropped blond hair and icy blue eyes set deep in a broad, angular face, turned toward Sister Katarin and stared at her with raised eyebrows. "I beg your pardon?"

"I'm almost one hundred percent sure a man's mind is powering that rescue beacon and he's not one of those rare friars whose ability approaches that of the sisters. This mind is too undisciplined, but it feels unusually powerful. We must find him, Captain. One such as he belongs in the abbey, not on a ruined world."

"If you can pinpoint his location, we'll send a shuttle."

Katarin gave him an amused smile.

"My abilities don't work like a targeting sensor. When we're in orbit, I shall give you the general area, then go with the shuttle so I can guide it to the precise spot."

"Understood."

"I should bring Sister Amelia with me. Experiencing a real rescue would serve her well."

"As you wish. There's plenty of room in the shuttle, even if I'll be sending an armed landing party." When he saw the question in her eyes, Kuusisten said, "We don't know what conditions are like on the surface nowadays. If I lose you and Sister Amelia because I neglected basic precautions, I might as well not go home."

Katarin inclined her head in acknowledgment.

"Of course."

After staring at Yotai's image on the primary display for a few heartbeats, Katarin rose and left the bridge to find Sister Amelia. She wanted her opinion of the mind behind the beacon now that they were closer. Katarin intercepted the younger woman as she emerged from her cabin, eyes bright with eagerness.

Amelia halted abruptly and bowed her head. "I was coming to see you."

"Why?"

"The mind of a man powers the beacon, one untrained in our ways."

"You reached this conclusion based on what evidence?" Katarin joined her hands loosely at her waist and watched Amelia with an air of anticipation, head tilted to one side.

"His thoughts are unfocused, undisciplined, yet powerful, but they seem more aggressive than those of our sisters and friars. I cannot tell you why I'm convinced a man carries that beacon, I merely know it is so."

Katarin nodded. "Agreed. Did Cory and Milene hear him?"

"They did, though not as clearly as I, and concur."

"Excellent. You will accompany me aboard the shuttle when we retrieve this wild talent."

Amelia inclined her head again. "I'm honored to take part in the rescue. It's been a long time since the last one."

"Then please prepare. We will leave before the end of the watch."

**

"Sisters."

Lieutenant Koris Leloup, *Dawn Hunter*'s second officer and, for the occasion, leader of the landing party, waved Katarin and Amelia up the shuttle's aft ramp. He, along with the dozen bosun's mates already aboard, was clad in black combat armor with matching battle harness and helmet. They wore the Lyonesse Navy's double-headed condor and anchor insignia above their helmet visors, badges of rank in the center of the chest, and the ship's crest, a stylized representation of the goddess Artemis superimposed on a rising sun on their right upper arms. Few noticed the irony of a pagan deity used to represent a naval vessel that once belonged to a monotheistic religious order. Still, Katarin always felt a spark of amusement every time she saw the badge.

She smiled at Leloup, whose seamed face was the only part of his body not covered by armor, though that would change once he lowered his visor. Commissioned from the ranks, like all Lyonesse officers save for those who once belonged to the Imperial Armed Services, he exuded a calm competence honed by years of salvage missions into the former empire's most dangerous parts.

"Is everything ready, Koris?"

"Indeed, Sister," he replied in a deep, gravelly voice. "Petty Officer Anton is at the controls and expecting both of you on the flight deck. Take the spare jumps seats so you can guide him to the target."

"While you sit at the gunnery station?"

A faint smile played across Leloup's thin lips. "Of course. And you'll stay on the flight deck once we land. Unarmored Void Sisters cannot leave the shuttle."

"And what if we wore the same tin suits as you?" Katarin reached out and rapped Leloup's breastplate with her knuckles.

"You'd still not be allowed out — Captain's orders. We don't know what the conditions are on Yotai and must assume we face a hostile environment. The Void Brethren might hold naval warrants, but you're still non-combatants."

"Understood." Katarin nudged Amelia and nodded at the door leading to the shuttle's flight deck. "Let's settle in."

A few minutes later, the small spacecraft nosed through the force field keeping the hangar deck pressurized when the space doors were open, giving Katarin a splendid view of Yotai from low orbit. At this altitude, the devastation wrought by Empress Dendera's Retribution Fleet a generation earlier was no longer visible, thanks to the fast-growing native flora. However, she knew the slightly discolored patches along major rivers and near most estuaries hid ruined cities.

Once the shuttle was clear, Petty Officer Anton set it on a course that would take them to the area surrounding the ruins of Yotai's former capital, Lena. As they descended, Amelia, under Katarin's close supervision, periodically reached out to touch the map displayed on a screen between Anton and Leloup's stations, her finger tracing ever-smaller rings around Lena and its former spaceport.

None of them spoke a word, though Anton acknowledged each of Amelia's indications with a nod while Leloup used the craft's sensor suite to scan the area. After a few minutes, he let out a grunt of surprise. One of the side displays came to life with an aerial view of what appeared to be the Lena Spaceport's runway, or what remained of it.

The sensor zoomed in with dizzying speed, focused on the wreckage of a small starship that seemed to have crash-landed recently. The surrounding vegetation still showed clear charring from out-of-control thrusters.

"Its crew must have vented the antimatter containment units before landing. Otherwise, there would be nothing left of that ship. Our sensors are picking up one life sign."

"That's it," Katarin said with finality. "Our man is there."

"In or near the crash site?" Anton asked.

"Yes."

Amelia nodded once. "I concur."

"How close do you want me to land, sir?"

The lieutenant glanced at the aerial view.

"That semi-bald spot one hundred meters south-east of the wreck should do. It's almost sunset there, and feral creatures come out after dark on every planet I've visited, so I'd rather not wander across hell's half-acre hoping we won't light up the night. Make sure we land facing it. Our topside weapon station is live."

"Aye, aye, sir."

Upon hearing Leloup's words, Katarin felt a shiver run up her spine. Feral creatures indeed. Now that he'd raised the subject, she could sense a chaotic background murmur of psychic energy, much of it from non-human sources, though what seemed human felt primitive, menacing, and not entirely sane. She exchanged an involuntary glance with Amelia and saw the same thoughts reflected in her eyes.

"A fallen world," the younger woman murmured in a voice pitched for her superior's ears only.

"One of many in a fallen galaxy," Katarin replied in the same tone. "Be thankful we cannot sense the souls of the dead. Otherwise, we would be overwhelmed. Countless millions died here a quarter-century ago."

"I am thankful, Sister." Amelia paused for a few seconds. "Yet I cannot fathom how many disembodied souls are wandering the Void without hope thanks to Dendera and her cursed dynasty. Billions?"

"Many billions. Based on what I've seen and what the other expeditions reported over the years, I daresay three-quarters of our species was immolated on the bonfire of imperial vanity. A catastrophe unmatched by anything in human history." Katarin reached out to squeeze the younger woman's hand. "And yet, we shall prevail."

"From your lips to the Almighty's ear."

"The Void giveth, the Void taketh away."

"Blessed be the Void."

They fell silent again as the shuttle shed its forward momentum and dropped straight down at an ever-slowing rate, riding on its keel thrusters. The wreck's image grew on the side display, but nothing seemed to stir around it, despite Leloup's life sign reading. Surely any human would hear a shuttle's whine slice through the still air of a late afternoon on a depopulated world. Perhaps he was hiding, fearful they might present a danger to his life. Few starships visited Yotai these days, and those that did were almost invariably salvagers interested in digging up tech, not rescuing survivors, unless they worked the slave trade.

The sensation of falling eased away as Petty Officer Anton gently settled them on the cracked, weed-infested tarmac, facing the wreck. Up close and seen from the side, it seemed in worse shape than the aerial view suggested, as if a giant had stomped on the ship's hull, flattening it.

"Definitely a sloop. Damn thing pancaked," Anton muttered. "Her thrusters probably went wonky at altitude. The pilot in me can't help but think it's a sickening sight. How did someone survive that crash?"

Leloup shrugged.

"Maybe he's not a survivor but local talent who took up residence in the wreck. Or he's just scavenging." The second officer paused, then added, "I can see a name on what's left of the starboard hyperdrive nacelle. *Antelope*. No registration number, no energy signature. She's as dead as the empire."

"He's inside the ship," Katarin said in a soft voice. "And he knows we're here. I sense confusion, fear even."

"And anger," Amelia added in a puzzled tone.

"Can you ask him to come out?"

A faint smile creased Katarin's face.

"It doesn't work like that, Petty Officer. We sisters are set to receive only. We can't transmit."

It wasn't the complete truth. Even though the Order's head, Abbess Gwenneth, had decreed they would admit the sisters possessed empathic talents, the fact there were stronger minds among them capable of projecting, remained a closely guarded secret.

"Never mind." Leloup pointed at the primary display. A human figure was emerging from the wreck's shadows. "Drop the aft ramp, Petty Officer.

He stuck his head through the flight deck door. "Chief?"

"Sir," the voice of *Dawn Hunter*'s bosun came from the passenger compartment.

"Disembark and form a security cordon around the shuttle. I'll join you in a moment."

"Aye, aye, sir." A pause. "All right, people, let's go earn our landing party bonus."

Now that she saw the man's face, albeit from a distance, Sister Katarin could sense his emotions in more granular detail, one of the talent's quirks. Centuries ago, visual contact was the only way sisters could connect with another mind. The Order's most powerful teachers eventually overcame that limitation, leading to the invention of rescue beacons and ultimately the survival of many Brethren in the Coalsack Sector after Admiral Zahar unleashed his pogrom.

She touched Lieutenant Leloup's arm as he freed himself from the seat restraints.

"That is a severely damaged human being, Koris. Physically, mentally, and spiritually. Be careful and treat him with kindness. It might become necessary I speak with him, which means leaving the safety of the shuttle despite Captain Kuusisten's orders."

"You'll invoke chaplain's privilege, Sister?"

"My duty to the Almighty and my fellow human beings sometimes trump the captain."

Leloup stared at her for a few seconds, then acquiesced with a nod.

"Okay. Just don't leave the shuttle until I say so. Otherwise, my guts, not yours, will adorn *Dawn Hunter*'s commo array."

— 4 —

Sister Gwenneth, the abbess of Lyonesse and the Order of the Void's de facto leader, stood at her second-floor office window and watched a group of friars installing a Void Orb in the middle of the abbey's central quadrangle. A tall, slender woman in her eighties, she seemed ageless, with unlined, ascetic features beneath a shock of iron-gray hair and intense lilac eyes on either side of an aquiline nose.

Gwenneth didn't quite know how she felt about the Orb, a sphere easily two meters across. Glassy, filled with black matter to symbolize the Void and small sparkling crystals representing stars, it gave the impression of infinite depth. The Order's Rule required major abbeys, those heading sectors, and of course, the motherhouse on Lindisfarne to display such a monument to the Brethren's Creed. She could certainly accept that the Lyonesse Abbey was now the Coalsack Sector's leading house of worship and reflection because of Admiral Zahar's pogroms.

But the Orb slowly floating into place down on the plaza matched that of Lindisfarne, not the smaller, less sophisticated models commonly used for a sector's chief abbey, such as that which once stood on Yotai, where so many of her Brethren were murdered in cold blood.

Gwenneth knew of the growing faction that wanted her to declare Lyonesse the Order's new motherhouse, under the presumption Lindisfarne suffered the fate of every former imperial planet visited by Void Ships during the last two decades. Sister Marta's visions, at least the few she shared with the Brethren, did nothing to dispel that notion.

If truth be told, Gwenneth sensed a mournful emptiness whenever her thoughts reached for the stars. The Lyonesse Abbey could well be her Order's last house, just as this star system might be all that remained of humanity's star-faring civilization.

A faint tap on the open office door broke her contemplation of the Orb and the expectations behind its installation at the heart of the abbey's sprawling complex.

"Sister?"

A welcoming smile lit up Gwenneth's face as she turned.

"Mirjam. Please come in and sit."

The new arrival, one of the Brethren saved during the Void Ship rescue operation, was a short, stout woman in her sixties with the same ageless features beneath a short, practical haircut as most of the old breed sisters. She wore the loose, black, one-piece garment favored by the Order beneath a long, hooded cloak and calf-high soft boots.

"I trust you're well?"

"The Almighty still smiles on me," Mirjam replied, as the office door closed behind her. "And you?"

Gwenneth let out a burst of humorless laughter.

"As well as can be expected under the circumstances, I suppose."

Mirjam studied her superior with amused eyes.

"One might almost suspect you're tired of being our abbess."

"Perhaps. Yet, strangely enough, the Brethren still aren't tired of my leadership."

Abbesses were elected by the members of her abbey and its outlying priories every eight years. Those called upon couldn't decline or resign for anything other than health reasons. And Gwenneth, still spry at an advanced age, was more than halfway through her third consecutive term.

"It is because you stay strong and give us continuity."

Gwenneth snorted.

"It is more because of the abbey's intricate relationship with secular Lyonesse. The work involved in maintaining the delicate balance that keeps the abbey both part of the people and apart from them is too daunting for most."

"Granted. It was easier in the old days when the Order wasn't so intimately involved in preserving a spark of civilization during these grim times. We appreciate your keeping the abbey and its relationship with the government on an even keel."

Gwenneth waved Mirjam's praise away with a dismissive hand gesture.

"How was your trip back from the Windy Isles?"

"Surprisingly comfortable. The new Phoenix Clippers are just as fast as the old Navy shuttles, but more elegant."

"So I'm told. Hecht Aerospace designed a winner. The Defense Force people must be happy."

"Our flight crew were certainly enjoying themselves."

"And the project?"

A pleased smile spread across Mirjam's face.

"We made a breakthrough at last."

Gwenneth's eyes widened slightly.

"Tell me more."

"The three original volunteers underwent a full personality realignment."

"Is it permanent?"

Mirjam nodded.

"We successfully wiped the engrams responsible for their pathologies and removed the memories of their lives before their arrival on Lyonesse without leaving traces. They retain everything else and function as adults of normal intelligence and ability. As planned, they are aware they were sent to the Windy Isles because of past crimes so terrible we could not allow them to live within reach of civil society. They also recall volunteering for personality realignment in the hope of softening their exile. But they will never recall those crimes, nor revert to their earlier selves."

"Congratulations. And the Correctional Service?"

"Governor Parsons and his people believe we achieved our results through psychological treatment, though none of them are convinced we permanently changed the test subjects' personalities. And since we can't reveal our mind-meddling abilities…"

Gwenneth raised a restraining hand.

"One step at a time. Will Parsons at least allow the volunteers to enter the Windy Isles Priory as postulants?"

"He will. That's why I'm here. Since the land on which the priory sits belongs to the Correctional Service, technically, the volunteers will still be exiles serving out a life sentence in the Windies. They can become full-fledged friars for all Governor Parsons cares, but they will never leave the archipelago short of a presidential pardon.

However, he will not assume responsibility for their behavior once they enter the priory and wants a personal statement from you confirming the Order becomes liable for problems involving the subjects."

"Not unexpected. Although Parsons is a progressively minded individual who fervently believes in rehabilitation, our dear penal colony governor remains a bureaucrat through and through."

"I wonder how he would react upon hearing we found a way of permanently curing antisocial personality disorders through engram manipulation. Wouldn't that be any rehabilitation expert's dream come true?"

Gwenneth grimaced.

"It would more likely become the nightmare of any freedom-loving citizen concerned about coercion by a tyrannical government even though personality realignment requires the subject's willing cooperation and cannot be forced."

"I know. But just between you and me, if we wanted, we could find a way of forcing it on non-cooperative subjects."

"Perhaps, but I dislike experimenting without the knowledge and consent of the Lyonesse government, which it would not give in this instance, for ethical reasons if nothing else. Admiral Zahar's actions were warning enough against antagonizing secular rulers. I agree the potential gains of the voluntary treatment far outweigh the risks, but let's not make things riskier by treading where we might violate our own Rule. We shouldn't speak of it again."

"Yes, Abbess. However, I can't stop imagining a society where the mental deficiencies causing chronic criminality are eradicated thanks to our gifts."

"Yet you must push away such thoughts, Mirjam. Concentrate on the three you and your team will take in as postulants. Three souls saved and turned to good works. That's more than most of us achieve in a lifetime. And that's without even counting the next batch of volunteers from among the permanently exiled.

Now, this statement for Governor Parsons, I trust a video recording will suffice?"

The younger woman inclined her head.

"It will, though he wants it authenticated and hand-delivered."

A cold smile briefly touched Gwenneth's lips.

"Parsons is a true bureaucrat. We can quit the empire, but some things will never change."

"Speaking of change." Mirjam hesitated for a second. "I noticed a new Void Orb in the quadrangle when I arrived. Am I correct in thinking it is larger than the normal sector abbey orb?"

Mirjam saw resignation reflected in Gwenneth's eyes as she responded.

"It is. You wouldn't have heard the latest movement among the Brethren, isolated as you are in the Windy Isles Priory, but I face increasing pressure to declare this abbey the Order's motherhouse under the presumption Lindisfarne was destroyed."

"Will you? Or should I not ask?"

"I'm not sure. Doing so means admitting this might be the last abbey of the Order left anywhere in the galaxy. Are we ready for such a momentous step?"

"The Void Ships certainly haven't recovered any Brethren in years, even though they've ranged far and wide across the empire's remains. We could well be the last of our kind." Mirjam tilted her head to one side as she studied Gwenneth. "Or do you fear naming our abbey as the Order's motherhouse might trigger demands we turn Lyonesse into a copy of Lindisfarne, governance, and everything?"

Gwenneth let out a soft snort.

"You always were perceptive. Yes, a few among us might contemplate just that."

"Because it could allow the Order to seize control of the Knowledge Vault. A dangerous path. The military might cheerfully use us as chaplains, counselors, healers, and more, but they'll easily turn against the Order if we overstep our bounds. Surely, everyone is aware of that." When she saw the expression on Gwenneth's face, Mirjam paused as if struck by an idea. "I see. You fear someone might misuse the talent and subtly bend senior government and military leaders to their will."

"It's been done before. The relevant lines in our version of the Hippocratic Oath and the conditioning we impose on sisters who can reach out are no guarantees against misbehavior, just roadblocks. Pendrick Zahar's hatred for us wasn't merely based on scurrilous accusations."

Mirjam's eyes lit up with understanding.

"Oh!"

"Oh, indeed. Do not share this conversation with anyone."

"You may rest assured of my discretion."

"I know."

"And this is why you forbade me to mention involuntary personality realignment again."

"In part."

"Then your fears are genuine."

Gwenneth shrugged.

"Perhaps. Mind you, I could be borrowing trouble when none is brewing. Yet, something is stirring among the Brethren. That motherhouse Void Orb outside is merely the first tangible manifestation. But why now, after over two decades on Lyonesse, when every major issue is settled?"

"Because they are settled? Restless souls will deliberately seek out or manufacture new issues so they may feel alive by debating them. We of the Void are no different in that regard."

"Without a doubt. Perhaps I should identify the most restless among the Brethren and send them on exploration treks across parts of this planet that remain untrod by human feet. We still barely know what lives in most parts beyond the settlement area. I read that many of the native life forms on Isolde differ, sometimes radically, from those native to Tristan."

"Send Tristan to seek Isolde, is that it?" Mirjam's lips twitched. "Not a bad idea. If we can convince Governor Parsons to seek limited presidential pardons, my three realigned personalities would make suitable candidates for an expeditionary group."

"Why? Because they're expendable?"

"No. Because they're keen to serve the Order in whatever capacity that may be. I daresay you'll find them less concerned with comfort and security than most in this abbey. Isolde isn't for the faint of heart."

"She never was," Gwenneth replied with a wry grin.

A soft chime stilled her next words.

"Friar Loxias for the abbess," her aide, Friar Landry, said.

Mirjam gave Gwenneth a wry look.

"Let me guess. He wants you to inaugurate the Void Orb his cronies just planted in the middle of our formerly peaceful quadrangle."

"Probably. Loxias has become, if anything, an even greater annoyance in recent times. If he weren't such an effective chief administrator, I'd send him as far from here as I could."

"Will you inaugurate the Orb?"

"Do I have a choice? Loxias is hardly alone in wanting to enhance our profile." Gwenneth stroked the screen to activate its voice pickup. "Please enter, Friar Loxias."

The door slid aside silently, admitting a tall, heavyset man with short silver hair and a beard framing a square face that was all angles. Hooded dark eyes on either side of a boxer's flattened nose briefly rested on Mirjam before they met Gwenneth's. He bowed his head and said in a basso profundo voice, "Abbess, the Void Orb is ready for your blessing and dedication."

"Very well." Gwenneth stood, imitated by Mirjam. She glanced at the younger woman. "You're welcome to join me."

"Yes, please do. I'm sure the Brethren of the Windy Isles Priory will enjoy a description of this blessed event from your lips, Prioress Mirjam." There was more than a hint of unseemly pride in Loxias' tone, at least to the latter's finely-tuned ears.

"I wouldn't dare miss it," she replied with a straight face.

— 5 —

Lieutenant Koris Leloup stopped within earshot of the solitary figure standing in the shadow of the wrecked sloop. He saw a man who seemed prematurely aged by privation and injury. Tall and whipcord thin, raggedly trimmed salt-and-pepper hair and a short dark beard framed a craggy, worn-out face. It was bisected, on the left side, by an angry red slash running from the bridge of his nose to his ear. Sunken eyes lit by a feverish glint studied him intently.

The man's posture and involuntary twitching hinted at as-yet-unseen injuries, perhaps from the crash. He held an ancient-looking plasma carbine loosely in his hands — although its muzzle was pointing away from Leloup — and wore a spacer's overalls, stained and torn in many spots. A dull metal disk, about the size of an adult man's palm, hung from a chain around his neck — the beacon.

"Who are you, and what do you want?" The man asked in a raspy voice that, to Leloup's ears, seemed distorted by chronic pain.

"My name is Koris Leloup. I'm a lieutenant in the Republic of Lyonesse Navy and second officer of the Void Ship *Dawn Hunter.*"

"Republic of Lyonesse Navy? Void Ship?" He sounded incredulous. "Are you kidding me? I've never heard of Lyonesse, let alone seen an organized naval force in the last twenty years that wasn't just a robber baron's pirate squadron."

"Believe it or not, I'm glad you never heard of Lyonesse. We prefer keeping a low profile. It reduces the chances of attracting barbarians intent on stripping us of advanced technology."

A tortured bark of laughter escaped the man's throat.

"No one has advanced tech anymore, at least not outside what's left of the empire's core. The mad empress blew everything away."

Leloup gestured at the shuttle.

"My ride, built on Lyonesse two years ago, says differently. In any case, we're here to pick you up and bring you with us to Lyonesse."

The man's eyes widened.

"Why?"

"That amulet around your neck is a beacon. We picked up its signal as we were crossing the Yotai system on our way home."

"Bullshit." The man wrapped a hand around the disk and held it up to his eyes. "This is just a hunk of stamped metal."

Leloup spread out his arms, palms facing upward. "And yet, here we are."

"Why should I come with you?"

"Because it's a chance at life on a world the mad empress didn't ravage. A place where things are more or less as they were fifty or a hundred years ago, except we've been a republic, independent of the empire, since the days of the Retribution Fleet. There's nothing for you on Yotai. If you came down in that ship, you'll surely have noticed the absence of lights visible from orbit on the night side. The few humans left here live in pre-industrial tribes and practice subsistence agriculture. They never finished terraforming Yotai, which means survivors will die out when the native fauna and flora reclaim everything."

The man didn't immediately reply as he digested Leloup's words.

"I still don't understand why you landed to offer a stranger sanctuary on a planet I never heard of. You don't know who I am or what I am." He tapped the beacon. "And I still can't believe this thing brought you here."

Leloup hesitated, searching for words. Then, he figured telling the truth, or at least some of it would be best.

"Do you know about the Order of the Void?"

"Sure. Religious types who specialize in good works — teachers, healers, spiritual counselors, that sort of thing. Some folks think they're mind-meddlers, but I figure that's garbage. There was a minor abbey on my homeworld before the mad empress torched everything. Or maybe it was a priory. I never found out. They abandoned it years ago."

"That amulet is a Void beacon. The Lyonesse Navy uses Void Sisters aboard starships. Because you unwittingly activated it, our chaplain, Sister Katarin, believes you're someone who could join the Brethren."

Another incredulous bark of laughter erupted. It quickly turned into a coughing fit. When the man finally recovered, he said, "You're saying the Order of the Void wants to adopt me sight unseen? Doesn't that beat everything? But what the hell. I won't live long in this wilderness, not with my injuries."

"You were aboard that ship when it crashed?" Leloup indicated the wreck with his left hand.

"*Antelope*? Sure. A piece of garbage held together with wire and tape. She shouldn't even be here in the first place, but Barnett — Captain Euclid Barnett, the damn thing's late owner — wouldn't surrender when we came across one of those robber barons I mentioned. Since our crappy guns were no match for theirs, we ran instead. Unfortunately, Barnett's chosen course took us further away from home, and we ended up in this star system aboard a ship low on antimatter fuel and with dying hyperdrives. I'm the only one who came through the crash alive, though most days I wish I'd died too. You could say I'm the last of Barnett's privateers; the Almighty damn him. Give me a moment to fetch my dunnage."

"What's your name?"

"Stearn Roget," the man tossed over his shoulder as he limped toward the gaping airlock.

He reappeared a few minutes later with a duffel bag dangling from his right hand. His left still held the battered plasma carbine.

"Lead me to the promised land, Mister Lyonesse Navy."

"You can leave that gun here, Stearn. Our armory is well equipped and with much newer weapons."

Roget stared at the weapon as if seeing it for the first time.

"No doubt. This thing is as cracked as our main guns were. Nothing worked properly on that damn ship, not even the bloody landing thrusters at the end, which is why we pancaked on the tarmac."

He tossed the carbine to one side and stepped off with grim determination and a visible limp.

"I look forward to hearing your story." Leloup fell into step beside him.

"It's a sad tale, Lieutenant." Roget pulled a palm-sized, gray plastic case approximately one centimeter thick from an inner pocket and offered it to Leloup. "Here, I made a copy of *Antelope*'s database and log before the batteries ran out, just in case."

Leloup accepted the memory card and tucked it in his combat harness pocket.

"Thanks. I'm sure our intelligence folks back home will find that useful. And what about you?"

"Me?" Roget scoffed. "I spent most of the cruise wishing I were back in Shearbrook. That's my hometown, on Scotia Colony, a crappy, barely habitable place out in the ass-end of the Aeolus Sector. It's about as far from Yotai as you can travel and not leave the empire's old sphere. Last I was there, it boasted exactly one barely working spaceport, a place called Haligon."

"Sorry, no idea where that is. I was born on Lyonesse and didn't venture out into the galaxy until well after the empire collapsed. The Navy's pushed out into neighboring sectors on salvage and reconnaissance runs since the mad empress' last strike, but we've pretty much remained in our little galactic neighborhood."

"Then, we share something in common. Neither of us knows about our respective birthplaces. Though yours isn't as screwed up as mine if you have a proper Navy. I suppose I should thank your chaplain for picking up a signal I wasn't aware of transmitting."

"She's aboard the shuttle, watching us from the flight deck and listening in on our conversation, along with her understudy, Sister Amelia."

"Two of them. You must feel blessed."

"Four, actually. Our crew also includes a pair of healers from the Order. The Navy's Void Ships go out on lengthy cruises, many as long as a year, and we need their special abilities for our health and sanity."

Roget glanced at Leloup. "Why do you call them Void Ships?"

"Because the ships that carry out these reconnaissance and salvage missions belonged to the Order before the mad empress' last rampage. Once every surviving sister and friar they could find settled on Lyonesse, the Order turned its fleet over to the Navy. We use the ships to monitor the galaxy while our cruisers and frigates protect the little dead-end wormhole branch we call home. I can't remember when the name Void Ships first came into use, but it was before my time."

As they neared the armored bosun's mates surrounding the shuttle, Roget examined them silently, his eyes moving from one to the next. Leloup led him around to the aft ramp and found both sisters standing just inside the passenger compartment, waiting for them.

"Say hi to Sister Katarin, and her understudy, Sister Amelia. Katarin was part of the first Brethren contingent to settle on Lyonesse."

Roget politely inclined his head.

"Sisters. I understand I should thank you for my improbable rescue. My name is Stearn Roget, of Scotia Colony and the ill-fated sloop *Antelope*."

"I know. We were listening. I'm sure you're extremely curious about why you attracted our attention, and we will answer your questions in good time, but right now, we should leave this place. The sun will drop behind the horizon in a few minutes."

"Excellent idea. We probably don't want to meet the things wandering around in the dark. I barricaded myself inside the wreck every night, but that didn't prevent me from finding signs someone or something tried to break in come morning."

"When did you land?" Leloup gestured at Roget to walk up the ramp.

"Twelve days ago."

"Which explains why the good sisters didn't pick up your beacon on our way through this system when we were outbound."

Sister Katarin pointed at three seats near the door leading to the flight deck. "We will sit there for the return trip since our presence up front is no longer required."

Leloup made a gesture of acknowledgment.

"Sure thing."

At his signal, the landing party climbed aboard with commendable speed, and the aft ramp rose, sealing them in. Moments later, the gentle whine of spooling thrusters reached their ears as Leloup took the gunner's station. Then, they felt the shuttle rise vertically.

"If I never see this place again," Roget said, "it won't be too soon."

"An understandable sentiment," Katarin replied. "What is the extent of your injuries?"

"You name it, I got it — torn ligaments, bruises everywhere, concussion, cracked ribs. My internal organs took a beating if the blood in my piss is any indication. And still, I'm the lucky one."

"How did you alone survive?"

"I was *Antelope*'s second engineer, which means I knew every nook and cranny of that blasted tub inside out. When we were on final approach, something told me things were going pear-shaped. I raced for the most heavily armored part of the ship, a compartment that held both our computer core and served as an auxiliary bridge. I was operating on pure instinct, you understand. I just had time to vent our remaining antimatter fuel and strap into a crash seat when the thrusters seized up. Then everything happened at once, and I lost consciousness. When I woke up, *Antelope* was on the ground, and everyone else aboard was dead."

Katarin and Amelia exchanged a glance before the latter asked, "How many?"

"There were twenty-one of us, from Scotia, all recruited by Euclid Barnett with his damned promise of getting rich as salvagers while helping our planet repair the damage left by the war. Now he and the others are dead, and I'm hundreds of wormhole transits from home." Roget fell silent for a few seconds before continuing in a hushed tone. "They took such a beating during the crash that most were barely recognizable as human. I buried them at the edge of the tarmac as best I could."

Katarin laid a soothing hand on his forearm.

"The Almighty is caring for their souls now. And we shall care for you in the Almighty's name."

"I'm not a man of faith, Sister."

"And yet you are destined to become one of the Brethren."

"Yeah. Lieutenant Leloup mentioned that, but if it's the same to you, I'd rather find a way home. Scotia might not be much, but it's where I was born and where my family lives. I don't care if it takes me years."

Katarin gave him a sad look.

"You won't find one. Even our Void Ships, arguably the best, fastest, and most enduring human starships navigating the wormhole network nowadays, can't make it that far. Besides, the empress ravaged most star systems between Scotia and Yotai, as you might have noticed. The chances of finding someone headed for a no-account minor wormhole junction at the edge of human space are almost nil."

"Sure, but that doesn't help me stop wishing I could see Shearbrook again. So, tell me, why will I become one of the Brethren? You know nothing about me."

"As I said earlier, in good time."

Katarin, trained by the Order to block the emotions of others instinctively, so she didn't go mad, opened her defenses momentarily, and touched Roget's mind. She almost recoiled at the strength of his emotions, at the turmoil he felt, but saw nothing reflected in his eyes. He wasn't aware of himself yet.

A sigh escaped Roget's lips, and he seemed to deflate. "Fine. In good time. Who am I to argue with my saviors?"

She patted his arm. "That's the spirit. First, we will heal your body. Then we can discuss the future."

— 6 —

"Might I be henceforth known as Erasmus, Sister Mirjam?" A deep voice asked in a respectful tone.

She stopped and turned to face the three gaunt, almost ascetic looking men in their late fifties who were following her into the twilight of the priory's entry hall, a refreshing oasis from the humid, tropical air. They wore gray prisoner coveralls with identifiers stamped on the left breast and carried small bags containing the sum of their worldly possessions.

After delivering Gwenneth's release to Governor Parsons upon landing on Changu Island, the atoll's principal landmass, Mirjam fetched the criminals whose antisocial personalities she and her assistants had successfully realigned and led them to the Windy Isles Priory. A simple, yet sprawling stone structure, the priory was nestled among tree-like fern analogs and isolated from the main facilities in its private garden at the far western end of Changu.

The priory was part of the penal colony and within its security perimeter like every one of the inhabited islands straddling Lyonesse's equator at the heart of the World Ocean, almost one hundred and eighty degrees longitude away from Lannion. Those living here were always twelve hours ahead of most humans on the planet. When the sun rose on Changu Monday morning, it was setting over the capital on Sunday evening.

The man who spoke, the eldest of the three, wore what Mirjam thought of as a fresh convert's glow on his narrow face, the sort that smoothed out the deep lines around his prominent nose. Even his silver hair seemed to shine preternaturally, but it was merely an optical illusion caused by the stained glass windows on either side of the wide door. Although he appeared as serene as any of the Order's friars, the frequent bobbing of his prominent Adam's apple betrayed a remnant of unconscious inner agitation. Bright brown eyes deeply set beneath heavy brows watched her intently.

The man had been, until recently, the most dangerous criminal on Lyonesse, someone condemned to exile for life on the imperial prison planet Parth because of his family connections instead of being executed for his crimes. He'd been saved from a slow and agonizing death because a twist of fate put him in a stasis pod aboard the Imperial Correction Service Ship *Tanith*, along with hundreds of political prisoners who'd fallen victim to Empress Dendera's rampant paranoia.

President Morane, at the time captain of the former imperial cruiser *Vanquish* and commander of the 197th Imperial Battle Group's remains, had salvaged *Tanith* after Grand Duke Custis' adherents ambushed and abandoned it. Morane brought her to Lyonesse, where the authorities separated the real criminals from the politicals and ensured the former served out their original sentences.

The man who wanted to call himself Erasmus, along with his two companions, were the most dangerous humans carried in *Tanith* and, therefore, the most dangerous on Lyonesse. But since the empire hadn't ordered their execution, Lyonesse's high court declined to change the original sentence of exile for life. So, they were transported, along with others, to the newly independent republic's version of Desolation Island, from which escape was impossible due to distance, deadly storms, and insanely aggressive aquatic megafauna.

"You may — Erasmus. Why that name?"

He shrugged.

"I can't rightly tell you. It came to me in my dreams last night and feels right. A suitable name for someone who will henceforth be an unselfish person, a servant of the Almighty. It celebrates my rebirth."

"Fair enough." She looked at the other two men. "And you?"

"I'm content to stay known as Shakib," the youngest of the trio, a dark-complexioned, black-haired man with hawk-like features, replied in a soft voice.

"And I as Marnix," the third, a tall, bald, painfully thin individual with leathery skin and a permanent squint said. "Although I feel reborn in the same way as friend Erasmus, no new name came to me in my dreams, and I'll take it as a sign from the Almighty that my current designation is satisfactory."

Mirjam led them on a familiarization tour of the priory, explaining each room's function and the associated protocols along the way, before ending in the dormitory. There, she assigned each a small, monastic cell no different from those occupied by members of the Order including Mirjam. The size of cabins aboard small starships, these cells contained nothing more than a bed with a side table, a small desk with a chair, and a shelving unit for clothes and other items.

"How many of the Brethren live here?" Erasmus asked after carefully unpacking his meager possessions.

"We are forty, all of whom either work as healers, counselors, or agricultural advisers for the inmates and penal colony personnel."

"And what will our role be?"

"You will undergo the training given to every postulant, and then, depending on your aptitudes, you will help the Brethren in carrying out their duties and work in maintaining the priory and its grounds."

"I see." Erasmus met Mirjam's eyes. "And when will we be permitted to leave the Windy Isles?"

"Not for some time, if ever. The president must commute your sentences before you can reintegrate into normal society, which means Governor Parsons or one of his successors will have to convince the Secretary of Public Safety you no longer present a risk. Considering the magnitude of your crimes, you may well spend the rest of your lives as members of this priory, even if the procedure you underwent removed any chance of re-offending."

"I see," Erasmus repeated. His tone betrayed no emotions, not even resignation. "We are no longer prisoners in the penal colony but remain exiles in the isles. What is your Order's saying? The Void giveth, the Void taketh away."

"Blessed be the Void," Mirjam responded. "That is indeed our saying. You will find life among us meaningful and rewarding. Serving others as a way of expiating the sins you no longer remember will repair the damage to your souls. The evening meal is at eighteen hundred hours. You will meet everyone else at that time."

"Will there be an initiation rite?" Shakib asked.

Mirjam shook her head.

"Not for postulants. Should you show yourselves ready to become friars at a future date and Sister Gwenneth, who leads us, approves, we will formally induct you into the Order. You will find clothing in your cells. Please shower and change now, then dispose of the prison garb by adding it to the proper bin in the laundry. Once cleaned, we will return everything to the Correctional Service."

The men inclined their heads by way of acknowledgment.

"Afterward, I recommend silent contemplation in your cells until mealtime. You will find printed copies of our holy books and a treatise on the Order's Rule in your desks."

With that, Mirjam pivoted on her heels and left the dormitory, headed for her office on the principal building's upper floor where the friar assigned as the priory's property manager and now a trainer for the new postulants waited.

As she entered the spacious room overlooking the atoll's central lagoon, Friar Rikkard, one of the many rescued by the Order's fleet of ships and brought to Lyonesse during the empire's collapse, climbed to his feet and bowed from the neck in greeting. Stocky and muscular. with a broad face tanned by the sun and wind, he had bright, observant brown eyes beneath thick brows and wore a neatly trimmed beard, though his skull was as devoid of hair as Marnix's.

"You observed our arrival?" Mirjam nodded toward the bank of displays on the far wall.

"I did. They appear untroubled, but then, their sort are chameleons, able to become whatever others expect of them."

Mirjam dropped into the chair behind her simple wooden desk.

"Still not convinced?"

"I've never seen a violent criminal suddenly develop a conscience. The Almighty might work in mysterious ways, but I doubt men of that sort can be saved before they're called into the Eternal Void."

"And yet our tests prove they no longer show the brain anomalies that took away their humanity."

"Which still doesn't give them a soul, and that means they're what?" After a momentary pause, Rikkard shrugged and answered his question. "Empty vessels, I suppose."

"Ready for your teachings."

"Aye. And I'll do my best to see they become useful members of the Order. Or failing that, non-consecrated servants, since I doubt the president will ever pardon them, and we certainly can't send them back to the penal colony."

Mirjam gave him a brief smile.

"I know. That's why I chose you as postulant master."

Rikkard let out a soft snort of amusement.

"Considering the dearth of friars in this priory, there's not much choice."

"I could have arranged for one of the teaching friars from the abbey."

"True."

"Besides, you possess enough of the talent to detect something going wrong up here." Mirjam tapped the side of her head with an extended index finger. "And that means I need not divert a sister from her duties to watch them."

"Aha! You're not fully convinced either, are you?" A smile split Rikkard's gray beard. "I knew it."

"Oh, I'm convinced the changes we made to their engrams are permanent and removed every last trace of aberrant thought, but Gwenneth urged caution nonetheless."

"And how is our abbess these days?"

"Dealing with internal politics, as usual. How she's done it for so long without tiring is beyond me."

"I hear they erected a motherhouse-sized Orb while you were there. Does that mean Gwenneth will declare Lyonesse the Order's new home?"

"Perhaps. There is growing pressure among the Brethren to do so and break with the past."

Rikkard raised a skeptical eyebrow.

"Just break with the past? I seem to remember the Order exercised a lot of secular power in the Lindisfarne system."

"Gwenneth will never go down that path. Nor will the republic's citizens allow us to meddle in matters of planetary governance."

"Fair enough." Rikkard stood with a vigor that belied his age. "If there's nothing else, I'll introduce myself to the postulants and get a better sense of their characters. One can only divine so much via the security system."

— 7 —

Stearn Roget's eyes fluttered open of their own volition. Within seconds, a blurry face filled his field of view.

"Awake at last, are we?" A low-pitched woman's voice asked. "You gave us quite a scare."

"W-what?"

"Take it easy." The face that came into focus as he adjusted to his surroundings was round, pleasant, and unmarked by age or privation. However, her intelligent brown eyes seemed almost ancient with wisdom, though he also saw a hint of mischief. They met his gaze without guile, and he felt a sense of calm envelop him. A gentle hand landed on his forehead. "Your body was in worse shape than anyone figured. It's a miracle you survived so long after the crash. You collapsed moments after entering my sickbay. We placed you in a medically induced coma."

"H-how long?"

"Seven days. I'm Sister Cory, by the way. *Dawn Hunter's* medical officer. Sister Milene, the assistant medical officer, and I took turns caring for you. She'll be here in a moment. Your internal injuries were extensive. How you survived almost two weeks before we picked you up is a question only the Almighty can answer. But life is vigorous within you, my friend. Extraordinarily so. Your healing has progressed beyond my wildest hopes, which is why I decided it was time to end your coma. We're on our last leg home in case you were wondering. Once we cross this star system, we'll enter the Lyonesse Branch, a wormhole network dead-end well defended by the republic's naval forces. I daresay your troubles are almost over."

"Which system?" Roget's words came out as a broken croak.

"Arietis."

"Never heard of it."

"I'm not surprised." Cory laid a warm, dry hand on his cheek. "Most of the people who lived there when the empire pulled out either emigrated to Lyonesse or found other homes. Last we checked, there were no longer any humans on Arietis. Even the barbarians bypass it, but this system is a major wormhole junction with six termini. One of them leads home, and the one we just exited leads back to where the empire once ruled. The other four connect to star systems on what was once the imperial frontier and were overrun by barbarians, if not outright sterilized."

Roget felt his skin tingle beneath her hand. It quickly spread across his face and into his skull, and the residual throbbing he'd felt moments earlier vanished. But before he could comment, the ship's public address system came to life, though it wasn't nearly as loud in the sickbay as elsewhere aboard.

"All hands now hear this. The traffic control network detected five bogies exiting Wormhole Arietis Three less than four hours ago. The last known course was in the direction of Wormhole Six."

A frown creased Cory's smooth forehead as she withdrew her hand.

"Unless the Navy sent out an expedition during our absence, that's not pleasant news. Wormhole Six is the terminus of the Lyonesse Branch."

Roget sat up slowly, eyes darting everywhere.

"You run a traffic control network in an uninhabited system?"

"Yes, and a subspace relay. We occasionally need to replace the odd wormhole traffic control buoy that didn't go silent fast enough after reporting intruders. But they can no longer surprise the picket ships at the Corbenic end of Wormhole Six, where the Republic of Lyonesse begins. Few survive the attempt even if they make it through the minefield, and none try a second time, because they're either destroyed or captured."

"You mean Lyonesse has the technological base to produce sensor buoys with subspace transmitters?"

Cory nodded.

"And more. We even began building faster-than-light starships from scratch, though none are yet in service. The Navy's combat vessels are former imperial units, and the Void Ships such as *Dawn Hunter* once belonged to the Order of the Void's commercial arm, which means they're old and wearing out. Captured units aren't any better."

"Like *Antelope,* no doubt."

"Oh, based on ship's gossip, she was in even worse shape." When Cory saw the question in Roget's eyes, she chuckled as she raised the diagnostic bed's upper half, transforming it into a backrest. "If you'll recall, you gave Koris Leloup a copy of *Antelope*'s database and log. He uploaded the data and made it accessible. Since we're a little short on fresh entertainment, a lot of crew members are reading up on what happened to your former ship."

Roget leaned back and nodded.

"Of course."

"The fact it took you ninety-one days to reach the Montego system from Scotia has our navigator shaking his head in despair."

A scowl briefly flashed across Roget's face.

"While fixing one failing component after another during the entire trip. Euclid Barnett was a cheapskate and a fool. Oh well. The crash smashed his head like a giant egg, so I suppose he got his comeuppance for what he put us through, the Almighty damn him. The universe is better off without his sort."

"Any man's death diminishes me," Cory quoted in a soft tone, *"because I am involved in mankind. And therefore never send to know for whom the bell tolls; it tolls for thee."*

She gave Roget a tight smile.

"John Donne, from his poem 'No Man is an Island.' He lived two thousand years ago, yet his words still resonate. If you take vows and join us, you'll become familiar with his work and his thoughts. Donne's argument that it was better to examine one's religious convictions with care rather than blindly follow any established tradition — a revolutionary idea at the time — was in many ways a precursor to the Order of the Void's underlying philosophy."

"And when will I find out why I should become one of you, if I may ask, Sister?"

"After a lot of thought and discussion among us, Sister Katarin, who leads our little contingent in *Dawn Hunter*, has decided you should meet our abbess, Gwenneth, on Lyonesse before any further discussion about your future in the Order."

"If I ask why, I suppose you won't tell me."

She patted his arm, then stood.

"You're catching on. And you'll stay here until we're home. I released you from your coma, but you still need around the clock medical attention and plenty of rest. Sister Milene will be here shortly with a light meal, and there's a reader on the side table, connected to the ship's non-classified data stores. Read whatever you want on Lyonesse and the Order of the Void. I must report to Sister Katarin and go through my daily meditation regimen."

"Thank you for everything, Sister."

"Healing is what I do, Stearn. Best thank the Almighty for the vitality he gave you. It made all the difference. Without that physical toughness, you wouldn't have lived until our fortuitous arrival."

"Why would the Almighty care about me? I'm not a man of faith."

"Perhaps the Almighty has plans for you."

With that, Cory left the compartment. Roget picked up the reader and activated it. If he was stuck in an otherwise empty sickbay, he might as well acquaint himself with his saviors.

**

"Reivers?" Lieutenant Joyann Prusak, *Dawn Hunter*'s first officer, and currently officer of the watch, asked as she turned to face Captain Kuusisten.

"It can't be a convoy of Badlands Revival Collective ships intent on saving Lyonesse from the Empress of Darkness. They went out of business when President Morane was just an imperial captain dreaming the impossible dream."

Prusak smirked at her commanding officer's questionable sense of humor.

"Do you think there's any point in contacting the Outer Picket ships and advising them we're inbound?"

"Probably a good idea, even though any situation that might develop will be resolved by the time we reach Wormhole Six." Kuusisten glanced at the communications watchkeeper. "Are we hooked into the subspace relay?"

"Yes, sir."

"Make to Outer Picket. Hunter is plotting the final leg at Wormhole One. Understand bogies traveling FTL between Wormholes Three and Six. Advise if we should wait."

The communications petty officer repeated Kuusisten's message verbatim, and when she received his nod, she sent it off, encrypted, on the Lyonesse Navy's emergency subspace frequency.

"Joyann, we will hold off on going FTL until Outer Picket replies," Kuusisten said.

"Understood, sir." A pause. "Captain?"

"Yes?"

"Sister Cory reports our passenger is awake, lucid, and on the mend."

"Excellent. Ask Sister Katarin if she can meet me in sickbay. I'd like to speak with this mysterious Stearn Roget. If Outer Picket says we can go ahead, take us FTL at once."

"Aye, aye, sir."

Kuusisten and Katarin reached the sickbay door simultaneously.

"Do you still intend to stay silent on exactly how and why we found him?" The former asked.

"Yes. Since Stearn is unaware of his abilities, it's best if we let Gwenneth make the call in a controlled environment such as the abbey."

"You fear he might not be controllable?"

Katarin allowed herself a faint grimace.

"Possibly. We know little about male talents and almost nothing about wild ones. Besides, we should make sure his body's energies are focused on healing."

"I would still like answers about how he found that beacon, Sister. It's been bothering me ever since you first sensed it."

"As would I. Let me ask any questions. Just in case. He may not be aware of his abilities, but they nonetheless manifest through heightened instincts, what laypeople call the sixth sense."

Kuusisten dipped his head in acknowledgment.

"I bow to your greater judgment."

With that, he led the way into the sickbay's recovery room. Its sole occupant raised his head from the reader and stared at them.

"Stearn Roget, I'm Lieutenant Commander Alwin Kuusisten, Republic of Lyonesse Navy and *Dawn Hunter*'s captain. I didn't have a chance to greet you before you collapsed upon arrival. Welcome aboard. I understand you're healing rapidly."

"Thank you, Captain, and apparently, I am."

"Stearn would be dead by now if not for our arrival," Sister Milene said as she entered with a tray from the galley in her hands. A younger version of Cory, with a similar trim to her short, black hair, she nodded politely at her superior and the captain. "A few more days, and he'd have fallen into a natural coma before dying as his internal organs shut down."

Roget's eyes went from Milene to Kuusisten.

"Then I truly owe you my life."

"Saving lives is part of our job, Mister Roget, and we're good at it." He smiled at Milene. "We won't be long, Sister. I know better than standing between a man and his first meal in a week."

A loud rumble came from Roget's stomach, and he gave his visitors a wry grin.

"What I was eating on Yotai wasn't much either."

"Could I just ask about one thing before we let you sample the cuisine?" Katarin asked.

"Anything, Sister."

"Where and how did you acquire this beacon?" She produced the disk in question with the panache of a professional prestidigitator. "It is normally only issued to members of my Order, mainly the sisters, in case of emergency. We rescued every living Brethren in this and the neighboring sectors, and they brought their beacons with them."

Roget's eyes met Katarin's without a hint of guile.

"I found it among the ruins of the Kingstown Spaceport on Montego Colony. We were looking for salvage, and it attracted my attention."

"Why wear it around your neck?"

He shrugged. "Why not?"

"Because it isn't exactly a lightweight piece of jewelry."

"No idea, but whatever instinct drove me proved to be right."

"Fair enough. We can discuss matters after your meal."

"How long until we arrive on Lyonesse?" He asked as Milene put the tray on the bed's swing-out table.

"Three wormhole transits and a little over three and a half star system crossings considering where Lyonesse is on her orbital path at the moment. Call it five more days, provided the bogies currently in this star system don't cause trouble."

"Thank you, Captain."

Katarin touched Kuusisten's arm and nodded at the door.

"Let's leave Stearn to eat in peace."

Once out in the passageway, Katarin made the beacon vanish in one of her garment's many pockets and sighed.

"I'm afraid he's lying."

Kuusisten cocked an eyebrow at her.

"What makes you say that?"

"He's not particularly good at controlling his feelings, though he keeps a remarkably good poker face. But there's something else. We engrave beacons with a mark identifying the abbey that fabricated them. The abbey on Montego Colony didn't make this one. It came from the Valamo Abbey on New Karelia. The same sector, but almost a hundred light-years apart. I'm having a hard time wrapping my head around how a Valamo beacon ended up in the ruins of a Montego spaceport. Sisters, and those few friars with enough talent, activated them only if they thought or knew a *Dawn* ship would cross their star system back during the empire's collapse, when the rescue efforts were underway. Granted, we'll likely never find out what happened in the Aeolus Sector or anywhere else in that part of human space. However, we can take it as a given that beacons don't make a dozen wormhole transits on their own. Not if they hang around the neck of someone running for sanctuary, which in that part of the old empire would be Lindisfarne. Our fleet of Dawn ships never made it that far."

"Why would he lie?"

"Search me. Stearn's mind does not feel tainted, let alone malevolent, although it's so chaotic I can't sense anything useful. I spent enough time in the Windy Isles, working with the worst of the exiles who came with us in *Tanith*, to have met true evil. Roget is undisciplined, but he feels, for lack of a better word, clean."

"Are you afraid he might have taken it from a living member of the Order?"

"Everything is possible, I suppose." Katarin gave Kuusisten a helpless look. "But until we're home and Abbess Gwenneth rules on Stearn Roget's future, there isn't much more I can do, lest I somehow make him aware of his abilities."

— 8 —

The soft chime of an incoming call broke through Lieutenant General Barca's concentration. Since the tone indicated it was her aide, she finished reading the current paragraph while absently stabbing at the screen embedded in her desk.

"What is it, Rian?"

"Message from the operations center, sir," Lieutenant Colonel Rian Krupak replied in his clipped accent. "Outer Picket reports five bogies entering Wormhole Arietis Six. Sensor data from the traffic control buoys show they're not configured as merchant ships. *Dawn Hunter* arrived in the Arietis system at the same time, inbound from her mission, and is holding by Wormhole One at Outer Picket's orders. I've forwarded the buoy imagery to your workstation. Admiral Sirak is monitoring the situation."

"Thank you."

Barca sat back in her chair and swiveled it to face a large window overlooking the Haven River, which lazily wound its way past the republic's government precinct at the heart of the capital.

The first Chief of the Defense Staff worked out of the old garrison commander's office, an aerie with a spectacular view carved into Lannion Base's cliffside. But when the newly formed republic stood up a proper Defense Department, its first elected president, Elenia Yakin, insisted Rear Admiral Morane and his staff move into purpose-built headquarters near Government House on the Haven River's banks. Then Major Barca, along with most officers, breathed a sigh of relief when the service chiefs and their retinues moved out of the Defense Force's main ground installation.

As she stared at the river, Barca called up, from memory, the names of the warships currently assigned to Outer Picket. Since the day Admiral Morane implemented the concept of forward defense, Outer Picket and the string of traffic control buoys and subspace relays were the most critical components of Lyonesse's naval strategy. But unless the senate finally voted enough funds for an orbital shipyard capable of manufacturing frigates or even cruiser-sized vessels, the pickets would gradually lose their punch as the former imperial warships were decommissioned because of age.

The Coromandel class cruiser *Savage*, Outer Picket's lead ship for this rotation, was over fifty years old, and its companion, the Kalinka class frigate *Ivan Rebroff*, wasn't much younger. Still, the first domestically produced faster-than-light man-o-war, a corvette, was rapidly taking shape along the shores of the Middle Sea, south of Lannion.

She would be commissioned as the Republic of Lyonesse Ship *Standfast* early in the new year. Then the Navy would no longer be composed of warships older than their crews, captured reivers of dubious quality, and the equally ancient Void Ships. Another, to be commissioned as *Prevail*, was under construction in an adjoining slip while the components for two more were being assembled nearby.

Barca turned back toward her desk after a fruitless search for the shipyard's outline on the hazy horizon and called up the imagery from the traffic control buoys. Those were not merchant ships. They looked almost exactly like the reivers who had tried their luck in the Lyonesse Branch five years earlier.

Besides, the last honest trader visited Lyonesse nearly fifteen years ago and judging by the Void Ship reports over the last decade, there no longer was any commercial traffic worth mentioning in the Coalsack Sector. Not that Lyonesse was a significant trading hub even well before Dendera lost her mind and then her empire.

Barca's fingers danced on the desktop for a few seconds. Ossian Vara, who commanded *Savage* and Outer Picket, was under standing orders to capture any intruders who entered Corbenic. The star was formerly cataloged as ISC668231-2 until Morane baptized the two sterile systems between Arietis and Lyonesse because he got tired of remembering their numbers. The other now bore the name Broceliande.

But those reivers didn't look like they were in good shape, even to her Marine Corps-trained eye. With Lyonesse's shipbuilding resources focused on the corvettes, there was no point in seizing more dubious hulls that might need scarce materials and parts. Besides, crews for additional ships would be limited until the next few classes went through naval basic and trades training in preparation for the Navy's upcoming expansion.

Perhaps she should rescind those standing orders. Let Vara destroy them if they offered battle or, if they turned tail, let them run. Reivers wanted easy pickings. Allowing this lot to run and spread the word that the Lyonesse Branch of the former imperial wormhole network was well defended might keep future intruder-wannabes from even trying. It wasn't as if the various competing worlds who still possessed the means for faster-than-light travel would suddenly coalesce and form a fleet capable of attacking an obscure planet few remembered even before the empire's destruction.

Barca reached for the intercom, then decided she might as well stretch her legs and walk down one floor to where Rear Admiral Nate Sirak, the Chief of the Naval Staff, had his office. Sirak's aide rose the moment Barca entered the CNS' domain and came to attention. She gave him a friendly wave and crossed the antechamber, ears picking up not only Sirak's voice but that of Major General Devin Hamm, Chief of the Ground Forces Staff, and the first Lyonesse-born officer to reach flag rank.

Both two-stars fell silent the moment she cleared her throat and let out a gentle 'Good afternoon.'

"Sir." Sirak stood while Hamm, who'd been sitting on the edge of his naval counterpart's desk, jumped up and straightened.

"Am I right in thinking your discussion centers on the bogies coming through from Arietis?"

"You are," Sirak replied. "This is the most excitement we've had since the last batch came looking for an easy target."

"What would you say if I rescinded part of the Morane Doctrine and let Ossian Vara give them the chance to reconsider and run?"

Sirak, a lean, black-haired, and dark-complexioned man in his early sixties, considered Barca's question for a few heartbeats.

"We don't need more crappy little ships, and until the corvette program wraps up, we won't have the wherewithal to upgrade them so that they're slightly less crappy little ships. Never mind that the Navy is tight on personnel as well. But I'm not telling you anything you don't already know. That leaves either expending ammunition or letting them run, and though I'm sure

Ossian's gunners would be delighted with a little live-fire training, waste not, want not."

"Those were my conclusions, as well. It's time we move away from the idea of a mysterious Lyonesse Branch, the starship graveyard from which no intruder returns. Let's shake things up and leave would be intruders thinking our wormhole cul-de-sac is too risky short of using a full naval battle group. At some point, star systems desperate for advanced tech will think of bypassing a heavily defended part of the wormhole network and try to cross interstellar space in FTL, as we did before our ancestors mapped stable wormholes. Provided they can enlarge their antimatter containment units, of course, which I believe isn't that difficult."

The CNS shook his head.

"It isn't. Magnetic containment fields are simple in comparison with the rest of an FTL starship's systems. I'll send Ossian orders to scare the bogies and let them run. That is if they don't pick a fight with him."

"Go ahead. Consider the capture or destroy part of the Morane Doctrine shelved. While I have both of you, did our intelligence network pick up anything new on this Lindisfarne Brethren matter?"

"Yes. I intended to mention it at the next command conference," General Hamm replied. "They erected a Void Orb at the heart of the abbey, one that is apparently of motherhouse size rather than normal abbey size. One of my reservists saw its dedication by Sister Gwenneth, who didn't appear overly enthusiastic. Going through the motions were the words he used. Has President Morane spoken with the abbess yet?"

"Not that I know, but he figured it could wait until the next time Gwenneth visited him and Chancellor Reyes, so we don't appear concerned by a matter internal to the Order of the Void.

Considering all they've done for Lyonesse and the Knowledge Vault over the years, it might appear uncharitable."

**

Commander Yulia Zheng, *Ivan Rebroff*'s commanding officer, raised a skeptical eyebrow — or at least her hologram did — when Captain Ossian Vara told her they were to scare away the incoming bogies instead of capturing them.

"Did HQ finally decide the Navy has enough worn-out hulls? If so, I can't say I'm unhappy. It's a given we run the largest naval force in this and the neighboring sectors. Otherwise, one of the Void Ships would have reported something, or the Outer Picket would face more than just an occasional wolf pack. Why shouldn't scavengers, reivers, and other assorted scum find out they can't mess with us? Making ships vanish is good for mystery, not so good for deterrence."

Vara made a face at his younger colleague.

"You're not wrong, but part of me remains a tad cautious about advertising a Navy is protecting the Lyonesse Branch. It'll make the wrong sort of sentient beings wonder how valuable our home system is."

"Perhaps. In any case, the top brass decided. What are your intentions?"

"Pretty much the same procedure as always. Go silent shortly before the reivers are due to cross the wormhole's event horizon, give them a few minutes so they can shake off any disorientation, then light them up with our targeting sensors. Once we have their attention, I'll let them know they can either leave or die instead of demanding they surrender or die."

Zheng, a hard-faced woman in her forties with intense dark eyes and short, jet black hair, let out a soft snort.

"Leave or die just doesn't sound right."

"True. But if we'll no longer operate our version of a black hole that makes ships vanish without a trace, so we keep Lyonesse just as mysterious as her legendary Earth namesake, a softer tone is necessary. It'll be at least another six hours before they exit the wormhole, so I'll call the picket to battle stations at four bells in the dog watch. We'll go silent once both ships are ready."

"Understood, sir."

"Vara, out."

Ossian Vara was a heavy set, dark-haired man in his early fifties, with deep-set brown eyes that missed little. Although he was one of the Republic of Lyonesse Navy's most senior officers, he'd been a mere lieutenant in *Savage* when Task Force 160A's flag officer, Commodore Reginus Bryner, defected to Lyonesse with his five ships more than two decades earlier.

When news came of Yotai's scouring by Empress Dendera's Retribution Fleet, even the most skeptical among the task force's crews had nothing but praise for Bryner's decision. But part of Vara still longed for the days when imperial starships patrolled the wormhole network and kept order throughout a fractious empire.

Since trading the imperial crown for a gold, double-headed Vanger's Condor and anchor emblem, he'd spent almost half his time in space standing guard at this wormhole terminus as part of the Outer Picket. A necessary job, but a boring one, unless hapless reivers peeked down the cul-de-sac. And they were becoming scarce as fallout from the human empire's collapse affected more and more star-faring worlds in this part of the galaxy.

He couldn't even remember the last time an honest trader asked for admittance, but he'd still been a lieutenant, or perhaps a freshly promoted lieutenant commander. It was long before he became the second most senior starship captain in the fleet after Tupo Hak, who commanded *Vanquish*, the Navy's flagship and most powerful unit.

Back then, the crews came from elsewhere. Now, most of them were born on Lyonesse and had no memories of the mighty Imperial Fleet. The fast attack cruiser *Vanquish* was the largest warship they'd ever seen, even if she wasn't particularly powerful compared to the long-vanished heavy cruisers and battleships that gave the empire its mighty fighting power. Few of them ever left the three star systems Lyonesse claimed as her own, other than those who volunteered for Void Ship expeditions, and they were carefully selected.

Vara let out a soft sigh. He had no regrets about his choices, but now and then, he felt nostalgia for a bygone era and a distant birth planet even though both seemed more like fading dreams. He tapped the screen embedded in his day cabin's desk.

"Captain to first officer."

"Sir," Commander Senga's voice replied a few seconds later.

"We will call battle stations at four bells in the dog watch."

"Aye, aye, sir."

— 9 —

"Sensors are picking up heightened radiation levels from the wormhole terminus, sir," *Savage's* combat systems officer announced when Vara entered the cruiser's combat information center. "Fifteen minutes at most until the bogies emerge. The optical commo link with *Ivan Rebroff* is live, and the mines are ready to accept our command codes."

"Thank you." Vara settled into the throne-like command chair and studied the holographic tactical projection dominating the CIC's heart. It showed the position of both ships, the wormhole's terminus disk, and the hundreds of command-detonated mines scattered along the expected exit path.

This would be his first action against intruders as captain, though he'd been *Vanquish's* first officer when she intercepted the last wolf pack that tried its luck. Yet, Vara felt little by way of trepidation, which pleased him. Five sloop-sized reivers against a Coromandel class cruiser and a Kalinka class frigate? It wasn't even a contest, despite the age of both former imperial warships. One broadside would suffice. Two if they raised shields before Vara ordered his ships to open fire.

He heard the door open and knew Sister Brienne, *Savage's* chaplain, was taking her accustomed seat behind him. He turned and nodded politely at her, a gesture she returned with equal formality. Brienne, who'd come to Lyonesse from Arietis as a refugee with her parents when she was barely ten years old, belonged to the new generation trained by Sister Marta, the Order's most revered teacher in living memory. Though only in her mid-thirties, Brienne had so far proved to be an exceptional ship's counselor, capable of dealing with the most troubled souls. Small of stature, with sparkling blue eyes in an elfin face topped by a cap of gleaming auburn hair, her straightforward manner inspired trust.

Yet Vara found her ability to connect with others almost preternatural and kept a professional distance rather than use her as a sounding board and confidante, like so many of his fellow commanding officers did with their chaplains. Vara had noticed those least comfortable around Void Sisters even after so long were almost invariably old-time imperial officers who'd defected with Commodore Bryner and not the survivors of Morane's 197th Battle Group or the Lyonesse natives. Much of that discomfort probably stemmed from the late Admiral Zahar's hatred of the Order.

The minutes seemed to drag by as Vara and his crew waited for the bogies to cross the wormhole's event horizon. Neither he nor anyone else made attempts at small talk. Intercepting intruders was such a rare event nowadays that the tension in the CIC was almost palpable as the crew focused on their duties to the exclusion of everything else.

"Radiation levels are peaking," the sensor chief announced almost precisely fifteen minutes after Vara's arrival.

Those words pulled him from his idle contemplation of the tactical hologram.

"Thank you."

Less than a minute later. "Emergence traces. Five distinct signatures that match the traffic control buoy's sensor readings."

Within seconds, five red icons appeared inside the three-dimensional projection, joining the blue icons representing *Savage* and *Ivan Rebroff* and the green icons denoting the mines.

"Assigning targets," the combat systems officer announced.

Three of the red icons turned into squares, making them *Savage*'s while the other two became triangles, meaning they belonged to the frigate.

"*Ivan Rebroff* confirms."

"Go up systems. Targeting sensors on."

"Up systems and sensors on, aye," the combat systems officer replied in a smooth voice. "Their threat boards should be screaming."

"I make two hundred or so life signs per ship, sir. It seems a lot for small hulls."

A sudden and unexpected gasp came from the back of the CIC. Vara turned and saw Sister Brienne's face twist in anguish, a novel, and unnerving sight. Her voice when she spoke sounded far from its usual, melodic self. It was a hoarse, deep-throated thing that belonged in the furthest circle of hell.

"There is an evil aboard those ships like I've never encountered, nor read of in the Order's annals. You must destroy them. Now."

A chill ran up Vara's spine, though whether it came from Brienne's words or her tone, or both, he couldn't tell.

"Why?"

As she replied, her voice lost most of its eeriness.

"You must remove them from the universe, Captain, lest their evil contaminates everything good."

"How can you tell?" When Brienne gave him an exasperated look, he said, "Right. You just know."

"Captain." The communications petty officer raised his hand. "One of the bogies is calling, text only, in Anglic. They demand to know who we are and why we're targeting them."

"And they raised shields," the sensor chief added.

Two volleys it was.

Vara felt indecision rob him of his plan. He turned away from Brienne, whose eyes still reflected an unearthly glow. But before he could decide on a course of action, she spoke again.

"You wish to open a visual link with the ship calling ours instead of unleashing *Savage*'s cleansing fire. Those are your orders. Know this. They will not appear as you and me, though they are human, at least outwardly. But their souls, if they still have them, are no longer anything the Almighty can recognize. That which animates them is alien. Unfathomable. Something twisted them beyond recognition, and they are a peril to us. One we cannot let escape and infest other worlds still untouched by this corruption, let alone our home."

The certainty in Brienne's tone made Vara hesitate even more. He suppressed the instinct to glance back at her over his shoulder and focused on carrying out his mission, mystical visions be damned.

"Signals, open a visual link with the ship querying us and make sure *Ivan Rebroff* sees everything we see."

"Sir." A few seconds passed. "*Ivan Rebroff* is connected."

"Confirmed," Commander Zheng's disembodied voice reached their ears almost at once.

"And we're linked."

The being whose image swam into view on the primary display was still identifiably human, but barely. Vara ignored Brienne's strangled intake of breath behind him and studied the man intently.

His head was hairless, down to missing eyebrows. Ritual scars and piercings adorned a bony face with sunken cheeks and deep-set eyes while undecipherable tattoos wound their way around his scalp. Irregular greenish-blue splotches marred his scalp and neck while his sclera had turned a deep, unhealthy orange. When he opened his mouth to speak, Vara saw blackened teeth filed to a sharp point.

"Who are you?" His gravelly voice almost matched that used by Brienne moments earlier when she demanded the intruders' destruction.

On impulse, Vara avoided mentioning the Republic of Lyonesse or its Navy.

"I am the guardian of this wormhole junction. You are not welcome here. Turn around, leave, and never come back."

A cruel smile split the man's nightmarish face.

"No. I hear there's an oasis of advanced tech at the end of this wormhole branch, and we will find it."

"Why?"

"Advanced tech means advanced medicine."

Brienne's soft voice caught Vara by surprise. "They're dying, Captain, every single one, though it's a painful and protracted death."

"Who said that?" The man asked in a querulous tone.

Vara's eyes narrowed with suspicion.

"Are you dying? You certainly don't look healthy to me."

"None of your business. If you want a fight, we'll fight, and the devil take the loser. Or you can move out of our way and let us find help." He shook with barely suppressed rage.

"We don't allow visitors."

"Destroy them," Brienne urged once again in a tone pitched solely for his ears. "No one, not even the Almighty, can save them, nor can we allow them near healthy populations."

The man's face turned into a mask of pure hatred.

"Then we'll invite ourselves."

"They're powering weapons," the sensor chief announced.

Vara knew he no longer had a choice. His aging ships couldn't afford a lucky hit from the bogies.

"Open fire."

He felt the vibrations from *Savage*'s launchers almost before his words died away. The Navy carried less advanced Lyonesse-built missiles after withdrawing the last of the old imperial stock from service years earlier. But against indifferently maintained reivers no bigger than imperial sloops, they would suffice.

A howl of rage came through the speakers while the barbarian frothed at the lips. It died just as suddenly when the missile volley struck the bogies' shields. They collapsed with breathtaking speed after cycling through the spectrum of colors from green to deep violet in the blink of an eye.

Streams of plasma erupted from both warships' main guns as the communications link died. Moments later, Vara and his crew watched with something akin to awe as the plasma ate through hulls, creating geysers of flash-frozen air. A weak volley erupted from the bogies' smaller guns, but in vain. They broke apart one after the other as their antimatter fuel containment fields failed, turning them into tiny novae. Secondary explosions continued to dot the wreckage for a few more minutes, and then it was all over.

"I'm not picking up any life signs," the sensor chief finally said, breaking the silence that enveloped *Savage*'s CIC.

"Neither is *Ivan Rebroff*. What the hell just happened, sir?" Zhang, who didn't hear Brienne's warnings, sounded more than a little puzzled. Her hologram popped up in front of Vara's command chair.

"Did that maniac look healthy to you?"

Zhang exhaled slowly. "No."

"Did your ship's counselor pick up anything strange about them?"

"She was unnerved by their appearance, more than I've ever seen, but said nothing." A frown creased Zhang's forehead.

"Sister Brienne believes they were slowly dying from something, which explains why they wanted to find Lyonesse."

"We should retrieve a body and their computer cores so we can find out what was ailing them."

"No!" Brienne's vehemence startled both captains, and they stared at her.

"They were diseased, and we cannot expose ourselves to whatever they carried. The symptoms I detected are so unusual we might face something never seen by our species before now. And if it is new, we almost certainly have no cure."

"Seems to me the guy was rabid at the end," the combat systems officer said.

Brienne inclined her head toward him.

"A good observation. We might indeed find the barbarians suffered from something that attacks the central nervous system. But we must carry out our investigation remotely and cannot bring any of the equipment used back aboard this ship. When we're done, you must incinerate the debris so that no passing ship unwittingly salvages contaminated wreckage."

Something about Brienne's intensity forbade any dissent, and he nodded once.

"It shall be done. Can the medical staff work with the engineering section and modify one of our probes for medical analysis?"

"Yes. I'll let them know right away."

Vara glanced at Zhang.

"Want to tackle finding and remotely downloading one of their computer cores?"

"Sure."

"Excellent. Please go ahead. Signals, call *Dawn Hunter* and let her know she can transit the wormhole at her convenience. In the meantime, I'll draw up a preliminary report for HQ."

As he headed for his day cabin after standing the Outer Picket down from battle stations, Vara couldn't get the image of the unnamed man out of his mind, and it unnerved him more than he cared to admit.

— 10 —

"Good heavens!" Vice President Charis Sandino, a grandmotherly woman in her late fifties with thick, silvery blond hair, sat back in her chair at the foot of the conference table, wearing an alarmed look. Lieutenant General Barca had just finished relaying Vara's report, vividly illustrated with the video of the brief conversation between him and the barbarian. The other attendees, members of Morane's cabinet, seemed equally dismayed. Only the president maintained his inscrutable demeanor. "You're telling me there's a pandemic somewhere out in the badlands and barbarians are spreading it across the former empire?"

"Possibly, Madame Vice President. We don't know what that is yet, but Outer Picket should find answers for us within the next few days. The only thing we can say for sure is that the man who spoke with Captain Vara showed symptoms of something never seen before, and both ship's counselors picked up intensely disturbing brain waves. *Savage's* counselor recommended Vara destroy the reivers at once, which should tell you something. Void Sisters aren't the bloodthirsty sort."

"I trust they'll apply the strictest quarantine protocols," Wevers Rauseo, the Health Secretary and a medical doctor with four decades of practice, said.

"There will be no physical contact between Outer Picket and the intruders' remains, Mister Secretary. They will do everything remotely with droids and probes. The equipment they're using will be destroyed rather than recovered, along with the wreckage." Barca saw nods of approval around the table. "We must assume that this thing is spreading if those affected are traveling through the wormhole network, which means closing off the Lyonesse Branch to traffic until we find out more. Once *Dawn Hunter* is back, I'm suspending Void Ship expeditions until further notice."

"How can we be sure *Dawn Hunter* isn't carrying the disease if it is a disease and not something worse?" Jonas Morane asked.

"We don't, Mister President. I've given orders that *Dawn Hunter* goes no further than Outer Picket. Once *Savage*'s medical people figure out what was wrong with the barbarians, they'll see that *Dawn Hunter*'s medical officer tests everyone aboard. Chances are the crew will be clean. This is the first we hear of an epidemic, and those five ships came from the badlands via Peralka, whose other connections with the Coalsack Sector are rather convoluted."

"What if the people in *Dawn Hunter* caught whatever ailed the barbarians?"

"She'll stay quarantined away from Lyonesse until we develop a cure."

Morane didn't ask what would happen if they couldn't find a cure because he and the other cabinet members already knew the answer. Lyonesse's survival as a world with advanced technology, including faster-than-light travel, was paramount. After more than two decades of isolation in an increasingly hostile galaxy, everyone understood that principle, especially those at the highest levels of government, because their oaths of office explicitly referred to it.

"As well," Barca continued, "I've ordered the Navy to intercept any ship entering the republic's star systems via interstellar space under the presumption it could carry infected crew and passengers. If this group of barbarians was seeking a place with advanced medical capabilities, others like it might do the same but avoid the Arietis wormhole so they can slip past our pickets."

"What are the chances of that?" Sandino asked.

"Impossible to say, Madame Vice President. Not high in my estimation, because any ship attempting such a crossing would need larger antimatter containment units. But the chances aren't zero either. It's, therefore, best if we consider any starship approaching our space as infected until we can prove otherwise. That includes *Dawn Hunter*."

"And Outer Picket, if they screw up the quarantine protocols," Rauseo added in a sour tone.

"They won't. I have full confidence in my people and the Void medical personnel aboard their ships. Both Outer Picket units will stay at least a thousand kilometers from the wreckage, and I've already written off the equipment they'll need for the remote analysis."

"You said none of Outer Picket's healers could identify the ailment based on the symptoms that barbarian displayed."

Barca turned to Defense Secretary DeCarde.

"That's correct, Madame Secretary. And they searched the medical database afterward. I also passed copies of the recording *Savage* made to infectious disease specialists at the Lannion Hospital and the university's medical school, as well as to the Lyonesse Abbey's foremost healers. None could come up with a known illness that would present such symptoms. Chances are we're dealing with a new pathogen. Perhaps it's something that incubated out beyond the empire's sphere for generations and is only now spreading along with barbarians desperate for advanced tech they can't build themselves and can no longer easily steal from outlying imperial worlds."

"Or there could be another source," DeCarde said with a grim expression.

Morane cocked an eyebrow at her.

"Such as?"

"Biological warfare, sir, whether intended or unintended."

Rauseo scoffed. "How can biowarfare be unintended?"

"Simple. The empire operated bioweapon labs. It wasn't exactly a well-guarded secret within the armed forces. Fortunately, the empire built those labs in isolated star systems along the frontier, where accidents wouldn't threaten entire sectors. What if barbarians stumbled across one such lab, broke in so they could salvage tech and accidentally infected themselves with any number of pathogens that they then brought home and spread throughout the badlands during raids?" When she saw her colleague wince, DeCarde nodded sympathetically. "Empress Dendera's final, if unplanned revenge."

"You have a way of making a nasty situation seem even worse, Brigid."

She winked at him. "What can I say, Wevers? It's a natural talent."

"What security classification did you put on this news, General?" Morane asked.

"Top secret special access code name Crichton, sir. Only a few of my people saw Captain Vara's report before I clamped down. The experts at the hospital, the university, and the abbey already held the necessary clearances. They will make sure this doesn't reach civilian ears before we have the facts."

"Good. Once we know what we face, I will decide the next steps, and I'll be the one to tell our citizens of this new threat."

"Of course."

"Was there anything else?"

"No, sir."

"Thank you, General."

Barca drew herself to attention.

"Mister President, Madame Vice President, members of the cabinet. Always a pleasure."

"I wouldn't exactly call this a pleasure," Wevers Rauseo muttered, but Barca and Rauseo's colleagues ignored the comment.

When the conference room door closed behind Barca, Morane looked around the table.

"On to other business. Who's next?"

**

"How did they take it?" Rear Admiral Sirak asked when Barca entered the antechamber to her office. He, along with Major General Hamm and Rear Admiral Atman Au, Chief of the Lyonesse Defense Force Support Command, had assembled moments earlier, warned by Lieutenant Colonel Krupak that Barca was back from Government House.

"About as you'd expect. Secretaries Rauseo and DeCarde, along with the president, were pretty much the only ones who instinctively understood the ramifications. I'm not sure the vice president did, but she said the right things. DeCarde figures we face the results of barbarians breaching containment in one of the empire's old bioweapon labs along the frontier."

Sirak nodded appreciatively.

"Not a bad theory. That barbarian looked like one sick puppy."

Barca waved them into her office and gestured toward the settee group around a low table in one corner.

"Considering our Brigid is rarely wrong, I'd say it's a decent theory. But we'll likely never find out." She dropped into one of the chairs and exhaled. "However, it means we must cut Lyonesse off from the rest of the galaxy until we find a way of protecting ourselves from whatever is running rampant out there. Vara's private notes concerning what Sister Brienne sensed are disquieting. And should it spread across the former empire, there's no telling what that might mean for humanity's survival."

"More the reason for an impenetrable quarantine bubble around Lyonesse," Sirak said. "Nothing enters our wormhole branch, let alone this system, other than our warships. We might not only end up protecting the Knowledge Vault but the human genome itself."

Au made a face.

"I figured the last few years were too quiet."

Sirak reached out and patted his colleague on the shoulder.

"Cheer up, Atman. We could have sent reconnaissance missions into the badlands and unwittingly brought the crud back ourselves. At least Vara and his chaplain figured it out quickly enough and took the right containment measures two wormhole transits away."

"True. So, no more Void Ship missions?"

Barca shook her head.

"No. We can't risk our people, and I doubt *Dawn Hunter*'s expedition netted us much. That means we would need to send the next ones further out, and I'm leery of doing so now that our industrial base looks like its growth might be self-sustaining."

"Would you order *Dawn Hunter*'s destruction if her crew is infected, and we can't find a cure?" Hamm asked.

She raised her hands, palms facing upward, in a gesture of helplessness.

"Do I have a choice?"

"I suppose not."

"Is Sister Gwenneth aware of this?"

"Yes. I spoke with her before roping in the abbey's chief healer."

Hamm cocked an eyebrow. "And what did she say?"

"Trust in the Almighty."

Sirak rolled his eyes theatrically. "The Void giveth, the Void taketh away, blessed be the Void."

—11—

"Sir." The bridge sensor tech raised her hand. "I'm picking up a radiation spike at the wormhole terminus."

Lieutenant Stefan Norum, *Savage*'s assistant combat systems officer, swiveled the bridge command chair to face the sensor station.

"Unless the wormhole went rogue and connected to another star system, that should be *Dawn Hunter*."

"We'll find out for sure in fifteen minutes tops, sir."

"Yep." Norum stroked the screen embedded in the command chair's arm. "Bridge to the captain."

A few seconds passed. "Vara here."

"Officer of the watch, sir. The wormhole terminus radiation levels are spiking. *Dawn Hunter* should cross the event horizon in about fifteen minutes."

"Excellent. Thank you. Vara, out."

Norum turned his eyes back on the starboard secondary display showing the remotely piloted medical probe sifting through the wreckage, looking for a suitable corpse. Though it was a horrible sight, everyone aboard who could do so watched with grim fascination. Piloted from the CIC, the probe carried a small medical lab in its payload compartment instead of the usual sensor package. A medical droid who would manipulate the selected corpse and extract the required samples under its operator's control augmented it.

Ten minutes later, the door to the bridge opened with a sigh. Norum glanced over his shoulder and immediately sprang to his feet.

"Captain on the bridge."

He stepped away from the command chair and waited until Vara sat before reporting.

"Radiation levels at the wormhole terminus are still rising. The medical probe found a suitable corpse, and *Ivan Rebroff* reports they recovered a relatively undamaged computer core."

"Thank you, Lieutenant."

Vara usually kept out of his people's way after issuing orders so they could get on with it. So far, he'd been successful in avoiding the CIC, which served as the recovery effort's operations center. But he felt an overwhelming need to speak with Alwin Kuusisten the moment *Dawn Hunter* crossed the wormhole terminus' event horizon. That last glimpse of the infected man frothing at the mouth just before his ship blew apart was haunting Vara's every waking moment.

"Radiation surge leveling off, Captain," the sensor tech reported shortly thereafter. "And here she is."

A third blue icon appeared inside the bridge's tactical projection, joining those representing *Savage* and *Ivan Rebroff.*

"Signals, open a link with *Dawn Hunter.*"

Moments later, Lieutenant Commander Kuusisten's square face appeared on the primary display.

"*Dawn Hunter* reporting to the Outer Picket, sir."

"Welcome home, Alwin. And welcome to Outer Picket."

"Sir?" A puzzled expression creased Kuusisten's forehead.

"The last twenty-four hours were just a tad strange. We need to talk."

"Those bogies?"

"Yes. I would like this to be a private conversation on your end, so you can decide how you'll handle things. My crew already knows everything."

"Give me a moment, sir. I'll shift to my day cabin."

"Go."

Kuusisten's face vanished as *Dawn Hunter* paused the link, but less than a minute passed before it reappeared, this time with a different background.

"Ready, sir."

Vara recounted everything in detail, adding Defense Secretary DeCarde's suspicion the pathogen might come from an old imperial bioweapon lab. Then he let Kuusisten watch the recording he'd sent back to HQ. As Vara spoke, he saw Kuusisten's face lose its usual ruddy glow.

"The Lyonesse Branch of the wormhole network is officially shut. Now that you've arrived, no one else gets in, and no one leaves. The moment I reported this, General Barca issued the order to consider any vessel approaching Lyonesse either via this wormhole or through interstellar space as a plague ship that should be at the very least stopped and quarantined, *Dawn Hunter* included. You're not going any further until we figure out what happened and make sure no one in *Dawn Hunter* is affected. It means your ship is now part of Outer Picket and under my command."

"Yes, sir. Understood. But so that you know, we're healthy here."

"Perhaps, but since we're in the dark so far, you are quarantined. Nothing leaves *Dawn Hunter*. Not even a shuttle.

If you need supplies, we'll send containers over, and we won't ask you to return the empties, just as we won't recover the probes currently sifting through the wreckage."

When Vara noticed the obvious worry reflected in Kuusisten's eyes, he said, "Spit it out, man. Something's eating at you."

"We rescued a stranded spacer on Yotai. I sent down a landing party, which included two of my Void Sisters. What if they unwittingly picked this virus?"

Vara's right eyebrow crept up. "Talk to me, Alwin."

Kuusisten recounted the events in the Yotai system.

"Damn." Vara, wearing a grim expression, shook his head. "We're hoping those bogies were the first to come out of the badlands with the disease, but there's no telling whether others might have contaminated former imperial worlds in the sector, such as Yotai. And since we don't know what it is, let alone how it's transmitted…"

Kuusisten's shoulders twitched in a helpless shrug.

"My medical officers will run physical exams of the crew and our passenger while we wait for the results of your investigation, just in case. As they say, prepare for the worst and hope for the best. That should be the Navy's unofficial motto if you ask me."

"Never take counsel from your fears, Alwin. The odds are in your favor. If this Stearn Roget was infected on Yotai, chances are good the disease would have manifested in some way by now, considering the weakened state he was in when you found him."

"True." Kuusisten exhaled loudly. "What a mess. Can you imagine if a fatal sickness spreads across the galaxy with the help of rabid reivers? We might be the last humans left in a few years."

"I'm trying hard not to think of it."

"Well, if there was nothing else for the moment, I'll convene my department heads and pass on the joyful news."

"After which, your counselor and medical officers should speak to mine and *Ivan Rebroff*'s."

"Absolutely. With your permission, sir?"

"Go. *Savage*, out."

**

"This bizarre-looking thing," Sister Laerta, *Savage*'s chief medical officer, pointed at the conference room's main display, "is our culprit. A virus unlike any other ever seen, but despite its disturbingly demonic appearance, the pathogen is one that thrives in organisms whose ancestors evolved on Earth. That means it's almost certainly not of alien origin, nor, I suspect, is it of natural origin."

Two tense days had passed since *Dawn Hunter*'s arrival and the medical probe's recovery of a barbarian corpse suitable for analysis.

Vara shook his head in disgust. "Wonderful. So, Secretary DeCarde could be right. It might come from an imperial bioweapon lab looted by barbarians."

"Perhaps. Or this pathogen is natural but has mutated beyond recognition and became something that bears no resemblance to known viruses. We won't be able to tell where it comes from and what it does without further in-depth study. I focused on getting a clear identification so we can search for its presence in *Dawn Hunter*. Besides, we neither have infectious disease specialists nor the proper equipment. Perhaps the Navy could set up a remotely operated lab here — say one module for the lab itself and one unconnected module for researchers — and work with the specimens we've already extracted. If this is spreading throughout human space, we will face it again."

"What about an antiviral?" Lieutenant Commander Kuusisten, or rather his hologram, asked.

Laerta gave him a rueful glance. "Sorry. I'm a generalist, so that would be well beyond my competence. But my findings are already in the hands of the finest specialists back on Lyonesse. And now that we know what to look for, Sister Cory can test whether your crew picked up a nasty little hitchhiker. She'll test your environmental filters as well. If the pathogen is present in the air, it will show up."

Sister Brienne let out an exasperated sigh. "Why would anyone deliberately develop such a horrible thing?"

"Why do humans insist on periodically slaughtering each other in wars of unimaginable destructiveness?" Vara raised his hands, palms up. "Imagine if our major wars hadn't happened. There would be enough humans to colonize half the galaxy by now."

"And do so in peace, one would hope." Laerta looked around the table at *Savage*'s department heads. "I'm open to questions, but beyond identifying the virus, I can't tell you much more about it."

When no one spoke up, Vara tapped the tabletop with his extended fingers.

"Clearing *Dawn Hunter* is the immediate priority. She's been away for the better part of a year, and her people need Lyonesse's pure air in their lungs again. HQ will rule on anything beyond that, but I'll suggest the Navy set up a fully equipped lab that can study what, for lack of a better term, we'll call the Unidentified Virus for now. Any last-minute comments or questions?"

He gave those present, either in person or via hologram, a full minute to respond. No one did.

"Since there's nothing more to discuss at the moment, thank you. Commander Kuusisten, I look forward to your report once Sister Cory and her staff run the tests."

"Sir."

"Dismissed."

The holograms of *Ivan Rebroff* and *Dawn Hunter*'s captains vanished as the department heads stood. Sister Brienne gave Sister Laerta a barely perceptible sign, and both lingered until only they and Vara remained in the conference room.

He looked expectantly from one to the other. "Yes?"

"Even if Cory finds no trace of the pathogen in *Dawn Hunter*'s crew or environmental filters when she runs her analysis," Sister Laerta said, "I'm sure Lyonesse will impose a lengthy quarantine once the specialists back home study my findings. I didn't raise the matter in front of Captain Kuusisten since I'm not qualified to make recommendations, let alone decisions. But we don't know how well this virus can hide, nor what its incubation time is. *Dawn Hunter* could still be a plague ship even if her last contact with a planetary atmosphere was two weeks ago."

"Understood. We'll wait until the experts on Lyonesse pronounce judgment before we let *Dawn Hunter* leave Outer Picket. Until then, she's legally under my command. Captain Kuusisten won't act without my permission. He's a solid officer. One of the best."

"Our survival as the last bastion of advanced humanity, or at least one of the last bastions, may depend on it."

A skeptical expression crossed Vara's face. "I'm not sure it's quite so dramatic, Sister."

"Are you willing to take that chance?"

—12—

"Gwenneth. Welcome!" Jonas Morane beamed at her as he swept his arm toward the open door behind him when the head of the Order emerged from her aircar carrying a small valise.

She returned his affectionate smile with one of her own.

"Jonas. You look as hale and hearty as ever. I didn't notice your guard detail on the way in."

"They noticed you and let me know the moment you crossed the perimeter. We changed protocols, so Emma and I could enjoy more privacy without affecting our security." He nodded at the woods beyond the estate's imitation forged iron fence. "I shouldn't tell you this, but there's a guardhouse hidden among the trees, one undetectable unless you stumble over it. From there, my security team can detect any intrusion and deal with it."

Gwenneth climbed the broad stone steps and followed Morane into the modest two-story house. Sitting on a rise overlooking one of the Middle Sea's many secluded inlets, the home built by Lyonesse's second president and his partner, Emma Reyes, was clad in pinkish-gray granite and topped by a dark green metal roof. It could withstand the worst Lyonesse's weather might throw at it during the stormy season while still allowing for a quiet, genteel life in a subtropical environment. Morane and Reyes had official quarters in a wing of Government House but rarely used them.

The inlet, renamed Vanquish Bay in honor of Morane's former command, was a mere fifty kilometers southwest of Lannion. Less than an hour by land and only fifteen minutes in an aircar — an easy commute for both the republic's president and his now-retired partner.

"You arrived just in time." Emma Reyes, a lithe woman whose silver-tinged red hair and delicate features belied a long life on Lyonesse and other imperial worlds, smiled warmly when they entered the plant-filled solarium. She gestured at the broad expanse of south-facing windows made from transparent aluminum. Menacing clouds were piling up over the open sea at an alarming rate. "I figure it'll be one heck of a soaking, and I so love sitting out a monsoon downpour in here. Watching all that water cascade off the roof will be fun. Are you staying overnight for a change?"

"If you don't mind."

"Of course, we don't mind. You're almost part of the family. Are your Brethren becoming tiresome again?"

"A few of them." Gwenneth gave Morane a nod of thanks when he took her bag.

"It'll be in your usual room. Tea?" He waited for both women to reply before leaving the solarium.

Reyes gestured at well-padded chairs facing the windows.

"Shall we sit and watch the storm?"

"As opposed to discussing the other sort of storm closing on us?" Gwenneth asked with a mischievous smile.

"I'm sure Jonas will guide the conversation in that direction. He was getting a tad bored with his role as president now that the administration is working like a finely-tuned engine. But recent developments perked him up again."

"The unknown pathogen."

"It has everyone in the upper echelons of government and the Defense Force spooked. Or to be more precise, the idea that hordes of rabid barbarians infected with a deadly disease are heading for Lyonesse because they heard we're still an advanced society utterly terrifies them. Did Government House warn you that *Dawn Hunter* would stay with Outer Picket until we're sure no one aboard is a carrier?"

Gwenneth nodded.

"A confidential call from Brigid DeCarde. They're keeping the news closely held. It might be months before *Dawn Hunter* receives permission to come home."

"That's what she discussed with Jonas."

"Who discussed what with me?" Morane, carrying a tea tray, asked as he came through the kitchen door. He placed it on the low table by the chairs and sat across from both women, his back to the increasingly gloomy sky.

"Brigid, concerning *Dawn Hunter*."

"There's no reason she absolutely must come home right away. She's a sound ship, with a crew used to long periods of inactivity in deep space, and she still carries plenty of supplies. If they hadn't landed a party on Yotai, I wouldn't be worried, but Yotai is well within range for roving barbarian wolf packs like the one Ossian Vara destroyed." When he saw the question on Gwenneth's face, Morane said, "He commands the cruiser *Savage*, which is currently Outer Picket's lead ship. A solid officer. One of Reginus Bryner's men back in the day."

An ironic smile lit up Reyes' face. "See what I mean?"

As Morane frowned at her, a distant rumble of thunder reached their ears, and they turned their eyes on a now black horizon.

"I understand the storms lashing Isolde's northern coast this time of year," Reyes waved toward the window as if indicating the southern continent, whose shores lay over a thousand kilometers away, "are much worse than anything we see here."

"And that is why the first humans who colonized Lyonesse settled here rather than there." Morane offered Gwenneth a steaming cup while Reyes helped herself, then he picked up the third and settled back, studying the abbess over the rim of his mug. "Since we're caught up on the plague ship scare, how are you doing, Gwenneth? Do I see a hint of fatigue in your eyes?"

She sighed softly.

"Some days, many days, in fact, I wish I could become the Void's equivalent of an elder stateswoman and spend the rest of my years as a simple sister. But so long as I am sound of mind and body and the Brethren keep electing me, I'm bound by the Rule and must serve as abbess."

"What's driving you to distraction these days?" Reyes asked after glancing at her partner.

Gwenneth took a sip of tea before replying in a thoughtful tone. "Internal politics, if you can believe it."

"Surely you deal with those frequently. No organization is immune, not even a monastic order."

"The latest bit isn't quite as simple." She paused when thunder, this time louder, punctuated her rueful words. "A growing faction among the Brethren believe we're likely the last functioning Void abbey in existence and believe I should declare us the motherhouse. The new Lindisfarne, if you will. Everyone knows about the new and rather large Void Orb now adorning the abbey's quadrangle, one which, not coincidentally, is perfectly sized for a motherhouse. The group calling themselves the Lindisfarne Brethren erected it."

Morane nodded. "We heard. But do I detect reluctance on your part?"

"Very perceptive of you, Jonas. Declaring Lyonesse the new motherhouse has huge psychological implications for the Brethren. It would mean admitting we're the last of our Order, or at least our abbey is the last house still standing. We once numbered in the millions, with abbeys and priories on every human settled world, a fleet of starships, and much more."

"Such as a star system governed by the Order under an imperial charter," Reyes said, eyes on the horizon.

"Yes, that too," Gwenneth admitted without a trace of hesitation. "Though we kept it quiet, for obvious reasons. What an emperor kindly disposed toward the Order can grant, one not so well disposed can take away."

"I'm surprised the Ruggero dynasty let you keep running Lindisfarne."

"Dendera didn't have time to turn her venom on an unremarkable star system far from the imperial capital, and her predecessors were more cunning. They knew incurring our ill will would deprive them of a useful resource."

Another prolonged rumble of thunder, this one still closer, rolled over them, and for the first time, they saw lightning connect the black clouds to an increasingly wild sea. A gust of wind slammed into the house, though they couldn't feel its strength behind the solid walls. The surrounding trees, however, took the full brunt, and their branches danced with alarming vigor.

"Once word of the new pathogen gets out," Gwenneth continued, eyes fixed on the rapidly nearing storm, "the Lindisfarne Brethren will increase their pressure. They will consider it a sign from the Almighty that Lyonesse was chosen as the Order's ultimate sanctuary."

"A tad dramatic, no?" Morane, who'd turned his chair around so he could watch the storm, glanced over his shoulder at Gwenneth.

"Some of my people live for drama, especially now that our existence is mercifully one of quiet contemplation and good works. The Almighty only knows where their teachers went wrong."

Morane snorted.

"You mean friars like Loxias? I can't begin to understand what he's doing among the Brethren."

"Funny you should mention Loxias." Gwenneth's gaze broke away from the horizon as a frown creased her forehead. "He's the leader of the Lindisfarne Brethren and is responsible for the motherhouse-sized Void Orb."

"I'm not surprised. The man always struck me as a blowhard. He should be a politician instead of a monastic."

"Yet he's an accomplished chief administrator. And now you understand why internal politics are draining my energy and patience." Gwenneth drank the rest of her tea and set the cup down with care. "You know friars cannot occupy most of the senior positions within the Order, that sisters always lead abbeys, priories, and minor houses while friars take care of the Order's worldly matters, right?"

"Sure." Reyes nodded.

"I might head the Lyonesse Abbey, but senior friars under Loxias oversee its day-to-day operations. Lindisfarne's governance was this principle writ large. The friars held the levers of worldly power over an entire star system. The most senior friar was the de facto equivalent of a colonial chief administrator, while the Abbess of Lindisfarne was more like an imperial governor with little actual power. Running Lindisfarne gave the most ambitious among our friars an outlet."

"One which the Order no longer has," Morane said in a thoughtful tone. "I think I can see the nub of your problem with restless friars."

At that moment, the first curtain of rain lashed against the windows and glassed ceiling, and they could no longer see Vanquish Bay, let alone the Middle Sea. Furious thunder hammered the air outside while lightning danced as if the demons of hell were loose on Lyonesse.

"At this moment, I feel much like your house, my friends. Beset from every side by a storm and fearing the one brewing in my abbey."

Morane gave her a searching look.

"Am I correct in assuming more than just Loxias and his merry band is bothering you?"

A smile tugged at Gwenneth's lips.

"Could it be I finally know something you don't?"

"You know more than I can ever imagine, Sister."

She gave Reyes a knowing look.

"The republic's leading statesman and yet so modest."

The latter rolled her eyes. "You have no idea."

"I am here, you know," Morane protested half-heartedly even as another barrage of thunder drowned out any possibility of rational thought.

Though it was still mid-afternoon, night had fallen over Vanquish Bay, and the solarium felt like a transparent bunker assailed by the elements yet safe from them.

"*Dawn Hunter* didn't send a landing party to Yotai's surface for just any reason. Do you know who serves as her chaplain and counselor?" When Morane and Reyes shook their heads, Gwenneth said, "Sister Katarin, who you might recall was my companion when we first joined *Vanquish* during our mad rush for safety."

"I remember her well," Morane replied. "As does everyone who was with us."

"What the government doesn't yet know is that Katarin sensed a Void beacon when *Dawn Hunter* entered the Yotai system on her way home, one amplified by an extraordinarily powerful mind. Katarin tracked it to a wrecked starship that crashed on the Lena Spaceport tarmac. Yet it wasn't a Void trained mind but a wild talent that somehow came into possession of a beacon. Extraordinarily, it turned out to be that rarest of all, a male." Gwenneth related the story of Stearn Roget's rescue as reported by Katarin, and how he ended up on Yotai in the first place.

"Katarin believes he might be as strong as Marta Norum and just as ignorant of his ability and destiny as Marta was when she first landed on Lyonesse. She's not told him of his talent, preferring I decide whether the Order takes him on. Some minds cannot be tamed and will inevitably cause strife. But now he's stuck in quarantine, where we can't decide whether he's a threat or a boon."

"Who can make that determination?" Reyes asked.

"Only a few of us. Myself. Sister Marta. A few of the psychologist sisters. Katarin, but she would rather defer to my judgment."

"Is he a danger to *Dawn Hunter*'s crew?"

A grimace briefly crossed Gwenneth's face. "I don't know. My Brethren can block his undisciplined mind, but that doesn't mean he's no threat to the unaware and untrained."

"Aren't Void Ship crews chosen specifically for mental resilience?"

Both Morane and Gwenneth nodded. The latter made a dubious face. "If Katarin is right, this man is in a class of his own, Emma. He should be in the abbey sooner rather than later."

"Wait a minute." Morane sat up as something Gwenneth said finally registered. "He's not one of the Brethren, but he carried a Void beacon. How did that happen?"

The abbess opened her mouth to reply when a bolt of lightning briefly lit up Vanquish Bay before the ensuing thunder drowned out everything else.

Once the sound faded, she said, "He claims he found it in the ruins of the Kingstown Spaceport on Montego Colony, which is plausible since there was a priory in that star system. But the beacon's identifying mark shows the Valamo Abbey made it on New Karelia, a dozen wormhole transits from Montego. Which begs the question, how did it get there? And what happened to the sister or friar who wore it? Katarin thinks Roget is lying but won't pursue the issue until *Dawn Hunter* is home."

"And what do you think?"

"Roget claims his ship was cruising for salvage to help the crew's homeworld stave off collapse. There's not much of a step between salvaging and piracy in these evil times."

"You figure he took it from the neck of a Void sister?"

Gwenneth made a dubious face.

"Anything is possible, but based on Katarin's report, until we can discipline his mind, we can't separate truth from lies with any degree of assurance."

A sardonic expression twisted Morane's features. "Maybe you should send him directly to the Windy Isles Priory upon arrival. Just in case."

"Don't think I'm not considering it. But let's discuss more pleasant things. How is Michael these days?"

The smile of a proud father replaced Morane's earlier, world-weary look.

"Within weeks of graduating basic along with his best buddy Konstantin DeCarde, Brigid's budding Marine heir. By the end of the month, he'll be posted in one of the ships for on-the-job training as a bosun's mate. And Konstantin's off to Ground Forces Battle School. If Michael's still interested in a naval career after doing his three years as a rating, I'm sure he'll pass the officer selection boards without problems."

"The president's son?" Gwenneth grinned. "I should hope not."

Morane wagged his finger at her.

"I don't believe in nepotism, as you well know. And I'll no longer be president by the time he finishes his three years."

The abbess waved away his remonstration.

"I merely meant the son of two people like you and Emma will have more than enough character and intellect for a commission in the Navy."

He snorted, smiling. "Nice save."

— 13 —

"Mister President! Please come in." Lieutenant General Adrienne Barca, imitated by the other four guests, climbed to her feet when Morane entered the Chief of the Defense Staff's private dining room. His close protection officer stopped before the threshold and stepped to one side. "We're glad you could join our little biweekly get-together far from curious ears."

"At ease, please, and good evening everyone." He went around the table to shake hands with Barca, Brigid DeCarde, Rear Admiral Nate Sirak, Major General Devin Hamm, and Rear Admiral Atman Au before taking the single unoccupied chair. "Thank you for the invitation."

"How is Emma?" DeCarde asked once she and the rest were seated.

"In fine fettle, as always. And you'll be glad to know we hosted Sister Gwenneth last week when that big storm hit the coast. I broached the subject of the Lindisfarne Brethren."

Morane reached for the wine bottle and served himself. Two white-jacketed mess employees entered moments later bearing trays with the first course. Once they were alone again, DeCarde and Barca looked at Morane expectantly.

"She brought the name Lindisfarne Brethren up," he said after taking an appreciative bite of the smoked ham. "Our abbess is not a fan of Friar Loxias and his followers. And even though a motherhouse-sized Void Orb now graces her domain, she'd rather not take the ultimate step and admit hers is probably the last surviving abbey. At least not voluntarily."

"Can they force her?" Nate Sirak asked.

Morane nodded.

"If two-thirds of the Brethren formally vote in favor. But historically, communities don't go against the will of long-serving and highly respected abbesses."

"Did you touch on the matter of governance?"

"We did. Gwenneth freely admitted her Order ruled the Lindisfarne system under an imperial grant dating back several centuries but considers it an anomaly in the Void's history, one which any sovereign could easily have corrected by revoking the grant. She made it clear the Lyonesse Abbey would never interfere in the republic's affairs."

"While she's the abbess, perhaps," Devin Hamm said in a skeptical tone. "But how about her successors? Gwenneth is what — in her mid-eighties? How much longer will she lead the Order?"

"If she remains in good health, many more years. Although Gwenneth talks about the joys of becoming one of the Order's elder sisters, living a life of teaching and contemplation without leadership responsibilities, I think she enjoys running the place too much."

"Sounds like our republic's second president, who would gleefully accept a third term if the constitution allowed it." Mischief danced in DeCarde's eyes.

"Hardly. Unlike Gwenneth, I'll enjoy being an elder dispensing wisdom without the burden of presidential responsibilities."

Light conversation accompanied the second and third courses, soup, and roasted chicken, but when the cheese plate and port wine took center stage, Barca steered them back to business.

"I received word from the researchers just before leaving HQ tonight. They cracked the barbarian pathogen's genome, which means they can now work on an antiviral."

The Lyonesse Navy had packed a remotely operated infectious disease research lab into a container and shipped it out in *Dawn Trader* three days earlier, along with a group of researchers who would run the lab from the safety of the ship.

Morane gave her a questioning look. "Barbarian pathogen? Is that what we're calling it now?"

"Among us, yes. The scientists gave it a proper designation, but once the virus becomes public knowledge, our nickname or a variation thereof will stick. At this point, they're fairly confident the pathogen isn't of alien origin but was created in an imperial bioweapon facility."

"Meaning there could be many virulent diseases now running rampant along the frontier and slowly making their way into the old empire via reiver incursions."

Barca nodded. "A distinct possibility, sir. Thankfully, so far, the people in *Dawn Hunter* show no signs of carrying it. They're tested by the ship's medical staff every twenty-four hours."

Morane accepted a glass of port and studied the cheeses on offer.

"How long will *Dawn Hunter* stay in quarantine?"

A grimace briefly crossed Barca's face.

"If it were up to the bureaucrats in the Health Department, a year, no doubt. News that it's a pathogen created in a bioweapon lab will only make things worse. They'll believe Dendera's regime created it as an ultimate means of retribution, with an almost one hundred percent fatality rate."

"What do the scientists believe?"

"The same as us military folks. Creating a bioweapon that remains dormant for weeks inside a human body defeats the entire purpose while giving it a chance to spread beyond the intended target. They're testing live samples in lab-grown human tissue now. We'll know what the pathogen's incubation time is soon enough. Until then, there's no point discussing *Dawn Hunter*'s return home. And that," she said, looking around the table, "was my news of the day. Who wants to go next? Brigid?"

DeCarde inclined her head. "Something interesting came to my attention via one of my colleagues a few days ago. The sisters in the Windy Isles Priory are doing more than just giving the exiles spiritual, medical, and psychological support. They cured three of the worst sociopaths condemned to the Windies for life, men we brought here in *Tanith*."

Morane cocked a skeptical eyebrow at her.

"Did they now? Why am I finding out through you?"

"I'm sure it'll be mentioned during the next cabinet meeting. The men are now postulants and will, in due course, become friars in the Order."

Hamm scoffed. "And won't the good sisters be surprised to find their throats slit when one of these miraculously healed friars backslides."

"Gwenneth seems convinced enough she formally absolved the Correctional Service of responsibility should any of the three commit an offense while living in the priory."

"Are the rest of the exiles for life lining up to become friars and sisters after miraculously finding the Almighty?" Sirak asked in a comical tone. "Talk about a get out of jail scheme."

"They're not getting off the Windies without a presidential pardon, which I won't sign. That means they'll remain at the Windy Isles Priory for the rest of their lives, ministering to the other prisoners." Morane popped a morsel of blue cheese in his mouth and chased it down with ruby red port wine, the kind he enjoyed most. "How did they come up with a way of deprogramming sociopaths without lobotomizing them when medicine has been stumped for fifteen hundred years? Counseling doesn't help develop empathy in uncaring individuals."

"I don't know, and neither does anyone else outside the Order. When questioned, Gwenneth invoked the patient-healer privilege. But she's confident of the results. Didn't she mention this experiment during one of her visits to Vanquish Bay, sir?"

"No, which is passing strange. We often engage in metaphysical discussions over a late-night dram of single malt, so you'd think the matter would have come up, considering they've probably been working on it for a long time." He took another sip of port. "Why use those three hardened criminals who should have died on Parth long ago and not Lyonesse natives for the experiment, I wonder. If you're developing a new procedure, wouldn't it be easier if you experimented on less extreme cases?"

Since no one could answer his question, Barca nodded at Nate Sirak.

"Your turn."

"At this rate, it seems likely our Void Ships won't carry out salvage and reconnaissance missions beyond the Lyonesse Branch for years, if not decades, seeing as how the rest of the old empire has become a cesspool of pestilence. Besides, we'll need more patrol vessels in case intruders bypass the wormhole network. As a result, I'm placing the *Dawns* on regular patrol duties, albeit with half the expeditionary crew strength since they'll stick closer to home port. It means those who've been on post-cruise furlough the longest are being recalled a little early. *Dawn Seeker* and *Dawn Runner* will join 1st Squadron in two weeks. *Dawn Mercy* and *Dawn Glory* will join 2nd Squadron three weeks after that."

Sirak paused for a taste of his port.

"Once *Dawn Hunter* is cleared from quarantine, and provided she presents no maintenance problems requiring time in dry dock, we'll change the crew and send her out. She'll join 3rd Squadron, which will guard both of Corbenic's wormhole termini, in case of an enterprising barbarian skipping the Arietis wormhole via interstellar space. I'm keeping *Dawn Trader* in reserve once she finishes her duties as a deep space virus laboratory. That'll give us five more armed FTL ships capable of discouraging intruders. So far, the reasons for the reassignment of the Void Ships aren't public knowledge, but eventually, we'll need a rationale so we can squash rumors. After twenty years of Void Ship cruises into the former empire, turning the *Dawns* into regular patrol vessels and halving their crews will make tongues wag."

"Point taken, Nate," DeCarde said. "But making the news public is the president's prerogative."

"Of course. I'm just taking advantage of having him among us informally to pass on a message." Sirak glanced at Morane. "As he knows, navies sail as much on rumors as they do on antimatter-powered hyperdrives. The trick is ensuring those rumors push our ships in the right direction."

Morane gave him a nod. "Noted."

"Anything else?" Barca asked.

"No, sir. That's my contribution for this week."

She turned to Devin Hamm. "Anything from the Ground Forces?"

"Nothing much, though I've asked my planning staff to consider purely fictional pandemic scenarios involving large-scale quarantines — just as an intellectual exercise."

"Not a bad idea."

Hamm gave her an ironic, albeit seated bow. "Thank you."

"And what about Support Command, Atman?"

"Same old, same old, General. *Standfast* and *Prevail* are still on track for their appointed launch dates. Construction of the components for the next two is also moving along. Assembling them once *Standfast* and *Prevail* clear their slips will be quick. Say what you want about Hecht Aerospace, they do an outstanding job. Now, if we could convince the senate to green-light construction of the orbital shipyard, we might finally think about building frigates. I can even suggest a historical name for the first one, something I found perusing the history of the human-Shrehari war eleven centuries ago. It would fit with our Navy's pugnacious self-image."

"I think the current crisis might finally convince our esteemed senators it's time we took the next step in building our infrastructure," Morane replied. "But again, no promises. We politicians prefer focusing on the present instead of a future well past our time in office, no matter how vital it might be for the republic's survival."

"I've noticed."

Barca turned her eyes on Morane. "Anything more you'd like to add, sir?"

"No."

"In that case, since our guest of honor is a former naval officer, I'll propose the toast while seated." She picked up her glass of port. "To the Republic of Lyonesse."

The three service chiefs, DeCarde, and Morane, imitated Barca.

"To the Republic. We shall prevail."

— 14 —

"All hands, now hear this." Lieutenant Commander Kuusisten's deep voice over the public address system instantly silenced a mess compartment filled with crew members accustomed to hearing the first officer make routine announcements. Whenever Kuusisten took over, it meant more important news than usual. "The government lifted our quarantine. We will shortly resume our trip home."

Deafening cheers erupted spontaneously. Kuusisten must have expected them because he waited for almost half a minute before continuing.

"I know the last eight weeks loitering within two wormhole transits of Lyonesse after being away for so long sucked. But if we weren't the sort who can deal with prolonged boredom and uncertainty, the Navy wouldn't have selected us for Void Ship duty, right? But that's done. The medicos declared us free of the Barbarian Plague. The duty watch will go to cruising stations. FTL jump in five minutes."

A dozen crew members hastily downed their teas or juices, jumped up with newfound energy, and dropped their meal trays off on the way out of the mess. No one wanted to spend a minute longer than necessary at Outer Picket.

"I guess I'll finally set foot on your sanctuary world, Sister." A faint, yet unmistakably sardonic grin danced on Stearn Roget's lips. "I was wondering whether that would happen before we died of old age."

He and Cory sat at one of the corner tables, enjoying a second mug of tea after yet another reconstituted breakfast.

"It is your sanctuary world now as well," the latter replied. "And if nothing else, our delay has given you the chance to heal in a controlled environment, and I daresay you healed faster than you would have on Lyonesse."

Roget inclined his head by way of acknowledgment. "I'll defer to your greater medical expertise, but why?"

"For two reasons. One, because *Dawn Hunter*'s environmental systems create a more antiseptic atmosphere and two because you faced no outside distractions and could concentrate on Katarin's teachings. Daily meditation, coupled with mental discipline exercises, helps the flesh heal by calming the mind. She says you learn at an extraordinary rate."

"Katarin is a skilled instructor."

"One of our best. You're fortunate to learn from her instead of a regular postulant master. She usually works with sisters intent on becoming counselors and psychologists."

"Isn't her job being a starship counselor?"

Cory made a so-so hand gesture.

"The Defense Force is not a long-term career choice for us. Counselors, chaplains, and healers from the Order generally serve in regular Navy ships for two years before moving on. Void Ships are part of the Navy but separate from the fighting squadrons and aren't continuously in commission like warships. The Navy crews them only for missions, and that's when the abbey sends its strongest volunteers, preferably those with prior service in a warship. Most of us go on one long-range cruise in our lifetimes. But a few, Katarin among them, did two or three over the years."

"And you?"

"This is my first and almost certainly my last. The Void Ship missions won't continue, not if there's the slightest risk of them bringing back something like the Barbarian Plague. If the government kept us quarantined for eight weeks even though we've known for over a month that the incubation period is twelve to twenty days, it won't let our starships leave the Lyonesse Branch for years, perhaps even decades. Certainly not until this virus and any other released from plundered bioweapon labs burn themselves out."

"Meaning Lyonesse will—"

The one minute to jump klaxon sounded three times, followed by the officer of the watch's verbal warning.

"—become an autarky."

Cory nodded.

"In a nutshell. We can only thank the Almighty he gave us over twenty years to prepare. A deadly pandemic in the early days of the republic might have destroyed us."

"Oh, well." Roget shrugged. "It's not like I was contemplating a Void Ship mission at some point. I'm done crossing the wormhole network looking for salvage, and I suppose that in time, I'll accept the idea of never seeing Scotia again."

"As did those of us who settled on Lyonesse with Jonas Morane or who immigrated before the empire collapsed. We still remember the friends and family we left behind, but Lyonesse is our home. And it is now yours."

The jump klaxon sounded again, and then, the universe twisted into a psychedelic mess so nauseating, Roget wished he would have skipped breakfast. But the sensation faded as quickly as it came on.

"What happens when we get there?"

"You'll come with us to the abbey where Sister Gwenneth will test your suitability as a postulant. If she agrees, which is likely, you'll start training under a friar appointed as a postulant master. Later on, we'll figure out what your path should be and make sure you receive the right education, either at the abbey, the university, or as an apprentice."

"Do I get a say?"

"Of course, but by that time, your choices will agree with your superiors' determination. Right now, you're merely a vessel filled with potential, albeit somewhat older than the usual postulants. Your training will turn that potential into abilities which will serve the abbey and the community."

Roget glanced at his empty cup as if wondering where the tea had gone, then up at Cory again.

"What if I don't want to become a friar?"

She gave him an encouraging smile.

"We'll cross that bridge once Sister Gwenneth meets you. However, Lyonesse is a vast planet with less than three million inhabitants. It offers rewarding work for everyone. The abbey will find you a job and a place to live."

"If you say so." He glanced at the time readout on the far bulkhead. "And I'm due for a class with Sister Katarin in five minutes. Thank you for being my breakfast companion."

"Always a pleasure."

**

"That is our home." Sister Katarin, a pleased smile on her face, glanced at Stearn Roget, who stood in front of the mess compartment's main display along with several off-duty crew members, watching Lyonesse's image as *Dawn Hunter* made her final approach. "We'll be on the ground by this afternoon."

"And not a moment too soon." Able Spacer Barrand's face took on a comical air of longing. "I can't wait to breathe fresh air after over a year in this tin can."

"It looks peaceful. Untouched."

"Lyonesse *is* mostly untouched." Barrand pointed at the display. "Ninety percent of the settlements are within a hundred kilometers of Tristan's southern shore, roughly from there to there. No one lives on Isolde."

Roget gave him a curious look. "Why?"

"Too hot, too stormy, and with too many deadly native critters."

"Yep," Ordinary Spacer Carp said. "And we dump our deadly critters on the Windy Isles, which we'll see when we do our orbital pass before landing."

Another crew member snorted derisively.

"Good luck with that. If it's midday in Lannion right now, it'll be nighttime there. We might see a few lights if we're lucky." He slapped Roget on the shoulder. "Make it your life's goal to avoid the Windies, my friend. Other than Correctional Service people, only the worst criminals go there. Most don't come back, and you can't escape."

"Don't forget the Order has a priory on Changu Island," Katarin said. "We take care of the inmates' and correctional staff's medical and spiritual needs."

"Of course, Sister. Forgive me. I avoid thinking of the Windies."

"I figure you should try harder, considering your habits." Barrand's quip drew amused chuckles from his comrades. "Navy personnel aren't exempt from exile."

"All hands now hear this," Lieutenant Prusak's melodious voice on the public address system cut through the banter. "Secure for landing stations. I say again, secure for landing stations."

"We might not even do a full orbital pass at this rate. But who am I to complain?" Barrand grinned at his mates. "Talk to you lot again on the ground."

The spacers filed out of the mess while Katarin beckoned Roget to follow her. "Protocol for off-duty crew and idlers is strapped into your bunk during landing maneuvers."

"And what if my gut tells me the thrusters are failing? Where do I hide?"

She gave him a reproachful look.

"This isn't the *Antelope* you keep damning, and Alwin Kuusisten isn't Euclid Barnett. We'll settle down on the Lannion Base tarmac as gently as can be. I've done more landings in a Void Ship than I care to remember, and none of them ended with so much as a lurch, let alone a bump."

"From your lips to the Almighty's ears, Sister."

Katarin allowed herself a rather worldly snort. "I'm sure the Almighty would rather I keep my lips to myself."

**

"Wow." Stearn Roget's head moved from side to side as he took in Lannion Base's vast expanse when they stepped off *Dawn Hunter*'s belly ramp. "This is something I thought I'd never see again. A working, undamaged spaceport."

Four Void Ships were neatly parked at one end of the tarmac, watched over by aerospace defense emplacements both on the ground and on the heights above. Phoenix Clippers, along with shuttles and military aircraft sat in orderly rows at the other end.

Uniformed personnel, on foot and aboard ground vehicles painted a dull gray, went about their daily business.

"This is the Lyonesse Defense Force's primary base. Most of the installation is inside and beneath the cliff, as you might note from the doors and windows. It was home to an imperial Marine regiment and a naval supply depot long ago. The base has grown a lot over the years. Back when we first arrived, there wasn't enough room on the tarmac for five Void Ships, let alone space left over for the smaller craft. They burned a lot of extra rooms and corridors into the cliff as well. If ever you're interested, perhaps we can arrange for a tour once you've finished your training."

"I'd like that."

A smaller ground car, this one painted black, broke away from the row of parked vehicles and headed toward them.

"The Almighty be thanked. Our ride is here," Sister Milene said in a tone oozing relief. "I, for one, cannot wait to enter the peace and calm of the abbey."

The car glided to a stop beside them, and doors on either side opened as if by magic. A bearded but youthful face popped out on the left, grinning.

"Hail the exploring heroes come home unscathed by the evils of a fallen galaxy."

"Landry! You're a sight for tired eyes," Katarin replied in an affectionate tone. "This is Stearn Roget, who we picked up on Yotai. He might join the Order."

"Welcome, Stearn Roget. Now hop in. Sister Gwenneth awaits."

They complied, and within moments, the car was speeding across the tarmac, headed for Lannion Base's main gate. Roget turned back to study the imposing installation through the rear window until they turned off the primary east-west road and onto a secondary leading away from Lannion. After a brief but silent trip, they spied a sign marking the boundary of Lyonesse Abbey's land grant and passed through fields heavy with ripening grain swaying gently in the breeze before sighting a cluster of gray stone buildings, a few up to three stories high.

What started as an assemblage of old shipping containers when the Brethren rescued by Jonas Morane's 197th Battle Group first moved out of Lannion Base's disused barracks, became, over the years, an imposing replica of a pre-spaceflight Earth monastery, but with every modern convenience. Katarin pointed out and named the various structures for Roget's benefit: administration, dormitory, cloister, refectory, school, hospital and, separate from the main complex, the agricultural and mechanical annexes.

When Landry drove the car onto the quadrangle, the returning sisters noticed the new Void Orb for the first time, and Katarin let out a faint gasp.

"There's a sight I've not seen since Pendrick Zahar leveled the Yotai Abbey." A pause, then, "Wait a minute, that's not an abbey-sized Orb, is it, Landry?"

The young friar shook his head. "No. It's a perfect replica of the Orb on Lindisfarne. Friar Loxias and the Lindisfarne Brethren installed it several weeks ago."

"The what now?" Cory asked.

When the car stopped in front of the administration building, Landry looked over his shoulder at his passengers.

"There is a growing sentiment shared by many that Sister Gwenneth should declare this abbey the Order's motherhouse and Lyonesse the new Lindisfarne. So far, she's dismissed the notion, even though she dedicated the Orb."

An exasperated sigh escaped Katarin's lips.

"Only Loxias could come up with a scheme that essentially declares us the Order's sole survivors and writes off anyone still out there, among the stars. Oh well. Thank you for fetching us, Landry."

"A pleasure, Sister. See you at supper."

They climbed out with their luggage and followed Katarin up the short flight of steps leading to the main door, which stood wide open on such a warm, sunny day. As they entered the wood-paneled lobby, a tall, slender, gray-haired figure in black came down the stairs.

"Welcome home, Sisters. And welcome to what I hope will be your home as well, Stearn Roget."

— 15 —

"I thank the Almighty for sending you back to us in good health." Gwenneth embraced the sisters, then offered her hand to Roget. "And for guiding Katarin to you. I'm Gwenneth. I lead this abbey."

"Sister. I've heard much about you during our long quarantine."

A mischievous gleam appeared in Gwenneth's eyes.

"Don't believe everything Katarin says. She's as good a storyteller as she is a counselor."

"And a wonderful teacher. She showed me ways of controlling some of my inner turmoil, which, I understand, helped my physical injuries heal faster."

"If you join the Order, you will learn even more advanced techniques so you can always be at peace with yourself."

"This abbey certainly strikes me as a restful place. When we arrived, my spirit became lighter, as if I were shedding a burden I've been unwittingly carrying for a long time."

Gwenneth and Katarin exchanged a glance full of significance.

"Many who come here for the first time experience that sensation. This is a place in harmony with the universe. I will speak with Katarin and Stearn in my office. The rest of you may unpack and relax. Friar Herbert won't seek you out for the mission debrief until tomorrow."

Cory, Milene, and Amelia bowed their heads in acknowledgment before filing out of the lobby and back into the sunshine.

"Please follow me." Gwenneth spun on her heels and led them up the polished wooden staircase. Once in her office, she gestured at the chairs grouped around a low table. "We'll be more comfortable there."

Once they were seated, Gwenneth mentally reached out and touched Roget's mind. Only decades of practice allowed her to keep an impassive face when she sensed its strength.

"Katarin told you we take in people who show certain characteristics and train them as sisters and friars so they can serve others by fully developing their hidden traits."

"Yes. But she didn't tell me what these characteristics are, so I'm not sure why I should become a friar instead of finding a regular job. I'm good with my hands and know a lot about starship engineering and mechanical things in general."

"Becoming a friar does not negate that. On the contrary. Most friars carry out work essential to the abbey's good functioning." She studied him for a few seconds. "You're probably not aware of this, but humans have six senses and not just the five physical ones. The sixth," she tapped the side of her head with an extended index finger, "is mental. Most people experience it as instinct or gut feeling or strange impressions, that sort of thing."

"Like when my gut told me *Antelope* was in trouble as we were landing on Yotai. That saved my life."

"Precisely. In a few, the sixth sense is much stronger, and those are the ones who seem to enjoy unbelievable luck. In a tiny minority, this sixth sense is extremely well developed, to the point where they can detect the emotions of others. Most, if not quite all, are women. You, my friend, are part of that tiny minority even though you're a man."

An expression of sheer disbelief crossed Roget's face.

"Sister, my gut instinct may be pretty decent, but I'm neither lucky, nor can I sense the emotions of others."

"Yet you activated that rescue beacon. Only someone with a powerful sixth sense, what we call the talent, can do so." When he made to speak, Gwenneth raised a hand. "Upon meeting you, Katarin knew right away yours was much stronger than most, whether male or female. And I agree with her. You may not be aware, but your sixth sense is awake. That sensation of peace upon entering the abbey you talked about downstairs? It's what an untrained mind experiences when it no longer strains against unfiltered mental emanations, uncontrolled brain waves if you like. Everyone here, sisters and friars, can block them out so we don't go mad, and we keep our minds shielded so we don't disturb others."

She paused and watched Roget closely as he absorbed the full meaning of her words. When understanding lit up his eyes, she continued.

"The Order of the Void was first created almost two thousand years ago to give humans with a woken sixth sense sanctuary and remove those who might be tempted to use the talent for nefarious ends from society. Over time, it became what you see now, a monastic order serving the community as counselors, healers, and teachers. Servants of the Almighty who sense the pain, confusion, and hunger of others can help them more effectively than those without the talent. Your mind is undisciplined right now. It's unbearably loud to those of us with the talent, and that affects your mental and physical wellbeing in ways you cannot yet comprehend. But once you undertake the Order's training and understand that extraordinary gift from the Almighty, many things about your past life will make sense at last, and you will, for the first time, find inner peace. Katarin set you on the path of enlightenment by teaching you basic techniques while *Dawn Hunter* was under quarantine. Perhaps you already see a difference in yourself."

He thought about it for a few heartbeats, then nodded. "I don't find myself quite as angry at my fate as I did before."

"If you do not wish to join the Order, then at least undergo part of the training so you can shut out the mental emanations of others and discipline your mind. We simply won't instruct you in the advanced techniques."

"You mean so I can be at peace everywhere, not just here?"

Gwenneth nodded. "Precisely. And you might find your gut instinct a bit sharper as a bonus."

Roget shrugged.

"There's nothing else for me right now. I humbly accept your offer. Perhaps along the way, I'll discover a desire to join the Order, but I make no promises."

"A wise choice. You may find the journey of self-discovery difficult at times, but oh so rewarding in the end." Gwenneth turned her eyes on Katarin. "We started a postulant class ten weeks ago — four aspiring sisters. Much younger than Stearn, of course, but that shouldn't matter. Would your training place him at approximately their level?"

"Yes. Besides, he's a quick learner."

"In that case, you may introduce Stearn to Friar Rinne right away, which solves the question of who guides him during his stay here and where he'll sleep." She gave Roget a slight smile.

"Rinne is a hard taskmaster, but a kind soul. He settled on Lyonesse with us back in the day but traveled a lot before the empire collapsed. He will understand where you're coming from and how your experiences affect you. The other postulants were born and raised here and might benefit from your adventures."

"Thank you."

"We will speak again. For now, settle in and find your bearings. Familiarize yourself with the abbey and follow the teachings of Friar Rinne and those who help him." Gwenneth turned her head toward the open door. "Landry?"

The young friar appeared within seconds. "Yes, Sister?"

"Stearn will join the postulants as a new trainee. Please introduce him to Friar Rinne."

"Will do." He grinned at Roget. "Follow me, my friend."

Once they were alone, Gwenneth and Katarin visibly relaxed.

"That is quite the chaotic mind you brought home. Those eight weeks in quarantine must have been a trial for you and the others."

"Not so much us sisters since we quickly learned to block him, but I suspect the random brain waves he sent crashing around the ship affected the mood of a few crew members. We certainly cannot allow him out in the community before he has his mind under control. I wonder to what degree he was unwittingly responsible for *Antelope*'s serial mishaps."

Gwenneth shrugged. "We'll never know since he was the sole survivor. Now, what about the beacon he wore around his neck?"

Katarin reached into her cloak's voluminous pockets and produced the palm-sized metal disk. She reached over the low table and offered it to Gwenneth, who studied the inscriptions stamped on the rim.

"As you noted in your report, it came from Valamo Abbey on New Karelia. How did it ever reach Montego?" Gwenneth looked up at Katarin. "You're sure *Antelope* never went near New Karelia?"

"According to her logs, no."

"Could someone, perhaps even Stearn, have falsified them?"

"Certainly. Anything is possible. But why? Neither he nor anyone else aboard could know they would come across a regular Navy ship, and I doubt he did so when we rescued him. There wasn't enough time. We could always ask the Navy if there is evidence of tampering."

Gwenneth tapped a finger against her chin.

"Perhaps I'll reach out to Adrienne Barca and see what she can do, but I'd rather wait until Stearn gets his mind under control. Involving the Navy at this point might be counterproductive. Once Stearn is no longer a walking vortex of mental chaos, we can question him again and decide whether he's told you the truth."

"Agreed, and if there's nothing else, I would sell my soul for a long bath and wash away the cares of our trek."

"Of course. You're free to do what you want for the next six months, just like any other Void Ship crewmember after a mission. You can serve the abbey or your own needs, as can Amelia, Cory, and Milene — after Friar Herbert's debriefing. But I'm sure Sister Marta would be pleased to hear your evaluation of Amelia's performance."

"I will speak with her no later than tomorrow, and perhaps I might offer a few hours of my time each week as a teacher for Friar Rinne's postulant class."

"If you're inclined to help, then please do so with my blessing."

"Thank you. I enjoy teaching, and the challenge of taming a mind like Stearn's is irresistible, though I think my abilities won't be enough."

"I know. Marta will become his primary teacher once he masters the basics. Now go soak your old bones, my friend."

Gwenneth watched Katarin leave her office, then turned to face the window overlooking the quadrangle and its large Void Orb. For reasons she couldn't explain, Gwenneth knew *Dawn Hunter*'s return signaled Lyonesse was on the brink of another change. It could be one as momentous as that which occurred when she and Morane foiled a plot aimed at wresting control of the precious Knowledge Vault from the military.

But Gwenneth couldn't pinpoint what this new change might entail. However, the growing fear of rampant and deadly disease spreading across human worlds, a fear turning Lyonesse in on itself and hardening her heart against outsiders, would certainly influence it. The republic's motto, "We Shall Prevail," would take on more importance from now on in every decision by its government. It meant Lyonesse's complete isolation from the rest of humanity, a fate Gwenneth had expected for years, would finally come to fruition. There would be no more Void Ship expeditions. The first age of humanity across the stars was truly over. Whether there would be a second one, even a seer such as Sister Marta couldn't tell.

A sudden urge to visit Jonas Morane and Emma Reyes at their seaside retreat overcame Gwenneth, and she reached for her communicator.

—16—

"Radiation levels at the wormhole terminus are spiking, Captain."

Ossian Vara, who'd been morosely contemplating what would happen in a few minutes, looked up at the CIC's tactical projection. Four ships like the ones he'd destroyed over three months ago and coming from the galactic badlands as well, were about to enter Outer Picket's free-fire zone. Under orders from the President of the Republic of Lyonesse, Vara would offer them no parley, no warning, and no chance at turning around. Morane made a public announcement declaring the republic's three star systems closed to any non-Lyonesse traffic when he revealed the Barbarian Virus' existence during *Dawn Hunter*'s extended quarantine.

Anything coming through the Arietis-Corbenic wormhole or entering the republic via interstellar space was a target. The best scientific minds on Lyonesse couldn't find a cure for the Barbarian Virus, and no one knew when, if ever, they would. But they'd established a few things from the tests using lab-grown human tissue.

Its incubation period was between twelve and twenty days. It attacked the nervous system, much like rabies, as well as the circulatory system; the outcome was almost invariably fatal, and it would take infected humans months to die while suffering from increasingly debilitating pain. Which meant the unprovoked destruction of ships filled with infected intruders was an act of mercy rather than one of murder. Or so Vara told himself.

The status board was unchanged since the last time he looked. Both *Savage* and *Ivan Rebroff* were at battle stations, their fire control systems active, and the command-detonated directional mines covering the wormhole terminus' exit vector were live and waiting. Vara briefly wondered how he'd react if ships entering the Lyonesse Branch weren't of the typical reiver configuration, that they corresponded to those used by ordinary, harmless traders throughout the wormhole network when the empire still controlled it.

He answered his question with a mental shrug. Orders were orders, and for all they knew, the Barbarian Virus was infesting every world within two hundred light-years by now. But the day when the fast attack cruiser *Vanquish* and the Kalinka class frigate *Aleksandr Borodin* relieved *Savage* and *Ivan Rebroff* couldn't come soon enough. Unfortunately, it would be another two weeks before they headed home.

Once in orbit around Lyonesse, Vara and Zheng would turn their ships over to maintenance teams from the naval engineering branch and enjoy an extended leave after more than half a year away. When they returned, many old faces among both crews would be replaced by new ones as people took up new assignments.

The mere thought of a vacation with his family made him smile. This tour guarding the entrance to the Lyonesse Branch had been more tiring than any he remembered. Vara felt as decrepit as his command. He knew he wouldn't serve long enough in the Navy to see new major combatants, both frigates and cruisers, join the fleet and take over from ships long past their original retirement dates, but with luck, he might witness their launch.

Still, barring unforeseen events, he would be back in *Savage* when *Standfast* lifted off for the first time and witness the corvette's maiden hyperspace jump since the cruiser would spend her next operational tour in the Lyonesse system. Several of *Savage*'s crew members, including the assistant combat systems officer, were joining the new ship after their vacation.

"Emergence. Four bogies matching the readings from the traffic control buoys in the Arietis system," the sensor chief reported. "Their shields are up, and their fire control sensors are active."

"I'm assigning targets." Four red icons joined blue and green markers in the tactical projection. A pause, then the cruiser's combat systems officer said, "Mines going active. We're opening fire, guns only."

The intruders never stood a chance. Between the directional mines and the guns of the two Lyonesse warships, they turned from functional, if feeble, faster-than-light starships into wreckage before anyone aboard could react. Four miniature novae fueled by four antimatter containment units failing lit up the wormhole terminus for a few, brief seconds before dying away.

"Checking for survivors." Almost a minute passed before the sensor chief raised his hand. "One chunk of the wreckage shows life signs, Captain. I fed the targeting information to gunnery."

"Confirmed," the combat systems officer said.

"Destroy."

A brief plasma stream, less intense than the first salvos, erupted from *Savage*'s main guns and chewed through what remained of a starship's primary hull, turning it into smaller, glowing chunks of alloy.

"Life signs eradicated."

Though he should ask his sensor chief to determine how many lives were aboard the wolf pack's ships, Vara couldn't quite make himself do so. Should HQ ask, he would give an estimate. It didn't matter if there were a hundred in each vessel or four hundred. If the Barbarian Plague was indeed ravaging human planets in what was once the empire's Coalsack Sector, the casualty rate would dwarf what Outer Picket's two ships just racked up.

Vara swallowed a heavy-hearted sigh and tapped the control surface in his command chair's right armrest.

"Cancel battle stations."

"Canceling battle stations, aye," the first officer answered from the bridge. Then, after a few seconds, "*Ivan Rebroff* acknowledges."

"Resume regular patrol route."

✶✶

"The Outer Picket laboratory has finished examining the remains of the intruders aboard those ships, Mister President," Lieutenant General Barca said the moment Jonas Morane accepted her call.

"And?"

"Infected as well. We estimate there were between six and seven hundred of them. A more accurate count is unfortunately not possible. Outer Picket opened fire the moment they crossed the wormhole terminus' event horizon and thoroughly destroyed them."

"Thank you, General. Sometimes I wish we could simply collapse that damned wormhole. Perhaps a massive antimatter bomb might do the trick. Once Lyonesse-built starships become operational, we won't need the wormhole network anymore."

"We will eventually wish to venture out again, sir. Perhaps not during our lifetimes, but once we find a way of immunizing ourselves against the Barbarian Plague, our descendants might do so, and using the wormhole network will make reuniting our species that much easier."

He grunted. "I suppose. How is work on an antiviral progressing?"

Barca grimaced. "We're still a long way from finding one, I'm afraid."

"Then, we can only hope the disease runs its course before more intruders enter our star systems."

Unvoiced, but clearly understood, was Morane's fear infected reivers might come at Lyonesse via interstellar space and stay undetected until it was too late. Barca knew the risk was small but still higher than zero. The Navy couldn't set up a cordon sanitaire around the entire Lyonesse star system with its limited fleet of starships, nor was its sensor network capable of continuously watching every single approach.

A reiver might conceivably sneak his way past the planet's outer moon before being detected and destroyed, leaving a trail of wreckage in a decaying orbit. Should that wreckage not burn up during entry into Lyonesse's atmosphere, it might release the virus.

"They won't get past the Navy, sir. Our republic is and will remain secure against intrusion from anyone, especially as we grow both in size and capability."

"I wish I shared your unshakable confidence, General. Nevertheless, I will show no doubts when I share this latest development with the people of Lyonesse. Thank you for letting me know. My announcement will go out over the net within the hour. Was there anything else?"

"No, Mister President."

"Thank you and goodbye, General." Morane cut the link, leaving Barca to stare at a blank display.

"You're welcome, sir," she murmured as she climbed to her feet. It was almost time for the weekly command conference, which meant stopping by the break room for a fresh cup of tea. Barca vaguely remembered the taste of coffee and still mourned its disappearance even though it was two decades since the last few roasted beans met their demise in a grinder. Coffee plants simply couldn't adapt to Lyonesse's soil, but caffeine was caffeine, no matter the source, so tea it had been ever since then.

Five minutes later, cup in hand, Barca entered the conference room where her principal officers and the Lyonesse Defense Force Sergeant Major waited for her arrival.

"Good afternoon, everyone." She took the chair at the head of the table. "Please sit. I've just informed the president that the latest batch of reivers was infected by the Barbarian Virus as well."

"How did he react?" Nate Sirak asked.

"The way one would expect. He took it as confirmation that the first wolf pack wasn't an isolated case but the harbinger of a pandemic. He, just as I, will be happy once we beef up the Navy's patrol and surveillance capabilities."

"Does that mean certain large-scale projects will be approved soon?"

"It wouldn't surprise me if he uses this as a cudgel to pry more defense money from our notoriously skinflint senate. Now, on to the agenda. Nate, you're up."

**

"You heard about the four new plague ships that came through the Arietis wormhole?" Jonas Morane asked once Sister Gwenneth settled into her usual solarium chair facing Vanquish Bay.

Unlike her visit several weeks earlier, the sky was a bright blue with small puffy clouds marching off into the west, pushed by gentle upper winds. The sun still hung a few hand-spans above the horizon, but the lengthening shadows spoke of a waning afternoon. Morane had retracted the wall of transparent aluminum windows, turning the solarium into a covered veranda filled with the warm scents of the surrounding native vegetation.

She nodded.

"I caught your announcement before leaving the abbey. Whether further proof the Navy is protecting us will help ease the general anxiety about the Barbarian Plague or whether evidence of more infected reivers with eyes on our medical technology will worsen those fears is up for debate."

Emma Reyes entered with a tray bearing three tall crystal glasses.

"I thought we'd enjoy gin and tonic instead of tea on such a glorious, sunny day."

"A good thing the Order's Rule doesn't forbid spirits before supper."

"Or the consumption of alcohol in general." Reyes passed out the drinks and sat. She raised her glass. "I propose we toast the men and women protecting us from the ills of a fallen galaxy."

PART II - MOONRISE

—17—

"Marta! Please come in and sit." Sister Gwenneth smiled fondly at the abbey's preeminent teacher. Marta was a daughter of the imperial nobility who came to Lyonesse as a refugee during the old empire's last days rather than let herself be used as a rival empress in a doomed attempt at creating a new realm centered on the Coalsack Sector. She not only possessed one of the strongest talents Gwenneth ever encountered but also a fully open third eye, rare even among the sisters. Her abilities had only grown in the decades since she first arrived. Many within the Order also believed Marta was prescient.

"Thank you for seeing me, Gwenneth." Marta, a pale, slender, sixty-something who wore her short, ash-blond hair in the same practical cut as almost everyone else, entered the abbess' office and took one of the chairs in front of her desk.

"You're always welcome." An amused look crossed Gwenneth's face. "Let me guess. You would like to witness *Standfast*'s launch with me tomorrow."

"Stefan will be aboard as first officer."

Gwenneth heard quiet pride in Marta's voice. She'd thought her twin children, Stefan and Sigrid, gone forever when the late Grand Duke Custis made her prisoner. Yet by the grace of the Almighty and the tireless work of Void Ships on rescue missions throughout the Coalsack Sector, they were reunited on Lyonesse. Her son was now a career Navy officer while her daughter Sigrid was one of the engineers working for Hecht Aerospace. Tomorrow, Stefan would lift off in the starship his sister helped design and build.

"Of course you can come with me, Marta."

The latter inclined her head in gratitude. "Thank you. I'm also here to discuss Stearn."

Gwenneth gestured at her to go ahead.

"By now, he can keep his mind from disturbing others and do so instinctively using the discipline developed through meditation exercises. Stearn is no longer a source of turmoil who'll disturb those in his immediate vicinity. But I will confess a talent that powerful was difficult to tame, and I'm sure he'll backslide every so often until his new habits become ingrained. I usually develop a normal postulant by stimulating her native talent and making it flower, a much easier proposition than reining in a psychic hurricane."

Marta let out a soft sigh.

"There is still much work ahead. But Stearn must leave the abbey and encounter minds other than those of the Brethren. His development is only half-finished, and this environment is too well controlled. It doesn't offer the sort of challenge he needs so he can build defenses capable of blocking the mental turmoil of others. Since he has not yet decided whether to join the Order and is not ready for normal society, I recommend he spends the next few months at the Windy Isles Priory and continue his training under Sister Mirjam. Because of her work with the disturbed psyches of sociopaths, I'm sure her insights will be valuable."

Gwenneth tapped an extended finger against her chin. "An intriguing proposition."

"I've reached the limits of what I can do for him since he won't take vows."

Gwenneth's eyebrows rose at the admission. "Really?"

Marta lowered her eyes for a few seconds.

"Stearn often confounds me. If I thought he exercised the same level of self-control as any of the sisters, I might almost suspect he was toying with his teachers, myself included."

"I see. That's interesting. When should we send him to the Windies?"

"Any time. I will supervise his self-study while he remains here, but I can no longer train him unless he enters the Order. He knows everything we may teach a layperson."

"Then warn him of his impending departure. Landry will book the next available seat on one of the Phoenix Clippers."

"Thank you."

"Is there anything else on your mind?"

"At what time will you leave for the launch tomorrow?"

"Thirteen-hundred hours. And I believe it's customary to wear one's best attire for such an occasion."

**

"Even though I've seen it many times before, I remain impressed." Marta's soft voice was tinged with awe as the abbey's aircar came within sight of the sprawling shipyard complex on the shores of a deep bay south of Lannion, where the Haven River joined the Middle Sea. "Especially now they've removed the scaffolding around *Standfast*. What a beautiful vessel. And so much larger than the Void Ships."

"Way better armed too," Friar Landry said from the control station. "That is a warship, through and through. And look how far they've progressed on *Prevail*."

"Indeed." Three pairs of eyes turned toward the large scaffolding assembly partially hiding what looked like an almost completed ship.

As they got closer, they could make out markings on *Standfast*'s dull gray hull: her name, the Navy's double-headed condor and anchor symbol, and a letter and number combination which Gwenneth assumed was the registration number. She seemed menacingly sleek from this distance as if one of the shark-like apex predators prowling Lyonesse's oceans had come ashore. Hyperdrive nacelles hanging from short swept back, wing-like extrusions framed a hull studded with weapon emplacements while huge sublight drive nozzles festooned her stern.

A makeshift parade ground was laid out on the ship's landward side, with reviewing stand, seating for spectators, flags flapping the breeze, and row upon row of military personnel in dress uniform preparing for the launch ceremonies.

Landry, under orders from traffic control, veered to the left and aimed the aircar's nose at a section of tarmac beside the cavernous ship assembly building turned into a parking lot. Mere minutes later, he brought them down with barely a bump and switched off the power plant. Around them, other cars were either landing or coming up the road from Lannion. Watchful Lyonesse Defense Force troopers wearing battle dress and carrying carbines stood at regular intervals or patrolled in pairs, to make sure no spectators went astray, let alone wandered off so they could examine *Standfast* from up close.

Gwenneth, with Marta and Landry on her heels, headed for the spectator seats, nodding politely at those who acknowledged her. A Lyonesse Rifle Regiment sergeant intercepted them and pointed at the VIP section, reserved for leading figures in the community and family members of *Standfast*'s crew. Landry left the sisters and looked for acquaintances among the many off-duty Defense Force members who were present to witness a momentous day in Lyonesse history — the liftoff of her first domestically built faster-than-light warship.

As they settled into their seats, Gwenneth and Marta saw former President Elenia Yakin, her partner, Brigadier General (retired) Matti Kayne, and the entirety of President Morane's cabinet arrive, along with every member of the Lyonesse Senate. Then, battalion-sized Defense Force contingents marched on by element: Ground Forces, Navy, and Support Command, under the colonel commanding the Ground Forces' 1st Brigade.

Once they were in place, the service chiefs climbed the reviewing stand one-by-one to receive the general salute, first Major General Hamm, then Rear Admiral Sirak, and finally Rear Admiral Au. Lieutenant General Barca, driven to the reviewing stand in a sleek, black staff car bearing small red plates adorned with three silver stars, followed them less than a minute later.

No sooner had Barca taken the salute that another staff car, this one with a small Republic of Lyonesse flag flying from a short pole on the roof, crossed the makeshift parade ground and stopped in front of the reviewing stand. Everyone in attendance stood while those in the military and police services came to attention.

The president's naval aide, a commander with gold aiguillettes on his right shoulder, jumped out, opened the back door, and saluted as Morane, wearing an admiral's uniform, emerged from the car. He climbed onto the dais for a presidential salute from the Defense Force contingent while aide and car cleared the area.

Moments after the salute's last drum roll faded away, a distant voice called out indistinct orders and to the onlooker's surprise and delight, *Standfast*'s crew, led by her captain, marched down the ship's belly ramp as the band struck up the Navy march. In contrast to their comrades already on parade, they wore dark blue battledress uniforms with their ship's crest, an armored gauntlet holding a sword, on the sleeves.

The fifty-two men and women who would take the corvette on her maiden patrol made their way around the battalions. They came to a halt in front of the reviewing stand where the captain, Lieutenant Commander Laurent Lisiecki, ordered a presidential salute. He then led Morane, Barca, and Sirak through the ranks on an inspection tour. Every member of *Standfast*'s crew glowed with pride, though both Gwenneth and Marta could sense an undercurrent of apprehension at the upcoming liftoff.

After the inspection, Morane climbed back onto the dais, and his amplified voice rang out.

"Citizens of Lyonesse, in the next minutes, we will witness a momentous event which will live on in the republic's history for as long as Lyonesse exists. The first Lyonesse-designed and built faster-than-light warship, *Standfast*, will lift off and join the fleet. She is, without a doubt, the newest, most modern, most advanced vessel in human space, capable of defending our republic against any comer. But before she can slip the surly bonds of Lyonesse and trod the high untrespassed sanctity of space, we must launch her in the time-honored manner. Our republic's first president, Elenia Yakin, has graciously accepted to become *Standfast*'s sponsor and will become a permanent honorary member of her crew."

Morane turned to Yakin, and with a gesture, invited her to rise. "Madame President."

The naval aide stepped forward with a bottle of champagne in hand. As if on cue, Lieutenant General Barca, Rear Admiral Sirak, and the Defense Force Sergeant Major formed an orderly group that followed Morane and Yakin as they made their way to the corvette.

Once they were on the other side of the battalions, the parade commander ordered his troops to make an about-face so they could witness the christening while the announcer asked the spectators to stand.

Yakin and the launch party, dwarfed by the corvette's hull, stopped at one her massive landing struts where Morane's aide offered Yakin the champagne bottle. She held it up by the neck so everyone could see and said in a voice that echoed across the parade ground,

"*They that go up to the stars in ships;*
That do business in the great galaxy;
These see the works of the Almighty, and the Almighty's wonders in the Void."

Yakin smashed the bottle against the strut.

"I name this ship *Standfast*. May the Almighty bless her and those who sail in her."

A roar of approval erupted from the massed troops while cheers and applause filled the air behind them. When it died away, Lieutenant General Barca turned to face the parade.

"*Standfast* will join the fleet."

"Sir!" Lieutenant Commander Lisiecki snapped off a crisp salute. "Ship's company will go to liftoff stations. In column of route, right turn. Ship's company, MARCH."

Morane and his party returned to the reviewing stand as the crew, heads held high, arms swinging, headed for the belly ramp.

"While we would no doubt rather watch *Standfast*'s departure from where we sit," the announcer said, "security concerns demand that we clear the tarmac once the president departs. I would, therefore, ask you to head for the parking area at that time."

After a final salute, Morane climbed into his staff car and left for a vantage point near the ship assembly building, where Hecht Aerospace had laid on drinks and canapés for the VIPs and the families of crew members who would head there on foot. Gwenneth and Marta fell in with Admiral Sirak while the troops marched off.

"I've been wondering how *Standfast* will receive its first injection of antimatter fuel," Gwenneth said. "She can't sail to the refueling station at sublight speed without going relativistic."

"*Narwhal*," he replied, naming the replenishment ship that accompanied *Vanquish* and Sirak's former command, the frigate *Myrtale*, to Lyonesse after the remnants of the 197th defected. "We don't use her in a refueling capacity that often. But the crew practiced. She'll give *Standfast* enough to light up the hyperdrives and see she reaches the refueling station with a good reserve."

"Ah." Gwenneth nodded. "Of course. I should have guessed."

While they walked across the tarmac, the reviewing stand, chairs, flagpoles, and every other bit of parade finery vanished, leaving a cleared space of several hundred meters around *Standfast*, whose belly ramp had retracted into the hull. Speakers came to life behind them, surprising the guests.

"Lannion Traffic Control, this is the Republic of Lyonesse Starship *Standfast*, corvette, Laurent Lisiecki commanding."

"Welcome to the network, *Standfast*," a female voice replied. Gwenneth recognized it as belonging to the chief controller, taking a turn at the console for the occasion. "May your service to the republic be long and honorable."

"Our identification beacon is active."

"Beacon confirmed," the chief traffic controller replied. "We have registered you."

"*Standfast* requests permission to lift off on a vertical vector to ten thousand meters. At ten thousand meters, she will change her angle of attack to twenty degrees from the vertical until entering orbit at an altitude of two thousand kilometers."

"Your flight path is empty of all air and spacecraft up to two thousand kilometers. You are cleared for departure."

Gwenneth and Marta exchanged amused glances. The back and forth between starship and traffic control was obviously rehearsed even though it would sound natural to anyone else's ears.

"It'll be okay, Mom," a soft woman's voice said, startling Marta.

She was so focused on pushing away the anxiety at her son riding a new and unproven starship straight up into the sky that she didn't sense Sigrid's arrival.

"I helped build *Standfast*. If I didn't think she was perfectly safe for our people, I wouldn't let Stefan aboard." The young woman, a close copy of her mother when she was that age, smiled confidently.

A rapidly growing whine reached their ears as the corvette's thrusters spooled up, making any further conversation fruitless. Marta reached out and grasped her daughter's hand instead. Bright streams of light appeared under *Standfast*'s hull, and as she rose, her landing gear broke contact with the tarmac.

"We are feet up, Traffic Control."

"Acknowledged. Godspeed, *Standfast*."

When she was ten meters above the ground, her landing gear vanished, retracted into the hull. She kept rising on bright pillars of light, straight up into a sky so blue it almost broke Marta's heart.

"Passing through ten thousand meters. All systems nominal."

Standfast gradually turned into a speck that soon vanished from view, though everyone at the shipyard, and indeed across the settlement area, kept their eyes glued to the heavens. Captain Lisiecki reported each increment of ten kilometers until reaching one hundred, then each increment of one hundred kilometers.

With the ship no longer visible to the naked eye, the guests in the VIP section mingled while Marta let Sigrid take her around so she could meet her daughter's colleagues, the people responsible for *Standfast*'s design and construction. Finally, the report she'd been waiting for came through the hidden speakers.

"*Standfast* is in orbit around Lyonesse at an altitude of two thousand kilometers and preparing to take on fuel for the hyperdrives."

The enthusiastic round of applause told Marta she wasn't the only one who'd been tense during the corvette's ascent.

"Acknowledged. Lannion Traffic Control is turning you over to the Navy. Fair winds and following seas, *Standfast*. Lannion, out."

—18—

Stearn Roget, wearing the Order's loose, black garment and carrying a small valise, stepped off the Phoenix Clipper *City of Lannion* and took a deep breath of the warm, salt-tinged tropical air. The setting sun's harsh rays stung his eyes, and he snorted with amusement at his momentary feeling of displacement. When the Clipper lifted off from Lannion Spaceport an hour earlier, it had been in the fresh pre-dawn air. Here, in the Windy Isles, the day was already over. But when the sleek, white shuttle returned to Lannion, it would go back in time and arrive just after breakfast, while he was eating his supper.

Roget suddenly became conscious of a tall, silver-haired man with a narrow, ascetic face and a prominent nose framed by intense brown eyes watching him intently from the shade of a tiny landing field hut. He also wore the Order's garment. When their eyes met, the man pushed himself away from the wall and walked toward Roget with long, deliberate strides.

"I am Erasmus, a postulant at the Windy Isles Priory, and you must be Stearn." He held out his hand.

"That would be me. A pleasure to meet you, Erasmus." They shook, and Roget noted the other man's sturdy grip.

"You're joining our postulant class?" Erasmus asked as he fell into step beside Roget, leading him toward the checkpoint guarding the landing field's entrance.

"I've not decided yet if I will join the Order. Call me a lay trainee or something of the sort. I'm here to continue my training under a Sister Mirjam."

Erasmus nodded. "Our prioress. A remarkable servant of the Almighty. Extraordinarily gifted if I may say so. You will learn much from her."

The correctional officer at the checkpoint waved them through after scanning Roget's identification. Once outside, Erasmus pointed at a collection of low stone buildings partially hidden by vegetation in the distance.

"Our priory." He then aimed his finger in the opposite direction. "The penal colony is in that direction. It occupies most of Changu Island and the neighboring cays of this atoll."

"It's charming, I'm sure."

Erasmus gave Roget a curious look. "It isn't when you're inside the penal colony."

"Right. You'd know from ministering to the exiles."

"Postulants do not, as you say, minister."

"Oh?" Roget glanced at Erasmus through narrowed eyes.

"Sister Mirjam and her assistants cured two other prisoners and myself of our turmoil as part of an experimental rehabilitation process. We three are now in training to become friars, though we will serve the Windy Isles Priory for the rest of our lives."

"Really? How interesting." As they walked along a crushed seashell path, Roget's eyes never remained on one spot for long. They took in the shockingly green vegetation, liberally dotted with neon reds and yellows, the spindly trees with fern-like appendages sprouting from their tops, and the bright blue of the lagoon beyond, its surface shimmering under the setting sun.

"Did you witness *Standfast*'s departure by chance? We watched the video feed, although it was past midnight here."

Roget shook his head.

"Not in person. Most of us at the abbey saw the same video feed, though once she cleared the shipyard, I watched her fly up into the sky. Mind you, at that distance, she wasn't much more than a speck. Abbess Gwenneth and Sister Marta were at the launch, though. Marta's son is *Standfast*'s first officer, and her daughter was part of the ship's design team."

"I don't believe I ever heard of this Sister Marta."

"She was one of my trainers, and they say she has the strongest mind among the Brethren. I certainly found her impressive, perhaps even a bit frightening."

"May I ask why the Order is training you if you've not yet committed to joining it?"

A crooked smile lit up Roget's face. He tapped the side of his head with an extended index finger.

"Apparently, I'm the proud owner of an out-of-control sixth sense. It used to run amok, and Sister Marta thinks it's still not totally tamed, which is why I'm here."

"I see." Erasmus waved him through an open garden door and along a flagstone path ending at the main building's equally open front door. "You're blessed with the talent, just like the Brethren."

"I'm not sure blessed is the right word for it, but yeah. Mine is stronger than the normal friar version."

"The Almighty has plans for you, my friend."

They entered the lobby and Roget blinked a few times while his eyes adapted to the lower level of illumination. When he could see clearly, he spotted a familiar elfin face framed by blonde hair coming down the curved wooden stairs. She stopped half a dozen steps before they ended.

"Amelia! What a pleasant surprise."

Erasmus briefly stared at Roget before turning his eyes on the sister.

"You know each other?"

"She was in *Dawn Hunter* when they rescued me from impending death on Yotai. Lyonesse really is a small world."

"Stearn." Amelia inclined her head, smiling. "Welcome to the Windy Isles Priory. Gwenneth transferred me here four months ago as part of my development as a counselor under Sister Mirjam, who asked I bring you to her office. Thank you for fetching him, Erasmus. You may resume your regular duties."

Erasmus bowed at the neck. "Sister."

Then, he vanished into a ground floor hallway, his footsteps fading rapidly.

"You seem more serene than when we last spoke, Stearn."

"Sister Marta taught me how to control my mental turmoil — one which I didn't even know bedeviled me until Sister Gwenneth explained my affliction."

She smiled.

"We knew about that turmoil even before our shuttle landed on Yotai. Trust me, the difference in you between that day and now is breathtaking, and though we might have been the only ones who heard it clearly, it affected everyone around you."

"Then I'm happy I've progressed, even though I don't quite understand."

"Come." Amelia turned and climbed back up the staircase. After a moment of hesitation, Roget followed her.

When they entered Mirjam's office, Roget decided she was another of those sisters whose age one couldn't possibly guess. She stood and came around her desk.

"Welcome to the Windy Isles Priory, Stearn."

Something about the physical contact as they shook hands felt a little strange, as if that same hand were brushing against his mind. He shook off the sensation and returned her open smile with one of his own.

"Thank you, Sister."

She gestured at the chairs around a low table in one corner.

"Please sit. You as well, Amelia." She took a seat across from them and met Roget's open, curious gaze. "Marta updated me on your progress. When I mentioned Amelia was doing her advanced training under my guidance, she suggested I let the two of you work together, since you already know each other."

"What sort of work will that be?"

"Amelia is a counselor and helps the condemned deal with their sentences, work through the mental issues that led them into crime and prepare those whose exile isn't permanent for reintegration with civil society." Mirjam studied Roget for a few heartbeats. "You don't seem particularly thrilled at the idea."

When Roget didn't react to her accurate assessment, she added, "And you're wondering how I figured out so quickly. That's what we counselors do. We read people so we can guide them."

"The talent."

"Yes. It makes us more sensitive to the emotions of others. But only members of the Order are trained to interpret what they pick up."

"Then why will I work with Sister Amelia? Marta focused my training exclusively on taming my sixth sense."

"You won't be helping the prisoners, although you'll be observing Amelia. No, this is for your development. Many of the prisoners on this island suffer from diseased minds they cannot control. They may even possess a smidgen of talent — what laypeople would call natural cunning. You will sense them. They will even repulse you. But being in their presence will force you to take the next step and learn how one blocks out the minds of others."

Roget nodded in understanding. "I see. I'm here because everyone at the abbey is so self-controlled."

"Partially correct. Now that Marta's teachings put you in touch with your talent, you will find yourself consciously affected by those filled with strong negative emotions if you don't develop a protective shell. The best place to do so is where negative emotions flow like white-hot lava — such as the atoll where Lyonesse sends its worst offenders."

"Do all Brethren pass through here?"

Mirjam shook her head.

"No. There are other ways of teaching this skill to those who join the Order. But since you remain undecided, Marta thought a stint here would be an adequate substitute, and I agree. Once I consider you ready, you can leave us and find a place in secular society, if that is your decision."

Roget inclined his head. "Understood."

"You'll live with the three postulants now in training and do your daily exercises with them."

"The cured prisoners this Erasmus mentioned?"

"Yes." Another pause. "You find it hard to believe we can cure sociopaths."

"I guess so."

"Did Erasmus make you feel uneasy in any way?"

"No."

"And yet he was the angriest, most manipulative and most violent man on the Windy Isles before he volunteered for the experiment. The negative emotions he felt before his treatment would overwhelm you on such close contact. The other two weren't much different. You'll be living with them for the next few weeks. Judge for yourself if they seem cured of their antisocial personality disorders."

"I will, Sister."

"Amelia will take you to Friar Rikkard. He is the priory's property manager and postulant master for the current class, which will include you for matters other than those involving postulant studies. I will allow you two days of acclimatization before joining Amelia on her daily sessions with the prisoners."

Roget stood and bowed his head respectfully.

"Yes, Sister."

She watched both leave her office, wondering what the future held for Stearn Roget. His mind was indeed one of the strongest she'd ever encountered. It would be a shame if he didn't join the Order. Marta opening his third eye could prove hugely beneficial for the Void and the community at large. He could even, with the right training, join her team and help cure more of the disordered souls living inside Changu Island's Supermax complex. Many of them didn't react well to sisters. Perhaps they would accept a friar who possessed the same capabilities.

Mirjam mentally shrugged. Roget would do as he must. *The Void giveth and the Void taketh away. Blessed be the Void.*

— 19 —

Stearn Roget let out a soft gasp as he and Sister Amelia entered the Supermax compound occupying Changu Island's far end, almost directly across the lagoon from the priory, after passing through a guardroom.

Amelia glanced at him over her shoulder. "What is it?"

"I don't know." He shook his head. "A darkness is pressing against my mind, I suppose. It's as if my soul took a deep breath and inhaled a noxious cloud of—"

When she saw him search for the right word, Amelia said, "Evil?"

"Yes. That's it. Evil." Roget hesitated. "Strange. I've never believed in its existence before, but there truly is such a thing."

"You and most humans." She gave him an encouraging smile. "Few can detect its manifestation in sentient beings, and thus, the majority long ago stopped believing it exists. Sadly, at the same time, they also abandoned the notion of goodness because one cannot exist without the other. Yet once you abandon the idea some things are truly black or white, morality becomes a gradation of gray with no absolutes and no limits to human depravity."

"With Dendera's vengeance being the ultimate expression of such limitless depravity, right?"

"Just so. Clinicians would tell you she suffered from a severe form of antisocial personality disorder. Still, if she was a psychopath, she was also an utterly evil being, the product of a corrupt dynasty. Most who suffer from the disorder live reasonably normal lives and don't engage in criminal activity, let alone genocide. But the ones you'll meet in here, for a variety of social or environmental reasons, gave full expression to their disorder and crossed the line into committing horrific acts. They cannot feel regret for what they did, and they don't fear consequences."

Roget studied his surroundings as they walked. A two-meter tall, wire-topped stone wall separated the Supermax compound from the medium and high-security parts of the Windy Isles main penitentiary complex. Within, it resembled a miniature military installation — single-story barracks in neat rows, a dining facility, several other buildings, and an exercise yard, currently devoid of life. Amelia led him to one of the structures set apart from the barracks.

"There are two broad varieties of extreme antisocial personality disorder," she said, continuing her discourse, "the psychopaths and the sociopaths. We don't deal with psychopaths because, despite our best attempts, there is no cure for the genetic abnormality in their brains. The ones condemned to exile will die behind prison walls. Sociopaths, on the other hand, have a reasonably normal brain, meaning they can differentiate right from wrong at a subconscious level. Our treatment seeks to amplify that ability and grow it. None will develop true empathy, but reversing the damage caused by social and environmental stressors will, hopefully, suppress their depraved instincts and let them act more like ordinary people."

"The evil I'm picking up comes from the psychopaths?"

She shook her head as she reached for the door.

"No. Even the best of us can't sense much from their minds. We suspect the genetic abnormality provides a sort of built-in defense against mental threats. However, maybe because they cannot recognize the existence of good or evil, they feel no turmoil. There's another theory that posits psychopaths are human vessels devoid of souls, and what we sense with our talent is, in large part, the soul. What you sensed upon entering the compound were the disordered emanations from sociopaths, who know, at some level, what they did was wrong even if they don't understand. If you belong to the soul theorists, you might say theirs are blackened and tattered beyond human recognition."

"Pardon me for saying so, Sister, but I don't think I could become a counselor."

She ushered him into a calm, softly lit lobby with cream-colored walls, a white ceiling, and a light blue tile floor.

"Once you can shield yourself from others, you will only sense evil if you peek behind the curtain."

"I understand that. I meant wanting to work with such beings. Aren't you repulsed?"

"I was at first." Amelia took him across the lobby and into a corridor pierced by eight pairs of doors on each side. It, too, was devoid of decorations. "But after meeting Erasmus, Shakib, and Marnix, I knew we could save these men and women from the darkness within them. Besides, advanced counselors must deal with the worst our species offers. Otherwise, we're no good to anyone. Regular counselors can help normal people."

She stopped at the second pair of doors and pointed at the one on the right.

"Observation room. There will always be two correctional officers watching us. If the prisoner becomes threatening, they will enter the interview room via a connecting door."

"Does that happen often? I mean a prisoner becoming threatening?"

Amelia shook her head.

"No. The ones seeking our help are volunteers who hope counseling will allow them off Changu Island and, if not back to civilization, then at least the limited freedom of the low-security colonies on the atoll's other islands. Attacking one of us would end that dream. But they are manipulative, almost reflexively so, and not shy about trying to play us."

"Friar Rikkard gave me chapter and verse, Sister."

"How are you now?"

Roget examined his inner self and grimaced. "I can still detect evil."

"Don't worry, it won't twist your mind, though it will tire you out. With any luck, you'll find ways of warding off those mental emanations by yourself quickly enough. After all, that's why Sister Marta suggested you spend time with us."

Amelia touched the door. It slid aside with a sigh, revealing a surprisingly informal day room with four comfortable looking chairs around a low table which bore a water jug and four cups. Roget noted the connecting door leading to the observation room and instinctively headed for one of the two chairs facing it. When he glanced at Amelia, he caught a glint of approval in her eyes as she took the other seat.

"Our subject for this session," she said, making herself comfortable, "is Seled Hyson, fifty-two years old, born on

Wyvern. She came to Lyonesse in *Tanith* along with others condemned to the imperial prison planet Parth."

Roget nodded.

"I read the story of the 197th Battle Group's trek and Jonas Morane's work to create the republic."

"Seled experienced a tough upbringing, filled with parental neglect, lack of restraint or suitable role models, and most importantly, in an environment which catered to her every whim. I also suspect there was a fair amount of abuse, though she won't discuss it. Those factors, in conjunction with a predisposition for antisocial behavior, sent her down a dark path that ended with multiple murders. Interestingly, she was born into a family of senior imperial bureaucrats and enjoyed the advantages of an upper-class childhood. Yet, she is not a good person and will never become one. But Seled volunteered, and she is trying, if only to leave this compound, and we must work with volunteers. I'll introduce you as my trainee. Please don't speak a word during the session. Also, please keep your body language neutral and your face expressionless, no matter what you hear. It's good training even if you don't join the Order."

"Yes, Sister."

She pulled a communicator from the folds of her robe. "Sister Amelia and Trainee Stearn in Suite number three, ready for Seled Hyson."

"On our way," a male voice replied moments later.

"Thank you. Amelia, out." The communicator vanished again. "Do you sense someone in the observation room?"

"No."

"And you'd be right. Pay close attention to the moment that changes and let me know what you detect."

"Is this part of my training?"

Amelia gave him a brief smile. "Call it curiosity. Since you felt evil before even coming face-to-face with a prisoner, I'm interested to see if you can sense the correctional officers."

"Why?"

"Humor me, please."

Almost a minute passed in silence, then Roget sensed the cloak of evil that weighed on him since entering the compound shimmer as if caught in a breeze. An enormous part of it darkened almost oppressively, and he immediately understood it was because Seled Hyson was near. But another, almost imperceptible part became brittle as it hardened.

"Is there an officer in the observation room?" He asked in a low voice.

She nodded. "Well done. You must describe—"

The hallway door opened, and a tall, slender woman wearing an orange one-piece garment and sandals entered. She had a narrow, deeply tanned face beneath short, off-white hair, a patrician nose framed by watchful brown eyes and thin, almost bloodless lips. Hyson didn't appear particularly dangerous. One could still detect a woman of privilege and grace beneath the coarsening of years on Changu. But Roget couldn't recognize a soul, malevolent or otherwise, peering back at him through those eyes, though he could almost see the aura of corruption enveloping her, and it squeezed his mind like a vise. A familiar migraine accompanied by nausea surged as he fought for self-control.

"Sister." Hyson settled into one of the two chairs facing them and crossed her legs. Her pleasant, alto voice sounded slightly hoarse. "And who is your friend?"

"Stearn. He's training under my guidance."

"Is he now? How delightful to see a male face from the outside. You're cute enough for my tastes, Sister, but I could use a bit of variety." She gave Roget a feral smile, then blew him a kiss. "I wouldn't mind training under you, handsome."

When Roget didn't react, let alone reply, a disappointed moue twisted her lips.

"Carved from stone, eh? Well, a hard man *is* good to find. How about it, Amelia? A little three-way play? I don't mind the COs watching from next door."

Amelia, who'd kept an equally expressionless face, waited for a few heartbeats after Hyson fell silent, then said, "Shall we pick up where we last left off, Seled?"

—20—

When they walked away from the Supermax compound shortly before midday, Roget breathed a sigh of relief as the iron bands of the worst migraine he'd ever experienced evaporated in the warm sun.

"Any longer in there, and I would be on the verge of blowing my brains out. How can these people live inside their minds?"

"They do not hear their minds. Otherwise, madness would overcome them."

"Do some reach that point, though?"

"Hear themselves? Yes, it happens. Eventually, the darkness within eats away at their soul. Their lives end prematurely. Most commit suicide in rather spectacular ways." After a few more steps, she asked, "How did you notice the correctional officers?"

Roget thought about her question for several seconds, then said in a tentative voice, "When I sensed Seled's approach, I also picked up something hard and brittle. It wasn't so much the opposite of her mind as it was a wall built to block it out."

"Nicely done." Amelia gave him a smile of approval. "It takes a special person to become a correctional officer and walk among evil daily. Most of those who succeed do so because they instinctively close in on themselves and block out everything. That is the hard, brittle thing. The ones who can't close in on themselves or find their shell cracking after years here move on to guard habitual criminals or leave the service altogether. They are, in a way, continual victims of the people imprisoned here, though neither inmates nor correctional officers know about it."

Roget made a face. "And another career choice struck from my list."

"Once you learn to block out others, you won't see or hear evil unless you look for it."

"If I learn to speak no evil on top of that, can I audition for the role of the three wise monkeys?"

"You know about them? I'm impressed."

He shrugged.

"It's Marta's doing. She introduced me to Mizaru, Kikazaru, and Iwazaru when we discussed the links between mind, speech, and action from the perspective of those with a well-developed sixth sense."

They walked on in silence for a few minutes before Roget glanced at Amelia again.

"Did you ever discover people with antisocial personality disorder in your midst?"

"You mean among consecrated sisters or friars? Yes. Highly functioning psychopaths with a strong sixth sense, the sort who don't suffer from criminal impulses. We don't necessarily detect all of them, but those we identify invariably tell us they joined the Order because they wanted an environment that would make sure their lack of empathy didn't take them down a grim path."

"They recognize their condition. That's fascinating."

"We find those with a strong sixth sense have enough self-awareness to know they can't differentiate between good and evil in the same way as normal humans. In response, they adapt by taking cues from religious or moral teachings and the people around them. They don't care about others but made a conscious decision that they would do no harm. By living under the Order's Rule and within a community where everyone engages in the same behaviors helps them achieve that goal. They integrate by mimicking those around them even though they don't believe in the Almighty or the Void."

"The human mind is an incredible thing."

She nodded.

"I agree, which is why I'm training to become more than just a normal counselor. You could do so too if you join the Order."

"One more question." Roget halted as he chose his words. They were halfway between the priory and the maximum security compound, where administrative buildings and correctional officer lodgings lined the crushed coral streets. "Erasmus, Marnix, and Shakib were once like Seled Hyson. They no longer are since I don't pick anything up when I'm around them. Not even the mental auras of normal people. Did this cure turn them from violent sociopaths into highly functioning psychopaths?"

Amelia studied him for a few heartbeats.

"I wasn't involved in that project and never quite looked at it that way. But you could be right. Perhaps I will ask Sister Mirjam in private one day."

**

"What did you think of Supermax?" Erasmus asked when Roget joined the postulants for lunch in the priory's small dining hall.

The three were already halfway through their meals — soup and raw vegetables from the priory's greenhouses.

Roget put down his tray and sat across from him.

"Terrifying is the first word that comes to mind. That's a seriously bleak place. Gave me a massive headache, though it's fading."

Marnix snorted.

"And don't we know it? Everyone there belongs in the Seventh Circle of Hell." When Roget cocked an amused eyebrow at him, he frowned. "What? Did you think we weren't getting the full classical education given to every postulant? Just because we were exiled for life and don't have a normal friar's talent? We can debate metaphysics and philosophy with you until the end of the universe, my friend."

Roget raised his hands in surrender.

"Sorry, Marnix. I didn't mean to offend you. After what I experienced this morning, I wasn't expecting Dante's Inferno, but I agree with you about the Seventh Circle of Hell. So how did the sisters cure you guys?"

"They peered deep into the Void where a normal person keeps his soul," Erasmus replied, "and cauterized our psychological and spiritual wounds. I can't describe it otherwise. After each session, a small part of the evil living within me was gone, along with the associated memories, until no trace of darkness remained. Sure, I lost a fair bit of myself in the process and often think I'm a hollow man, but for the first time since I can remember, I'm at peace."

"Ditto." Marnix and Shakib nodded in agreement.

Roget popped a baby carrot into his mouth and chewed thoughtfully. After swallowing, he asked, "Why didn't the sisters cure more of the Supermax prisoners? The difference between the ones I saw this morning and you three is incredible."

"Only the sisters can answer that question, though I doubt they would, especially with an outsider. All I know is that the sisters vetted us thoroughly over several weeks before they offered us places in the experimental program. During the treatment, they kept us segregated from the rest of Supermax." Erasmus gave Roget a humorless smile. "Apply to become a friar, and once you take your vows, join their counselor training program. Maybe they'll let you in on the secret."

"I'm not interested in working with deranged people. My tolerance for humans, in general, took another nosedive this morning. What'll you guys do when you take vows?"

"Anything the Order needs. Since we don't have a shred of talent, I suspect it'll be manual labor in and around the priory."

"Those who sweep floors and rake leaves also serve the Almighty's purpose," Marnix intoned with mock seriousness. "But that still beats spending the rest of our lives in Supermax surrounded by the most violent humans in the republic. You're going back with Amelia tomorrow?"

Roget nodded.

"Yup. Until I can shut out those violent human minds."

"Good luck staying sane."

"Some of it is interesting." Roget took a sip of his iced tea. "I didn't believe until this morning that evil was an actual thing. The discovery is making me question a lot of my assumptions about life and the universe."

"Aye." Erasmus raised a water glass, as if in salute. "Take it from a former practitioner of evil. It's too bloody real."

"Tell me something." Roget gave the man a speculative look. "You said the sisters cauterized your psychological and spiritual wounds bit by bit."

"Sure. They burned out that which made us sociopaths."

"But you still can't experience empathy for others."

Erasmus shook his head.

"No. Not a shred. Yet I'm not under a compulsion to harm others or fulfill evil ambitions. What I want, what we want, is to live a life of service and repay the Order that gave us peace."

"Can you remember your thoughts before the cure?"

"No. We cannot even remember our crimes."

"Do you remember your lives before the cure?"

The three men glanced at each other with an air of puzzlement on their faces.

"We remember a few things, but they're rather vague. Does it matter? This is now our destiny, a second chance by the grace of the Almighty and the Brethren."

"How do you know the Order gave you peace if you don't remember your turmoil?"

Erasmus didn't immediately reply as he cast about for an answer.

"I can sometimes glimpse a faint echo of my former madness. It reminds me of whence I came."

For reasons he couldn't explain, Roget knew with certainty Erasmus was telling the truth, though the man's mind was a complete blank compared to Seled Hyson's, as were those of the other two postulants.

**

"How did he do?" Mirjam gestured at the chairs in front of her desk when Amelia entered the prioress' office.

"About as we expected. He's recovering from what must be the worst migraine of his life and will probably spend the rest of the day sleeping. After witnessing Stearn's distress, I think the shock treatment Marta envisioned might simply be too much for such a well-developed talent. If only he would join the Order so we could use the teachings instead."

"Stearn is far stronger than you give him credit. This morning was a shock because he could not conceive of sensing such violent chaos in others until encountering it for the first time."

"He told me it changed his views on the existence of evil as an actual phenomenon."

"As opposed to a social construct invented by the religious so they could condemn behavior they don't like?" An air of amusement lit up Mirjam's eyes. "Will he be a soul theorist or a more prosaic believer in twisted psyches?"

"We didn't discuss the matter in any significant detail once he made the discovery."

"It'll be easier for him tomorrow now that he knows what to expect. We will continue the process as Marta directed."

Amelia, hearing her superior and not her sister in the Order speak, lowered her gaze for a few seconds. "Yes, Prioress."

"Now tell me about your progress with the prisoners. I'd like another two or three for the new treatment, including a woman if possible, and neither Mette nor Teresa can come up with likely candidates," Mirjam said, naming two of the priory's counselors. Both had worked on developing and implementing the treatment that cured Erasmus and his fellow prisoners.

A grimace briefly twisted Amelia's face.

"Seled Hyson is the least damaged of the women I'm counseling. But she doesn't strike me as the sort who would relinquish her memories of the past for a chance at becoming the priory's indentured servant, which is all she would be since I've not sensed any sign of the talent. Seled's goal is living in an exile colony on one of the other islands."

"Are you sure she's bereft of the talent? It could be latent, hidden beneath the chaos that is her mind, and be driving Seled's antisocial personality disorder." Mirjam sat back, a thoughtful expression on her face. "And wouldn't *that* be an interesting experiment? I'd like to examine this Seled myself."

—21—

"Sister Gwenneth?" Landry's tone was soft and respectful as usual, but she knew him well, and he sounded mildly irked to her ears, which could only mean Friar Loxias and his delegation were in the outer office. Gwenneth let her eyes roam over the abbey's quadrangle one last time, consciously avoiding the Orb that seemed to mock her.

The stone buildings glistened with rain under a dishearteningly gray sky that matched her mood, and though the building was climate-controlled, she could almost feel the suffocating humidity as if it were a thick blanket. Southern Tristan's monsoon season was mercifully short, but everything seemed waterlogged. Northern Isolde faced much worse, with storms barreling at it from the World Ocean every week.

"Friars Loxias and Sandor along with Sisters Emilie and Keleos for the abbess."

Gwenneth suppressed a sigh and turned away from the rain-streaked window to take her place behind the large but plain wooden desk.

"Please usher them in."

Landry had lined up four unpadded chairs in front of the desk at her orders. Gwenneth did not want her visitors made comfortable in a less formal setting around the low tea table. She hoped it would send an unmistakable message but feared it might be an empty gesture instead. Loxias shrugged off insults, overt and implied, with the disdain of a self-righteous man convinced his truth triumphed over all others.

She remained seated but gestured at the chairs as the delegation entered the office.

"Brethren. Please sit."

The four wore respectful expressions but couldn't hide the triumphant gleam in their eyes as they bowed their heads in greeting. Gwenneth studied them in silence one-by-one as they sat. Keleos joining Loxias didn't surprise her. A Void Ship rescued both from the destruction of the Hatshepsut Abbey during the empire's collapse. They had entered the Order at almost the same time and knew each other well.

Neither was Gwenneth taken aback at seeing Sandor, a survivor from the Mykonos Abbey. She'd long ago marked him as one of the most conservative, if not reactionary friars. Emilie's presence in the delegation, however, was unexpected. Lyonesse born and bred, she knew no other abbey than this one and no abbess other than Gwenneth. She hardly fit in with the Lindisfarne Brethren, who were mainly older and from somewhere other than Lyonesse.

"What is your purpose?" Gwenneth asked, turning her attention on Loxias.

"We must move forward and declare this the Order's motherhouse, Abbess."

"Surely, you understand my position, Loxias. Absent evidence Lindisfarne was destroyed, I cannot in good conscience do so."

"Our community includes members rescued from hundreds of abbeys and priories destroyed during Dendera's madness, and our Void Ships found no evidence of survivors after countless expeditions into what was once the human empire. We are the last. I do not doubt it."

"That's not evidence Lindisfarne no longer exists." Gwenneth wanted Loxias to speak openly about the Lindisfarne Brethren's true motivations. She already knew what they were, of course, but no one dared voice the truth. "Tell me, why are you and your followers so keen on a symbolic gesture that changes nothing about our lives and our duties?"

"Do the Order's teachings not say we should face reality, especially in trying times? Yes, finally admitting we are the last Brethren left in the galaxy might be traumatic for some, but it can also be liberating. As motherhouse of the Order, we can chart a new course and better prepare ourselves for the day when the republic finally ventures out and reunites our species under its banner."

"Fair enough. But I don't think that's your primary motivation."

Loxias adopted a mildly affronted air. "I'm not sure I understand what you're getting at, Abbess."

"We can do everything you just mentioned, even without usurping Lindisfarne's primacy. Tell me, why do I think this push for me to declare us the motherhouse is more because of the way the Order governed Lindisfarne?"

Loxias' affronted air took on a tinge of self-righteousness.

"Why shouldn't we play a bigger part in the republic's affairs? Our destiny is irrevocably entwined with it, we serve the community in ways rarely seen throughout the Order's history, and yet we dare not raise our voice. Many of the Brethren feel this just isn't right, including many sisters born here, such as

Emilie." He glanced at the younger woman. "This isn't just about a bunch of sisters and friars who remember the good old days and wish to recreate them."

"The good old days?" Gwenneth cocked a mocking eyebrow. "You mean when the Order ran an entire star system like a medieval fief, denying the laypeople a voice? Or when so many of us were rightly or wrongly accused of meddling in secular politics and massacred? What good old days do you mean?"

When Loxias, clearly surprised at her cutting tone, didn't reply, she said, "I've spent the last twenty-five years making sure the Order stays far away from secular politics and governance. Otherwise, we could well incur the wrath of citizens who came here or whose parents came here to escape imperial oppression. They'll certainly not accept theocratic rule, Lindisfarne-style."

Loxias made a dismissive hand gesture.

"Please give me some credit, Gwenneth. We don't plan on making Lyonesse a theocracy. But we deserve a say in the government, especially with deadly diseases running rampant across human space. Or did you forget we provide most of this star system's medical services, among others?"

"And you think declaring our abbey the Order's motherhouse, thereby turning me into the Order of the Void's *Summus Abbatissa,* will accomplish that goal?" She let a hint of incredulity color her words.

"It's a first and essential step. It makes you an equal to any cabinet member and the head of the Defense Force and will give us a way of sitting on the republic's highest councils from where we can influence the course of events. Perhaps we might even convince the government it should transfer control of the Knowledge Vault *we* built, from the military to the Order."

"Again, why? The last time abbesses meddled in secular politics, it didn't end well for their abbeys. Perhaps not on

Hatshepsut since its abbey suffered at the hands of Dendera's Retribution Fleet rather than the local viceroy. But I can assure you on Yotai and every other planet in the Coalsack Sector it was a different story. I witnessed Admiral Zahar's troops wantonly murdering our Brethren by the thousands, as did those of us who arrived here in *Dawn Trader* and founded this abbey. I will not allow such a thing to happen again, and that means we steer clear of politics, period. There are still plenty of people on this planet who don't quite trust us, including government leaders such as Defense Secretary Brigid DeCarde. It takes only one hint the Order is attempting to influence government policy, and our good works will be for naught. Once we lose the trust of the people, we're finished."

Loxias shrugged as if her words didn't matter.

"Then we work through friends in high places."

"We already have friends in high places."

"Jonas Morane? His second and last term as president is ending soon. After that, he might still wield a bit of influence by dint of his stature as an elder statesman, but it will fade over the next few years. Emma Reyes? Same thing. Elenia Yakin? She's no longer in the public eye. Sure, you enjoy excellent relationships with General Barca and many of the senior officers in the Defense Force. Still, they're a far cry from being the sort of friends who can nudge policy decisions at our behest."

"This discussion isn't leading us anywhere." Gwenneth let her eyes shine with suppressed exasperation. "I see no reason we should take on Lindisfarne's mantle, and I definitely will not scale back our policy of non-interference in secular matters. If you're that concerned about the Order charting a new path and preparing itself for when the republic sallies forth into human space, you will heed my words and leave things as they are. The path you propose could well make sure there is no Order of the

Void left when Lyonesse re-enters the wormhole network in a few generations. To repeat, if we lose the trust of the people, the Order will die."

A smug expression appeared on Loxias' face.

"I believe most Brethren support us becoming the new Lindisfarne, especially those who entered the Order on Lyonesse and aren't burdened with memories of our past. They believe we deserve a say in the affairs of this star system. My colleagues here can attest to that. Put the question before the community and let us decide together."

Gwenneth ignored the supportive nods.

"I lead this house. The decision is mine and mine alone. We will not repeat the Order's mistakes, nor will we assume a title that is not ours."

Loxias inclined his head, but he did not mean it as a gesture of acceptance. If anything, his smug expression widened.

"For as long as you are abbess, I agree the decision is yours. But since you will not even put the question before the community, we four, who represent the Lindisfarne Brethren, have assembled enough signatures for a leadership review." He fished a data wafer from a hidden pocket. "You will find the petition and signatures duly recorded on this. As per the Rule, you must now convene the community within fourteen days. Until then, you may not make any decisions beyond those necessary for the abbey's day-to-day operations."

"And who will you name in my stead if the Brethren remove me?"

"Someone who will seek a better future for the Order. We might even vote on amending the Rule so friars can become abbots and priors." A smile touched his lips. "Heresy, I know. But, if we find more men like Stearn Roget with a talent as good as, if not better than that of our leading sisters, then I see no reason why men cannot shoulder the top leadership responsibilities alongside them."

He placed the data wafer on Gwenneth's otherwise bare desk, but she pointedly ignored it even as she wondered how Loxias managed to gather enough signatures for a leadership review. Did she miscalculate support for his position that badly?

"I've said what needed saying," Loxias continued, "and with your permission, we shall leave so you can consider the matter."

"And your colleagues have nothing to say? Or are they merely a mute Greek chorus whose role is witnessing your performance? I was at least expecting some commentary on your mummery." When she saw the surprise in his eyes at her unaccustomed sarcasm, she waved a hand at him. "Never mind. You may go."

The foursome retreated with more alacrity than Gwenneth expected, and Landry, perceptive as always, mercifully closed the office door behind them, leaving her to contemplate what was, in essence, a monastic coup d'état. Loxias was no dummy. Somehow, he'd assembled a coalition capable of defeating her if she didn't bend to the Lindisfarne Brethren's will. Otherwise, he would still be biding his time.

For a few seconds, Gwenneth wished she could call upon Jonas Morane's wisdom to help her through this, but Loxias' mutiny was an internal matter, not one for outsiders, even though Morane and Reyes were her closest friends. The Rule demanded she be discreet. Gwenneth faced the possibility she would no longer be abbess by the time her fourteen days of grace ran out.

If that happened, she could only watch from the sidelines while the Lindisfarne Brethren wrapped themselves in a cloak of righteousness so those with unseemly ambition could get a taste of power and take them all down when their hubris outstripped reality. Even after over two decades on Lyonesse, Loxias and his followers from the old Order still didn't understand the Lyonesse mentality. Apparently, neither did the children of those who fled the empire and chose this as their home.

— 22 —

"All these years on Lyonesse and I never figured Gwenneth capable of sarcasm," Friar Sandor said as they left the administrative building.

Sister Keleos, a thin, elderly woman who wore a perpetual frown, sneered. "So long as she's capable of following the Rule regarding a leadership review, she can be as sarcastic as she wants."

"Our abbess is nothing if not scrupulous." Loxias' long stride carried them across the quadrangle under what he knew were Gwenneth's watchful eyes. Her composure throughout had been remarkable considering his provocative attitude, save for that barb at the end, which told him he'd finally scored a direct hit. "She will bow to the inevitable once she sees the vote go against her."

Sandor nodded. "Agreed. A shame Stearn Roget hasn't joined the Order. Someone with a talent that strong would be a shoo-in as our first abbot."

"Even if he took vows now, it would be years before a majority considered him ready," Emilie replied, "if not decades."

Loxias glanced at her over his shoulder. "Perhaps. But considering how rapidly he learned to control a mind so disordered, I daresay he could rival our strongest sisters faster than anyone might expect. I should speak with Rikkard and see if he can coax Stearn into taking vows."

"We might be more successful if I spoke with Amelia. She doesn't broadcast it, but she stands behind the Lindisfarne Brethren, and Stearn is continuing his self-control training by observing her work with prisoners. They spend a lot of time together."

"Even better. Speak with Amelia, and I'll talk to Rikkard. If we can entice Stearn into the fold as the strongest male talent on record, it will bring many waverers to our side. Considering Gwenneth will do her best to woo them before and during the leadership review, we should take advantage of anything that helps our cause. I don't just want her defeated; I don't want any doubt that a firm majority supports us. It'll ensure the remaining naysayers fall in line."

"It would be even better if we could enlist Marta. She's the strongest among the sisters and respected by almost everyone."

Loxias turned his gaze on Sandor. "I tried and failed, and one doesn't try again with Marta once she's given her answer. She can reach into our minds without us knowing if she's so inclined, and that scares me."

"A shame. She would be so useful in helping us guide government policy."

"Let's not discuss such matters, especially out in the open. The Rule forbids sisters with an open third eye from influencing others without their knowledge."

"Then it's time we rewrote the damn thing. If we're taking the Order on a new path, then perhaps we should remove every obstacle."

Emilie winked at Sandor. "Heretic."

"Gwenneth's warning on the trust of the lay people is valid," Keleos pointed out. "We don't dare risk confirming our mythical reputation for mind-meddling is anything but. I would ask we never discuss the matter again. We will influence government policy without reaching into politicians' minds. I'm sure we can use other ways of swaying elected officials and bureaucrats. You friars are redoubtable poker players for a reason while we sisters can not only read body language but emotions."

"Understood," Sandor replied in a grudging tone, aware Keleos could become the next abbess. She was the most experienced and talented sister among the Lindisfarne Brethren, and those stronger than her wouldn't want the job in the first place.

They entered the refectory where the Lindisfarne Brethren leadership waited for a report of the delegation's visit to the abbess' office. Four dozen pairs of eyes belonging to friars in senior administrative positions and sisters from every discipline turned on them as conversation died away. Their most notable feature as a group was that none of them were survivors of the Yotai Abbey's massacre, one of the most violent pogroms against the Order of the Void in its entire history.

"It went as expected, my friends," Loxias said, beaming. "Gwenneth denied our community a chance of voicing its opinion on the matter of declaring this the motherhouse and taking a greater role in governing the star system, as Lindisfarne did before the empire collapsed. I presented her with the call for a leadership review, and she did not refuse it. We will settle this once and for all within the next fourteen days."

Enthusiastic applause greeted his words.

"It is time we shed the old ways." Loxias walked among his followers, wearing a mask of humility. "The universe has changed, and so must we, otherwise I fear our Order may not survive this dark age. Lyonesse could well be the last bastion of human civilization and we the last of our kind."

**

"This is utter madness." Sister Katarin's eyes blazed with suppressed anger. She'd stormed into Gwenneth's office uninvited moments after seeing the message calling the Brethren together a few days hence. "You can't let these idiots sacrifice everything on the altar of ambition."

"The Rule is clear," Gwenneth replied in a resigned tone. "They gathered enough signatures for a leadership review. I have no choice but to face the Brethren and let them judge."

"Well, I won't stand for it. And neither will those who saw the bloody result of our Order interfering in secular governance. Lyonesse may seem like an oasis of reason, but we both know how fast a society can turn against those they perceive as threatening their future. Pendrick Zahar was a point in case I never wish to experience again."

"Sandor is a member of the Lindisfarne faction, yet he barely escaped with his life when Jorge Danton wiped out the Mykonos Abbey at Zahar's behest. There are more than a few survivors from the Coalsack Sector pogrom who support Loxias."

"Fools, the lot of them, worthy of excommunication."

"I doubt I'll find a two-thirds majority among the Brethren to excommunicate anyone, let alone a Loxias follower. Matters must take their course as they will, according to the Almighty's plan."

Katarin scoffed. "Trust the plan? Is that it? I still remember a time, long ago, when you helped Jonas Morane force events and eliminated a threat against the Knowledge Vault. Where is the Sister Gwenneth who helped him push Rorik Hecht and the scheming former imperial nobles out of Lyonesse politics forever?"

Gwenneth let out a soft sigh.

"She's older and considerably more tired. Look, I hope sanity will prevail. Speak with those you trust. Spread the word that the Lindisfarne Brethren's path could end with another Yotai massacre if they're not careful. And trust in the Almighty. At least get Marta out of her endless mystical trance so she can school the abbey on the risk of a future filled with fire and blood if we play secular politics again."

"Marta will intervene when it suits her and not before. If she intervenes. Look up the word unpredictable in the Encyclopedia Galactica. Her image will accompany the definition."

A scornful expression crossed Katarin's face.

"Very funny. This could trigger an existential crisis, Gwenneth. Loxias won't stop at installing an abbess of his choice and declaring this the motherhouse. He wants a seat on the republic's most senior councils."

"Don't you think I know that?" Gwenneth's voice cracked over Katarin's head like a bullwhip.

"Speak with Jonas Morane. You must warn him."

"How can I? A leadership review is an internal matter which doesn't concern anyone outside the abbey, even if we know the motivations behind it. The Rule is clear on that."

"Bugger the Rule."

Gwenneth snorted. "That sounded exactly like something Loxias or his followers would say."

"If I weren't a well-disciplined sister of the Order of the Void, I'd say something thoroughly impolite right now."

"Don't hold back on my account."

"I'm holding back on the Order's account, and because you're my abbess, one which we cannot afford to replace with a sister whose gaze goes beyond the abbey's walls." Katarin exhaled loudly. "Bugger Loxias and the fools who follow him. Please let Jonas know what's happening. He'll keep our secrets while helping, or at least providing wise counsel."

"I'll think about it."

Gwenneth's eyes slid to one side as she considered, once again, the possibility of their sociopathy 'cure' being used for more nefarious ends by those intent on taking control of the republic. That was the one thing she couldn't discuss with outsiders. Even Katarin was still unaware. So far, Mirjam and her assistants were staying well away from the Lindisfarne Brethren, in no small part because of their isolation in the Windies, where abbey politics seemed no more than a mirage on the horizon.

But if another sister sat behind this desk and radically changed the Order's path? Mirjam wasn't a survivor of Admiral Zahar's pogroms and didn't have those soul-searing massacres imprinted on her deepest engrams. She, along with most of Loxias' supporters, hadn't seen with their own eyes what happened when the Order was suspected of meddling in politics.

"While you do that, I'll rally everyone with a shred of sanity, and we'll stop this madness before it turns into an unmitigated disaster." Katarin, eyes blazing with unexpected fervor, stood. "Surely, there's more of us than there is of them."

"Do as you will. But keep in mind the words of a pre-diaspora statesman whose nation slipped into civil war. A house divided against itself cannot stand. If we draw battle lines between the Lindisfarne Brethren and those who don't care a whit about secular governance, we might well split the Order in two with little chance of recovery."

A frown of concern creased Katarin's forehead. "You sound defeated."

"Lately, I've wondered whether my time as abbess and leader of our Order is over, whether I represent a past that imprisons us."

"Then help choose a successor who believes we must give to Caesar the things that are Caesar's, and to the Almighty the things that are the Almighty's. You of all people know theocracies never end well. Entire religions self-immolated on the pyre of theocratic rule to the point where no one remembers them nowadays, though they once numbered billions of faithful."

"I will do my duty and protect the abbey; you can be confident of that. But if the Almighty no longer wishes my service as abbess, then I shall no longer do so."

Katarin shook her head. "You go ahead and trust the Almighty. I'll rally the troops. We'll see who gets results. Believing there's a divine plan is nice and well, but the Almighty gave us free will for a reason and hasn't taken it away even though we misuse that gift, otherwise the empire would still be intact."

"Or Dendera's madness and the empire's destruction are part of the plan." When Katarin made to reply, a wry smile softened Gwenneth's features. "I know. You don't believe in predestination, and I'm not sure about it myself since I've always enjoyed discussing the nature of causality. But I lack the energy for a debate as old as humanity right now."

— 23 —

"Mister President." Defense Secretary Brigid DeCarde and Lieutenant General Adrienne Barca rose as the former's executive assistant ushered Jonas Morane into her office. "We appreciate you making time for us."

"My agenda isn't particularly full these days, and I always enjoy the brief walk here from Government House. Besides, my close protection detail can use the exercise. They spend way too much time sitting." He dropped into a chair facing both women. "Now, what is it that couldn't wait until my regular Friday night visit to the Officers' Mess?"

"Information from the abbey that will stun you."

"Gathered by the Intelligence Company's irregulars among the university student body, no doubt?"

Barca nodded.

"Indeed. The Brethren are keeping a lid on word spreading beyond the abbey walls, but Gwenneth faces a formal leadership review in a few days."

An air of disgust crossed Morane's face. "Loxias and those infernal Lindisfarne Brethren, am I right?"

"You are. That they found enough support to force a leadership review worries us."

"A shame they're attacking the woman whose force of character pulled them through those tough, early years on Lyonesse. But Gwenneth will soon turn ninety, and as I mentioned a few weeks ago, dealing with political shenanigans is taking a toll. I'm not convinced she was overly pleased when they reappointed her the last time." Morane shrugged. "At this point, the leadership review is an internal matter for the Order alone and none of our business. But ·if a sister from the Lindisfarne Brethren replaces Gwenneth and shows more than just a passing interest in secular politics, we'll pay close attention."

"Our thoughts precisely," DeCarde said. "We can't let mind-meddlers interfere with the proper governance of the republic as mandated by our constitution and the will of the people."

"I doubt it'll go that far. None of the Brethren who came to Lyonesse from other parts of the old empire ever served in the Lindisfarne star system government. The Order as it is here, today, has no institutional memory of running anything more than a monastic house."

Barca made a dubious face. "Not having an institutional memory doesn't exclude yearning for a return to a more glorious past."

"They should round up those troublesome friars and make them build a monastery on Isolde," DeCarde grumbled. "That would take care of their ambitions and yearnings."

"At least they stopped recruiting male postulants. Other than reformed exiles, that is, and they don't count since they'll never leave the Windies, meaning the problem will eventually solve itself when the surplus retires or passes on."

DeCarde scoffed. "But in the meantime, Loxias and his crew can cause a lot of mischief. What's the old saying? Idle hands are the devil's workshop? Ironic, isn't it."

"Only if the Brethren choose an abbess who's under the man's thumb should they vote Gwenneth out, and if I've learned anything about the Order of the Void over the years, it's that the sisters are in charge, period. The friars make sure the abbey and the priories function on a day-to-day basis. They don't make policy, let alone decide what path the Order takes."

"Yet the friars governed an entire star system and might still do so if Lindisfarne survived the empire's collapse," DeCarde pointed out.

"Under the overall direction of the Order's *Summus Abbatissa*, who laid out the colonial government's policies."

A smirk twisted her lips. "You're determined to make us think this leadership review isn't a big deal, aren't you?"

"Because it's not a big deal for anyone outside the Order. Yet. But I think I'll speak with Gwenneth nonetheless, though she won't thank me for prying into abbey affairs."

"That's what we hoped you might do."

Morane cocked an amused eyebrow at DeCarde.

"You want Gwenneth to reassure us the republic is not in danger of a theocratic takeover? I doubt the abbey's policy of sticking to spiritual matters and good works in the community will change. But I'll suggest the Order consider establishing a friars-only house on Isolde. If nothing else, she might find humor in the idea."

"Thank you. I've never trusted the mind-meddlers. For the longest time, they didn't confirm rumors sisters can sense the emotions of others, the reason they're sisters in the first place. What else did they not tell us? Imagine a world where their sort can influence politicians with no one being the wiser." DeCarde shook her head.

"We already live in that world, Brigid. Except they're called lobbyists who use flattery, favors, and donations to influence policy, which is mind-meddling of another sort." He winked at her. "While I'm here, anything new on *Standfast*?"

"She's what we wanted and more. The shakeout cruise has brought no major issues to light. Minor ones, sure, but that's normal. Hecht Aerospace did a superb job."

"They also received a superb payment. When's her first wormhole transit?"

"Tomorrow," Barca replied.

"Hopefully, it will go smoothly. Maiden wormhole transits have a way of making design flaws glaringly obvious. Still, since she already pushed into the upper in-system FTL bands during her shakeout, they know about hidden problems, especially those related to hull integrity."

"They red-lined her three days ago on two ten-hour jumps. No issues."

"Then I'd say that's a good omen."

**

"How did you find out? Or should I not ask?"

"About what?" Morane gave Gwenneth a penetrating stare as she slipped into the booth across from him. He'd invited her for a late lunch after leaving DeCarde's office, and she, like Morane, was a lifetime member of the Lannion Base Officers' Mess. In her case, it was for services rendered as the first Defense Force Chaplain General in the republic's early days.

"The leadership review." She glared at him. "Why else would you ask me here with no warning on a random Wednesday?

Normally, you wait for one of my weekend escapes from the abbey to question me about private matters concerning the Order."

"Guilty as charged, *Summus Abbatissa*."

The despair that briefly crossed Gwenneth's face made her seem twenty years older for a fleeting moment. "Please, Jonas. Not you too."

"Little remains secret for long on Lyonesse. It may be a big planet, but our human community isn't much more than an overgrown village by comparison. Yes, I invited you so we could talk about the leadership review Loxias and the Lindisfarne Brethren rammed through. Some of us wonder what it means for the future of the Order vis-à-vis the republic."

"Well, thank you for coming straight to the point, Jonas."

If Morane didn't know better, he'd think her tone and words held a sharp edge of exasperation.

"We've been friends for too long, Gwenneth. Anything less than complete honesty between us would be improper." He nodded at the buffet table. "Shall we fetch our meal before discussing the matter?"

She inclined her head. "Certainly, though thinking about Loxias is doing wonders to keep my calorie intake down these days."

They sampled the remaining cold dishes moments before the mess staff, who'd been waiting for the president and his guest, closed the buffet now that the midday meal hour was over.

Gwenneth took a bit of smoked fish and let out an appreciative if soft groan. "I really should send the abbey cooks here for a stint so they could learn from the mess' head chef."

Morane snorted. "You say that almost every time we sample the mess cuisine, but we're still waiting for you to act on the notion."

"Mostly because my cooks would mutiny if I even hinted they weren't as skilled as their military equivalents."

"And yet you face a mutiny nonetheless, or something similar."

She let out a heartfelt sigh. "Loxias and his faction are acting under the Order's Rule. I cannot deny them the leadership review because they drummed up enough support among the Brethren. There's no mutiny involved."

"Figure of speech. They don't like your policies, and since you won't change them, they'll remove you. That's not much different from a mutiny in the naval sense. Of course, your lot is doing it under a cloak of legitimacy, however thin, because of the Order's Rule."

"Contrary to the Defense Force, the Order of the Void is a limited democracy where the rank and file can remove their general or admiral with a simple vote. My opponents will make their case before the assembled community, I will present my rebuttal, and the Brethren will decide." She put down her fork and sat back. "Frankly, I'm not even sure I can find the energy to oppose Loxias. I've been abbess longer than most I've seen in my decades with the Order. Retirement is increasingly appealing. I could easily spend the rest of my life in quiet contemplation, perhaps occasionally helping the teachers and, if asked, be a wise elder and counsel my younger sisters."

"You're in excellent health. That retirement could easily turn into thirty years without a firm purpose. A quarter of your lifespan."

Gwenneth chuckled.

"Irony, thy name is Jonas. I could say the same about you. Except you're younger than I am and could easily face forty or fifty years without a firm purpose once your term is up. I suppose it's tragic in the sense that you entered the highest office in the republic at a relatively young age. You've nowhere left. Sure, you could make a post-retirement career offering your wisdom to whoever asks, but let's face it, most would find the prospect overly intimidating. You are the father of the sacred Knowledge Vault and the man who made sure Lyonesse survived the empire's demise."

"Granted. But we're speaking about you and the Order's future, not me. Besides, I'm in discussions with Brigid DeCarde and Adrienne Barca to create a Defense Force Command and Staff College after the next election."

"Don't worry about me, let alone the abbey. Yes, we're blessed with a greater proportion of friars than is usual, which accounts for the restlessness of the most ambitious, since there aren't many senior leadership positions open to men. But sisters still outnumber friars by a wide margin, and I daresay a plurality, if not a majority, are content with the status quo. My ouster as abbess is far from being a certainty."

"Good to hear. But I worry about what might happen if a sister who agrees with Loxias replaces you, whether next week or in ten years. And I'm not alone. If your friars become involved in politics, things might turn sour between the republic and the Order because you'll be suspected of using your secretive and mystical talents to influence government policy."

A sigh escaped Gwenneth's thin lips.

"I know, and I remember Pendrick Zahar's destruction of the Order in the Coalsack Sector on suspicion of involvement with imperial authorities, as do the others who survived. But by now, the Brethren rescued from other sectors or who joined on Lyonesse outnumber us. I've made that point to Loxias and his closest followers, without much success. I'll make it again when I face the entire community at the leadership review. After that, it'll be in the Almighty's hands."

"Trust in his plan, is that it?"

She raised a restraining hand. "I had that very discussion with Katarin yesterday, and I'm not in the mood for a repeat."

"Fair enough. If the Brethren declare Lyonesse the Order's motherhouse and make you the *Summus Abbatissa*, that's an internal matter which doesn't concern the republic. I'll send you my official congratulations. But since you're already invited to major state events as it is, taking on the title of top abbess won't change anything with the way the citizenry regards you or the Order."

"Loxias wants more than that. He wants the abbess to sit on councils of state as a co-equal with the cabinet and the legislature."

"Of course he does and it wouldn't surprise me if he found supporters both within the government and among certain segments of the population."

A frown creased Gwenneth's forehead. "Why?"

"The Order has a lot of admirers out there who wouldn't think twice about giving it a greater say in how the republic is run. And some people are still unhappy our constitution established a unicameral legislature whose members aren't beholden to political parties. That makes it harder for special interests who want to influence policies and legislation behind closed doors so the voters can't overhear them. Adding a player would give those special interests another avenue of approach. I'm sure the Order of the Void isn't immune to a bit of friendly backscratching. I'll wager one of your predecessors negotiated quite an understanding with the reigning emperor and his government when they gave her the Lindisfarne star system, and it probably wasn't spiritual in any way, shape, or fashion."

"Then what can I do?"

"Ever read a little book written about four thousand years ago by a Chinese general called Sun Tzu?"

— 24 —

"All hands now hear this. Prepare for wormhole transit in five minutes. I repeat, prepare for wormhole transit in five minutes. That is all."

Lieutenant Stefan Norum switched off the public address system and sat back while his eyes sought out the holographic tactical projection dominating *Standfast*'s bridge. At its heart, two blue icons were rapidly nearing the orange disk that marked the wormhole's event horizon. One represented the corvette, while the other marked her constant companion since the beginning of the shakeout cruise, the Republic of Lyonesse Starship *Dawn Seeker*. The latter was now part of the Navy's 1st Squadron after General Barca suspended the Void Ship program for an indefinite period.

Dawn Seeker fulfilled two purposes. The first was as *Standfast*'s safety in case she suffered severe problems and required outside help or, the Almighty forbid, evacuation, while the second was acting as a telemetry station and reporting on the corvette's performance as seen by an outside observer.

Norum's ears picked up a door opening behind him and turned around, knowing it would be Lieutenant Commander Lisiecki. The door leading to the captain's day cabin made a slightly different whisper than the main entrance.

"Systems are green, sir. *Dawn Seeker* is synced and ready to cross the event horizon in tandem with us."

Lisiecki dropped into the throne-like command chair behind the navigation and helm stations and rubbed his hands with gleeful anticipation that was only partially feigned.

"This is where a starship meets the true Void."

Norum, who wasn't quite as skilled as his captain at disguising a twinge of apprehension, nodded enthusiastically.

"The third and last of *Standfast*'s three baptisms. Finally."

"She's done better than expected so far, Number One. Her first wormhole transit should be as boring as it is momentous in the Republic of Lyonesse's naval history."

"It would be equally momentous if the Void swallowed us," Chief Petty Officer Husam Bracker, *Standfast*'s coxswain and her helmsman for the first wormhole transit, said, grinning at Norum over his shoulder. "We might find out whether it's true that wormholes are direct conduits to the Almighty."

"Let's concentrate on using wormholes as shortcuts between star systems, shall we?" Lisiecki gave the coxswain his best 'I'm not amused' look.

"Aye, aye, sir. A shortcut we shall take."

The timer in the lower right corner of the primary display ticked away the minutes and seconds with inexorable precision and Lisiecki could feel the tension on the bridge. Every spacer knew ancient tales of malfunctioning starships entering a wormhole and vanishing forever, stories so old no one could dredge up examples, let alone names. Even the Navy's exhaustive database, which held centuries of imperial history, contained no records of vessels lost in such a manner. Lisiecki had checked. Of course, that didn't mean it never happened. At the height of the empire's glory, the entirety of human shipping must have made over a million crossings each year, not all of them between systems with operational traffic control infrastructures.

"All hands now hear this — wormhole transit in one minute. I repeat — wormhole transit in one minute. That is all."

The two blue icons in the tactical hologram were already touching the orange disk. For *Dawn Seeker*, which was older than anyone in *Standfast*, it would be just another plunge into a tunnel connecting star systems dozens of light-years apart, one of hundreds during a long career in service of both the Order of the Void and the Republic of Lyonesse.

Lisiecki realized he was clenching his fists and forced himself to relax. In a few seconds, the wormhole would draw them in. Once that happened, no one aboard could control what came next. They would come out on the other side in eight hours, or they wouldn't.

"Crossing the event horizon in three, two, one," Bracker intoned.

The universe turned into a pretzel of psychedelic colors that threatened to burn a hole through Lisiecki's brain, but the sensation vanished as quickly as it had come on.

"Status."

"Systems are nominal," Norum reported after a few seconds. He glanced at the primary display. Where they'd seen stars moments earlier, there now was nothing but unrelieved black. "We are transiting as per normal parameters."

Lisiecki, who'd joined the Navy over twenty years ago and served on two Void Ship expeditions, knew in his bones everything was right, that his ship *felt* right. He nodded.

"Excellent. I expected nothing less. You have the bridge, Number One. I'll be in my quarters."

"Aye, aye, sir."

**

"A few things knocked loose, but nothing we can't fix with a turn of the wrench," Lieutenant Padraig Younis, *Standfast*'s chief engineer, reported once he finished surveying the corvette after she emerged from the wormhole on the Broceliande end. "She's working as designed."

"How long before we—"

Lisiecki's communicator chirped for attention. "Bridge to the captain."

He tapped it. "Captain here."

"Officer of the watch, sir. Sensors are picking up three hyperspace trails aimed at the wormhole terminus. If this is their destination, they'll drop out of FTL in no more than ten minutes."

"A patrol from 2nd Squadron?"

"The traces are too small for either Void Ships or frigates, or any Lyonesse units allowed to leave the home system. *Dawn Seeker* confirmed our readings."

Lisiecki bit back a curse as he and Younis exchanged a knowing look.

"Put us at battle stations and make sure *Dawn Seeker* does the same, then broadcast a general alert to all naval units and HQ."

"Aye, aye, sir."

The battle stations klaxon sounded seconds later, followed by Lieutenant Norum's voice warning the crew this was not a drill — unknown FTL ships were inbound and unlikely to be Lyonesse-flagged.

"How are there intruders in this system?" Younis asked. "No way they slipped past Outer Picket and 2nd Squadron unseen. We would have, at the very least, received a signal from the traffic control buoys when we arrived or found them offline altogether. Yet the ones in this system are functional and not reporting unauthorized transits."

"Interstellar space. That's the only answer."

"Arietis is the closest wormhole junction and getting here from there in FTL only would be a stretch for your standard reiver junk."

Lisiecki shrugged. "They either enlarged their antimatter containment units without exploding, or they're running on fumes right now. Desperation will drive people to risk everything on a single throw of the dice. We'll find out momentarily."

"Aye. Well, thank the Almighty we're building our ships using pre-imperial standards. *Standfast*'s containment units can take on enough antimatter fuel for a thousand light-year trip in the highest interstellar hyperspace bands." Younis climbed to his feet. "I'd best make sure engineering is ready for battle."

"And I'm due in the CIC."

Lisiecki remembered reading corvettes in the defunct Imperial Fleet didn't offer the luxury of a combat information center. Still, he was glad the Lyonesse Navy insisted on them for the new class of warships. After running battle drills from the bridge of a Void Ship, he much preferred fighting from a CIC while the first officer took care of *Standfast*'s systems and navigation on the bridge, even if it that CIC was tiny compared to the ones in Kalinka class frigates.

As he entered, Lieutenant Vera Strade, the combat systems officer, rose from the command chair and stepped to one side.

"We're at battle stations, shields are up, and weapons are loaded. *Dawn Seeker* is linked in and ready to take our gunnery orders."

As the larger and more powerful ship, as well as the only purpose-built warship of the two, *Standfast* automatically took the lead, even though *Dawn Seeker*'s captain boasted just over a year more seniority as a lieutenant commander than Lisiecki.

"Thank you."

Lisiecki's eyes turned to the holographic tactical projection dominating the heavily armored compartment. Three red icons surrounded by equally red circles indicating the positions were approximate, seemed directly aimed at the two blue symbols hovering near the wormhole terminus disk.

"How did word get out we were blocking the entrance to the Lyonesse Branch if no ships escaped Outer Picket in years, sir?"

"Your guess is as good as mine, Vera. Maybe someone was supposed to report back. When they didn't, the reivers figured we were guarding our end of the Arietis wormhole and decided bypassing Corbenic altogether would be a splendid idea. Fear can push people into doing things they never would ordinarily."

"Makes sense."

Strade took her station to the command chair's left and ran one last check on the ship's offensive and defensive systems, if only to keep her mind off what she suspected would be another outright slaughter, just like the ones at Outer Picket. She didn't quite know how she would deal with that possibility. Her previous tours at Outer Picket had been dull and bloodless.

"Just remember, we're as desperate to keep the plague from Lyonesse as those infected are to find a star system with a functioning medical system," he said in a voice pitched for Strade's ears only as if he'd sensed her doubts. "Our duty is to our own."

"Yes, sir." She kept her eyes on the weapon systems status board.

"Sir." The communications petty officer raised her hand. "Incoming from Commander, 2nd Squadron."

Lisiecki turned toward the signals alcove. "Yes?"

"Text only. One word — destroy."

He took a deep breath. The senior 2nd Squadron officer in this star system exercised control over all traffic from wormhole terminus to wormhole terminus despite the fact *Standfast* and *Dawn Seeker* were under Navy HQ orders during the corvette's shakeout cruise. Per protocol, ships in one of the republic's three star systems came under the local commander for the duration should an emergency arise. Unknown intruders coming at a wormhole terminus from interstellar space in a time of galactic plague was about as big an emergency as Lisiecki could conceive.

"Acknowledge."

"Aye, aye, sir."

"Guns, once we determine the incoming ships are not of Lyonesse origin, target and prepare to fire for effect."

His words notwithstanding, Lisiecki knew the intruders wouldn't broadcast a beacon identifying them as belonging to the republic. No Lyonesse ships had left the republic's star systems since *Dawn Hunter*'s return a year earlier, and she'd been the last of the Void Ships sent out to pick through the empire's remains. Whoever was coming at the wormhole terminus *Standfast* and *Dawn Seeker* were unexpectedly guarding didn't belong. And they would die just as surely as if the plague had felled them on their homeworlds.

"Sensors are picking up three emergence signatures." A pause. "Sloop-sized, no beacons. Their emissions and hull profiles do not match any Lyonesse-flagged starship. They're accelerating toward the wormhole terminus."

"Targets marked. *Standfast* will take Tangos One and Two, and *Dawn Seeker* will take Tango Three." Numerals appeared beside the red icons in the tactical projection. "We are locked in and ready to open fire."

Moments later, a voice by Lisiecki's right elbow said, "Incoming transmission from one of the Tangos, Captain, audio-only. They claim to be disease-free and are demanding we give them asylum."

Lisiecki glanced down at his first officer's hologram. "Demanding? That's not how sane refugees would phrase a request for mercy."

"I know. And the fact there's no video component to the transmission speaks volumes. Those are plague ships for sure."

"Tangos are within effective weapons range," Strade said without turning away from her console.

Lisiecki took a deep breath. This would be the first time in his entire career he gave the order to kill sentient beings. But there was no choice. The safety of the republic came before everything else.

"Fire."

— 25 —

"It is time, Abbess." Landry, wearing the Order's formal cowl just like his superior, filled the open doorway to Gwenneth's office.

She turned away from the window overlooking the quadrangle and the Void Orb and smiled at him.

"It is indeed."

"The abbey's Brethren are assembled in the chapter house — standing room only. Those from outlying priories are connected via comlink, including the Windy Isles, though it's the middle of the night there. Sister Mirjam and her people will probably vote for you just because Loxias interrupted their sleep."

"I should hope they will vote on the merits of the review, not based on the inconvenience it poses."

"Human nature, Abbess. We're not immune, no matter how much we might try."

Gwenneth gave Landry a tight smile as she swept past him and into the corridor. They took the stairs to the ground floor and passed through the main door. Although the chapter house was a stout stone structure with thick walls built to survive for millennia and sitting at the far end of the quadrangle, Gwenneth could sense minds jostling for space within even as she stepped out into the open.

They were nowhere near as chaotic as those at the citizens' assemblies she'd attended with Jonas Morane in the months after their arrival on Lyonesse. Still, the fact she could hear them at all spoke to the turmoil Loxias' maneuver created among the Brethren. They'd never witnessed a leadership review because no abbey had conducted one in living memory. Pushing away the press of agitated thoughts, she walked past the Void Orb without giving it so much as a glance, and her mind focused on what lay ahead.

The chapter house was a high-ceilinged space used for community assemblies, classes, and occasional entertainment evenings. It was a close cousin to the Lyonesse Senate building, designed by the same architect. Rows of tiered benches lined its long axis on either side of the floor with observation galleries above them. Another set of seats reserved for the abbey's senior leadership filled one end, facing the main doors. Stained glass windows above the galleries, several over two meters high, let in a watery, mid-afternoon glow which complemented the light globes floating at regular intervals near the arched, neo-Gothic ceiling.

Though the heavy wood doors stood open, Gwenneth heard no voices, no hint of conversation, and she smiled to herself. Even on this momentous occasion, at least outward discipline prevailed. As she crossed the threshold, heads bowed respectfully and remained so as Gwenneth swept down the center aisle toward the abbess' seat, a simple, high-backed wooden chair upholstered in red fabric.

As she turned and faced the hall, she glanced at the wall of displays above the main doors, showing live video connections with the outlying priories, then let her eyes roam over the assembly. The chapter house was full, the priory chapter rooms appeared full, and she knew the abbey's overflow, mainly junior Brethren, watched from the refectory next door. Only those aboard warships or on duty in the various hospitals and clinics weren't attending in some fashion. Should any vote be within the margin of absence, it wouldn't be certified until those not in attendance sent in their ballot.

"We will now ask that the Almighty guide us and grant us wisdom during this extraordinary gathering of the Brethren on Lyonesse." Gwenneth's voice resonated clearly and without effort, thanks to the excellent acoustics, as she led her flock into prayer. When the last words faded away, she took her chair and said, "Please be seated."

After the rustling of robes faded away, she turned her head toward Loxias, who, as the abbey's chief administrator, sat on her right.

"Since you requested this assembly, the floor is yours."

Loxias inclined his head.

"Abbess."

He stood and took an orator's pose — confident, shoulders squared, head held high, eyes sweeping over the assembled friars and sisters.

"Brethren of the Order of the Void. You know why we are assembled here today, even though we were called together at what some might consider unseemly short notice." Gwenneth didn't react to the implied criticism, though a few Yotai Abbey survivors in the assembly weren't quite as reserved. "We are probably the last of our kind left alive anywhere in the galaxy. Our motherhouse, Lindisfarne, surely did not survive the empire's collapse. None of the major wormhole junctions did, as our Void Ship expeditions found out. Worse yet, they've not found any surviving Brethren for well over a decade. My friends, we must accept the sad fact we are alone, saved by the Almighty for a purpose that is not yet clear."

Gwenneth hoped someone would point out the Void Ships visited less than half of the old empire's sectors, and those were considered the hardest hit by Dendera because they were rebellion strongholds, however, no one stood to rebut Loxias.

"Many of us believe our abbess should recognize this new reality and take appropriate steps." Loxias glanced at her for a few seconds before continuing. "Chief among them is declaring this the motherhouse, another Lindisfarne if you will, and, as a result, working on a new relationship with the republic's government. If we consider ourselves the last consecrated servants of the Almighty in his Infinite Void, we must step beyond the walls of our abbey, our priories, our schools, and our hospitals. For Lyonesse, for its citizens, and the future of humanity among the stars so that when the republic sallies forth and reunites our species under a new banner, we will be ready to go with it and spread the Almighty's teachings once more."

No one could deny Loxias was a skilled orator. His deep voice, his reasonable tone, and his measured cadences resonated, both physically and intellectually. He might not fire up a secular crowd at a political event, but his style suited the Brethren, and Gwenneth saw many heads nod with approval as he spoke.

"Sadly, Gwenneth has rejected our calls to take this abbey in a new direction, even though I know many of you, perhaps a majority, know it must be done. The status quo is no longer good enough for the Order and Lyonesse. Just as our proud Navy launched the first of a new fleet so it can protect Lyonesse's future, we must launch ourselves on a new path." He paused for dramatic effect, eyes roaming over the assembly and across the video displays. "I, therefore, ask the assembled Brethren judge

Abbess Gwenneth's leadership of our community. Many among us, enough for a formal review, are no longer confident she is acting in the Order's best interests."

Loxias sat with a solemn expression on his face, but those watching closely wouldn't fail to notice the triumphant glimmer in his eyes. He glanced at Gwenneth.

"As per the Rule, we await your rebuttal, Abbess."

She stood and, as Loxias did, surveyed the audience, video feeds included.

"Brethren, I've been your leader for almost a quarter-century. I daresay you know me better than I know myself in many respects, and you've witnessed every moment of my time as abbess. You know everything I do is to make sure the Order thrives as it serves the people of the Republic of Lyonesse and that it will continue to thrive for the ages. I won't see humanity reunited under a single banner. But I will make sure the Order is on the right path to prepare for that glorious day."

Gwenneth glanced at Loxias, imitating his earlier gesture.

"Our honorable chief administrator spoke eloquently just now, and the points he raised are compelling." She was pleased to see a faint air of suspicion cross his face and smiled at him. "But I submit the following before calling a vote on whether the Brethren have lost confidence in me as your abbess. First, I propose that the Lyonesse Abbey proclaim itself the motherhouse of the Order of the Void. Then I propose we hold a vote to appoint the *Summus Abbatissa* who will lead both the Order and this abbey until such a time as we establish a second one. At that point, she will relinquish leadership of the Lyonesse Abbey and focus solely on the Order."

A rustle of robes filled the air as Brethren turned to each other in surprise, though none raised their voices. Gwenneth stepped forward, pivoted on her heels, and faced the senior leadership, many of whom seemed stunned at her unexpected words.

"What say you?"

One after the other, in order of ascending seniority, the abbey's most influential sisters and friars bowed their heads by way of assent, until only Loxias remained. He gave Gwenneth a hard stare before signifying his agreement. However, Katarin, who headed the abbey's military chaplaincy division, couldn't repress a smile of delight.

Gwenneth turned toward the assembly again.

"By the grace of the Almighty, I declare Lyonesse the new home of the Order of the Void, and this abbey its motherhouse. Let it be written in the annals and proclaimed across the galaxy."

She raised her hands and over a thousand voices intoned, "The Void giveth, the Void taketh away, blessed be the Void."

When they faded away, a grizzled sister sitting in one of the two front rows reserved for elders rose to be recognized.

"Brethren," she said in a surprisingly loud voice when Gwenneth gave her the nod. "I nominate Sister Gwenneth as the new *Summus Abbatissa*."

An equally weathered friar across the aisle from her stood. "I second the nomination."

Loxias, face set in a neutral expression, also climbed to his feet. Presiding over the election of an abbess was the chief administrator's responsibility.

"Do you accept the nomination, Sister Gwenneth?"

"I do."

"Are there any other nominations?" He glanced at the abbey's senior leaders, eyes briefly resting on Sister Keleos, who gave him an almost imperceptible shake of the head. When none were forthcoming, Loxias said, "Sister Gwenneth is hereby elected

Summus Abbatissa of the Order and abbess of the Lyonesse Abbey by acclamation."

He bowed formally at Gwenneth, though his eyes told her he didn't believe for a single second that she'd converted to the Lindisfarne Brethren viewpoint. But it didn't matter. The immediate crisis was averted, though there would be another one when Loxias and his followers realized she would never involve the Order in the republic's politics, let alone challenge the Defense Force's custody of the Knowledge Vault.

"I hereby withdraw my request for a leadership review."

— 26 —

"For someone who runs an entire religious order as *Summus Abbatissa*, you don't seem any different. No special robes or brooches?" Morane held out his hands to greet Gwenneth as she stepped out of her aircar.

"We don't do ostentatious, and my status is essentially unchanged since my flock is no bigger than it was before today's assembly." She gave him a radiant smile. "I can thank you for the result, however."

"Not me, but Sun Tzu." Morane led her up the steps and into the house. "Give me your bag and head for the solarium. Emma is making us celebratory gin and tonics."

When he, Reyes, and Gwenneth were sitting in their usual chairs, glass in hand, facing a Vanquish Bay shimmering under the setting sun, the latter said, "You know this isn't over by a long shot."

"I'd be a fool if I thought otherwise, but you drained the antimatter from Loxias' hyperdrives. He expected a show of stubborn defiance. Instead, you agreed and amplified, letting him coast with no way of boosting his cause. I'm sure Loxias lost more than a few supporters the moment you laid out your proposals."

"No doubt. But he'll get them back once they realize I won't be attending weekly cabinet meetings or visiting Government House regularly."

A mysterious smile softened Morane's craggy features.

"I think we can arrange things and make you appear like an honored friend of the powerful and sit at their tables without actually having you interfere in secular governance."

"I should mislead the Brethren?"

"Would it be misleading if you attended the president's weekly cabinet breakfast once a month? We invite community leaders regularly. The only reason you've never attended is because you never accepted the invitation."

"I was making a point." Gwenneth gave Morane a mildly exasperated glare. "Render unto Caesar and all that."

"Don't I know it. My attempts at enticing you out of the abbey over the years were for naught." He gave her an annoyed glare of his own. "Just play along. I know you can do that. From now on, you'll be the honored guest every last Thursday of the month. Enjoy the meal, chat with the secretaries. Exchange suspicious looks with Brigid DeCarde. Have fun. The food is pretty good too. Then go home knowing Loxias and his crew saw nothing more than their abbess breaking bread with the most powerful in the republic. There's no misleading if they believe what they want. Simply say that whatever you heard came under the banner of cabinet confidence and keep silent."

Gwenneth took a sip of her drink, eyes on the bay's dark waters, then said, "Very well. I can play that game in the interests of keeping the peace."

"Excellent. Expect a formal invitation by the end of the week."

"Thank you, Jonas. Though I think Loxias will eventually see through the ploy when he notices nothing much has changed in the way we interact with the government."

"It's called buying time so you can figure out another way of bleeding off your friars' excess energy and ambition. Perhaps you should set up a men-only priory or sub-abbey or whatever you want to call it on Isolde and charge it with opening the first permanent settlement. Brigid came up with the idea, by the way."

An amused chortle escaped Gwenneth's lips.

"Oh, dear. I can't see many of them volunteering to hack a new house out of the wilderness, separated from the rest of us by the expanse of the Middle Sea. My flock isn't exactly known for its pioneering spirit. But I'll propose it nonetheless, out of sheer devilment. Who knows? I might find a few dozen takers; in which case I'll speak with the Home Secretary at one of those breakfasts and offer the abbey's help with efforts to open Isolde. But enough about my problems. How is your retirement plan to create a Defense Force Command and Staff College progressing?"

"Surprisingly well. The university finally accepted our proposal we build it next to the Lannion campus so we can share facilities and personnel. The plague ships seem to have muted those among the faculty who dislike anyone in a uniform."

Morane didn't mention the latest incursion, which bypassed Outer Picket. That news was still embargoed at his orders until the Navy examined the wreckage and adjusted its dispositions. Nor did he tell Gwenneth progress on developing an antiviral was going nowhere. The Barbarian Plague had stumped the finest minds in the republic.

**

"She's visiting with President Morane at his private residence again." Sister Keleos dropped into an empty chair at Loxias' table in a private corner of the refectory. The evening meal was still more than an hour away, and the Lindisfarne Brethren leaders had the hall to themselves. "He's probably behind her unexpectedly giving in to our demands."

Loxias nodded.

"Morane is a shrewd operator, as he proved before and during his time in office, and he won't want us involved in secular governance, let alone taking charge of the Knowledge Vault. Which means Gwenneth is playing us for fools. This isn't over yet."

"Then you'd better find another way of ousting her. We looked like right fools during that assembly, after the lobbying we did to convince folks it was time for an orderly transfer of power."

Though Keleos kept any hint of emotion from coloring her words, everyone at the table knew she expected to become the next abbess and was therefore thoroughly annoyed Gwenneth not only didn't step down but became *Summus Abbatissa* instead.

"I will. A shame we couldn't make our move today, but everyone will see soon enough what a sham her proclamation was. We've waited this long. A few months more won't make a difference. Once Morane leaves office, things will change. I'll talk to my non-Brethren friends and see how we can build support on the outside now that we're formally the motherhouse."

"Making an end-run on Gwenneth and Morane's little machinations, eh?" Sandor gave him a skeptical glance. "Now that she's wise to our plans, it could be harder than you think."

"Perhaps." Loxias scratched his salt-and-pepper beard. "But here's something Gwenneth might not realize. As *Summus*

Abbatissa, she can amend the Rule if enough Brethren vote in favor and said amendments don't violate Canon Law. Canon Law doesn't cover a lot of the Order's current policies and practices. For instance, abbesses ruling unchecked by a Council of Elder Brethren, or appointing only sisters as heads of abbeys and priories."

"The latter practice exists," Keleos said, "because Brethren leading houses are those with a strong talent, for obvious reasons, which rules out friars. That's reality. Besides, the Order was women only for the first half of its history, pretty much until we needed a fleet of starships under our control, which means most consider it an unwritten clause in the Rule. As for a council? I can't think of a single abbey with one in living memory."

A sly smile split Loxias' face.

"Other than Lindisfarne, you mean? It had *the* ruling council, the one governing the entire Order."

"Oh."

"Oh, indeed. Surely you didn't think I'd be without a backup plan. Since this is now the motherhouse, Gwenneth can hardly resist calls for a Council of Elder Brethren based on a venerable precedent. And as for friars with insufficient talent, if we can convince Stearn Roget his future lies with us, he'll be the perfect candidate for our first prior and then abbot. Gwenneth's victory will be short-lived. In fact, I think this outcome could be even better for us in the long run."

**

Roget sensed Seled Hyson's vicious mind lashing out unconsciously on the other side of the door before it opened. He steeled himself for another bout of migraine while embarking on one of the meditation exercises Sister Mirjam taught him as a way of developing defenses. When Hyson entered the interview room, the mental assault intensified. She gave Roget her usual lewd wink and blew him a kiss. For a fraction of a second, he felt an unaccustomed surge of rage at her behavior, and something in his head slammed shut like a starship airlock.

He no longer picked up Hyson's roiling emotions, and a wave of indescribable relief washed over him. It must have shown in his face because Hyson gave him a curious glance as she sat across from them. That glance caught Amelia's attention, and she gave him a brief, but searching stare, then a nod of understanding. For the first time since Roget started accompanying Amelia to her counseling sessions, he felt no fatigue when their hour with Hyson ended, let alone his usual migraine.

When the next prisoner entered for his turn with Amelia, Roget felt nothing, to his immense relief. Nor did he sense the emotions of the third, though he was tempted to open that mental airlock just a wee bit and see if he could close it at will. As they exited the Supermax compound at midday after a three-session morning that usually left Roget semi-catatonic, Amelia gave him a smile of encouragement.

"You finally did it, didn't you?"

He nodded.

"Yes. But don't ask me how. All I remember is getting pissed at Seled's crudeness when she entered, and that was it. A mental shield sprang up from who knows where. I didn't dare crack it even a bit in case I couldn't raise it fully again. I cannot express my relief at no longer dealing with the madness consuming those deranged souls."

"Excellent. Mirjam was hoping you'd experience a breakthrough of this sort."

"Does that mean I no longer need to sit in on your counseling sessions?"

"You don't enjoy my company?" Amelia asked in a playful tone.

"You're delightful. The prisoners, not so much."

"I'm afraid that until we know for sure you can raise and lower your mental shields intuitively in any given situation, you're stuck with me, and you'll be seeing more of dear Seled and her fellow sufferers."

Roget let out a sad grunt. "Figures."

"Did you give any more thought about taking vows and joining us? Rikkard mentioned you've been sitting in on classes with the postulants and going through the recommended reading list."

"Yes," he replied after a moment of hesitation. "Part of me enjoys the priory's peaceful environment, and the abbey's as well. I lived a turbulent existence until I landed on Lyonesse, and I now realize it was so even before I boarded *Antelope*. It might be possible I left Scotia to escape and not because of a desire for adventure."

He tapped the side of his head with an extended index finger.

"That dratted sixth sense in there is probably to blame."

"Quite likely. Most of those with a latent but strong talent don't live tranquil lives before coming to us, and yours is stronger than any I've seen. You could do a lot worse than become a friar and live among people who understand. Now that Sister Gwenneth has declared us the Order's motherhouse, we'll see a lot of new opportunities for friars and those sisters who aren't interested in the traditional monastic disciplines."

Roget gave her a curious look.

"Why does it matter? An abbey is an abbey, and since we don't know whether any others survive out there," he jerked a thumb at the cerulean sky, "Lyonesse might not be mothering a damned thing."

"The motherhouse may change our Rule, provided those changes don't affect Canon Law. It means we can adapt to our new circumstances and take a more active part in the republic's future. One day Lyonesse will venture out into the galaxy again and reunite humanity. The Order of the Void will go with those starships and plant fresh seeds on human worlds devastated by the empire's collapse."

"Sounds romantic, though I doubt either of us will live long enough to witness that."

"Nor will the next few generations of Brethren. Yet our role is preparing the Order for that day by strengthening it and ensuring it has a say in the republic's future. Since Gwenneth is now the *Summus Abbatissa*, the Order's supreme abbess, she can do whatever is necessary."

"Still seems a little strange to me. Nothing's changed. There are no new abbeys, let alone Void houses on other worlds."

"That's because you don't see this as one of us. Everything has changed from our point of view. By becoming the new Lindisfarne, we're free of the past because we acknowledge we're the last survivors. And that makes us the first of a reborn Order of the Void with everything it implies."

A crooked smile softened Roget's craggy face. "You certainly seem enthusiastic about it."

"I'm one of the many who've been waiting for the day we became the Order's motherhouse and charted a new future. If you take vows, you could be part of that future." She gave him a sideways glance. "And you could put your talent to good use. There's so much more than just shielding your mind from others. We teach advanced techniques to those who forsake the secular world."

"What advanced techniques?"

She put on an air of mock exasperation. "I probably shouldn't mention them. Vow to serve the Order for the rest of your life, and all shall be revealed."

He snorted.

"Bull. You say nothing you don't mean. You and every other member of the Order. I've never met more self-aware people in my life."

"And that is one thing we teach postulants. One of many. Join us and become a man who makes a difference."

"I don't know."

"Think about it, Stearn. Surely you know by now we're an extended family. We take care of each other, and you're almost one of us. The Almighty gave you this gift for a purpose. It would be a shame to waste it."

— 27 —

One evening a few days later, after more counseling sessions in Supermax with Amelia during which Roget practiced raising and lowering his mental shields, he found himself hesitating at the foot of the staircase leading to Sister Mirjam's office. He was considering an irrevocable step, one which would commit the rest of his life to a cause he didn't quite understand yet. However, the idea he could do so much more with this strange sixth sense was irresistible, not least because Amelia continued to tease him with glimpses of unvoiced possibilities. Roget knew some of the sisters could do and see things beyond his imagination, such as Marta and her rumored gift of precognition. Why not find out?

"You might as well come up." Mirjam's amused voice wafted down from the upper landing, and Roget snapped out of his reverie.

"How did you know that was my intent?" He took the steps two at a time with uncharacteristic energy, as if he feared his newfound resolve might falter.

"Your mind isn't quite leak proof yet, at least not to a prioress. Follow me." She turned on her heels and walked back to her office.

"You can read thoughts?"

"Thoughts? No. Not even Marta can do that. But with our training, we sisters can infer many things from another's emotions, which is why we make such good counselors and healers." She sat and gestured at a chair in front of her desk. "Tell me why you're here."

"I want to enlist."

A smile briefly lit up Mirjam's face. "The nearest Defense Force recruiting office is half a world away."

"Not in the military but the Order."

"Ah. In that case, welcome to the nearest recruiting office. What finally convinced you?"

He shrugged.

"I can't exactly pinpoint it. Now that I'm in control of my sixth sense and can shut myself in and others out, curiosity about what else is achievable overwhelms me. Besides, among the Brethren, I'm at peace for the first time in my life. I'd rather not give that up for a secular life. Especially one among people I don't know on a world that is not my own."

"You would certainly be an asset to the Order. Both Amelia and Rikkard speak well of your efforts to learn and your Brethren-like demeanor. But before we make you a postulant, I must speak with Gwenneth. She has the final say on recruits." Mirjam glanced at the antique clock ticking away in solitary splendor on a sideboard. "In fact, why don't I do that immediately. She should be in her office by now."

Roget climbed to his feet. "I'll leave you then."

Mirjam stopped him with a hand gesture.

"No. Stay. Gwenneth will probably wish to speak with you." She touched the controls embedded in the desktop, and the wall display lit up with the image of a Void Orb. It faded moments later, replaced by Friar Landry's smiling face.

"Mirjam! How are the Windies these days?"

"Still as hot as Hades and filled with tortured souls."

"I guess nothing's changed. What can I do for you?"

"There's a man in my office who wants to join the Order, and I need Gwenneth's approval."

"Let me guess — Stearn Roget."

She nodded. "The very same."

"One moment, please."

Landry's face vanished, and the Void Orb returned, but not for long. When Gwenneth replaced it, Mirjam and Roget bowed their heads.

"Abbess. Thank you for accepting my call."

"I would never refuse it, Mirjam. Now, what's this Landry tells me? Stearn is applying to join the Order?" Gwenneth speared Roget with her eyes.

"Yes, Abbess." He inclined his head again.

"Are you sure? When you left the abbey for your stint with Mirjam, you didn't seem interested."

"The Brethren here opened my eyes while they taught me to shield my mind. I want to continue training so that I can unlock my full potential. Besides, I'm a stranger in a strange land, and the Brethren feel like family. I'd rather take vows and stay."

Gwenneth nodded slowly. "I've heard worse reasons. Do you believe in the Almighty?"

"I suppose so, though, in truth, I'm not asking to join because of my faith, which isn't particularly strong."

"Many of the Brethren took vows for reasons other than their faith, so you'd be in good company. The Order was first created so those with the talent could withdraw from the mainstream population and live in a place where they could harness and control their abilities and, at the same time, preserve their sanity. Our founder determined monasticism was the most appropriate means of imposing discipline on restless minds and avoiding scrutiny by outsiders. Emphasis on the Almighty of the Infinite Void came later, though our Rule has always been a variation of the Rule of Saint Benedict, who most certainly believed in God."

"So I understand. I've been studying with the priory's postulants when I'm not sitting in on Sister Amelia's counseling sessions."

"Stearn is quite advanced," Mirjam said. "Now that we tamed his talent, he could sit for the entrance examinations and skip the formal postulant period."

Roget gave the prioress a look of surprise but remained silent.

"Marta figured that might be the case when she read your last progress report. Very well." Gwenneth turned to him again. "Stearn, you will return to the abbey at the earliest opportunity where you will take the examinations for entry into the Order of the Void. If you pass them, and there's no reason you shouldn't at this point, I will allow you to take vows and become a friar. Then, you will undergo further training with Marta or any sister she might name while we decide what your specialization will be. As we unlock your abilities, we will discover what would suit you best. Since we've not seen a male with such a powerful sixth sense in living memory if ever, I'd say the possibilities could be endless."

"Thank you, Abbess."

"Don't thank me. Thank Mirjam and Amelia by becoming a model friar who will use what the Almighty gave him and do good in a fallen universe."

"I'll see he gets on tomorrow's Clipper," Mirjam said. "There's no point in keeping him here any longer than necessary."

"Was there anything else while we're at it?"

"Yes." Mirjam glanced at Roget. "You may announce your upcoming departure."

He stood and bowed his head, first at Gwenneth, then at the prioress before leaving her office. The door closed silently behind him.

"We've identified three more candidates for engram wiping, including one woman who's been under Amelia's care. I studied her from the observation room during several counseling sessions this week and think if she accepts the procedure, she might be suitable."

"Send me their files. Should Marta and I agree, I'll give you my authorization to approach the candidates."

"You'll get them within the hour."

"How are the first three doing?"

"Well. None of them show a shred of antisocial behavior, nor do their minds reveal any chaotic tendencies. They're as normal as could be. Too normal. I'd hoped the cure would uncover a hidden talent, helping prove the theory it might be one cause of personality disorders. Still, so far, only Erasmus' mind has the usual markers, and they're weak. Once the postulants pass their examinations and take vows, I'll work with them myself and see what we can do. And that is all I have for now."

"Then, I'll wish you a good night."

"And you a good day."

The display turned dark as Gwenneth cut the link. Mirjam busied herself with the candidate files, then turned her chair and stared out the window at the dark lagoon whose surface shimmered with the reflected light of Scilly and Gwaelod, two of Lyonesse's three moons.

**

"I'm so happy for you." Amelia beamed at Roget when he told her the news. "When are you leaving?"

"Tomorrow evening." He gave her a crooked smile. "It's your fault, you silver-tongued witch."

"No." She shook her head. "If you weren't ready, you wouldn't have asked."

"I won't miss this place." He gestured at the refectory's empty tables. "Or the sociopaths you're treating, But I will miss you."

"Ditto. It's been interesting working with a man whose talent is at least as strong, if not stronger than mine. I can't wait to see what you become when your full potential is unleashed. You could be the Order's first abbot when you're a little more seasoned."

Roget raised both hands, palms facing outward. "Whoa. Let's not make grandiose plans just yet. First, I sit for the examinations—"

"Which you'll pass with ease."

"Then, I take vows and become Marta's student once more. What I might be in the end, nobody knows. I could become a total flop, fit only for sweeping floors."

"Never."

"At least I won't see the dreadful Seled again, though she'll probably haunt my dreams for a long time."

"That's one thing you learn after taking vows — how to keep bad memories from giving you nightmares. The talent never sleeps."

"Sounds handy. What else can I look forward to?"

She gave him a wink. "You'll find out after becoming Friar Stearn, not before."

"Right. First, I learn the Order's secret handshake. Tell you what, give Seled my love and tell her I flew away to a better place."

**

"This *is* good news." Friar Loxias sat across from Sister Keleos, tea mug in hand, in the latter's monastic cell, one no different from that of any other sister or friar. "I trust you congratulated Amelia for convincing Stearn he belongs with us?"

"The only thing he's done so far is postulate," she replied. "We don't know that he believes in the Order as such, let alone our vision of it."

"We will soon make him one of ours. Stearn isn't burdened by fifteen centuries of dogma like many. If you teachers can make him an equal to any sister, he will see the same future as the rest of us."

"Gwenneth charged Marta with his further development."

"So? She's a mystic, divorced from the secular universe."

"And uninterested in our goals. A teacher imprints her views on her students, no matter how neutral she strives to be. That is reality."

Loxias shrugged, visibly unconcerned. "Then it falls to us. In other news, on Friday, I'm firing the opening salvo in our campaign to force Gwenneth's hand."

Keleos cocked a questioning eyebrow at him. "Oh?"

"Lunch with Gerson Hecht. I let him know our becoming the motherhouse creates opportunities for cooperation in areas beyond health and academia. Gerson still holds a grudge against the republic for the way Morane and Yakin pushed his father Rorik out of government. He blames it for Rorik's later ill health and premature death. I intend to convince him by working together, we can rehabilitate his father's memory and steer the republic on the path Rorik wanted."

"Aren't the Hechts making a lot of money from defense contracts?"

"Holding a grudge doesn't mean eschewing lucrative business deals. But they pretty much prevent anyone in the immediate family from running for public office or working within the administration." A sly smile crossed Loxias' lips. "If only the Hechts could call on friends with access to the powerful of the land, the sort whose interests are not the pursuit of filthy lucre but the welfare of the republic and its citizens."

Keleos nodded. "Us."

"Yes, and with Gerson's help, we'll befriend others, those capable of convincing President Morane our Order should join the Estates-General and be given standing on the various councils formed from it. Gwenneth can hardly refuse if the president formally invites us. She believes in cooperating with the republic's elected officials and bureaucrats. Besides, we'll have a Council of Elders up and running by then."

"When will you raise the matter of the council with Gwenneth?"

"You mean when will *we* raise it?" Loxias' smile returned. "As soon as we speak with the elders who should sit on that council. I can think of a few suitable candidates."

— 28 —

"Rise, Friar Stearn, and be welcomed among the Brethren."

Sister Gwenneth, Abbess of Lyonesse and *Summus Abbatissa*, held her hand out to a kneeling Roget who'd just publicly made the vows of obedience, stability, and conversion of life in the abbey's chapter house, as per the Order's ancient Rule, witnessed by hundreds of sisters and friars. He gripped her hand, marveling once again at its unexpected strength, and stood with the elegance of an athlete.

Marta, Roget's principal teacher, stepped up and draped a hooded cloak over his shoulders, completing his transformation from postulant to servant of the Almighty in his Infinite Void. Then, as he'd been taught, the newly minted Friar Stearn turned and faced the Brethren, then bowed deeply, a gesture those present, save for the abbess, returned with equal solemnity. And with that, the simple rite dating back to a time well before the first humans left Earth ended. Roget's training to unlock his mind's full potential would now begin.

As they filed out of the chapter house, Loxias caught up with Roget and gave him a friendly clap on the shoulder.

"Friar Stearn! How do you feel now that you're one of us?"

"Like I've found my family at last."

"Well said. I'll be monitoring your further development. As chief administrator, making sure friars enter a proper line of work is part of my duties. Once Marta's training makes that impressive talent of yours bloom, we must use it for the Almighty's greater glory and the Order's future."

Roget inclined his head politely.

"Without a doubt."

"And we should discuss that future at some point, my friend. Perhaps around a cup of tea one evening. You might play an important part in ensuring it unfolds properly."

"I look forward to it."

"Excellent!"

Loxias peeled off and headed for the abbey's motor pool where a car waited while Roget made his way to the teaching complex and his first session with Marta as a consecrated friar.

**

"Loxias. How are you?"

Gerson Hecht, looking more and more the spitting image of his late father, fierce eyebrows and gray beard included, stood and came around his marble-topped desk, hand outstretched to greet the friar.

"Hale, hearty, and hungry," he boomed as they shook hands. "And you, my friend?"

"Prospering, though with the latest plague ship scare, I expect Hecht Industries will prosper even more." He waved at an open connecting door. "The executive dining room awaits us. A light lunch from *Tristan's Table*."

"Nothing but the best." Loxias' smile broadened at hearing the name of Lannion's most elegant restaurant.

"For you? Always."

The two men first met years ago when Rorik Hecht still lived and Gerson ran the Lyonesse Mercantile Consortium, an umbrella organization speaking on behalf of the planet's primary commercial interests. Loxias, not yet chief administrator, but widely seen as an inevitable candidate for the top friar job, oversaw the abbey's procurement office and spent a lot of time hobnobbing with business executives as he sought deals for supplies, construction material, and more. He and Gerson discovered quickly they were kindred spirits looking for a more significant say in the republic's future but hampered by their roles. Hecht headed the largest government supplier, one whose dealings with the Defense Force were extensive, making him subject to conflict of interest regulations while Gwenneth's strictures restrained Loxias.

Hecht ushered Loxias into the dining room and pointed at one of the three place settings.

"Please sit. My assistant called *Tristan's Table* the moment the front desk announced you. Our meal should be here at any moment."

The Hecht Industries corporate headquarters occupied a newish six-story building in downtown Lannion, within walking distance of Government House, the legislature, and the Defense Force headquarters among other departments. And only a block away from the famous restaurant.

"Who is joining us?" Loxias settled in across from the panoramic windows overlooking the Haven River.

"Severin Downes," Gerson replied, naming Hecht Industries' chairman of the board, a former imperial count who'd ended up on Lyonesse with a few hundred of his peers, brought there in the same ship as Erasmus and his two comrades. But unlike the violent criminals sentenced to exile, he and the nobles were condemned by the late Empress Dendera for plotting against her at court. Or at least she suspected them of doing so, which in her deranged state made them guilty, nonetheless. "Considering what we'll discuss, I thought his insight might be valuable."

"Indeed."

Downes was another man with a longstanding and unshakable grudge against the republic's government, and Jonas Morane and Sister Gwenneth in particular. He was a practiced schemer who spent time in the Windy Isles long ago and was therefore barred from government appointments. After serving his sentence, Downes turned to the private sector and ingratiated himself with Gerson Hecht after Rorik Hecht's death, becoming in due course chairman of the board. Loxias wasn't sure he liked the man, but he couldn't argue his effectiveness at glad-handing and recruiting allies in the halls of power.

The dining room's other door opened, and a silver-haired man in his eighties with a sculpted face that could only come from genetic engineering entered with an energetic stride. He wore a pleasant smile, but his eyes held no more warmth than interstellar space. Though he and the other former imperial nobles lost their titles when Governor Yakin abolished them, Downes still cloaked himself in a vague aura of superiority.

"A good day to you, Gentlemen." He shook hands with Hecht and Loxias before sitting across from the friar. "I trust everything is well in your busy lives."

Moments later, two men in white shirts and black trousers entered, carrying covered trays. A young woman in a business suit — Hecht's executive assistant — followed them in with an uncorked bottle of red wine. Once the waiters served them and left, she poured the wine, placed the bottle in the middle of the solid wood table, and withdrew.

Hecht reached for his glass and raised it.

"To your health, my friends."

Downes and Loxias followed suit, the latter nodding with approval at the vintage as he swirled the first sip around his tongue.

"Dig in." Hecht nodded at their plates, now covered with cold meats, cheeses, and vegetables. "The floor is yours, Loxias, unless you'd rather wait until after lunch."

The latter nodded but took a healthy morsel before speaking.

"This morning, I witnessed our newest friar take his vows. A most extraordinary man, with an unusual background." Loxias told Stearn Roget's story between bites. "He has the greatest potential of any friar the Order has known in its history and will no doubt be highly influential in a noticeably short time. Stearn could even become the first *Summus Abbas* in our history. His abilities will probably eclipse those of our strongest sisters once he finishes training."

"And what does this mean for Hecht Industries, Friar, if I may be so blunt?"

Loxias gave Downes a tolerant stare.

"When Gwenneth declared Lyonesse the motherhouse of the Order of the Void, she did more than just take a stand on our status vis-à-vis the republic. She clearly stated we had a stake in the republic's future and its mission of reuniting human worlds under a single banner, rebuilding what the Ruggero dynasty rent asunder."

"Good and well, but why does this concern us?" Downes took a sip of wine.

"I'm not convinced the present administration, or the abbey leadership understands the implications of Lyonesse's mission as the last outpost of civilization."

"Aren't you part of the abbey's leadership?"

Loxias raised his hand, palm facing downward, and wiggled it from side to side.

"Yes and no. I run the day-to-day operations of the abbey's physical plant, but decisions about the Order's policies and plans come from a single source — the abbess. We will soon set up a Council of Elders to dilute her power and give the abbey a measure of democracy."

"Won't she resist?"

"A Council of Elders governed the motherhouse on Lindisfarne. Gwenneth cannot erase that precedent."

Downes picked up his wine glass again.

"Pardon me, Friar, but that still doesn't tell us why we're discussing politics instead of simply enjoying this fine lunch."

"I think we should explore how we can help each other." Loxias gave Downes a knowing smile.

A spark of curiosity appeared in the latter's cold eyes. "I'm listening."

"Those at the senior levels of Hecht Industries can't openly engage in political activities, and neither can the former imperial officials who served the late empress on Wyvern. It means two of the three men in this room cannot enter the halls of power."

Though neither Severin Downes nor Gerson Hecht spoke, Loxias could see vague annoyance in their eyes. Whether at the restrictions laid on them or his words, he couldn't tell.

"I think the Order of the Void should take its rightful place in the Estates-General, and from there become a force in the republic's governance. One which can represent the disenfranchised."

Hecht gave Loxias a knowing look.

"And you'd like us to use our connections within the community to see the Order becomes part of the Estates-General."

"If you would be so kind." Loxias' smile broadened.

"Again, what's in it for us, besides another ally in the Estates-General?" Downes asked. "We already have plenty of friends in that august body."

"For one thing, we would make it our mission to transfer control of the Knowledge Vault away from the military, as you wanted years ago, Mister Downes." Loxias glanced at Hecht. "And as your father wanted. If anyone has a chance of succeeding, it would be the people who filled that vault."

"You forget it's in the virtually impregnable basement of the Defense Force's main installation on this planet. No president will sign off on moving it to a lesser location, and the Defense Force will not give just anyone access."

"One thing at a time, Gerson. Morane's time as president is almost finished. If his successor designates the Order as custodians, the military will give us unfettered access. We can work on moving it elsewhere in due course. Perhaps a site Hecht Industries or one of its partners could build. The teachings tell us vengeance belongs to the Almighty, but you can help usher in the next best thing — a rollback of Jonas Morane's militaristic republican dreams."

The former count and Gerson Hecht exchanged a meaningful glance, then the latter nodded.

"We will see that the Order of the Void joins the Estates-General."

Loxias inclined his head in a gesture of humility that, not coincidentally, hid the gleam of triumph in his eyes.

"Please accept my heartfelt thanks."

— 29 —

"A Council of Elders?" Gwenneth looked from Loxias to Keleos and back with a slightly raised eyebrow that could convey either incredulity or contempt. "Don't you think we hold enough meetings as it is? And how would such a council differ in scope and composition from the abbey's operations committee? I consider every department head an elder of the Order."

"But not every wise elder is a department head. Marta, for instance," Loxias replied. "Or Rinne. Or many Brethren I could name. Besides, the operations committee focuses on the day-to-day management of this abbey, its priories, and its other dependencies. You're the nominal chair, but as chief administrator, I run it. Since we're the Order's motherhouse, we must create a council concerned with our policies, our plans, our future, our relations with the secular world, and more."

"That would be my job."

"As head of a regular abbey, yes. But you're now the head of our entire Order. Our traditions do not give the *Summus Abbatissa* sole power over Order-wide policies, such as changes to the Rule, nor when charting a new path, let alone one which might deviate from centuries of precedent. The head of our Order on Lindisfarne always summoned a Council of Elders to help her deal with such matters. It is time we establish one as well."

"The idea is finding a lot of support among the Brethren," Keleos said. "They feel that since we're the Order's head abbey, we should align our ways with how it was on Lindisfarne."

A mocking smile briefly danced on Gwenneth's lips. "If we forge a fresh path, should we not leave centuries of precedent behind us, such as overly complex structures?"

"In some matters, yes." Loxias nodded once. "But the changes we face in adapting to our new place in this fallen universe are momentous enough they demand the wisest among us work in unison. With all due respect, Gwenneth, you are but mortal, with a mortal's limitations and failings. You alone cannot bring about that which will become necessary. Where one mind and one soul will not suffice, it behooves us to join in. Our predecessors recognized this long ago and created the first Council of Elders, which eventually propelled the Order to greater glory in the Almighty's name."

"And who would you suggest sit on this council, apart from the three of us?" Gwenneth ignored the flash of triumph in Loxias' eyes as he sensed another win in the offing. "I imagine you think we should imitate Lindisfarne and appoint ten elders plus the *Summus Abbatissa.*"

"Precisely." He rattled off eight names, all highly respected within the Order for their wisdom, experience, and profound knowledge. Gwenneth couldn't fault any of the nominations, even if Lindisfarne Brethren were in the majority. It wasn't unexpected that the eldest among her flock would show the most support for the Order's hoary traditions.

"Let me guess, if I don't create a Council of Elders, you two and the other eight will demand I convene the Brethren in the chapter house for a vote."

"I don't think it needs to go that far, Abbess. Someone with your humility knows the task you face in creating a renewed Order capable of seeding other worlds with abbeys and priories when the republic sallies forth. You also know this task is best tackled with plenty of help from the wisest among us."

Butter wouldn't melt in Loxias' mouth, but she knew he'd outmaneuvered her. Besides, the constant internal politics took their toll. Let others share in the misery, even if it meant giving up power.

"Very well. I shall announce the creation of a Council of Elders at this week's chapter. Should I assume the nominees already signified their acceptance?"

"They did."

"Was there anything else?" Gwenneth contemplated her visitors with a detached expression as she sat back in her chair.

"No, Abbess. Thank you for listening. Under your continued leadership and backed by the wisdom of ten elders, the Order will no doubt grow in strength while it prepares for a return to the stars."

As Loxias and Keleos stood, Gwenneth asked, "How was your lunch with Gerson Hecht and Severin Downes the other day? Did you discuss anything I should know about?"

"Productive, as usual," he replied without missing a beat. "I think we will get preferential pricing offers when we issue this year's request for proposals."

Loxias was too smooth by half, Gwenneth reflected as Landry ushered them out. But at the moment, she couldn't think why his dining with Hecht and Downes bothered her. She wouldn't even know, if not for the Defense Force's incredibly efficient intelligence service, which kept her informed on matters concerning the abbey at Morane's behest.

Gwenneth swiveled her chair and stared out at the Void Orb. It increasingly struck her as something malevolent brooding at the abbey's heart, despite the fact she'd never felt the slightest reservations about the one she'd seen daily inside the Yotai Abbey for many years.

Loxias had blindsided her with the Council of Elders suggestion, and she blamed herself for not realizing it would be his next move in a relentless campaign aimed at reducing her power over the Order's affairs. She could claim tiredness, even existential fatigue, but in an organization that prided itself on respecting precedent, establishing a council of ten headed by the *Summus Abbatissa*, as Lindisfarne did long ago, was the next logical step.

**

Jonas Morane's gaze fell on Brigid DeCarde once Health Secretary Wevers Rauseo finished informing the president and his cabinet colleagues there was still no progress in developing a vaccine against the Barbarian Virus.

"What about the analysis of the intruders destroyed by *Standfast* and her escort?"

"Our mobile lab confirms the people aboard were infected with the same strain, Mister President."

"As we expected," Rauseo said.

"The Navy also analyzed the wreckage to determine how those ships made it from what we assume was Arietis via interstellar space. Theoretically, they should not be able to carry enough antimatter fuel, since that type is optimized for wormhole travel, unlike *Standfast* and the rest of her class. But we found indications among the debris they increased the size of their antimatter containment units."

"No good." Vice President Charis Sandino lightly tapped the wooden tabletop with her clenched fist. "We should have known that would happen. It's the easiest thing to modify on a starship."

DeCarde nodded.

"Indeed. It also means they likely found an old imperial astrogation database somewhere if they identified not only Broceliande's star but could make precise enough hyperspace jumps."

"Then why not aim directly at us here?" Sandino asked. "If they found an imperial database, they can easily find our star."

"Range. Whatever they did with their magnetic containment units gave them just enough fuel for Broceliande. They probably hoped it would take them around whatever was blocking the entrance into Corbenic."

Sandino exhaled loudly.

"Which means someone will eventually figure out they need even larger fuel tanks and take aim directly at Lyonesse. They were smart enough to bypass Corbenic after a few attempts."

"The odds they'll die of the virus before that happens aren't negligible."

Morane nodded. "We can only hope. Will the Navy change its dispositions?"

"In a limited fashion, Mister President. We can't keep permanent pickets on both wormhole termini in Broceliande and Corbenic while at the same time patrolling Lyonesse's heliopause and hyperlimit. We have neither the hulls nor the crews. Our lightly armed sloops wouldn't fare quite as well as the purpose-built naval units or the *Dawns* in a head-on fight with intruders, and we can't afford to lose a single vessel. *Prevail* will join the fleet in a few weeks, but even with accelerating the corvette program and building a third dry dock, *Repel* and *Repulse* are still at least twelve months from commissioning. The next two ships won't be ready for at least twenty-four to thirty-six months, and that's with Hecht Aerospace working flat out. We desperately need an orbital facility to build frigates, yet even with the best will and enough funding, it's still years away. The corvette program is taking up too many resources."

"Then what's the plan?"

"Use the traffic control buoys at both ends of the Corbenic-Broceliande wormhole as tripwires if intruders slip into our space behind Outer Picket's back and post 2nd Squadron's warships as an inner picket on the Broceliande side of the Lyonesse wormhole."

A thoughtful expression crossed Morane's face.

"So long as we keep enough warships in this system and our eyes on the heliopause, I suppose it'll do."

"The alternative would be pulling our units back, with a single picket on the Broceliande end of the Lyonesse wormhole and watch the rest of the branch via traffic control buoys. But in doing so, we effectively surrender control of anything beyond Lyonesse itself."

Sandino shrugged. "If intruders are bypassing the wormhole network anyhow, why not? There's nothing of interest in the other two systems."

"Until we run out of easily mined places around here," the Natural Resources Secretary said. "Both Corbenic and Broceliande have ore-rich, albeit airless planets."

"That won't happen for centuries. By then, the Lyonesse Navy will be the strongest strike force in the known galaxy, one whose ships, more importantly, will have large antimatter containment units so they can bypass the entire wormhole network if necessary."

A smile briefly lit up DeCarde's face.

"Only if we build orbital facilities, Madame Vice President. And that'll take a lot more material than half a dozen corvettes. But fair enough. However, picket duty is hard on crews, and each wormhole transit to rotate ships home for rest and recuperation takes a little more out of old hulls that the empire would have retired by now. The Navy is currently evaluating *Myrtale*'s fitness as a faster-than-light and wormhole ship."

"What happens if she's no longer considered capable?"

"Then Lyonesse gets its first crewed orbital installation in the form of a monitor." When DeCarde saw Sandino didn't understand the term, she added, "It's what the Navy calls smallish but heavily armed ships whose primary role is orbital defense."

"I see."

"We'll squeeze the last gram of life out of our warships until we replace each one by a comparable, newly built unit."

"I know, but what I fear is that last gram of life evaporating before we launch replacements."

"You and me both, Madame Vice President."

— 30 —

Friar Stearn entered Marta's training room and saw she was already there. He bowed at the waist, as a student does to his sensei. She returned it in the same manner but didn't bow quite as deeply since she was, in every respect, his superior.

"I trust you are well this morning?" She gestured at the meditation mats in the center of a softly lit, window-less, wood-paneled space that was at once spare and warm. Stearn always thought it a most appropriate reflection of Marta's character.

"I am."

"And eager, no doubt."

"That as well."

In the week since he took vows, Marta had reviewed basic mental disciplines with him and tested his mind so she could evaluate the strength of his defenses. When he wasn't with Marta, Stearn worked as a stationary engineer, maintaining the abbey's environmental systems alongside gray-bearded, long-service friars with only a smidgen of talent. He was impatient to expand his sixth sense and become more. That was why he'd entered the

Order in the first place, and today would mark the start of his next journey.

They adopted the lotus position, and for the next hour, Marta led him through the process of centering his soul and calming his mind, something he could do almost out of instinct by now. But Stearn knew better than to force anything with the abbey's foremost teacher. She could detect impatience and draw out the meditation as a lesson in patience. Marta wasn't much with words, like some sisters who'd taught him the basics, but she was uncannily aware and could convey volumes with a single glance or gesture.

Stearn blocked out any thoughts that might escape his shields and turned himself into a mental blank, as he'd done during every session since returning from the Windy Isles and resuming his apprenticeship under the Order's leading mystic. After a while, the same strangeness he'd felt since telling Sister Mirjam about his breakthrough overcame him, as if ethereal fingertips were brushing against the wall protecting his inner core. It vanished as quickly as it appeared, and not for the first time, he suspected the sisters could do more than just sense the emotions of others in the way he sensed the chaotic *thing* inhabiting prisoners suffering from a personality disorder.

"You are strong."

Marta's voice almost jolted Stearn from his trance, but he remained centered and ignored it, proud of himself for both noticing and dismissing without effort. Then, after a few seconds, he realized her words hadn't reach his brain via his ear canals, that she hadn't made a sound. His eyes fluttered open before slamming shut again as he fought for mastery of his feelings.

Marta? Are you in my mind?

No answer. Was it the wrong question, or was he asking on the wrong frequency? Stearn centered his thoughts again and let himself drift, wondering whether he was hallucinating or whether this was yet another test. The rumors of Marta's abilities seemed exaggerated, even as he learned under her tutelage.

The moment his internal clock told him the hour was up, Marta's gentle voice shattered the absolute silence of a well-insulated room.

"I think you're ready for the next step." His eyes opened, and he found her studying him intently. "Tell me if something out of the ordinary happened during your meditation."

"Partway through. It was as if feather-light fingers touched my mind. Was that you?"

She nodded. "Anything else?"

"Then you said, 'you are strong,' but it seemed as if you didn't speak those words aloud."

A mysterious smile tugged at her lips. "And?"

"I asked whether you were in my mind."

"Three for three."

Stearn returned her sphinx-like gaze with a questioning look.

"It happened? You touched my mind; you spoke to me without speaking, and you heard my question in return?"

"Yes. I belong to a tiny minority of humans whose sixth sense is almost fully evolved. Or as certain mystics would say, my third eye," she tapped her forehead with an extended index finger, "in here, is open. There are a few of us among the sisters in this abbey and its dependencies, but not many. In most, the third eye is only partially open, though they can see more than others. We keep our true nature to ourselves and undergo rigorous training, so we don't misuse the advantages it gives us. The Brethren know, of course, but not quite the extent of our talent. However, no one outside the Order is aware and that must stay so, lest people become wary, if not fearful of us. Distrust would not only impede our ability to serve as healers and teachers but might even endanger the Brethren at large. Bluntly put, we are the witches our distant ancestors burned at the stake."

She paused for a reaction, but Stearn kept his expression perfectly neutral and waited respectfully for her to continue.

"You are that rarest human of all — a male whose third eye can open and open wide. I sensed it when you first arrived. The abbey's records do not speak of any other like you in our entire history, though a man called Jackson Thorn founded the Order not long after our species first colonized worlds beyond Earth's star system. Unfortunately, we don't know whether his sixth sense was fully evolved or whether he only saw the diffuse light of something greater, like most friars."

Stearn gave in to an impulse and asked with a sly grin, "If you sisters are the witches of yore, does this mean you'll teach me how to use abracadabra in a non-ironic way?"

Marta gave him an exasperated look he suspected was mostly feigned.

"There is no way of using abracadabra or any other word of incantation in a non-ironic manner. Women with a partially or fully open third eye, though they didn't know what the talent was, were deemed witches in those dismal days because they had abilities beyond anyone's understanding. They didn't actually perform magic because there is no such thing."

"Too bad. I was hoping I might become a super friar, righting wrongs and making the universe a better place."

She shook her head, eyes raised to the heavens.

"Speaking of irony. What we will do over the coming months and years, is build on the discipline you've developed so far to keep your mind hidden from others and the minds of others from intruding on yours. When I touched you during our meditation, I sensed the strength of the shell you've developed, one which is now an integral part of your being. You didn't react, as some would, by lashing out against my mental touch, yet you heard my words clearly, which means you've instinctively developed the ability to separate directed signals from the general noise of random brain waves. Few can reach that point alone. I must normally teach my students how. Better yet, you projected a question at me, and I heard it, which means you also developed the ability to let directed signals out, another thing I normally teach sisters with a lesser talent than yours."

He inclined his head in acknowledgment of her praise.

"The first thing I will teach you is touching another mind and interpreting the emotions you sense without leaving a trace of your passage. It's a skill our healers possess. Those with the strongest talents specialize in treating people with mental issues."

"Like Amelia, Mirjam and a few others in the Windies."

"Yes, which is why they are spearheading the project aimed at treating Lyonesse's most disturbed minds. The healers who specialize in physical ailments use this part of the talent to analyze a patient's condition beyond what mere words or medical instruments can tell because of the close link between the mind and the body it inhabits. Healers must swear the Hippocratic Oath, with emphasis on clauses added by the Order. The first is I will not peer into another human being's mind except in the course of my duties as a healer. The second is I will not use my knowledge of another's mind for any purpose other than healing its owner."

"What happens if a healer breaks her oath?"

"She can't. Part of the training ensures healers would become physically ill if they tried, largely thanks to a prohibition imprinted on their minds. It means they can't simply reach out and touch someone sitting across from them during a poker game to decide if they're bluffing. But none would even try. Respect for the sanctity of others is a core tenet of the Order. But because of our training, we can pick up visual and auditory cues as well, cues humans don't know they're giving off, and draw surprisingly accurate conclusions from them. Healers can do most of their work without using the third eye. And the stronger one's talent, the better one becomes at reading people without invading their privacy. Many of the long-serving friars are highly skilled, even though their talent is weaker than a sister's."

Stearn chuckled. "Then I'd best not walk into the refectory with a deck of cards after the evening meal."

"On the contrary." She smiled again. "Playing games with skilled cue readers will help develop your ability to give off no signals whatsoever. Now, about the oath. Since you'll learn the same mental skills as healers, you will take it as well and accept the prohibition imprint."

"Of course. Whatever you ask of me. Who knows what path I'll take? Though I'm not currently inclined toward medicine or psychology, I might still enter one of those fields once you finish training me."

"One step at a time. First, we will see if your third eye will open. Not all of them can, and I don't know why. Many believe a human's soul looks out through it, and some souls would rather stay hidden."

"And the oath?"

"At the proper moment. Before I imprint the prohibition, I must know it's necessary by confirming you can reach out. We do not imprint a trainee's mind lightly. Every intervention has risks."

"Should I be worried?" Stearn's tone remained as calm and neutral as before.

"No. But my fellow teachers and I always think of that tiny chance we might harm our students rather than help them. It keeps us grounded, fends off the vanity that plagues human beings, and ensures we stay humble before the Almighty. Too much pain comes from unthinking and ultimately unearned self-confidence."

"Yeah. We call that the arrogance of stupidity back home."

"How pithy. Are you prepared for this path?"

"I am."

"Then let us begin."

—31—

"I understand President Morane, upon the advice of the senate, has invited the Order to join the Estates-General." Loxias, sitting across from Gwenneth in the latter's office alongside Keleos, studied the *Summus Abbatissa* with an expectant air.

"How did you hear of this? The matter is confidential unless I accept so that refusal doesn't create ill will."

"Come now, Gwenneth, surely you realize that as the Order's chief administrator, I'm well connected within the community."

"The Lyonesse Abbey's chief administrator, Loxias."

He made a dismissive hand gesture.

"Since the Lyonesse Abbey *is* the Order, I see no difference. Once we establish houses on other worlds, our successors can debate whether we should separate the post of motherhouse chief administrator from that of the Order. And if I may be so bold, accepting or refusing this invitation must be decided by the Council of Elders rather than you alone, since either choice entails wide-ranging consequences for every single Brethren."

Gwenneth understood he would force the issue if she didn't put this matter before the council. She also knew a good many among the sisters and friars were in favor of joining the Estates-General. They wanted a direct voice on issues affecting the republic rather than rely on their abbess working through close friends, such as Jonas Morane. Besides, if Loxias and Keleos knew about the invitation, then they too were quietly working with close friends outside the abbey, in which case she might as well bring matters into the open.

"Very well. I will convene the Council of Elders tomorrow after vespers, and we will debate the matter. If a majority are in favor, then so be it."

Loxias inclined his head in a gesture of respect.

"Thank you, Abbess. We must secure our future within the republic, and this is the best way."

Gwenneth heard an unvoiced 'for now' at the end of his statement, but let it pass.

When the council met the following evening, it was a foregone conclusion. The ten elders voted in favor after a perfunctory debate.

"Our *Summus Abbatissa* will, of course, take the Order's seat on the Estates-General," Loxias said after they adopted the motion to join. "But under the rules, we must name an alternate and appoint at least two observers. I propose the three come from this council."

Gwenneth saw nothing but nods around the table and could predict what would come next.

Keleos raised a hand and said, "I propose the chief administrator be the alternate."

Friar Sandor raised his hand as well. "Seconded."

"Does anyone want a vote?" Gwenneth asked. No one spoke. She looked at Loxias. "Do you accept?"

"I do."

"Motion adopted. Friar Loxias will be my alternate until such a time as I retire or he steps down from the post of chief administrator, whichever comes first. To make sure the alternate is aware of all matters concerning the Estates-General, he will be an observer if he's not replacing me." Gwenneth was pleased when she saw a look of surprise cross his face. "Which means we will nominate two more observers and their alternates."

"I propose Sister Keleos and Friar Sandor as primary observers." Loxias gestured toward his two principal followers, though he kept his eyes on Gwenneth so he could gauge her reaction.

"Seconded," she said before anyone else could speak. "Does anyone ask for a vote? No? Motion adopted. Sister Keleos and Friar Sandor will be the primary observers alongside Friar Loxias. The floor is open for proposals on the two alternates."

**

"Your devious plan to stay one step ahead of Loxias and the Lindisfarne Brethren is failing." Gwenneth dropped into her usual chair overlooking Vanquish Bay and accepted a cup of tea from Emma Reyes. She gave Morane a sideways glance. "Tomorrow morning, I will formally accept your invitation and join the Estates-General as representative of the Order of the Void after the council Loxias imposed on me voted unanimously in favor. He is my alternate and one of the observers, while the other observers are members of the Council of Elders, meaning Loxias supporters. I am no longer in full control of the abbey, it seems."

"At least not the part where it interfaces with the secular world." He took a sip, eyes on the bay's dark waters. Another storm was brewing on the horizon, but Morane figured it would stay away from land. The winds weren't quite right, nor was it the season. "This is not exactly unexpected but cheer up. As the Order's representative, you will control its interactions with the Estates-General."

"Until I'm no longer *Summus Abbatissa*."

"Which would have happened by now, had you not given way on declaring Lyonesse the motherhouse and agreed to imitate Lindisfarne by forming a Council of Elders. Some battles cannot be won. Wise people realize that sometimes the only course of action available is minimizing the consequences of a loss."

"Yet I fear for the Order if it gets too deeply embroiled in the republic's politics. The invitation to join the Estates-General was almost certainly engineered by Loxias. I wonder what debts he now owes, either personally or as the abbey's chief administrator."

"If you want, I could ask the intelligence service to find out."

"It's probably best if I don't know."

"As you wish."

Something in Morane's voice caught Gwenneth's attention.

"You'll do it anyway, won't you?"

"I suddenly feel an irresistible urge to find out who among the republic's notables is schmoozing with Loxias, apart from Gerson Hecht and Severin Downes, that is."

"Pardon? Loxias is *schmoozing* with Hecht and Downes? I thought it was only a business thing."

"That's what I'm told. He's rather chummy with Hecht." Morane gave her a knowing look. "Their relationship is longstanding, which is why Hecht's companies and those of his closest friends are the abbey's favored suppliers. Nothing corrupt or criminal that anyone can prove, but there's a lot of backscratching. Loxias isn't as friendly with Downes, which shows your wayward friar isn't entirely without good judgment.

But our dear friend Severin chairs the Hecht Industries board of directors and circulates in rarefied circles now that most forgot his brief stint in the Windies."

Reyes snorted dismissively. "Self-imposed amnesia, more like. The people in those rarefied circles forget nothing, not even the cost of that drink they bought you thirty years ago in a seedy bar on the Lannion docks."

"That sounds a bit too personal." Morane arched an eyebrow as he eyed his partner. "Is there anything about your life before we met you'd like to discuss?"

She stuck out her tongue at him. "Figure of speech, Mister President. Don't ask, don't tell."

"You know about my previous loves. Me, not so much."

"Your previous love is in orbit right now, and you named this bay after her." She gestured at the windows. "Big deal. The whole damned republic knows."

Gwenneth, seated between them, raised both hands. "Could you please save it for when I've retired to my room. We of the Order may not swear vows of chastity, but still…"

"Sorry," Reyes said, though her amused expression proved she was anything but contrite.

Morane drained his cup and placed it on the low table in front of them.

"Back to your situation. All I can suggest is work with what you have. Loxias forced the motherhouse issue, which resulted in a Council of Elders and a seat in the Estates-General. He's fired his guns. What else can he demand?"

She thought for a moment, then shook her head.

"Nothing. This is as far as he can force us without entering unknown territory. We've taken on Lindisfarne's mantle of leadership and accepted a seat on the third-highest council in the republic after the senate and the cabinet. A government influenced by the Order, let alone a theocracy such as the one running the Lindisfarne system during better times, shouldn't come about. Yet, part of me fears we've not seen the end of this."

"Maybe, but our constitution is designed to prevent anyone from circumventing the will of the people. Let Loxias enjoy his time in the sun because whatever he does will be inconsequential in the grand order of things. He will eventually become a friar emeritus and spend his waning years meditating on the future of humanity across the Infinite Void."

"What worries me is the damage he can do between now and that blessed day, especially since he is younger than me and will stay active long after I relinquish the duties of an abbess. As for the future of humanity across the Infinite Void, I fear he meditates too much on the subject already. For him, the centuries between now and when the republic goes forth to reunite our species don't exist."

"If I shared your faith, I would counsel that you trust in the Almighty's plan. But since I don't, would asking for your trust in the republic's resilience assuage your worries?"

"No."

—32—

"Sister!" Morane stood to greet Gwenneth as she swept into a mostly empty Lannion Base Officer's Mess. "We're the first arrivals. Brigid, Adrienne, and the service chiefs will probably travel together from HQ. Can I offer you a drink while we wait for them?"

"Thank you, but no." The elderly abbess settled into a chair across from Morane. "I'll save myself for a glass of that marvelous red Adrienne serves in the private dining room."

Morane raised a half-empty beer mug.

"As you can see, I'm long past saving. How are things at the abbey these days? You haven't visited Vanquish Bay in weeks, though I hear you attended the quarterly Estates-General session late last month."

"Things are quiet. As the old trope goes, they're almost too quiet. Loxias was in his glory at the Estates-General, sitting behind me as an observer along with his closest acolytes, Keleos and Sandor. They behaved perfectly and even complimented me afterward on the few interventions I made when we discussed matters touching on the abbey's services within the community.

Vice President Sandino was quite effusive in welcoming me, as were those who I suspect influenced her into pushing for the invitation. Loxias seemed rather chummy with them, more than warranted by his interactions as our chief administrator."

"You recall not wanting to know who was behind it?"

She nodded. "Of course."

"You do now, trust me. The Estates-General members who welcomed you so enthusiastically, including the trade unionists, lobbied Sandino. It wasn't just the Hechts and Downes who saw an advantage in the Order taking on a higher profile."

A wry smile twisted her lips. "Why do I suddenly feel like I'm the only one who thinks greater involvement in secular matters isn't a good idea?"

"Because you survived Pendrick Zahar's pogroms. I'm sure other Coalsack Sector survivors share your opinion."

"You may recall Friar Sandor, one of Loxias' closest confidants, barely escaped the Mykonos Abbey massacre, so it's hardly the lot of them."

Morane picked up his mug.

"Time has a habit of changing one's perspective. Besides, something good might come out of the Order sitting with the republic's leading citizens four times a year." He took a sip. "So long as it doesn't indulge in the petty politicking that goes on behind the scenes."

"Oh, I assure you, we will stay aloof and keep our own counsel on matters that don't touch the Order's work."

A mischievous expression lit up Morane's face. "Does Loxias know about that?"

"Why? What's he been doing behind my back?"

"So far? Nothing that I heard of. You're right, it is too quiet." He saw five figures come through the front door, one in a business suit, the other four in uniform. "Our dinner companions are here."

Morane drained his mug, then stood, imitated by Gwenneth.

"Good evening, Mister President, Abbess," Defense Secretary DeCarde raised a hand in greeting. "I thought we'd go right through."

"Whatever you say, Brigid. We're the guests here. And how are the republic's top military leaders today?" Morane bestowed a fatherly smile on Lieutenant General Barca and the service chiefs.

"In fine fettle, sir," Barca replied. "As always. Thank you for coming."

"Gwenneth and I aren't known for refusing a free meal. Nor is my close protection detail." He nodded at a pair of tough-looking men in civilian clothes a few tables over.

"It's hardly free if we're asking for your opinion and help on the sly," DeCarde said over her shoulder as she led the way out of the main room and into the corridor beyond. "You're our wise oracles."

Morane and Gwenneth exchanged amused glances.

"Only because we survived this long without scandals."

"Then either you're saints or experts at making the past vanish. I don't really want to know which it is."

Once they were seated around the table with the wine served and a simple cold meal in front of them — Barca didn't want interruptions from the mess staff while they spoke — DeCarde raised her glass.

"Here's to our continued good health in every sense."

After they took a sip, Morane asked, "Another plague ship incursion?"

"Yes." Nate Sirak nodded, a grim expression on his face. "Three hours ago. I found out just before leaving the office. Four ships. They bypassed Corbenic by crossing through interstellar space, just like the earlier attempts. Not unexpectedly, 2nd Squadron's picket at the Broceliande end of the Lyonesse wormhole destroyed them. The mobile lab will go through the debris tomorrow, but there's no doubt in my mind they enlarged their antimatter containment units, and we'll find the people aboard were infected. But in keeping with the previous bypasses, those ships were low on fuel, judging by the anemic explosions when containment failed, so they're not yet at a point where they can bypass Broceliande as well."

"But eventually, they'll make it here." DeCarde carefully set her glass on the table. "At this point, I recommend you announce that the Navy will withdraw from Corbenic, Mister President, making the inner picket in the Broceliande system our new Outer Picket, albeit reinforced now that *Prevail* has completed her shakeout cruise. We will, however, leave the traffic control buoys where they are. Whether we'll replace them if they fail or are destroyed by reivers is still up for discussion."

"Agreed. I'll issue the order in the morning," Morane said. "I chose Lyonesse for the Knowledge Vault based on threats using the wormhole network. If they're returning to interstellar FTL travel, time and distance be damned, then this system is no safer than any other."

"And we're still no closer to a vaccine, nor do we know how long the plague takes to kill a person or anything about the survival rate. Lab-grown tissue only gets us so far." DeCarde gestured at her plate. "Why don't we dig in."

After her first few bites, she took a sip of wine and sat back.

"The reason we're here tonight is that I figure it's time we discussed the unthinkable — plague ships reaching Lyonesse despite the Navy's best efforts. We can't watch this system's entire heliopause, not even if the entire Imperial 16th Fleet was at our disposal."

"We're concentrating our efforts on the area where ships inbound from Arietis are most likely to cross it," Sirak said. "But that's still a vast arc of space. It's more than likely the first warning we'll get is a reiver wolf pack appearing at Lyonesse's hyperlimit, which gives us only a few hours to intercept and destroy them. The terrifying scenario is if they come close enough that wreckage covered with the virus enters our atmosphere and doesn't fully burn up. True, seventy-five percent of the planet's surface is ocean and icecaps, but that still leaves plenty of real estate."

Barca picked up the thread when Sirak paused for a bite of cold chicken.

"The most frightening scenario, a chunk of a ship's contaminated environmental system surviving re-entry and crashing in downtown Lannion has next to no chance of occurring. But the possibility is not nil. We know the virus can survive for days, if not weeks, on various surfaces under the right conditions, which means any wreckage crashing near settlements are potential sources of infection. Sure, we can warn people away from any impact area, then use our energy weapons and burn the debris, but if it's airborne, a gust of wind in the right direction and suddenly we face an outbreak. Yes, again, very unlikely but not nil."

"Which means," DeCarde said when Barca popped a chunk of pickled squash into her mouth, "we must plan for quarantines, mass evacuations, and potentially widespread deaths. It might overwhelm our medical system, citizens will panic, and we could see a breakdown of law and order. Many people, even in the government, are not yet ready for a discussion on what we do if our worst fears come true, but we can't wait until they're ready because by then, it might be too late."

Morane gave her a knowing look. "So, that's why Gwenneth and I are here."

"Yes. We wanted to make sure beforehand that the plan we'll present to you and the cabinet meets your approval. You know the most about running the republic. It's your brainchild. And Gwenneth is not only a medical professional in her own right, but her Brethren form the backbone of our medical system."

"Then let me give you a straightforward answer." He sat back and took a sip of wine. "If wreckage contaminated with the virus enters the atmosphere, Lyonesse must already be under a curfew with everyone sheltering in place while the Defense Force finds the impact site. That means I'll use my emergency powers and declare martial law the moment reivers are inbound from our hyperlimit. The constitution allows for it in the face of a clear and present danger to the republic's survival. No one can argue the Barbarian Plague's arrival on Lyonesse is anything less. Once the Defense Force finds the impact site and isolates it, the curfew can be lifted everywhere except within the immediate vicinity."

"What about lifting martial law? With elections later this year, the senators will be twitchy and when they get that way…"

"Too bad. We'll keep martial law in effect until the danger is over, meaning the wreckage has been turned into its constituent atoms, and any trace of the virus erased. If that means scouring a square kilometer of the planet's surface, even if that square kilometer is downtown Lannion, then so be it. Figure out how far dust from the impact would travel, then double that distance."

"Triple," Gwenneth said in a soft tone. "Or even quadruple."

Morane inclined his head by way of acknowledgment.

"Quadruple, then. If any humans are within that radius, they'll be quarantined at once and transported to an offshore location they can't escape. Shoot anyone who evades the quarantine."

"Hence the need to keep martial law."

"If, and that's a big if, the Navy can track wreckage and determine the probable impact site, you can try to evacuate anyone near ground zero beforehand."

"Your plan will horrify most of the career civilians in the administration, sir."

"Perhaps not as many as you think. Fear has a way of concentrating the mind on simple solutions."

"True." DeCarde turned to Gwenneth. "What about an offshore quarantine location for those who could be exposed?"

"I'd suggest the Windy Isles, but considering it might involve hundreds, if not thousands of people, something closer would be more appropriate, somewhere you could easily resupply internees without exposing crews and aircraft."

Major General Hamm raised a hand.

"There's a Ground Forces jungle training camp on Kodo Island. The installation is only occupied when a unit rotates through and shuttered the rest of the time. It's pretty basic, but there's room for several hundred, and if need be, we can throw up shelters and double the capacity."

"Where is it?"

Hamm pulled a flat device from his tunic pocket and placed it on the table. A holographic projection of Tristan's southern coast appeared along with a small red dot approximately five hundred kilometers southwest of Lannion.

"While escape is not impossible, the distance from the mainland is more than a human can swim by several orders of magnitude, never mind the predatory marine life. We can put eyes on the island and know immediately if someone attempts the swim or launches a raft."

Gwenneth nodded.

"It should do. You'll also need a separate offshore decontamination facility for aircraft and the pressure suit of anyone who comes into contact with evacuees. I'd even include those employed in isolating a crash site. Fortunately, repeated tests by the mobile lab show a simple bleach solution is one hundred percent effective in destroying the virus. You'd merely need a way of dunking your soldiers in a vat filled with the solution, then move them to a sterile place before they strip off their suits. You could spray the aircraft inside and out, but it might be easier if you simply parked them away from the decontamination site and left them sitting for a few months. Getting bleach into every nook and cranny will probably be a lot harder than clearing the outside of a pressure suit."

"Thank you, Sister. There's another island we sometimes use for training, about a hundred kilometers closer. It has several large clearings at its center."

"Set up the decontamination site as soon as possible and make practice runs," Morane said. "You have presidential approval."

A smile briefly relaxed Hamm's solemn expression. "Great minds and all that, sir. I was about to ask General Barca for permission."

"Granted, Devin."

Sirak glanced at Morane. "In that case, perhaps I should put my aerospace defense crews through their paces."

"Sure."

Gwenneth raised a restraining finger.

"Whatever you do, don't shoot at wreckage once it's already in the atmosphere. We might end up with several contaminated impact sites."

"No worries, Sister. I may be a simple Navy man, but I'm not *that* simple. Although training a few of my better shuttle crews in using tractor beams to divert wreckage if it seems headed for a settled area might be interesting. Send them aloft as soon as the alert sounds with the mission of diverting debris, so it splashes into the ocean far from human life." A sudden thought occurred to him. "Sister, there's no chance of it infecting native Lyonesse life forms, is there?"

"No. The virus was specifically engineered for us, and while it might mutate enough to survive in other species that evolved on Earth, it would die shortly after entering a native animal. Dumping reiver ship bits and pieces into the sea far from land should be fine. But be cautious. Tractor beams can break up pre-stressed components if they're not applied evenly."

Barca cleared her throat gently.

"There's one last thing, Sister. If we evacuate and quarantine civilians on Kodo Island, they'll need medical and spiritual care."

"I know." A sad smile tugged at Gwenneth's lips. "We who serve the Almighty in his Infinite Void will provide without complaint or holding back."

"Thank you."

— 33 —

A soft grunt of surprise escaped Stearn's lips, breaking the discipline he'd developed through hard work and repetition over the previous year. He and Marta sat face-to-face in the lotus position, eyes shut, on her training room's floor mats. He couldn't describe the sensation that threatened to overwhelm him at that instant. But it was as if the mythical third eye Marta kept mentioning fluttered open for a fraction of a second, and he touched her inner being with his mental fingertips for the first time. Was he reaching the crucial point after weeks of frustration and exhaustion?

He sensed an emotion best categorized as encouragement from Marta, whose mind had been his target for weeks, and reached out again. This time, the third eye remained open for a few seconds, and he marveled at the calm permeating his teacher's hidden core, one which mirrored the unbreakable air of serenity she wore like a second skin. Then, unbearable fatigue overcame him, and the third eye snapped shut.

"We will end the exercise."

Marta's voice broke through his trance, pulling him to the surface after a dive into the darkest of waters. His physical eyes slowly opened, and he saw her watching him.

"It took longer than I expected, but you've made the desired breakthrough. You can reach out and touch other minds in a controlled manner."

"I wasn't able to do it for long." Stearn's voice sounded distant to his own ears as if part of him was still somewhere else.

"No one can focus on their first successful attempt. Building the ability so you can call on it whenever you want takes time and practice. A lot of it. What you experienced so far will seem like a mental vacation on a sunny beach down by the sea once we begin your training in earnest." When he suppressed a yawn, she gave him a compassionate smile. "Once you become proficient, you won't be exhausted every time. Tired, yes. It takes a lot of energy. But not to the extent you're feeling right now."

"Good, because I'd like nothing better than sleep for a week."

"That's natural. Because I saw your third eye open, you will take the oath before we continue, which means I will condition you against misusing the talent. It will take an incredible amount of energy from both of us, but we cannot continue training until that is done."

Stearn bowed his head.

"I shall do as you say, Sister. But with your permission, I would return to my cell and sleep. Perhaps my mind will process what just happened, and I'll wake with renewed determination."

"Your mind will. Expect vivid dreams. Under the circumstances, you're excused other duties for today, as well as attendance at services. I'll inform Friar Loxias."

"Thank you."

"And do not try the exercise on your own. Until you've gained experience under my guidance, it would be a recipe for migraines, unbearable exhaustion, and sleepless nights. Did you ever see ancient maps of Earth with notations that say *here be dragons*?"

"No, Sister."

"They marked dangerous or unexplored territory. You are now standing in front of such a notation. Do not take another step without my guidance."

"Yes, Sister."

"You may go."

**

"Marta. Please come in."　Gwenneth gestured at the chairs in front of her desk. "I was just about to send for you."

"Then, this is a fortuitous coincidence unless you believe in predestination." Marta sat and folded her hands in her lap. "And since you don't, there's no point in discussing the matter. Shall I go first, or will you?"

"Go ahead."

"Stearn has finally shown he can reach out. It was brief yet intense. He might well develop the sharpest third eye the Order has seen in generations."

"Sharper than yours?"

Marta's expression conveyed indecision.

"I don't know. It took me a good ten years before I surpassed my teachers."

Gwenneth scoffed. "Less than that, I think. But never mind."

"He is, as one would expect, deeply fatigued by the experience. The oath and conditioning will come when he regains his strength. Next week, probably."

"Then he'll enjoy a few extra days rest. You're headed for the Windy Isles on tomorrow morning's Clipper."

"A problem?"

"No. More like an opportunity. Mirjam and her team successfully erased antisocial behavior traits in three more lifetime prisoners, one of them the first woman to undergo the process. It seems as if she might have the talent. Amelia sensed a stirring not long after her last treatment."

A thoughtful air crossed Marta's face.

"Interesting. Perhaps I should spend time with the five men as well and see whether there is some latency. I've long thought there was merit in exploring whether those with undiagnosed talent are more susceptible to personality disorders. If there's a correlation, I'd be curious why Stearn and I are reasonably well adjusted even though we experienced our share of troubles while this woman in the Windies committed horrific crimes."

"Her name is Seled Hyson. You may take the time you need with Mirjam's former patients. If necessary, Katarin or I can take over Stearn's conditioning and administer the oath. I think this recent development is a greater priority. Besides, working under a different teacher right now might do him good."

"Should my stay in the Windies exceed four or five days, then please go ahead."

"Working with Stearn would make a pleasant change from dealing with abbey politics day in and day out."

"Loxias?"

"He and his cohorts are strangely quiet these days, which makes me wonder what they're cooking. No, it's the small stuff that can sometimes pile up too fast. But you're not here so I can burden you with my problems. Landry booked a seat on tomorrow's Clipper and will take you to the spaceport in the morning. All that remains is rearranging your teaching schedule."

"In that case." Marta stood and bowed her head. "I'll prepare for the trip."

**

Marta visited the Windy Isles regularly, but her first breath of flower-scented, warm, salty air always made it seem like the first time. The sense of irony that such beautiful islands housed some of the ugliest souls and most dangerous, soulless creatures that humanity could produce never left her either. She made her way from the landing strip to the priory at a leisurely pace and basked in the rays of the late afternoon sun, watching them bounce off the lagoon's softly rippling waters.

Perhaps she would take a dip in the morning. There weren't many spots on Lyonesse safe enough for humans to enjoy an ocean swim without risking attack by native predators. This was one of them. The Phoenix Clipper took off behind her with a loud roar. She stopped and glanced up at its rapidly receding shape. The sleek, white spacecraft was the closest thing to a time machine she'd ever experienced. In one hour, *City of Lannion* would land where most people were only now waking up to a day that was already waning here.

As she entered the priory grounds, a smiling Mirjam appeared on the front stoop.

"Marta. Welcome back. Thank you for taking the time."

"How could I resist? A successfully treated sociopath with a third eye hidden behind the mess her mind once was is a first in our history."

"If Amelia is correct." Mirjam ushered her in and headed for the guest quarters.

"You didn't check?"

"We don't know what we're dealing with. Wiping entire engram sequences to cure personality disorders is so new I didn't want to risk blundering in. Your touch is the lightest, while your skill at teasing out things most of us can't even sense is unsurpassed. And since we're on that subject, how is Stearn?"

"We made the first breakthrough yesterday."

"Oh." Mirjam laid her hand on Marta's arm. "I apologize for pulling you away at this juncture."

"No apologies necessary. Stearn needs rest after the experience. His really is a powerful mind, one which draws a lot of energy. Should I stay here longer, Gwenneth or Katarin will take him through the next steps."

"Fine teachers, both, even if our revered abbess hasn't worked with students in a while. Here we are." Mirjam let Marta enter the small, sparsely furnished room ahead of her and watched as she unpacked her travel bag.

"There, done." Marta, wearing an expectant air on her face, smiled at Mirjam. "When do I meet this Seled Hyson?"

"Tomorrow. She left the maximum security enclosure this morning, along with the two men we treated. They're settling in under Friar Rikkard's guidance. They'll eat alone before the rest of us. We'd rather not overwhelm them on their first day."

"What about the ones you treated last year?"

"They passed their examinations and took vows. We use them as general labor around the priory. Why do you ask?"

"I'd like to test all six, not just Seled. They may have a glimmer of talent hidden away somewhere."

Mirjam nodded. "The theory that an undiagnosed and therefore undisciplined strong sixth sense contributes to personality disorders. I'll make the arrangements. But let's leave that until the morning, shall we?"

"This is your priory. Tomorrow will be fine. Just point them out during the evening meal."

"Certainly."

Soft, but determined footsteps in the corridor made both glance at the open door. Seconds later, Amelia's cheerful face appeared.

"Sister Marta! Welcome."

"Thank you, my dear. How are your latest patients?"

"Much more patient than before their treatment. The difference is nothing short of astounding."

"Amelia was their counselor, so she saw the change up close and personal."

"And if Seled does indeed have the talent, I'd like to be her teacher, at least for the first level of training."

Mirjam cocked a sardonic eyebrow at the younger woman. "Are you asking me or Marta?"

"Both of you."

"Good answer." Mirjam gave Marta a wink. "I don't mind if our Order's most talented teacher doesn't."

"So long as you supervise. Amelia was a star student of mine, but that wasn't so long ago. Still, the experience she'll gain won't be wasted."

"Thank you. I think Seled might learn more easily under my tutelage. Though it wasn't plain before, she developed a certain trust in me."

"How so?" Marta asked.

"When we stripped away the chaos filling Seled's mind by selectively wiping the engrams that drove her disorder, deeply suppressed parts of her personality rose to the surface."

"Including the hint she might have a quiescent third eye."

"Yes."

"But you didn't sense the same thing from the two men we treated alongside Seled."

Amelia shook her head.

"No, Sister." She hesitated. "Do you think there might be a glimmer?"

"I won't know until I verify. That is why Gwenneth sent me. But as Mirjam said, we will let matters rest until tomorrow."

"Understood." Amelia glanced at the prioress. "With your permission?"

"Carry on."

Once Amelia's footsteps faded away, Marta asked, "How is my star pupil doing?"

"Amelia is a credit to your teaching. She is a formidable counselor, helping us with the most irredeemable prisoners, and she took part in the treatment without hesitation. I wouldn't be surprised if she ended up taking your place when you retire to a life of contemplation."

"Then she has a long wait ahead of her. I'm still as spry as I was the day my training began."

"No doubt. We should thank the Almighty that our talent comes with a few side benefits, like delayed aging."

**

Once the sun vanished behind a watery horizon, Mirjam led Marta into the refectory, where she went around and greeted the Priory's Brethren one-by-one. Most of them, save for the exiles, now friars of the Order, were old acquaintances, if not former students. When Mirjam introduced her to Erasmus, Marnix, and Shakib, she briefly looked into each man's eyes and gently reached out with her mind. They were unfailingly polite, though guarded, as if they'd heard about Marta's prowess as the Order's foremost teacher.

Later, Marta and Mirjam shared a pot of tea in front of the latter's open office windows so they could admire the moonlit lagoon on one of the rare nights when all three of Lyonesse's natural satellites, including Ys, were visible over the Windies. The triple shadows they cast no longer seemed as strange to Marta's eyes as they did during her early years on Lyonesse, but she still found the sight intriguing.

"What did you think of our new friars?"

Marta took a sip of tea and replied, eyes still on the silver ripples, "I'm not sure. I briefly reached out while you introduced us. Their minds seemed hollow, as if part of their personality has vanished, which I suppose makes sense since you wiped the engrams that drove their disorder and didn't replace it with anything else."

"We hoped their training would fill part of the emptiness, but so far, that hasn't happened."

"The mind of the one who calls himself Erasmus is stronger than those of his companions and didn't feel quite as bare."

Mirjam nodded. "He was a challenge. His disorder dwarfed those of every other prisoner in the Supermax section. The man he used to be was utterly malevolent."

"Then it's remarkable how peaceful he seems. You can't tell he once harbored a heinous soul." Marta turned and smiled at her colleague. "I confess I've been skeptical about your treatment, but no more."

"Really? Even though it was you who suggested we study whether we can use the process by which sisters are conditioned against misusing their talent to correct aberrant behavior?"

"I never thought it would be possible to cure lifelong sociopaths. Imagine if we identified those with behavior problems before they caused harm and treated them so they could enjoy a normal life. Yes, I know we can't go around telling parents their children will become serial killers or worse, because it would raise the question of how we know they faced such a fate."

"It is unfortunate. Imagine how many innocent lives we would save." Mirjam took another sip of tea. "You know we don't need the patient's consent for a successful treatment. We can enter a mind and wipe the relevant engrams at will."

"Really?" Marta's eyebrows arched up in surprise. "That raises so many ethical questions."

"Which is why we don't discuss it. Besides, if we cured unwilling prisoners, the wardens would soon figure out we're doing more than just counseling. Mind you, getting as many out of Supermax as possible and giving them useful lives, even though none will ever leave the Windies, remains a worthwhile endeavor."

— 34 —

"How are you this morning, Stearn?" Loxias' voice boomed across the empty refectory, now that most of the Brethren were off to their various tasks. Being exempt from work for the day meant Roget could linger after breakfast, and he didn't mind the solitude. His room in the dormitory seemed too confining, for reasons he didn't understand.

He bowed his head respectfully.

"I've regained my energy, though my mind keeps worrying at the strange dreams I experienced."

Loxias poured himself a cup of tea and took a seat across from the younger man.

"I wouldn't know about those dreams since I'm just a normal friar with little talent other than the ability to read people and influence them. But you made an extraordinary breakthrough, one which might end the sisters' exclusive rule over our Order. If only we could figure out what makes you tick, we might find a way of creating more friars with your abilities."

"I've only just begun. My capabilities might not be much greater than yours."

Loxias waved the objection away. "I've been watching you from day one, my friend. You're already more aware than most of my friars. Since you're at loose ends while Marta is gone, how about shadowing me for a few days? You would learn more about administering the Order and see how we interact with Lyonesse society these days. It wouldn't do any harm if you met some folks who'll be important for us in the coming years."

Roget shrugged. "Sure. Why not? I still don't know what I'll be doing once my time with Marta is over. But I don't like people enough to become a teacher, counselor, or healer, I didn't enjoy farming back home, and the abbey has little call for a starship engineer. No offense, but working on the environmental systems day in and day out isn't part of my long-term plans."

"I'm sure you'll become proficient at anything you want. But here's the thing. A man of your potential has a duty to seek the highest leadership positions so he can challenge the sisters when they insist on looking inward while our future demands we look outward. They disregard what we ordinary friars say, but they won't dare ignore one who matches them talent for talent. Especially if that man finds support among the Brethren and presents himself as our first abbot." Loxias drained his cup. "Ever heard of a pre-diaspora sage by the name Hilaire Belloc?"

"No."

"He famously said, *time after time, mankind is driven against the rocks of the horrid reality of a fallen creation. And time after time, mankind must learn the hard lessons of history—the lessons that for some dangerous and awful reason we can't seem to keep in our collective memory.* I consider it my mission to make sure the Order doesn't lose its collective memory of humanity's latest fall, which will happen if we keep looking inward and exclude everything else." Loxias stood. "Come. It's time for the morning rounds."

**

Seled Hyson seemed older and more worn out by life than Marta expected. She was watching the three new postulants from the shadows of an upper-story window as Friar Rikkard led them through a series of exercises designed to rebuild bodies wasted by decades behind bars. Marta didn't reach out and touch their minds. But she saw much in their postures, their facial expressions, and their eyes. Especially the eyes.

Whoever called them windows to the soul long ago didn't know the half of it. None of the three possessed one worth mentioning. Just like Erasmus and his companions. Did the treatment erase it? Or did those with personality disorders lack a soul in the first place? Marta had peered into the eyes of irredeemable psychopaths and found an emptiness that still haunted her worst dreams. Though it was a peace of sorts, without the chaos of disordered minds like the ones Mirjam and her counselors were treating.

The training session ended with the customary exchange of bows, then Rikkard led them back to the dormitory while Marta headed for the meditation room she'd requisitioned at the back of the priory's main building. There, she took one of the two chairs and composed herself while waiting for Hyson. She didn't nurture preconceived notions about the upcoming encounter and therefore let her thoughts wander aimlessly rather than dwell on what would happen shortly.

When her ears noticed the sound of two humans entering the corridor, one with a heavier tread than the other, Marta's eyes opened, and she pushed away the last tendrils of her light trance. Friar Rikkard's familiar shape filled the open doorway. He dipped his head respectfully.

"Sister, I bring you the postulant named Seled."

"Thank you. She may enter."

Rikkard stepped aside and waved Hyson in, pointing at the empty chair facing Marta.

"Please sit, Seled."

Both women studied each other in silence as Hyson obeyed Rikkard.

"Sister Marta is one of the Order's most revered teachers," he continued. "Second only to Abbess Gwenneth."

"Yes, Friar."

Marta glanced at Rikkard, her eyes silently telling him he could safely leave Hyson with her. He inclined his head again and obeyed without uttering another word. When he closed the door behind him, she gave the exile her full attention.

"What do you remember of the person who inhabited your mind before the treatment?"

Hyson's shoulders twitched in an involuntary shrug.

"Most of my past, I suppose. But there are many gaps which I'm told was where the sisters removed the memories of my crimes. They said endless rage once filled me, but I cannot remember how or why."

"And how are you now?"

Hyson bit her lower lip as she thought. "I'm not sure. Empty? I can recall having many emotions as a child, but they seem foreign."

"Do you recall emotions you experienced as an adult?"

"No. The sisters took my memories of them as well. I suppose my rage permeated everything once I grew up."

As they spoke, Marta gently reached out and touched Hyson's mind. She found an aching emptiness where she expected a riot of emotion in healthy humans. Hyson didn't seem as barren as the psychopaths Marta studied, but it was close. She certainly wasn't chaotic like Stearn before he learned to discipline his thoughts. That would make her training much easier.

As Marta ventured deeper into Hyson's mind, she found weak feelings, as if newly born, and an undefined aura of loss. Perhaps an unconscious part of her mourned the old Seled even though she'd been a tortured soul who spent half her life incarcerated where she couldn't harm another. Given enough time, the new Seled would surely fill at least part of the emptiness within her as she learned to feel again. Hopefully, Mirjam was right, and life in a controlled, peaceful, and loving environment would keep Seled's old rage at bay for good.

"Did you expect this emptiness when you signed up for the experimental treatment?"

Another shrug. "I didn't know what to expect."

"Any regrets?"

A tiny, tentative smile appeared for the first time.

"How could I regret losing a part of me I cannot remember? The treatment gave me a chance at a new life, even if I never leave the Windies, and for that, I will be eternally grateful."

Marta touched the faint stirrings within Seled to see if any were cause for alarm, but found nothing more than curiosity, a tiny spark of amusement and a strange awe at her radically changed circumstances. She also found a sixth sense, hidden away but stirring, looking for parts of a mind that no longer existed and trying to adjust. Amelia was right. Seled had the talent, but how strong was she?

Then Marta saw a third eye, one with movement behind the mental eyelid. She couldn't tell how awake it was, or if that eye would even open, let alone how it might work in someone so devoid of underlying human feelings. But helping Seled discover her talent intrigued Marta. She differed vastly from other female postulants.

Unfortunately, remaining in the Windies for long wasn't an option. Perhaps Marta could stay a few weeks, just to see if that eye might open, then let Amelia take care of Seled's further development.

"What do you think about becoming a sister in this priory?"

She shrugged. "I don't believe in the concept of a deity. Or at least I think I don't."

"It doesn't matter. The Order of the Void primarily exists to serve others. Belief in the Almighty is not compulsory, though everyone eventually reaches a point where they realize the existence of a higher power is necessary, otherwise the universe makes no sense. We would teach you several disciplines, physical and mental, beyond what we teach friars like your two companions from this round of treatment and the three treated previously. It won't help escape from the Windies, but it will give you a purpose in life like no other. You might even end up counseling prisoners and exiles like Amelia and her colleagues do."

A frown of incredulity creased Seled's forehead. "What a fascinating idea."

"I cannot stay here for long, but I would start your training, then let Amelia take over."

"When would I start?"

"Once Sister Mirjam approves. Though I am one of the Order's most senior teachers, she leads the Windy Isles Priory and has final say on what happens in her house."

"Understood."

Marta produced her personal communicator and held it to her lips. "Rikkard."

A few seconds passed, then, "Yes, Sister."

"I'm done with Seled for the moment."

"On my way. Rikkard, out."

The communicator vanished again.

"I'm sure you're full of questions, but they must wait. I can only answer them after you begin your transformation."

**

"And?" Mirjam looked up at Marta expectantly as the latter swept into her office.

"It's there, all right. A solid sixth sense and third eye, shut, but stirring. We can attempt to train her as a sister."

"I see." The prioress sat back with a thoughtful expression on her face. "Ever since Amelia raised the possibility, I've been wondering whether we should do it just because we can. Seled is the first woman to undergo treatment, and we still know so little about the long-term effects."

Marta took one of the empty chairs.

"You mean we know nothing about the long-term effects. What if an undiagnosed talent is a cause of personality disorders? Wouldn't Seled be at risk of backsliding if we do nothing?"

"I suppose." Mirjam frowned as she sorted through her thoughts.

"Then, there's the matter of finding out how the talent manifests in a mind with only the barest of newborn emotions."

A snort escaped Mirjam's solemn countenance.

"Aha. I see. You want to play sorceresses' apprentice."

"I've never worked with someone like her. We could learn a lot about what drives us sisters by observing the closest thing to a blank slate."

"May I assume you're not going back to Lannion on tomorrow's Clipper?"

"If you'll let me be Seled's first teacher for a few weeks, then no. But the decision remains yours. I will respect your wishes, notwithstanding my curiosity. Once I'm sure she responds well to training, I will let Amelia take care of her further development and rejoin the abbey."

Mirjam looked away for a few seconds, then back at Marta. "You have my blessing."

"Thank you. I'll examine the other former prisoners today and begin with Seled tomorrow."

— 35 —

"Good morning, my friend. I hear Marta is staying in the Windies for a while." Roget looked up from his mug of tea as Loxias dropped into a chair across from him. He'd noticed the chief administrator make a beeline for his table, even though the refectory was full of sisters and friars enjoying their breakfast before another day of work.

"Loxias. And a good morning to you as well. Yes, she's assigned herself a new student from among the prisoners treated by Sister Amelia."

"Any idea how long?"

Roget shook his head. "No. She said a few days, but knowing her, it could easily become a few weeks."

"What of your training?"

"Katarin will take over when she clears her current commitments. In a few days, maybe."

A pleased smile split Loxias' bearded face.

"Which gives you more time to learn how things work on this world. You'll attend the Lyonesse Chamber of Commerce meeting with me this afternoon and meet some of the republic's biggest players, men and women with influence who can help us advance the Order's interests."

"It would be an honor."

"While we're there, you can study a few who I'll point out and tell me afterward what you think. Many of them are devious characters in one way or another, people with hidden agendas of their own. However, we Brethren are the ultimate students of human nature and can see behind most masks. Especially friars with your skills."

"Which aren't fully developed yet." Roget decided against mentioning he'd not taken the oath and received the conditioning yet, although his third eye could open, albeit briefly. A few things remained between student and teacher.

Loxias made a dismissive hand gesture.

"Think of it as on-the-job training during Marta's absence. The Brethren have a higher calling than merely help humans who suffer from various ailments. We also guide those in power for the greater good of society."

"The history of what happened in the Coalsack Sector before the empire's collapse proves that sort of counseling can be fraught with mortal risk."

"An anomaly that didn't crop up elsewhere. Pendrick Zahar suffered from a longstanding hatred of the Order for personal rather than political reasons. Or so Marta stated for our historical records. You see, he could tell when a sister brushed his mind, and the very notion revolted him. Imagine if Zahar had become a friar instead of a naval officer. The Coalsack Sector's history would be quite different, at least where the Order is concerned."

"I see. And how does one tell if a mind can register our touch and react badly to it?"

"One can't. That's why the sisters are conditioned against entering another's mind, absent medical or psychological needs.

Even then, they proceed gingerly, ready to withdraw at the slightest hint of awareness." Loxias stood. "Meet me in front of the administration building at thirteen-hundred hours. Wear your best garments."

"Will do."

Roget watched Loxias wend his way across the refectory before vanishing through the main door. As he finished his tea, he found himself anticipating the Chamber of Commerce meeting with unexpected interest. It would offer a welcome antidote to Marta's endless training sessions and put him back in touch with the real world. Loxias was onto something when he accused the sisters of looking inward, even though this new and perilous era demanded the Order look outward as well. The future belongs to those who show up instead of meditating endlessly on the Almighty's various permutations in the Infinite Void.

**

A few minutes before the appointed time, Roget, wearing an immaculate, black friar's habit, crossed the quadrangle to where a ground car, doors open, waited silently. No sooner did he reach it that Loxias walked out the administration building's main entrance with his usual energetic stride. He was also clad in an immaculate friar's habit but wore a small, shiny Void Orb on a simple metal chain around his neck.

Loxias gave Roget a comradely thump on the shoulder.

"Shall we head into Lannion and promote the Order's interests with our republic's captains of industry?"

He didn't wait for an answer but climbed into the car. After a moment of hesitation, Roget took the front passenger seat.

"Stick with me. I'll do the introductions," Loxias said once they were beyond the abbey's walls, "and when we take our chairs, you just sit along the wall near my table. Listen and don't speak unless someone asks you a question. Now, remember these people, because I want you to watch them closely during my introductions and the meeting." He rattled off six names, including Hecht and Downes, then said, "They're sharp, so don't be obvious about studying them."

"May I ask why these particular individuals interest you?"

"Hecht is CEO of Lyonesse's largest industrial conglomerate, Downes heads that conglomerate's board of directors and the others because they run the second to the sixth-largest businesses in the republic. Collectively, those six enterprises and their subsidiaries own almost forty percent of the planet's economic assets. When one of their senior people speaks, the government listens, even Jonas Morane. They're our way into the corridors of power, my friend. As you rise through the Order's ranks, you'll spend more time with them, meaning it's important you learn what you can about their characters."

"You want me to peer into their souls and see what's there. If they have souls, that is."

A bark of laughter filled the car's passenger compartment.

"If I didn't know you were Marta's student, that statement would set me straight. I don't share her mysticism, but there's no denying her trainees are among the most powerful minds of their generation."

"I don't share her mysticism either, but after spending time on the Windy Isles, I can confirm what Marta calls a soul is real. We can debate whether it's a soul in the religious sense or not, but I've met prisoners who are utterly empty inside and others who are nothing but chaos. Are the empty ones devoid of a soul? And are the chaotic ones possessed? Interesting questions, don't you think?"

Loxias shrugged, as if unconvinced but willing to go along.

"Perhaps. It's no worse an interpretation than any other the Order has contemplated over the centuries. In any case, peer into the souls of our Chamber of Commerce grandees and tell me what you find. I already enjoy good relations with Gerson Hecht, though Downes doesn't like me much, and I can't figure out why. The others are friendly enough, but a bit standoffish. The one thing you'll notice is neither Hecht nor Downes like Morane and his cronies, such as DeCarde. Both harbor a deep-seated grudge against him for events that happened long ago. They're outwardly civil toward Morane and Gwenneth when she makes an appearance, but anyone trained the way we are can't fail but see it. Not that the president attends something as prosaic as Chamber of Commerce meetings, though most of the time, he sends one of the cabinet secretaries."

The car entered Lannion's northern outskirts, and they soon found themselves driving along the Haven River toward downtown and the stone, two-story Chamber of Commerce Building close to Government House. As Roget noted when he looked the Chamber up in the abbey's database, its headquarters was one of the oldest structures on the planet and housed the colonial administration during Lyonesse's early years as a distant outpost, one which the imperial government mostly ignored.

They soon turned off the capital's main avenue and entered a courtyard already filling up with various vehicles, both aerial and ground. A large sign over the building's front door grandly announced its only tenant. Loxias parked them neatly beside a luxury vehicle bearing the Hecht Industries logo. He and Roget climbed out of their car and headed for the entrance where a thin, dark-haired man in his early thirties wearing a business suit greeted them with a polite nod.

"Friar Loxias. Welcome. And who is your companion?"

"This is Friar Stearn, one of my most trusted aides, Mister Pitt."

"Welcome, Friar Stearn."

"Thank you."

"The members are assembling in the ballroom where refreshments await. Enjoy the meeting."

Loxias bestowed an avuncular smile on Pitt. "Your courtesy honors you, as always."

Roget could have sworn he sensed a mental eye roll from the man. "You're too kind, Friar."

As they walked down a broad, carpeted corridor whose walls were paneled with honey-colored wood, a growing murmur of conversation reached their ears.

"Sounds like a full house," Loxias remarked with an air of satisfaction.

Roget gave him an amused sideways glance.

"You enjoy this sort of thing, don't you? Hobnobbing with the republic's upper crust."

"It makes a refreshing change from the solemnity and single-mindedness of our Brethren, especially the sisters. Ah. Here we are." Loxias pointed at an open double door on the left as the buzz of voices reached a crescendo.

Upon entering, Loxias, a pleasant smile plastered on his face, headed directly for a middle-aged man in a severely cut business suit while nodding at people as they passed them. He stood near a long table covered with cups, jugs, fruit bowls, and pastries, talking to a tall, squarely built woman whose short blond hair was liberally sprinkled with silver strands.

"That's Ari Hodson with Defense Secretary DeCarde," he murmured in an aside to Roget. "Ari is the Chamber's president. I guess DeCarde is this meeting's sacrificial cabinet member."

When they came within earshot, Hodson broke off his conversation and turned to Loxias. "Friar! How nice to see you again."

"Ari, always a pleasure." Loxias bowed his head in greeting. "May I present Friar Stearn, my most trusted aide, and someone destined for glorious things in the Order?"

Roget imitated Loxias' bow.

"You know Defense Secretary DeCarde." Hodson gestured at the woman beside him.

"Of course. How are you, Madame Secretary?"

"Doing tolerably well, Friar." DeCarde glanced at Stearn. "Aren't you the one *Dawn Seeker* picked up on Yotai?"

"Yes, ma'am."

"Stearn is extremely talented, as you'll no doubt see over the coming years, Madame Secretary. Now, if you'll excuse us."

Another bow and Loxias led Roget around the room, introducing him to each Chamber of Commerce member in attendance before both took a cup of tea and a small pastry.

"You might have noticed DeCarde isn't a fan of the Order, something she shares with other members of Morane's cabinet. Hopefully, his successor's appointees will be friendlier."

Stearn thought it might be more a case of DeCarde not liking Loxias personally rather than the Order itself, but he knew better than pointing that out. Instead, since this was his first time among non-Brethren other than the Windy Isles exiles since arriving on Lyonesse, he wondered how ordinary human minds would seem to his partially trained senses.

He cautiously lowered his mental shields, expecting something akin to Supermax's cacophony, though perhaps not nearly as pronounced, but what he picked up was only the mental counterpart of the quiet conversations around him. Roget looked around the room to match what he sensed with individuals but in vain.

A bell tinkled, and most voices trailed off. Once he had everyone's attention, Hodson said, in a surprisingly strong basso, "Ladies and gentlemen, if you would please move to the banquet hall next door so we can start the meeting."

Roget followed Loxias, but once in the banquet hall, he peeled off to one side where chairs lined the wall while his superior joined Gerson Hecht, Severin Downes, and a few others at one of the many cloth-covered round tables. The room filled quickly as Hodson stood behind a rostrum bearing the Chamber's logo, a green double-headed Vanger's Condor clutching a banner with the words 'The Spirit of Enterprise' written on it.

While Hodson waited for everyone to settle down and face him, Roget scanned the tables looking for those Loxias named on their way here. Once he fixed their position in his mind, he turned his eyes on the rostrum, like everyone else present.

"Ladies and gentlemen, today is the last Lyonesse Chamber of Commerce meeting before this year's general elections. With the increasing peril posed by plague ships and the ensuing demands placed on us to support the Navy's expansion, our interest in who will form the next senate and elect President Morane's successor is greater than ever. Simply put, we must make sure our views are well represented. I propose we debate senatorial endorsements after dealing with regular business."

Roget noticed Loxias and Hecht exchange glances and idly wondered how close they were. Animated discussions soon broke out, but instead of listening, he focused on his targets, since he knew nothing about Lyonesse politics. Yet the more he studied them, the more frustrated he became. Despite everything Roget tried, he couldn't distinguish their minds from the background noise, and the physical tells he'd been taught to look for weren't much in evidence. It left him with the study of body language, tone, and degree of participation in the debate, things he couldn't yet analyze with any confidence. Loxias would be disappointed, but what did he expect of a partly trained friar, even one with a sister's abilities?

Unless he took a step into the realm of dragons.

Roget looked inward at the third eye Marta's training showed him. Opening it might allow his talent to zero in on individual minds without touching them and thereby match emotions with demeanor. Where was the harm in that? Brethren took every opportunity for self-improvement, so long as they didn't violate any article of the Order's Rule. And since he'd not sworn the oath yet, there could be no violation.

Who first?

His eyes rested on Severin Downes' sharp, patrician profile a few meters in front of him. Downes struck Roget as a weak man when Loxias introduced him earlier, though he couldn't figure out why. Perhaps it was Downes' supercilious demeanor and the almost discourteous way he'd returned Roget's respectful greeting. Roget knew from experience forceful characters rarely wrapped themselves in a cloak of superiority because they didn't need one. They knew their worth and their place. Weak characters, on the other hand…

He concentrated on the mental image he'd created of his third eye while staring at Downes. After a few moments that felt more like eons, his inner eyelid quivered, then snapped open, and he saw Severin Downes' soul, writhing within the controlled envelope of a man who would always be at war with the universe.

At that same instant, half a planet away, the Order of the Void's most powerful teacher woke with a start and checked the time, wondering what could disturb her sleep at the hour of the wolf, when night's black cloak smothered the Windy Isles.

PART III - THE HOUR OF THE WOLF

— 36 —

The more Stearn's third eye peeled back the layers of Severin Downes' personality, the more he pitied him. Downes' strongest emotion was smoldering anger deep within. It lived side-by-side with resentment, hunger for power, and an unfulfilled thirst for respect. He was an insignificant man whose role in the republic's future was almost nil, and deep within, he understood that.

After a few minutes, Stearn closed his third eye for a brief rest and turned his gaze on DeCarde. He'd already decided the former commander of the Lyonesse Defense Force and current Defense Secretary was perhaps the most honest individual in the room. She exuded self-confidence and openness. Stearn could well believe she'd backed Morane's proposal Lyonesse build a Knowledge Vault and make itself independent of the crumbling empire.

Her name wasn't on Loxias' list, but he wanted to look at her mind anyway. A few deep, controlled breaths, then Stearn opened his inner eyelid, though not without difficulty. It resisted him, as if under a spell. Yet when he looked at DeCarde, he saw nothing. It was as if she had mental shields of her own. Or perhaps she kept such a tight leash on her emotions that the inner woman mirrored her outer manifestation.

Curious, Stearn formed mental fingers and reached across the room so he could examine her up close, mindful he was broadening his violation of Marta's strictures. But what she didn't know couldn't hurt him, no matter how strong her talent. None of the sisters, not even Marta, could force her way into his thoughts, he was sure of that by now.

When his fingers brushed up against the energy field that was DeCarde's mind, he felt a strange tingle but no shield. She really was extraordinarily self-possessed. Remarkable. Unexpectedly, DeCarde glanced at Stearn, as if she detected the intrusion. He instantly withdrew and closed his third eye, fearful DeCarde was one of the rare people Marta had mentioned.

Both successful attempts proved Stearn could reach out at will, even without further training, although he couldn't yet manage the energy expenditure. Surely sisters who worked as counselors, the most mentally draining of jobs, knew how. And there were probably advanced techniques on interpreting another's brain waves with greater precision. Yet what he'd sensed from Downes and DeCarde so closely corroborated his initial assessment of them that Stearn couldn't help but feel a surge of pride unseemly in a friar.

He spent another ten or fifteen minutes listening while he recuperated before turning his attention on Gerson Hecht. The head of Hecht Industries was outwardly as self-possessed as DeCarde, though without the latter's aura of openness and palpable honesty. Stearn expected the same sort of quiet mind, one which needed a closer examination before revealing its secrets.

Yet when he reached out with his mental fingers, Stearn found nothing. Hecht was a man without feelings and without emotions. Perhaps even without a soul. At least as far as he could tell. Maybe the planet's leading industrialist was what Amelia called a highly functioning psychopath, one who avoided criminality and channeled his energies into legitimate pursuits. Being devoid of empathy would certainly present advantages in someone who led the republic's largest conglomerate. For one, he wouldn't waste time worrying about the welfare of those over whom he rode roughshod on his way to success.

Though weariness was settling in after three attempts, Stearn nonetheless studied the others on Loxias' list and found a mishmash of personalities, none quite as remarkable as either DeCarde or Hecht nor as perpetually furious as Downes.

**

"Though I'm always glad to speak with you, it's the middle of the night in the Windies. Why are you calling me?" Gwenneth frowned at Marta's image on her office display.

"What is Stearn doing at the moment?"

"I couldn't say. Hang on." Gwenneth raised her voice. "Landry, please find out where Stearn is."

The young friar poked his head through the door seconds later. "He's been shadowing Loxias since Marta left, and Loxias is at the quarterly Lyonesse Chamber of Commerce meeting this afternoon."

Gwenneth mentally rolled her eyes. The Chamber of Commerce had invited the Order to join it, or rather Loxias' allies arranged for the invitation, shortly after she'd first sat with the Estates-General. Though the Order's involvement in the medical and academic fields was extensive, the abbey wasn't a big commercial player, despite its traditional monastic food and drink production. However, hobnobbing with the republic's captains of industry kept Loxias happy, and so she'd accepted.

She glanced at Marta. "You heard?"

"Yes. Do me a favor and peel Stearn away from Loxias the moment they return, then see that he swears the oath and receives the conditioning. I should never have left him at this critical juncture in his development."

"What is it you fear?" When Marta didn't immediately reply, Gwenneth gave her a knowing look. "You felt a premonition, didn't you?"

"I wouldn't exactly call it a premonition, but something pulled me from my sleep. Since the bond between teacher and student is strong, and Stearn is a stronger student than any I've taught, I fear he did something he shouldn't during that Chamber of Commerce meeting, likely at Loxias' urging. Since Loxias shows an unseemly lack of restraint in pursuing his ambitions, I fear he might take Stearn down the wrong path."

Gwenneth would suspect any other sister with such fears of having an overactive imagination, but not Marta. She'd been right often enough over the years, eerily so sometimes.

"Katarin will resume Stearn's training next week. She's the most appropriate teacher for him but has a firm commitment right now — a patient undergoing treatment at the University Medical Center."

"Then either you do it now or forbid him from leaving the abbey grounds until Katarin returns. If he's been peeking into non-Brethren minds at that meeting with no inhibitions keeping him from violating their privacy, who knows where it'll lead. Especially if there's another Pendrick Zahar in the crowd."

"Understood. I'll keep Stearn here once he returns, then call Katarin and decide on the next steps."

"Thank you. We've never seen a male with a fully opened third eye and can't predict what a lack of restraint may bring, but it won't be good. Especially not with Stearn's grueling life experiences and almost fatal injuries on Yotai. Our records tell us how women in similar situations end up, and it's not pretty."

"The corruption of power, Void style," Gwenneth murmured.

Marta nodded. "Exactly."

"I'm sure it'll be okay in the end. Between us, Katarin and I will ensure Stearn's welfare."

"Good. Keep me aware of developments. Enjoy the rest of your day."

"And you the rest of your night."

Marta's image faded away, leaving a thoughtful Gwenneth to stare at the black display.

"Landry?"

The friar's face reappeared in the doorway.

"When Stearn returns from Lannion, please see he comes to my office right away."

"Yes, Abbess."

**

"You look tired," Loxias remarked once their ground car left the Chamber of Commerce in its wake. The low, late afternoon sun was casting long shadows into the streets, proof the meeting lasted well beyond its allotted time. "Still can't channel those energies efficiently?"

"No. I'm a rank beginner." Loxias' breezy tone irked Stearn.

"Tell me about the people I named."

He recounted suitably edited versions of his observations, both overt and via his third eye. All the while, Loxias nodded, as if Stearn was proving him right in every detail.

"I did as you asked. What is the value of this information?"

Loxias chuckled.

"Leverage, my friend. The more I know about the people who both help and oppose our efforts, the better I can advance the Order's interests. So, you think Gerson Hecht is devoid of any human feelings. Not surprising. He always struck me as a block of ice. I daresay he's using us as much as we're using him. How Gerson tolerates Downes is a mystery."

"Two sides of the same coin," Stearn replied without thought.

"Pardon?" Loxias gave Stearn a surprised look. "That's quite a profound conclusion.

"Hecht is cold and calculating, without emotions. Downes hides it well, but he overflows with feelings of anger, rejection, envy, and hate. Separately, they're each half a man. Together they form a whole, albeit a dark one."

"How did you come to this conclusion? Not that I think you're wrong, but I'm curious."

Stearn half closed his eyes in thought.

"It simply came to me. Perhaps my time in the Windy Isles, sitting in on counseling sessions with the worst humans on the planet, gave me a subconscious insight into the human psyche."

"Am I correct in assuming you touched their minds as a sister would?" When Stearn remained silent, Loxias chuckled. "Come now. A student of Marta's can only be exceptional."

"It was wrong for me to reach out."

Loxias made a dismissive hand gesture.

"Would the Almighty give you a great talent if you weren't meant to use it? You did well today, and you can do more for the Order and the Almighty in the future. Did you follow any of the discussion?"

Stearn shook his head. "I didn't understand much of it, and I was rather busy with the task you set me."

"Our principal ally, Gerson Hecht, supports several senatorial candidates who favor us. Between them, they can raise our profile on government committees and commissions."

"And make sure Hecht Industries keeps getting lucrative government contracts."

"As a wise sage from the dark ages before spaceflight noted, there's no such thing as a free meal. Quid, meet the pro quo." Loxias chuckled at his own wit. "You and I will think of ways we can support those senatorial candidates in the upcoming election. Perhaps through them, we might even get a say in who becomes the next president. Charis Sandino, though a decent vice president, is, at best, indifferent to the Order of the Void. She has ambitions, but nothing says a vice president automatically becomes president once the incumbent's second term ends. There are suitable candidates for the presidency who are more favorably disposed and wouldn't mind seeing us assume a bigger role in the republic's affairs."

"You would interfere in secular elections?"

"Supporting the best candidate is hardly interference. No, I simply want the best outcome for everyone."

Stearn let out a calculated snort. "With all due respect, how can you or I decide what the best outcome looks like?"

Loxias took no visible offense at the younger man's skepticism.

"If it strengthens the Order's place within the republic, it strengthens the republic itself. In any case, well done with your study of the Chamber's principal members. What we need now is for you to continue training so you can become our leading influencer."

"What do you mean?"

"Surely, you're aware the sisters who work as counselors aren't just listeners, they're influencers. They can nudge people or strengthen them without their knowledge."

"I was told such things are forbidden outside a clinical setting."

Loxias made a disparaging sound. "Our esteemed sisters can be hypocrites if they believe it necessary, Abbess Gwenneth included. Did you think Jonas Morane convinced the Lyonesse Estates-General to build the Knowledge Vault and sever ties with the empire on his own? Of course not. Sure, he has a certain charisma, but convincing a colony at the hind end of human space that radically changing course was a splendid idea takes more. Granted, I wasn't here at the time, but enough of my Lindisfarne Brethren lived through those events, and they figure Gwenneth helped Morane without the latter's knowledge."

"You're saying I should do as she did and help certain senatorial candidates?"

"Now you're getting it."

— 37 —

Gwenneth, who'd been staring out at the quadrangle, turned around when Stearn gently rapped his knuckles on the doorjamb.

"Landry said you wished to see me."

"I did. Please come in and sit." She gestured at a chair in front of her desk. "You were in Lannion with Loxias this afternoon?"

"Yes, Abbess." Stearn took a seat and looked her straight in the eyes. "We attended the quarterly Chamber of Commerce meeting."

"Was it interesting?"

"Not particularly. A large part of the discussion centered on whether the Chamber would endorse candidates for the senate in the upcoming elections. Since I know nothing about politics in this star system, the debate was rather academic, though I met a few well-known people and can finally put faces to names."

Gwenneth arched an eyebrow. "Such as?"

"Defense Secretary DeCarde for one."

"And what did you think of her?"

"The words self-possessed, open, and honest came to mind."

"A fair assessment. She was an exceptional Chief of the Defense Staff and is a fine leader. Who else?"

Stearn gave her a few names beginning with Gerson Hecht and Severin Downes.

"What did you think of Hecht?" Seeing a potential trap hidden within her question, his mind raced to figure out what a trained friar or a sister on receive only would deduce.

"As self-possessed as DeCarde but rather inscrutable." Stearn hoped Gwenneth didn't notice his moment of hesitation. "I looked for a soul but saw nothing."

"I see. And Downes?"

Stearn hesitated again for a fraction of a second.

"A man disappointed by life."

"Astute observations, all of them. Well done."

Stearn inclined his head. "Thank you."

"That being said, you will not leave the abbey again until you take the oath and either Marta, Katarin, or I implant the prohibitions. This is for your safety, the good of the Order, and the safety of the public." When Stearn made to speak, she raised a hand. "I know. You can't see any reasons why at the moment, but they will become clear as your training progresses. Believe me when I say an unschooled talent as strong as yours can be dangerous, hence the need for prudence until we know you've mastered it and internalized the restrictions on its use."

"Understood, Abbess."

"Good. You may go."

**

"Thank you for taking my call, Katarin." Gwenneth gave her friend a tight smile. "There may be a problem with Stearn."

She recounted her conversation with him and Marta's fears.

"Do you think he peered into minds unbidden?"

"Possibly. Stearn wasn't lying, but I sensed momentary equivocation, as if he were carefully selecting his words lest they betray him."

"Not good. Do you think Loxias put him up to it?"

Gwenneth let out an unclerical snort.

"Almost certainly. Loxias is the sort who'll bend the Rule and arm himself with insider knowledge if it helps reach his goals. But no more. I forbade Stearn from leaving the abbey until further notice."

"It would be better if you forbid him from speaking with Loxias."

"I know. However, Loxias is the head friar, and that makes him responsible for Stearn's employment. When our predecessors amended the Rule and allowed men into the Order, they didn't foresee a friar with a sixth sense so strong it puts most sisters to shame."

"Alas."

"How is your patient?"

"She's doing as well as can be hoped. I should be able to come home by Monday. Will you work with Stearn in the meantime?"

Gwenneth shook her head. "No. I'd rather not interpose myself for a few days when what he really needs is continuity. Besides, you're a better teacher than I am."

"And you're a better leader than I, but I'll take the compliment. Don't worry too much about Stearn. You should remember how keen we were to use our talent as young sisters when it blossomed. He's no different. Keep him in the abbey, and it'll be fine. A week from now, he'll be bound by the same inhibitions against mind-meddling as the rest of us."

**

Stearn didn't quite know what he should think of his brief conversation with Gwenneth. Did she suspect something, and if so, how? Was there more to this sixth sense and the third eye than Marta let on? Were the sisters truly mind readers, and did the abbess sift through his guilty thoughts?

That Gwenneth influenced Lyonesse's leaders as a group into supporting Jonas Morane's plan decades earlier seemed both mildly terrifying and strangely exhilarating. If only he'd possessed that ability during his time in *Antelope*.

He could have kept Captain Barnett and his favorites in check, thereby avoiding the horrors they'd inflicted and endured. He might even have returned home instead of ending up a broken man on a Yotai spaceport landing strip, staring imminent death in the face. Not that permanent exile on Lyonesse as a friar of the Void was an awful fate, although he knew he could never become a committed monastic, never mind a believer. And once his training ended, then what?

He looked up from his mug of tea when he spotted someone coming toward his table in a refectory still mostly deserted since supper was over an hour away. Loxias. He dropped into a chair across from Stearn.

"What did Gwenneth want?"

"She asked me about the Chamber of Commerce meeting and what I thought of the principal participants, like DeCarde and Hecht. Then she forbade me from leaving the abbey until further notice because of my arrested training regimen."

Loxias scratched his beard. "I see. Does she believe you overstepped the bounds Marta set?"

"Probably, though she didn't mention it."

"Any idea how long until your confinement ends?"

"No. Why do you ask? Is there an event I should attend in the next few weeks?"

The older man nodded. "Several, so we can help our favored senatorial candidates shine in front of the electors."

"Then you'll do so without me. I can't disobey the abbess."

"Of course not. Just get through your next phase of training as quickly as possible and remember the sisters with a powerful talent, like Gwenneth and Katarin, don't follow the Rule when it suits their goals."

Loxias rose and walked away without another word, leaving Stearn with an unexpected surge of irritation as he wondered whether the chief administrator saw him only as a means to an end and not as a valued colleague. He drained his mug and left the refectory as well but didn't head for his assigned workstation in the mechanical building where a small fusion reactor generated the abbey's electricity, and a stationary environmental system took care of water purification and sewage.

Instead, Stearn walked in the other direction, toward the farm complex that fed the Brethren and served as the Lyonesse University's on-the-job training facility for students in veterinary medicine, agriculture, and animal husbandry-related disciplines. Between them, Gwenneth and Loxias had annoyed him enough that he wanted another unconstrained chance at opening his third eye on a civilian before Katarin meddled with his mind.

Stearn found just the right candidate walking one of the colony's precious horses around the main paddock, a man in his early twenties with a fresh, open face tanned by the sun. He leaned on a wooden fence railing after giving the student a friendly wave of the hand and watched for a minute or two. The roan mare, visibly gravid, seemed placid as she trotted around in a circle, getting her daily dose of exercise. She was part of another project like the Knowledge Vault — preserving and breeding animals whose distant ancestors left Earth along with human colonists during the first faster-than-light diaspora fifteen hundred years earlier.

He shifted his eyes from the mare to her handler and briefly wondered how sisters directly affected another's thoughts. Then he concentrated on his third eye, willing it to open so he could study the student's inner self. Proving that practice makes perfect, the effort required seemed less than during the Chamber of Commerce meeting. He reached out and brushed against the student's mind, sensing what could only be contentment at exercising the mare under a late afternoon sky. Compared to those Stearn studied earlier in the day, this one appeared more straightforward, without sharp delineations and few strong emotions.

The young man's inner peace increased Stearn's irritation, and he pictured his fingers flicking at it. To his complete and utter astonishment, the happiness vanished, replaced by confusion and even a bit of anger. He immediately withdrew and cut contact.

Halfway around the world, Marta's eyes snapped open for the second time. The feeling of unease she'd experienced earlier was back and stronger than ever. Since the first hint of dawn was coloring the eastern sky, she climbed out of bed and began her morning yoga routine, wondering what Stearn was doing now and whether she should call Gwenneth again.

**

Stearn woke with a start in the middle of the night, bedclothes askew, skin soaked with sweat and heart beating a disjointed tattoo. Fear and loathing oozed through every part of his being while ghastly images haunted him like an out-of-control cinematic production. He'd not experienced a nightmare since boarding *Dawn Hunter* and couldn't remember ever having one of this intensity. Stearn entered a meditative state so he could regain control over mind and body and realized his third eye had opened unbidden. He understood almost at once it was the source of his distress.

The sisters taught him dreams, including nightmares, were the mind's way of processing emotions and consolidating memories. Perhaps those with open third eyes felt dreams more strongly than ordinary people who by and large possessed only a smidgen of the sixth sense that was so developed in the Brethren. But why did his eye open while he slept? Was repeatedly invading another's mind unbidden the cause? Or was there a more sinister reason? His physical reaction to the nightmare was so intense, Stearn could well believe it might have caused cardiac arrest in a weaker man. He reached for the water glass by his bed and found it knocked over, contents spreading on the stone floor.

The dormitory outside his room remained silent, a good indication his struggles were soundless. Although he worried about what the nightmare meant, he couldn't discuss the matter with Gwenneth or Katarin, let alone Marta. They would quickly find out he'd overstepped his bounds and touched other minds without the inhibitions demanded by the Order's Rule. He wasn't that good a dissembler. Not when facing the most talented human lie detectors on the planet.

So far, none tried to violate his privacy — at least not by delving deeply into his mind — and would never know of the grim memories he kept well hidden since mastering the art of self-control. He climbed out of bed, rearranged his bedclothes, then took the water glass, and padded down the hallway to the washroom where he refilled it from the tap.

Once there, he slipped out of his underclothes for a quick rinse in the showers. He returned to his cell stark naked and dripping but met no one along the way. The rest of his night passed without incident. However, he felt bone-weary when the *Prote Ora* bells sounded at first light, calling the Brethren to rise and perform their morning devotions before another day of service to the community and the Almighty.

— 38 —

"Good morning, Stearn." Katarin waved him into Marta's workroom, now temporarily hers, the following Monday.

"Sister." He inclined his head respectfully.

"I understand you went out into the community for the first time last Friday." She pointed at the meditation mat. "Please sit."

"Loxias took me with him to the Lyonesse Chamber of Commerce quarterly meeting."

"And how was it?"

"Interesting. I met several big names." He settled on the mat and adopted the lotus position. Katarin did the same, facing him.

"And analyzed them quite cogently, from what Gwenneth says."

"The abbess is too kind. I'm not a particularly astute observer of human nature."

"You picked up more on reading others since arriving here than you might think. And after learning to focus your talent, you'll notice even more. Marta says your third eye opened briefly before she left for the Windies. Could you please try again, then reach out and touch my mind?"

"Certainly." He closed his physical eyes and concentrated. After Friday and a weekend of solitary training, he found the exercise much easier than during Marta's last session. Katarin opened herself for a few moments, so she could confirm the strength of his touch before closing her mental shields again.

"Impressive. I've never taught a sister who showed such speed and skill within days of her first successful attempt."

"I've been practicing."

"Not on others, I trust."

Stearn shook his head. "No."

Katarin held his eyes for a few heartbeats, but knowing the question would inevitably arise, he'd carefully composed himself so he could hide any signs of guilt. Short of invading his mind and asking again, she would never find out. Stearn was aware of the irony that a fully developed sixth sense not only made someone a human lie detector but also a skilled dissembler, and his training reinforced a character trait he'd nurtured his entire adult life.

"You will swear the oath this morning, then open your mind so I can embed the concomitant inhibitions that'll make sure you won't invade another's consciousness short of pressing medical or mental health needs."

He bowed at the neck. "I am ready."

Katarin led Stearn through the Hippocratic Oath, including the two Order of the Void specific clauses: I will not peer into another human being's mind except in the course of my duties as a healer nor will I use my knowledge of another's mind for any purpose other than healing its owner. She told him to lie on his back, eyes closed, and enter a meditative trance while dropping his mental shields.

Over the next four hours, he could detect her ethereal touch etching new imperatives on his engrams. A wave of strange mental nausea threatened to overcome him several times, and she withdrew almost at once until it passed. The idea someone was changing a part of him, be it ever so tiny, at the very core of what made him Stearn Roget and modifying his behavior rankled each time the nausea struck, but there was no choice. They would not let him leave the abbey again without their safeguards.

A tired voice finally broke through his trance. "You may close your mind."

His eyes opened on a Katarin hunched over with fatigue. She gave him an encouraging smile, though it seemed as if she'd aged twenty years.

"Don't worry — conditioning a mind to keep the oath always drains my energy. And yours, as you'll realize in a few seconds. We are both excused from any further activities today. I suggest we partake in the midday meal and sleep until tomorrow morning."

As Stearn sat up, a deep weariness overcame him. "I see. Does this mean I can leave the abbey?"

"Not yet. You need a few sessions with me to reinforce certain mental habits. How many depends on how fast you progress. When I'm satisfied you won't present a risk to yourself or others, I will tell Gwenneth."

She stood with exaggerated care and held out her hand to steady Stearn as he did the same. His stomach rumbled with hunger, and they grinned at each other.

"I think we're both in need of sustenance," she said.

"And sleep."

"That too."

Yet a few hours later, Stearn woke in a cold sweat again, just like a few nights earlier, driven by the same indistinct but terrifying nightmare. With the dormitory empty on a workday afternoon, no one heard him, nor did anyone see him use the communal showers, and for that, he was grateful.

**

"Brigid DeCarde saw your head friar and his protege at the Chamber of Commerce meeting last week." Morane gave Gwenneth a chilled glass of gin and tonic beaded with moisture and took his accustomed seat next to her in the solarium overlooking Vanquish Bay. He raised his drink. "Cheers."

"Your health."

They took a sip, then Morane said, "Loxias introduced Stearn to the republic's biggest movers and shakers—"

"Brigid included. Stearn told me about it."

"During the meeting, Loxias sat with Gerson Hecht and Severin Downes."

Gwenneth gave him a half shrug. "Hecht Industries owns most of the abbey's supply and service providers. As chief administrator, Loxias has no choice but to make nice with Gerson. It keeps our costs under control. After all, we're a religious, not-for-profit organization desirous of saving every cred we can. We've never depended on charity and never will."

"Commendable, I'm sure. They spent a good chunk of the afternoon debating Chamber of Commerce endorsements in the upcoming senatorial elections. Loxias remained commendably silent, but Hecht and Downes threw their support behind candidates who might support the Order taking a bigger role in government affairs, which would also give Hecht an indirect presence in the corridors of power."

"I won't allow it."

"Short of removing Loxias and giving the chief administrator job to a friar who shares your views, I don't see what you can do. Hecht and Downes must stay at arm's length from every branch of government because of their extensive business dealings with the republic, notably the starship and orbital base construction projects. An ally with no secular ambitions or business interests who enjoys access to the Estates-General, the cabinet, and legislators can be invaluable. It'll happen no matter what we wish. Our republic, though it doesn't suffer from the same flaws as the Ruggero dynasty's empire, remains far from perfect, but we built it on solid foundations."

"The republic will be even less perfect if it takes on so much as a vague theocratic flavor. Make no mistake. The Lindisfarne Brethren's goal is to become an influential part of the Lyonesse government. They won't come out and say so, but I'm convinced of it. Remember, Lindisfarne was neither a republic nor a democracy. The secular colonists had no voice and no representation."

"I can't see that happening here. The Defense Force wouldn't let it."

The abbess took another sip of her drink.

"Not to that extent, no. But if Loxias can see that the head of the Order, or better yet, the chief administrator sits at the cabinet table, then he'll have the next best thing. And it won't upset the voters or the Defense Force. Find enough pro-Loxias senators to elect a president in favor of such an idea, and it'll be done."

Morane gave her a curious glance. "You think?"

"I know. Perhaps it won't happen this time, but the next for sure."

"Maybe." Morane took another sip of his drink. "There's one thing you must know about Stearn."

"Yes?"

"Brigid said he spent a lot of time staring at several attendees, her included — studying them no doubt. Brigid's not sure the others noticed, but she did. You know that eerie sensation someone's watching you?"

"Sure."

"She got it in spades, almost as if Stearn was breathing down her neck. Warn him that he should never do it with Brigid again. She still believes the Void Brethren hide unholy mind-meddlers in their ranks."

"Consider it done."

**

That Friday, after what Katarin said would be his last conditioning session, Stearn wandered out to the farm complex instead of taking a nap. He was looking for one of the university students so he could test the inhibitions planted in his mind because he felt no different than before.

Stearn found a young woman perched on a bale of hay by the barn, sunning herself while eating a sandwich. He leaned on a fence railing, as if admiring the trio of horses roaming around the paddock. After a few minutes of meditation, Stearn opened his third eye and reached out to brush her mind. He found it not unlike that of the other student — bright, contented, brimming with energy and purpose. So far, so good, but the inhibitions were against meddling, not sampling a mind's aura. As before, Stearn imagined himself flicking it with his finger. Almost immediately, the contentment vanished, replaced with confusion.

And he was fine. The inhibitions didn't take, something Katarin failed to notice earlier that day when she checked on her work. His first impulse was finding her and letting her know, but the realization he'd just violated the oath quickly suppressed it. No one told him about the penalties for doing so or what happened with mind-meddlers who couldn't be constrained and therefore posed a danger. He turned away from the paddock and slowly headed for his workstation, wondering why the conditioning failed and what it meant.

That night, he experienced his third hellish phantasm and woke up more distressed than ever. It was as if the suppressed memories of his time in *Antelope* were trying to resurface.

Gwenneth, believing the conditioning had taken hold, lifted his confinement to the abbey the next day.

— 39 —

"He doesn't seem particularly impressive," Stearn murmured after watching the senatorial candidate for Carhaix South deliver his stump speech.

"But he is in favor of the Order taking a larger role," Loxias replied in the same tone. "How does the audience feel?"

Stearn opened his mind and let it parse through the mass of feelings it picked up.

"Nothing negative that I can sense, but not much enthusiasm either."

They were in the Carhaix City Gallery, a high-ceilinged, expansive structure used for public gatherings of every kind. Thousands of voters variously sat on folding chairs or stood along the walls, listening to the man whose aim was unseating the incumbent after only one term. Unfortunately, his charm and affability worked best in one-on-one interactions, not with a crowd.

Stearn reached out and brushed the politician's mind. Violating the oath was routine by now, something he could do with an ever decreasing expenditure of energy, though if Loxias' stories about

Gwenneth were true, he wondered how effective conditioning really was. Nothing struck him as notable about the man's inner self. He was simply not that charismatic.

But if Gwenneth secretly helped Morane sell his bizarre Knowledge Vault proposal back in the day, surely Stearn could give the challenger a little boost. Following Loxias into the halls of power after the election was now an overarching goal as he faced the decision on what he would do once his training ended.

Counseling and teaching were out, as was spending decades tending the abbey's environmental systems until he could succeed Loxias as chief administrator or become the first abbot. Nothing else interested him in the least, and he often regretted taking vows that bound him to the Void for good. Why not use his abilities to advance the Order's interests if it meant he could find a better purpose?

Stearn visualized himself pouring energy into the candidate's mind, along with a greater sense of joy and self-confidence. Almost immediately, what was up to now a dull, meat and potatoes speech turned into a barn burner which energized the audience, even after Stearn stopped so he wouldn't pass out from fatigue.

Later, in the car, Loxias gave him a suspicious stare. "Did you do something in there?"

"You know how Gwenneth supposedly helped Morane sell his scheme to the Estates-General?"

"Sure."

"I just did something similar and didn't even cross the line into forbidden mind-meddling."

Loxias inclined his head in a gesture of respect. "Impressive. How?"

"I shared my energy with him. It can't really be explained if you've never touched another's inner self."

The chief administrator let out a pleased chortle.

"You will be abbot one day, my friend. Someone so powerful will rise to the top of the Order and break the sisters' stranglehold. Then we will remake it and assert our place on Lyonesse."

"We need not wait until I become abbot. If I can give a boring politician sudden charisma, think how I might influence the next president if enough of those who support the Order sit in the senate."

"You're taking quite an interest in the Lindisfarne Brethren's ultimate goals, aren't you?"

"If truth be told, I find the sisters increasingly irritating. Their horizons are annoyingly limited even though there's an entire universe beyond Lyonesse, albeit one that's still depopulating because of horrors like the Barbarian Plague." They drove on in silence for a few moments, then Stearn said, "What I did is something any sister with advanced training can do. Send the ones belonging to the Lindisfarne Brethren out there, supporting our preferred candidates, and use them as multipliers."

"I might just do that, even if it means pushing against the spirit of the Rule."

**

"How is Seled doing?" Gwenneth asked the moment Marta's face appeared on her office display.

"She's learning at an impressive rate. Whatever else Seled once was, she's highly intelligent."

"People with personality disorders often are."

"True. I just ran the last tests, and Seled can shield her mind in both directions. We can begin advanced training, which will confirm my suspicions her third eye is stronger than average. But I need your permission."

The two women held each other's gaze while Gwenneth wavered. Seled was the first woman to undergo treatment. The first three men who came through the program had so far shown no behavioral changes. But in Marta's estimation, their sixth sense was, at best, no more potent than that of an average human and therefore not worth developing any further.

They didn't know what opening a strong third eye in a mind that once harbored chaotic evil might entail. Yet if Marta stopped now, they never would. The Order had made considerable advances in its understanding of the human mind over the last few years by taking the sort of risks that would make a *Summus Abbatissa* on Lindisfarne blanch. As a result, the younger sisters trained on Lyonesse were more potent and more capable healers than their predecessors.

"There should be plenty of engrams available for an expanded conditioning process, inhibitions that will kick in if her sociopathic tendencies return," Marta said. "I'll do it before attempting to open the inner eye."

Gwenneth gave her a nod. "Go ahead."

"Thank you. How's Stearn?"

The abbess grimaced. "He's spending entirely too much time with Loxias out in the community now that Katarin took him as far as he should go."

"I gather he's still not interested in becoming a healer or counselor. A shame, but we can't force him. And since a mind like Stearn's won't find satisfaction in a regular friar's work, it's just as well he explores other outlets now that Katarin conditioned him. Whatever we think of Loxias, he is a smart, capable chief administrator who ensures the abbey's physical needs are met."

"Perhaps. But Jonas Morane tells me he's also becoming adept at backroom politics and cultivating several senatorial candidates in favor of giving the Order a larger say in the republic's affairs."

Marta shrugged. "The Order needs a well-connected chief administrator so it can work at peak efficiency. Besides, maybe he's right, and we should look beyond our walls from time to time."

A teasing smile lit up Gwenneth's features. "You're spending too many hours under the tropical sun, my friend. It's affecting your perception of reality."

"Doubtful, but the Windy Isles themselves might give me a fresh perspective on the world, the Order, and our place in the republic. Remember, I was once partnered with a star system governor general. My view of the universe is less parochial."

"May I infer you've gone native along with Mirjam and her flock?"

"Most of our recent advances in mental health originated here. I could do worse than go native. You don't need me at the abbey these days anyhow since we're not taking in as many postulants."

"Very well. Stay as long as you wish or until Mirjam tires of your presence, whichever comes first, unless I need you here."

Marta joined her hands beneath her chin and bowed her head. "Thank you."

**

"And that, Mister President, is the plan. We should adopt it now. If we wait until a reiver wolf pack filled with infected barbarians passes our inner moon, it'll be too late. Thank you for your attention." DeCarde stepped away from the rostrum and took her seat at the cabinet table again.

The secretaries shifted their attention to Jonas Morane, waiting for his reaction at hearing the proposal he use his emergency powers and declare martial law so he could impose harsh quarantine measures should a plague ship make it past the Navy.

Vice President Sandino was the first to speak.

"The optics of preparing for such extreme measures strike me as particularly bad, Mister President. Brigid is suggesting you suspend civil liberties and essentially turn the republic into a dictatorship. You know how bloody-minded the citizens of Lyonesse are about their freedoms."

A grimace briefly twisted Morane's lips.

"Faced with an existential threat, it's not just a necessity but an imperative. And existential threats are why I made sure the president's emergency powers were written into our constitution. We can't avoid it. The Defense Force and first responders need the unfettered ability to act rapidly and with decisiveness. Most of our fellow citizens will understand, even though they won't like it. Martial law is for the stubborn or simpleminded minority who won't let a deadly virus interfere with their lives, never mind the lives they're risking are those of others. I'm sure the intelligence digests you receive from Brigid's office discussed folks — mercifully not many — who think the Barbarian Plague is a fabrication by sinister elements in our administration intent on overthrowing the constitution."

"That's precisely who I was thinking of when I asked about the optics."

"You can't worry about conspiracy theorists, Charis. Sure, they'll raise Cain, but most of the people won't listen. I dare say a great majority will be reassured the government is taking their safety so seriously it's prepared to impose the harshest measures."

"I suppose you're right," she said with a slight shrug. "It's just that most of us here didn't serve in the military or police and never thought about law enforcement in worst-case scenarios. Suspending civil liberties is alien to us."

"Madame Vice President." DeCarde briefly raised her hand. "I lived through the breakdown of civil order on Coraline during the rebellion against Dendera's governor general there. A frightened or angry mob with power weapons can quickly overwhelm even the best-trained troops, and every household on Lyonesse has at least one hunting gun. Letting people know ahead of time will make a difference. The last thing we want is potentially infected folks spreading the plague because of insufficient controls or out of sheer ignorance. The president must invoke his emergency powers the moment reiver ships appear in this system so the military and the police can deal with matters unhindered. Once the danger passes, the declaration expires, and our civil liberties come back into force. At least until the next existential threat arises. Besides, the president can only suspend them for thirty days. After that, it takes a two-thirds majority vote in the senate to keep emergency conditions in place."

"Folks." Morane leaned forward and placed his hands on the tabletop. "This is one issue I won't discuss at length because there is no other way. That alone should convince you how serious I am. The Defense Department will issue a directive aimed at the civilian population, the military, and the police informing everyone what will happen the moment I declare an emergency. Once that's done, the uniformed branches will prepare contingency plans and carry out practice runs. To deal with an identified and immediate threat, the police will come under military control, and the chief constable will take his orders from General Barca."

He looked pointedly at the Public Safety Secretary, who signified his understanding with a silent nod.

"After this meeting, the Attorney General will draw up the requisite executive order invoking emergency measures, ready for my signature in case of need."

"It'll be on your desk by the end of the day, sir."

"Thank you." Morane stood to pre-empt any further interventions and left the cabinet room.

— 40 —

Stearn gave yet another senatorial candidate favoring greater political participation by the Order a burst of energy to strengthen her charisma as she addressed a thick crowd in downtown Trevena's main square under a tropical sun. While doing so, he idly wondered why many of the people backed by Hecht and his cronies seemed weak. Not physically, to be sure, but none so far struck him as displaying remarkable strength of character, the sort he'd sensed in someone like Brigid DeCarde. Was it because they could be more easily manipulated or influenced?

He gave Loxias a sideways glance, wondering whether Hecht was using the Order's chief administrator to advance his own goals. Did the industrialist know or suspect something about the talent, or was he secretly one of those who believed in rumors that the Brethren harbored mind-meddlers in their midst? Or did he think the Order silently supporting specific candidates by showing up at rallies, speeches, and events sufficed? Under Gwenneth's long rule as abbess, the Void Sisters came to be held in high respect if not awe for their selfless work as healers and counselors of exceptional skill as well as chaplains in the Defense Force.

When the crowd finally perked up as the candidate's speech took on a fierier edge, Loxias muttered 'well done' under his breath. Stearn withdrew his touch, feeling drained as usual. The fact he was doing the work while Loxias expected the glory became more irksome every time the chief administrator took him to political events or meetings with Hecht's cabal.

Like all Brethren, Loxias could shield his mind so nothing escaped and disturbed the abbey's peace, but he possessed only an ordinary friar's talent, which meant a smidgen more than the general population. Was it possible for Stearn to influence Loxias and take his place at the head of the Lindisfarne faction? Become the man who would enter the corridors of power instead of being a mere tool?

Yes, Loxias saw Roget as the first abbot, although it would probably not happen when Gwenneth finally retired but was a strong possibility once her successor did so. That would make him the Order's *Summus Abbas*, capable of charting their future within the republic, but how many years would he wait while doing Loxias' bidding?

Stearn believed he was more powerful than any sister by now, with a few exceptions such as Marta, and certainly outstripped every friar. Why shouldn't he spearhead the Lindisfarne Brethren's campaign and use Loxias as a figurehead?

He reopened his mind and sent tired tendrils to touch Loxias, looking for a reaction, something that proved the older man could sense him.

Nothing. Loxias' eyes remained on the candidate, now wrapping up her speech.

Stearn pushed against Loxias' shielding. He found it flimsy and unable to prevent unauthorized entry. Of course. The sisters would make sure the friars couldn't keep them out. So much for their pieties and oaths. Still no reaction from Loxias. He was unaware of mental tendrils working their way into his mind, tasting his aura.

Stearn felt a forceful character, which he expected, and something he thought might represent overweening ambition, also not a surprise, but no trace of the serenity common among the Brethren, especially the sisters. Loxias struck him as a driven man, looking for something to fill a hole in his soul and not knowing what.

But how to influence him so that Stearn might covertly become, if not quite the most powerful man in the republic, then the one sitting behind the presidential chair, whispering into the incumbent's ear, a sort of gray eminence. He projected joy at Loxias, aiming it toward the notional hole in his soul, and watched him out of the corner of his eyes. Almost immediately, the chief administrator's face lit up, and a goofy smile split his beard, proving friars, even the most senior among them, were just as vulnerable as the laypeople on whom Stearn tested his abilities. So far, so good. Then an idea struck him.

He projected an image of himself and a sense of love at Loxias. Moments later, the chief administrator looked at him and said, "I'm not sure if I ever told you this, but you're like a son to me, Stearn."

That night, the terror dreams returned, leaving Roget a sweat-drenched wreck.

**

"You look exhausted."

Amelia gracefully lowered herself onto the wooden bench beside Marta, who liked to gaze out at the peaceful lagoon before the hustle and bustle of the communal evening meal. The younger sister often joined her in silent contemplation or quiet conversation beneath the tall umbrella-like native tree.

"Probably because I am exhausted."

"Seled?"

Marta nodded. "We finally made a breakthrough this afternoon. The weeks I spent conditioning her weren't wasted."

"Excellent news. Congratulations. You truly are the Order's most skilled trainer."

A tired shrug.

"I merely use the Almighty's gift as intended."

"What now?"

"Now? I wait for dawn in Lannion and inform Gwenneth." Marta turned her head toward Amelia and smiled. "I know. That's not what you meant. I'm of two minds about Seled's future. What I glimpsed of her talent makes me believe it sits firmly in the mid-range for Sisters of the Void, which is to be expected since the treatment removed so much of her personality. Yes, you don't fully agree with me that what makes us capable of opening our third eye is informed by everything we are and experience. Still, Seled is changing and will continue to change our views on many subjects, including those beyond the purview of conventional psychology."

"Agreed. And what are your two minds about her future?"

"Do I leave well enough alone at this point? Seled is a functioning member of this community and will probably stay so for the rest of her life. She's highly intelligent and can be trained as a healer's assistant, serving both inmates and exiles. Or, I work with her a bit longer and see if she has the strength to become a counselor capable of helping the more deeply disturbed prisoners."

"Why the indecision? Don't I recall someone who looks remarkably like you tell me talents should be developed to the utmost?"

"And so they should. Except Seled can never become a normal Sister of the Void. Though she's no longer in thrall to her disorder, her past deeds are indelible. Even the Almighty cannot erase them."

"But the Almighty forgives."

"That isn't the same thing, my dear. Our actions leave spiritual traces, no matter how deeply the mind is cleansed of them."

"True." A pause. "Perhaps you should consider working with her just a bit longer so you can test the strength of her talent. It might help in deciding."

"An excellent suggestion. I shall do so."

As they watched Lyonesse's sun kiss the horizon, Marta said, "I've never seen the green flash you islanders think is one of this world's great wonders. Does it even exist, or are you putting me on?"

"It exists, and I've witnessed it, but the atmospheric conditions must be just so, and that happens only a few times a year."

"How about now?" Marta gestured at the horizon with a deeply tanned hand.

"No idea." Amelia gave her former teacher a wry smile. "As you might recall, even in your state of extreme fatigue, I'm trained as a psychiatrist, not a meteorologist."

A few minutes passed while the sun transformed the lagoon's rippling surface into liquid metal reflecting the heat of a thousand furnaces. The last moments of a tropical sunset passed with the rapidity Marta expected. But for a fraction of a second, a green glow seemed to overlay that final burst of light, and she gasped at the transcendent beauty.

"The atmospheric conditions were ideal."

"I know."

**

Seled, clad in a sister's tropical lightweight one-piece garment, stopped on the threshold of Marta's training room, and bowed at the waist.

"Sister."

Marta, already sitting in the lotus position on the mat, returned her formal greeting with an equally grave nod.

"Please enter and sit."

The former convict obeyed and settled on the mat facing her teacher. Their eyes met without hesitation or embarrassment.

"I am ready."

"As before, enter the meditative trance and allow me into your mind. Once you achieve balance, try to open your third eye again."

"Yes, Sister." Seled closed her eyes and slowed her breathing rhythm until it matched Marta's.

The latter reached out with her mental fingers and felt Seled's shields dissolve, revealing once more a curiously empty mind with the gaping hole where her chaotic disorder once lived. She truly felt unfinished, as if the Almighty stopped her development in early adulthood, or perhaps even before. But Seled's aura was suffused with the same calm as that of any other sister, the same serenity, and inner peace. Though Marta knew nothing about the old Seled, other than what was recorded in her file, she'd sat in on Amelia's regular sessions with Supermax inmates and experienced firsthand the sickness that ate at their minds and rotted their souls.

The lid covering Seled's third eye trembled — or at least that was how Marta visualized something no one could adequately describe. The previous day, her eye opened just enough to prove it could do so, but without allowing Marta more than a momentary glimpse of what lay behind.

With a suddenness that left Marta dumbfounded, the eye opened wide and unleashed a wave of horror that left her feeling as if she were suffocating. Her heart rate shot up as her mind slammed shut.

She broke out of the meditative trance and saw Seled slump to the floor, unconscious. Marta reached out and touched her neck, looking for a pulse because she could not bear the idea of checking on the former inmate with her extrasensory abilities. Seled was merely unconscious, struck by whatever came through her third eye. Marta fished a communicator from her garment's upper pocket. She tapped it.

"Infirmary."

**

Mirjam sat back in her chair, looking stunned after Marta described the incident. "Heavens above. How is that even possible? I've never heard of the like before today."

"We always knew our understanding of the third eye was nowhere near complete. At this point, I'd call it only rudimentary."

Marta sounded hoarse, her tone distracted, and her eyes never resting on a single spot for more than a second or two.

"My apologies. I'm still shaken. I can only think what I saw was as close to the perfect manifestation of evil as I can conceive. If it were anyone other than me with Seled, you'd have two sisters in a coma rather than just one. We cannot go any further with Seled — if she ever wakes. Whatever is bottled inside her where no one can reach must stay there forever."

"No arguments here. A shame, though. If there's a whole other dimension to the personality that can only come out through a third eye, Seled would be the ideal research subject, seeing as how so much of her overt characteristics were erased during treatment. It puts a new wrinkle on your theory about the origins of certain personality disorders. Perhaps what you saw was her actual soul. They say the evil we do accumulates within us and eventually rots a soul from the inside out until nothing more than a horrific presence remains."

Marta replied with a tired shrug.

"There are things we're not meant to see and places we're not meant to go. Science cannot answer every question and never will, especially when it comes to the human condition. The countless horrific genocides that resulted whenever misguided ideologues tried to improve or control that which they never understood provides irrefutable proof."

"It's about who exercises power over whom." When Marta seemed about to object, Mirjam held up her hand in a restraining gesture. "Yes, that's a simple way of summarizing a complex problem, but my words carry more than a hint of truth. Admit it."

"I wonder whether the hidden part of Seled, what you think of as her soul, would be capable of projecting such malevolence if we had trained her at a young age like most postulants?"

"Provided your theory is correct, taking her in when she was sixteen or seventeen would likely have ensured her salvation because she wouldn't have been tormented by her suppressed talent."

Another shrug. "I suppose. It makes me wonder about others we trained later in life."

"Like Stearn? If something equally horrific is hiding behind his third eye, you'd know. Mind you, he's what? Twenty years younger than Seled? His soul can't be corrupted by as much evil as hers was, so he should be okay."

A tired smile briefly crossed Marta's face. "The theologians among us would have a field day if they found out."

"If?"

"This remains between you, me, and Gwenneth. No one else will know, especially not Seled herself when she wakes. Imagine the chaos and confusion it would create among the Brethren should we even so much as hint that I saw another's soul through her third eye. Many of the sisters would look, and it's my belief we're not meant to do so. That, in fact, it would be harmful. And you will not train any more former inmates who show a hint of talent beyond teaching them to shield their minds. What happened today can never be repeated."

Mirjam nodded formally, signifying she understood Marta's words as a direct command. No one would dare gainsay the Order's most gifted teacher on such matters, not even Gwenneth. Especially now that she seemed a mere shadow of her usual self.

"Understood. And Seled?"

"Her path will be as a simple healer's assistant. We'll tell her she lost consciousness because opening the third eye took more than she could give and leave it at that." Marta slowly climbed to her feet. "I must sleep, and once the sun rises over Lannion, I will speak with Gwenneth. Would you be a dear and book me a seat on the next available Clipper?"

—41—

Gwenneth studied Marta's image for a few heartbeats once she finished her report. The latter looked as if she aged by several decades since their last video call.

"This development is worrisome."

"Only if we let it worry us. The treatment program can continue, but we cannot teach those who come through anything more than simple shielding, such as we teach friars, even if they show a strong sixth sense. And any active third eye is definitely out of bounds. Knowledge of what happened to Seled must be suppressed. So far, it's restricted to you, Mirjam, and me. I've already told Mirjam she must take the secret to the grave. You and I will do the same."

"A shame, though. But you're right. This is not meant for us. Are you coming home?"

"On tomorrow's Clipper. It's best if Seled doesn't see me again, should she ever come out of the coma. We can't tell when or even if that'll happen. Cautious scans by Amelia show her mind is in a catatonic state. She's simply not there. Perhaps the remnants of her personality were sucked in by the third eye as I slammed my mind shut against its emanations."

"I see." Gwenneth sighed. "Why do I think we've been playing sorceresses' apprentice with the human psyche over the last few years?"

"Because we have, and we must stop. Otherwise, we might unleash a force capable of wreaking havoc on the Order and on Lyonesse."

"Did you see something?"

Marta bit her lower lip as she nodded.

"In the hours after my session with Seled, I saw a potential future where we face our own Ragnarok — the end of everything you and Jonas Morane created. I didn't see what could trigger it, but I don't doubt it somehow involves our mind-meddling. We are messing with things beyond our understanding. I see that now. Our arrogance has been blinding us." A grim look hardened Marta's face. "On second thought, perhaps we should not continue the experimental treatment program, period, and use conventional methods before we inadvertently create an uncontrollable monster. So far, no one beyond a few of us knows about its existence. If word gets out because of an incident, we will face a crisis beyond imagining."

Gwenneth's ascetic features took on an air of indecision.

"The program is successful beyond our hopes, and I know we can release more of those with behavior disorders from their torment."

"On the surface, yes. But as Seled proved, we cannot heal a twisted soul. Only death will offer release from torment. If that." Marta sighed. "But perhaps I'm reading too much into my visions. Still, give my suggestion some thought. It may be prudent if we suspend the experimental program for a few years and watch those who've undergone the cure."

"I'll discuss the matter with Mirjam."

Marta inclined her head, accepting Gwenneth's answer — for now. "Is anything waiting for me upon my return?"

"I'd like you to resume working with Stearn."

A frown. "Didn't Katarin declare him for all intents and purposes done?"

"In terms of training, yes, seeing as how he's shown no interest in becoming a healer or counselor, and he has neither the faith nor the temperament to become a chaplain. But he's been spending entirely too much time with Loxias, out in the community, monitoring the senate elections and interacting with the leading business tycoons. Please resume your daily meditation sessions with him and check his behavior. I fear Loxias is using Stearn's abilities for his own purposes."

"Really?" Marta gave her superior a skeptical glance. "If you think Loxias is going against the Rule, call him on it."

"I can't because I saw no evidence, although I've heard whispers that Stearn's been experiencing frequent nightmares in recent weeks. He was seen showering in the middle of the night on several occasions. The only reason I can think of why he'd do so is because he's waking up in a cold sweat. Bad dreams. A guilty conscience. Perhaps he's been pushing against his conditioning, and we know that can leave the mind prey to every manner of self-punishment."

"He wouldn't."

"You and I have done so when required. Although we were taught how to bleed off the after-effects in a controlled manner. Stearn has both the smarts and the life experience to search for his limits and test them." Gwenneth exhaled noisily, a sure sign of exasperation. Something in Marta's expression gave her pause. "What is it?"

"The glimmer of an idea. What came through Seled's third eye was the stuff of nightmares. It could be Stearn's soul has its own problems, and they manifest as dreadful dreams leaking through an imperfectly closed third eye, one that wasted more energy during the day than it should."

"*Now* you're scaring me."

"Good. Stearn could easily become stronger than either of us. And if he's been breaking his oath while fighting the conditioning..." Marta let her words hang between them.

"I should never have indulged Mirjam and sent you to the Windies."

"Wallowing in regrets is pointless. We learned something important, perhaps even vital, about the essence of being human. Besides, I'll correct Stearn's trajectory, don't fear. There's plenty of good in him."

"And even more we don't know. He never gave us a full accounting of his time in *Antelope,* and I'm still not convinced he told us the true story of the Void Beacon he supposedly found on a world far from the abbey that manufactured it."

"By the time his mind cleared enough for a truth read, he'd developed shields I couldn't push through without leaving obvious tracks, which just proves my point about the speed at which his mind has been developing."

Gwenneth waved her hand in a dismissive gesture.

"As you said, regrets are pointless. Come home, reassert your role as Stearn's teacher and guide him away from the secular ambitions peddled by the likes of Loxias and his followers."

**

The electoral ads playing on every available display inside the Lannion Spaceport terminal's central hall struck Marta as more strident and darker than ever before in the republic's brief history. What little she glimpsed as she made her way through the cavernous, almost empty space advocated a wholesale replacement of the current senate and administration.

When Marta stepped out into the early morning sunshine, she suppressed a groan of dismay. She intellectually understood that what was early evening in the Windy Isles when the Phoenix Clipper *City of Carhaix* lifted off became dawn upon landing in Lannion. But being confronted by the fact she faced at least twelve hours until bedtime and not three made her heart sink. That brief, suborbital flight gave back the hours stolen from her weeks earlier, but the notion didn't make an interminable day any more appealing. Not when she still suffered the after-effects of Seled's collapse.

She found the abbey's ground car waiting by the curb, along with other vehicles destined for her fellow passengers. One of its doors opened, and Landry's smiling, bearded face appeared.

"Welcome home, Sister. How was your flight?"

Marta climbed in beside him and placed her bag at her feet. "The Clippers are amazing."

"Perhaps one of these days, I should volunteer for an assignment in the Windies or aboard a starship and experience them for myself." Under his deft control, the car pulled away smoothly and headed for the avenue leading into downtown Lannion at a comfortable speed, its anti-grav cushion absorbing imperfections in the roadway. Marta felt as if she sat in a comfortable reading chair.

"I didn't follow the elections but caught the advertising in the terminal. Is it just me, or is this campaign rather less civil than previous ones?"

Landry chuckled.

"You don't know the half of it. A lot of the races, especially in Lannion districts, are turning particularly nasty these days. I can't figure what's motivating it, but I'll happily stay far away from politics, unlike many Brethren. Could be we need an amendment to the Rule forbidding political discussions, let alone attending rallies like Loxias and his cronies. But considering how many among us want the Order to wield more secular influence, I doubt the abbess would get a two-thirds majority to support such an amendment."

This early in the day, traffic was light, and they quickly left Lannion behind, though not before Marta spied more political advertising on large animated displays. Some even referenced the administration's handling of the Barbarian Plague risk, promising their candidate would do better than the incumbent. She felt a sense of relief after the events of the last two days when they left the main road and entered the abbey's expansive land grant. Soon, she spied its buildings above green fields and trees in full flower. Home.

"Gwenneth asked that you come to her office upon arrival," Landry said, breaking through her reverie. "I'll take your valise to your room."

"Of course. Thank you."

Landry stopped the car in front of the administration building, and the passenger door opened soundlessly.

"Enjoy a blessed day, Sister."

"You as well."

Marta found Gwenneth staring out of a side window overlooking the fields. The abbess turned when she sensed her presence by the open door.

"Please come in and sit." She settled in behind her desk with a tired sigh. "Seled came out of her coma minutes after your Clipper took off."

"And?"

"It took four friars to restrain her. Mirjam says her mind resembled that of a wild animal driven by rage. It's as if her personality disorder was back, but without the restraint she could exercise before undergoing treatment."

Marta cocked a questioning eyebrow. "You just used the past tense. What else happened?"

"Seled died of cardiac arrest shortly afterward, thankfully before Mirjam called the warden and ask he take her back for everyone's safety. They'll carry out an autopsy when it's morning in the Windies, but Mirjam figures the heart attack was stress-induced."

Grief twisted Marta's features.

"The Void giveth, the Void taketh away."

"Blessed be the Void."

"At least the Almighty's mercy will now grant her the peace she never had." After a moment of silence, Marta said, "This means that the treatment likely doesn't address the true behavioral drivers. It merely removes the overt part. The sickness afflicting those unfortunates is much deeper and is probably impervious to any cure."

Gwenneth nodded tiredly. "A sickness of the soul. Yes. I ordered the experimental treatment stopped indefinitely. The other five who underwent it will be closely monitored for any signs of their disorder returning."

"I don't think that'll happen. If they cannot open the third eye, whatever lies behind it will stay walled off, and I checked — none of them has anything more than an above-average sixth sense." Marta shook her head. "Sorceresses' apprentices, indeed. I suppose it's a good thing this happened behind the priory's walls and not out in public where her condition would raise questions we cannot answer without imperiling the Order. What will Mirjam tell the warden about Seled's death and the termination of the treatment program?"

"As little as possible. No doubt, there will be lingering suspicions."

"Unavoidable, I suppose." Marta suppressed a yawn. "My body thinks it's bedtime."

"Head for the refectory and eat breakfast as step one in resetting your inner clock, followed by meditation."

"A wise suggestion." She climbed to her feet. "I would take a few days of rest before shouldering fresh duties."

"I only need you to deal with Stearn."

"I will do so." She bowed her head at Gwenneth and left the abbess to her thoughts.

When Marta entered the refectory, she noticed a cluster of Lindisfarne Brethren — friars and sisters — lingering after the morning meal, Stearn sat among them, looking as if he were holding court and not Loxias, the group's putative leader. Stearn briefly looked up at her, and their eyes met. Marta's heart sank when he gave her only a cold, dispassionate stare instead of the amused reverence he used to show for what he mischievously called his surrogate mother.

— 42 —

The next morning, Stearn stopped on the threshold to Marta's training room and bowed his head.

"I'm here as directed, Sister, though I can't understand why. Katarin taught me what I needed after you left for the Windy Isles. Since I will not become a healer, counselor, or chaplain, I don't need further instruction and should concentrate on my duties."

Marta, already sitting on her mat in the lotus position, gave him a hard look. "Duties that include taking part in secular politics?"

"Loxias is training me to become chief administrator one day. That involves accompanying him wherever he goes outside the abbey's walls."

"Please come in." She pointed at the mat in front of her. "We will meditate together every morning. That way, I can check your personal progress."

Stearn didn't budge. "Why?"

"Because the student I was teaching in the Windies died yesterday, shortly after my departure. She was, like you, a wild talent who entered the Order later in life than usual, and I want to watch you for signs of the same condition that struck her down."

His eyes narrowed with suspicion. "May I ask the student's name?"

"Seled."

The suspicion turned to incredulity. "That crazy old woman with delusions of attractiveness? They took her on as a sister?"

"She underwent treatment that erased her antisocial personality disorder, and once it was gone, we discovered she had the talent. Unfortunately, when she finally opened her third eye, things went terribly wrong."

"And you're afraid you'll lose another student. Sister, I've been opening and closing my third eye at will since you left, and as you can see, I'm alive and well. Please don't confuse me with a sociopath."

"It is how you open and close it that interests me." She pointed at the mat again. "Please, Stearn. Indulge me in this. The bond between teacher and student is one of the few things that can only be severed by death. And since we don't know what happens after we die, perhaps it continues across the Void for eternity."

"You know I'm not into religious mumbo jumbo." Stearn exhaled with just a tinge of exasperation. "Very well. For you, anything."

As he adopted the lotus position facing her, Marta said, "I've recently experienced something that makes me think at least part of what you call mumbo jumbo is real."

"Oh?" A skeptical eyebrow crept up Stearn's forehead. "I'm listening."

"Do you believe we have a soul, immortal or not?"

"I've never given it much consideration." He cocked his head to one side. "To be honest, I've never given it *any* consideration."

"Please don't speak of this with anyone else, but when Seled opened her third eye, I think I caught a brief glimpse of what I think was her soul."

"And then she died. Maybe we're not meant to see certain things."

"Funny you should say that. However, the real question is, what precisely are we not meant to see or do?" Marta closed her eyes. "Please enter a meditative trance."

Stearn followed suit and loosened the tight bonds that kept his thoughts in check. As expected, he soon felt the tendrils of her mind brush against his.

"Let me in." Her voice seemed to come from afar.

"With all due respect, I will keep my privacy intact." He hardened his mental shielding.

"You no longer trust your teacher?"

"Tell me why you want in."

"You've been experiencing horrible nightmares in recent times."

A moment of hesitation. "Yes."

"They always happened after you opened your third eye and pushed against the conditioning."

More hesitation. "Yes. How do you know?"

"Do you believe you're the only one who's ever tested his boundaries?"

"No."

"We all do because that's human nature. One of the most common reactions is disturbing nightmares, as if the soul was revolting while we're at our most vulnerable." When Stearn didn't reply, Marta said, "You won't let me in, will you?"

"No. I neither want nor need supervision by you or anyone else at this point. I simply wish to make my way in life by becoming one of the Order's administrators and follow in Loxias' footsteps.

We can meditate together, but that is the only thing you or Gwenneth can ask of me. The Rule does not mandate I allow anyone into my mind. And should you insist, I will invoke the oath."

"None of my other students have ever used such harsh words."

"I am my own man, *Sister*. My mind does not need supervision by you or anyone else." Stearn opened his eyes. "And I am no longer in a meditative state of mind, so if you'll excuse me, we can take this up again tomorrow morning. My duties await."

He uncoiled his legs and stood, bowed at the waist, then left her staring at his back as he walked away.

Loxias caught up with him on the way to the power generation plant. "How was your first session with Marta since her return?"

"Marta, like the rest of the older sisters, figures she understands the human psyche. She doesn't. None of them do. They play with it instead of facing the truth."

"I'm pleased you finally recognize that fact, my friend. Fortunately, the future is ours, not theirs."

**

"Brigid! Thanks for showing up a little early." Morane waved her into his office, pointing at one of the chairs in front of his desk, then gave his executive assistant a nod. He stepped back into the corridor and closed the door behind him.

"Always a pleasure, Mister President. I gather you read last night's intelligence report."

Morane nodded at his reader, lying on the desk. "Indeed. Did you check the latest opinion polls this morning?"

"Yes, and they dovetail nicely with the trends noted in the report. Something is happening out there that'll upend the political landscape come election day. A lot of first-term senators won't be getting a second one."

"And your operatives saw Order of the Void Brethren at most political events to support the challengers." Morane's tone made his words a statement.

DeCarde nodded.

"Loxias and Stearn are the most prominent, but they're far from the only ones. I know you don't share my views, but I smell mind-meddling of some sort. More first time candidates are ahead of incumbents than normal, and where the incumbent faces term limits, the leading replacements are cut from the same cloth as the challengers."

"This is only the fourth senate election in the republic's history. We can't really look back and decide what's normal and what isn't."

"My analysts checked the Colonial Council election history. Lyonesse generally gives its politicians a second term if they don't trip over themselves during the first, but this time around, plenty of solid senators seem headed for defeat. Charis Sandino's chances of succeeding you are getting slimmer. The newcomers will nominate their own candidates for the presidency and vice presidency."

"Any idea who they might put forward?"

She shook her head.

"Not yet, but as the preference cascade speeds up, we should find out, although my best analysts are betting on Viktor Arko. He's been a close friend of the Hechts since before we arrived and is well regarded by most people. I'm sure he'd accept the nomination."

Morane grimaced at hearing the name of the man who was Health Secretary in Elenia Yakin's cabinet, and before independence, ran the colony's medical system. Arko made no bones about his dislike of Morane and fought him on many issues related to health services for the Defense Force. When Morane offered to keep him on as a cabinet member after succeeding Yakin, at least on an interim basis, Arko refused point-blank, returning to private life, and busying himself with philanthropic pursuits.

"Viktor certainly likes the Order. The sisters and friars made his life as Health Secretary a walk in the park — inexpensive, devoted, and supremely capable doctors, nurses, psychologists, and orderlies. What's not to like? I wouldn't be surprised if your people were onto something."

"Could be. Arko doesn't worry me much. He's competent and smart, even if he's not one of your fans or a fan of senior military people in general. He spent enough time traveling around the empire as a young naval surgeon to have seen the worst of the old Imperial Armed Services. I'm mostly concerned about the undisputed fact someone is backing newcomers — other than the Chamber of Commerce grandees, I mean — but they're careful, and they're using Loxias' Lindisfarne Brethren. Whether it's via mind-meddling," DeCarde held up a restraining hand, "I know, you don't believe they do that, or simply by hinting that the organization basically running the republic's health care system is tacitly endorsing certain candidates."

"The Void Brethren are full citizens of the republic. They can take part in any lawful activity, including politics."

DeCarde made a face at him. "Easy for you to say, once the next session of the Lyonesse Senate votes in a new president, you no longer need to worry about mind-meddlers working their way into government corridors. Unless the Loxias faction decides it's interested in running the future Defense Force Command and Staff College."

A thin smile appeared on Morane's lips. "I am contemplating an annual security studies course that brings together senior folks from various parts of the republic, including the Order of the Void."

"Fortunately, I'm beyond attending that sort of training."

"But not beyond teaching."

"Recruiting faculty already?"

"It's never too early. Reginus Bryner signed up, sight unseen, as did Matti Kayne and Elenia Yakin. Since I figure you won't stick around as Defense Secretary under whoever succeeds me, and you've not yet cleared land for a garden on your property…"

"Perish the thought. We Marines have a red thumb, not a green one. Fine. I volunteer. Is there anything you'd like intelligence to focus on concerning the election?"

"Keep an ear to the ground and an eye on the perimeter. The electoral commission will make sure everything is honest."

"Could you speak with Gwenneth and see if she might rein in the budding political backroom operators in her flock?"

"I already did, and she told me the same thing I told you. The Void Brethren are full citizens of the republic with all the rights and responsibilities that entails, including the right to vote, and they don't meddle in the minds of others. The sisters are empaths, yes, but that means they're on receive only, and only for medical purposes."

"It's not the sisters I worry about, but Friar Stearn. I swear he peeked into my mind during the Chamber of Commerce meeting a few weeks ago."

"He's no different from the sisters and can't actually read your thoughts, though he will pick up on your distrust of his sort. The Brethren are the keenest students of human behavior you'll ever meet."

"And that's not creepy in itself?"

"You play poker. The best players are just as keen to refine their understanding of human behavior."

She gave him an exasperated grimace. "You always find a plausible answer for everything. I guess that's why you're the president."

"It certainly isn't because of my good looks."

"I'm sure Emma would disagree."

"Let's not go there." Morane glanced at the ancient clock on his office sideboard and stood. "Besides, it's time we head for the cabinet room."

"Saved by the bell," a clearly unrepentant DeCarde replied with a mischievous grin as she imitated him.

— 43 —

"Loxias, Stearn, thank you for coming. I wanted you to meet an old family friend who might come out of retirement after the senate elections."

Gerson Hecht invited the friars into his mansion with a sweeping arm gesture. The sun was setting over Lannion after another warm, muggy day. Still, here on the heights above the capital where many of the republic's wealthiest citizens owned sprawling estates, the air seemed lighter and less redolent of the Middle Sea. If Hecht noticed that Stearn preceded Loxias into the marble-floored foyer rather than the other way around, he gave no sign.

Stearn smiled at Hecht.

"Thank you for inviting us, Gerson. We're honored."

"I felt it was time. Our guest of honor had been the Order's friend ever since his days as Health Secretary and doesn't much like our current president or his policies, which makes his return to public life an opportunity none of us can afford to waste." Hecht glanced at Loxias, who so far hadn't said a word. "You might remember him from Elenia Yakin's time as president — Viktor Arko."

A smile split Loxias' beard.

"A friend of the Order indeed. I never met him but know his reputation as Lyonesse's foremost and longest-serving health administrator. Gwenneth holds him in high esteem."

"No doubt." Hecht led them through a broad, carpeted corridor whose walls were covered with art — paintings, prints, and other reproductions of ancient pieces that probably didn't survive the empire's demise. "I know he respects the abbess for her dedication to serving the community."

They entered an expansive salon where two dozen men and women stood in clusters, conversing, drinks in hand, shunning the sofa and easy chair groupings. Panoramic windows overlooked a star system capital lighting up for the rapidly oncoming subtropical night. Stearn could even spy the far end of the Lannion Base tarmac out of a corner. But where grounded Void Ships sat the day he arrived almost two years earlier, he saw nothing more than an expanse of gray concrete, underscoring the Navy's assertion all available ships were in space, on the lookout for intruders.

Most of the conversations trailed off as eyes turned on the bearded, black-robed friars who stopped and politely bowed at the other guests. Stearn recognized all of them save for one man in his late sixties. Tall, lean, with close-cropped gray hair and intense dark eyes, he dominated the room with his mere presence.

"Viktor, these are Friars Loxias and Stearn, two of our best friends inside the Order. Loxias is the chief administrator and, therefore, the abbess' de facto second in command. Stearn is Loxias' understudy, destined for the chief administrator's mantle in due course."

Arko didn't offer his hand, although he nodded.

"A pleasure. Gerson told me of your commitment to help elect senators who believe the republic's administration needs urgent changes in the face of an increasingly perilous galaxy."

"We of the Order must play our part in ensuring Lyonesse will one day venture forth and reunite humanity's other survivors," Stearn replied. "Between them, our abbess and President Morane keep us on the sidelines, but that must end."

"A good thing Morane's time is almost over, and to think he knee-capped himself by insisting on term limits for elected officials when we drew up our constitution." Arko's tone was even and unemotional, but Stearn's finely-tuned ears picked up more than a hint of sarcasm.

"Gwenneth's time will end soon enough as well. She is a prisoner of the past, and an increasing number of Brethren are looking to the future."

"Gerson told me you might become the Order's first abbot. Will you be taking Gwenneth's place?"

Stearn shook his head. "I'm still too young and too new, but our next abbess will be a sister who shares our views. May I assume you will vie for the presidency?"

"That's what my friend Gerson wants." Arko nodded at Hecht.

"Viktor would make a fine president, and if it weren't for Jonas Morane taking such an outsized role in Lyonesse affairs before his nomination, I daresay we'd both be speaking with President Arko right now."

"I suppose it was rather inevitable that the savior of Lyonesse would take over from our beloved Elenia, who I'm sure, had no involvement with Morane's political elevation." This time, the sarcasm in Arko's voice was noticeable.

"He got two terms," Loxias said. "I'm sure she wasn't stumping for him both times."

"A politician who doesn't trip over his own feet generally gets re-elected around here, Friar. Voters by and large are rather lazy and would rather not take the time to scrutinize candidates. They operate under the principle that the devil you know is always more attractive than the one you don't. It's among the reasons why we have term limits, one of the few things Morane pushed for that I like. In any case, it was a pleasure meeting you. Enjoy the rest of your evening."

With that, Arko wandered off and joined a small cluster of senatorial candidates by the windows. After pointing at a buffet table covered with finger food and groaning under the weight of countless alcohol bottles, Hecht joined him.

"There's a man who didn't leave public life voluntarily," Stearn murmured, "which explains his dislike of Morane."

Loxias nodded.

"Yes. I daresay Viktor Arko was hoping he'd replace Yakin only to see his ambitions thwarted by Morane's popularity. Offering himself up for nomination now and erasing Morane's legacy would be a fitting revenge."

As they helped themselves to the buffet, Stearn opened his third eye and reached out for Arko's mind, hoping he'd find someone as malleable as Loxias and the preferred senatorial candidates, people susceptible to his influence. But he didn't enter it for fear of triggering a reaction. Best to study the inner man from a distance first.

Arko's mind seemed as calm and self-possessed as the man appeared to the naked eye. Yet, it also felt hard, brittle, with little depth, much like Gerson Hecht or some of the Supermax inmates on Changu Island, those whom Amelia called soulless. It was a strange thing for a medical doctor and philanthropist. However, of greater interest was the fact he showed no evidence of mental shields. It meant he could touch Arko's mind.

"What chances do you give him?" Stearn asked his nominal superior.

"Fairly good, I'd say. He's a well-known quantity even among incumbent senators, and he has more charisma than Charis Sandino, the only other serious contender. Should he become president, we'll have a friend and ally at the very heart of Government House."

Stearn snorted softly. "Friend? No. He doesn't strike me as a man who has friends, although he most certainly can make people think otherwise."

Loxias gave him a strange look. "What do you mean?"

"I would venture that while Viktor Arko is a talented actor, a good manipulator, and a highly intelligent man, he cares little for others."

"You peeked at his mind."

"Yes, and if you believe there is such a thing as a soul, then I'm afraid I didn't find one. That doesn't make him evil. It merely means any empathy he shows will be feigned. He'll be our ally as long as we're useful, but never our friend. If he praised the Brethren during his tenure as Health Secretary, it wasn't because of friendly feelings."

Loxias chuckled. "One might almost think Marta trained you as a counselor. Well done. Now we must figure out how we make ourselves useful to the future President Arko in ways that transcend the Order's usual good works for the community."

"I can think of a few ways which don't necessarily involve divulging too much about my abilities. But this is neither the time nor the place."

"Of course."

Stearn waved his wine glass toward the other guests. "Shall we mingle?"

**

"As expected, reaction to your laying out what would happen in case of a barbarian incursion that reaches Lyonesse orbit has been mixed," Morane's public affairs director said after taking a seat in front of the presidential desk. "The majority consensus is in favor of strong action to save lives, though with concern about how long you'll suspend civil liberties. But a surprising number of people find the administration's plans objectionable, fearing a permanent loss of freedom which would transform the republic into a miniature version of the Ruggero dynasty's empire."

"Even though I made it clear the law prevented me from imposing emergency conditions longer than thirty days without a two-thirds approval by the senate." He shook his head. "Wasn't I explicit enough in stating I won't even consider prolonging it beyond what's necessary under the circumstances, which might be a few days at most?"

"Either the objectors don't trust you, or they didn't listen, never mind read the notification we sent every citizen afterward. More interesting are the prominent people among the objectors who decry a further militarization of the republic, such as former Health Secretary Viktor Arko."

Morane sat up. "Arko? He hasn't voiced an opinion in almost twelve years."

"True, but word on the street is that he's shown interest in presenting himself as a candidate for the presidency once your administration stands down after the elections."

Morane cocked an eyebrow. "Does word on the street give him favorable odds?"

"Too early to tell, Mister President. Viktor Arko only waded into the electoral discussion in the last twenty-four hours."

"Anything else?"

"No, sir. The written report will be on your reader by now."

"Thank you, Marc."

The public affairs director rose, dipped his shaved head, turned on his heels, then left the presidential office.

Morane swiveled his chair around and gazed out the window at the back lawn and the Haven River's broad, lazy expanse beyond it. If truth be told, he was looking forward to retiring as president after twelve years and doing something else. His tolerance for idiots was dramatically decreasing as his second term wore on, and he was encountering an ever-growing number of them. Standing up a Command and Staff College for the Defense Force was just the ticket for a satisfying life after politics, one which would still serve the republic for many more years.

If only he could finish his time as president without further incident.

— 44 —

"Stearn, Loxias, good day. Please come in." Gerson Hecht's welcoming smile didn't extend to his watchful eyes as he greeted the friars at the entrance of the private club in downtown Lannion where he'd assembled the senatorial candidates he and his faction supported. Their role was cheering when Arko officially announced he would accept a nomination as president from the next senate. "Viktor isn't here yet, but we expect him momentarily."

They quickly exchanged greetings with each of the attendees, then Hecht's amplified voice smothered dozens of low-key conversations.

"Ladies and gentlemen, may I present the man who we hope to call Mister President after the upcoming elections, Viktor Arko."

Enthusiastic applause broke out when Arko strode across the low stage, smiling and nodding as if he considered the plaudits his due. He stopped to face the audience and waited until a rapt silence settled over the room.

"My friends, thank you for the warm welcome. How about we get the formalities over with and then chat about what's going on in our beloved republic these days, yes?" He paused when a chorus of 'yeas' erupted from the crowd. "Let's do this. I, Viktor Arko, hereby propose myself as nominee once the next senate convenes and elects a new president."

Roars of approval underscored by applause even more exuberant than before greeted his announcement. After almost two minutes by Stearn's inner clock, Arko raised both arms, and the noise quickly faded away. During that time, the friar let his mind brush those of the people around him, and he tasted energy, ambition, eagerness, and warm regard for the man on the stage.

"I need not tell you about my qualifications for the highest office in the republic, nor go on at length about my achievements. Everything is public knowledge, and you'll agree I'm as good a candidate as President Morane's heir presumptive and the current favorite for the presidency, Charis Sandino. But Charis and I don't hold the same views, nor do we espouse the same philosophies, and therefore the next senate must choose wisely. Charis will continue in the same vein as Jonas Morane and Elenia Yakin. She'll espouse a militaristic republic focused on building a mighty faster-than-light warship fleet. Under her leadership, Lyonesse will become an impregnable autarky, closed to the rest of humanity. She'll keep our most precious jewel, the Knowledge Vault, under military control rather than hand this legacy over to the people."

Stearn reached out mentally and filled what passed for Arko's soul with a feeling of love and respect for the Order, though he knew violating another's inner being in such a manner would come at a cost.

"And she will keep some of our most valuable citizens from participating fully in the republic's political life. I speak of our friends the Void Brethren." Arko made a sweeping arm gesture toward Stearn and Loxias as he beamed. "No, we cannot allow the republic to continue as before. Especially now that President Morane has made his intentions clear by announcing he would impose martial law if ever intruders came within sublight distance of Lyonesse. Does anyone doubt Charis Sandino will keep that same policy in place if she succeeds him? Make no mistake, the mere act of considering martial law endangers our hard-won liberties. We don't want to become a new empire in all but name, do we?"

Shouts of 'no' filled the air.

"Then let us pray no intruders, real or imagined, show up between now and when the next senate votes for change in a few short weeks. I know Jonas Morane and Charis Sandino are honorable and want nothing but the best for the republic, but the allure of power is irresistible, which is why our constitution wisely sets inviolable term limits. Yet those limits can be ignored if parts of the constitution are suspended during a state of emergency and we know human history is replete with endless emergencies kept alive purely for political motives and not the welfare of the citizenry. If I become president, I will see our constitution is amended so an administration can no longer declare martial law without the consent of the senate."

More cheering and applause followed his declaration, and Stearn opened his mind so he could drink up the energy of several hundred people united by a fiery orator. Arko must become the next president. There was no other choice. Only through him would the Order of the Void take its rightful place within the republic.

When the inevitable dreams struck Stearn that night, he tried once again to harness them instead of fighting back. He wanted their energy so he could fill his depleted reserves after expending so much on strengthening Arko's appreciation of the Order. He knew he still faced plenty of work to make it a permanent fixture in the mind of a man with little empathy. Yet welcoming the nightmares as a source of strength proved difficult, and it left him disoriented for hours, unsure of what was real and what was a figment of his tortured soul.

**

"I find your trust in Jonas Morane's integrity disturbing, Loxias. Power corrupts, and he's been president for twelve years. Before that, he held sway over the Defense Force as chief of staff and Defense Secretary. This is a man who has bathed in barely constrained power for decades. He won't let a crisis go to waste. Viktor Arko said as much last week."

The chief administrator shook his head as he sighed in exasperation.

"If I didn't know better, I'd say you suffer from monomania. Jonas Morane has never acted in anything other than an honorable manner in the years I've lived on Lyonesse. He will most certainly not impose martial law on account of a non-existent barbarian incursion so he can cancel the upcoming elections and make himself president for life. If he invokes emergency powers, it'll be only for as long as necessary to preserve the lives of our fellow citizens from the ravages of the Barbarian Plague."

Stearn stood and began pacing Loxias' office, hands clasped behind his back. To the older friar's eyes, he seemed unusually agitated.

"Something is about to go very wrong. I can feel it. If we don't act, we might lose everything we worked for over the last year."

"Sit, Stearn. Your behavior is unbecoming a trained friar, and it's affecting my serenity."

The younger man stopped and gave his elder an incredulous stare. "Serenity? You've not enjoyed a serene day during our entire acquaintanceship. Someone grasping for power instead of living in the present doesn't even know the meaning of the word."

"You forget yourself, Stearn."

"No. I'm the only one who remembers what is right. What our goals are." Defiance replaced incredulity. "Thankfully, you've become irrelevant to the cause. I hold the keys that will unlock our future, and I will not allow Jonas Morane to impose a tyranny quashing our legitimate aspirations."

"What do you mean you won't allow?"

At that moment, both their communicators lit up with an insistent buzz.

**

Gwenneth glanced at her office display, ignoring the chime coming from an inner pocket, and read the advisory from the Lyonesse government. The long-dreaded day was finally here. The Navy had spotted intruders at Lyonesse's hyperlimit, intruders who came from interstellar space and not via the wormhole network. Government House was warning everyone the president might use his emergency powers and declare martial law within the next few hours.

Landry popped his head through the door.

"Shall I issue a notice that Brethren working outside should take shelter soonest?"

"There's still a little time. Warn them that they must wrap up whatever they're doing if it can be finished within the next three hours. If it can't, then they must suspend work at the most appropriate point within the next three hours." She checked the time. "Make sure the outlying priories acknowledge, especially the Windy Isles, in case they slept through the alert."

"Yes, Abbess. Though I daresay, Prioress Mirjam will be on top of things." Landry withdrew to carry out his orders.

The Brethren were as ready as they could be should the worst happen. A contingent of volunteers from among the medical sisters and friars stood by, ready to help the Defense Force if rigorous quarantining became necessary. Gwenneth had even visited the two offshore islands designated as quarantine and decontamination sites along with General Hamm and the Order's designated team leads. Now all they could do was pray the Almighty would let this poisonous cup pass Lyonesse.

She returned to her work and was so deeply absorbed that Landry's interruption caught her by surprise.

"Abbess, Sister Keleos just called. She found Loxias sitting in his office, catatonic. She cannot wake him or sense his presence."

Gwenneth reared up. A worm of suspicion stirred. "Call Marta and ask her to join us in Loxias' office."

"Immediately."

— 45 —

Gwenneth and Marta found Loxias sitting behind his desk on the ground floor of the administration building. His eyes were glazed over, and a string of drool hung from the corner of his mouth. Sister Keleos stayed by the door while Gwenneth entered to check his vitals.

"He still lives," Marta said in a strange voice. "You needn't take his pulse. But his essence has vanished."

"What?" Gwenneth stopped in her tracks and stared back at Marta while a gasp of terror escaped Keleos' throat.

"Something blasted his mind away. It looks a lot like Seled's did, only I sense much greater damage. There's nothing left."

Stretcher-bearers from the abbey's hospital pushed their way past Keleos, followed by the duty healer, a young sister doing her residency. Gwenneth, Marta, and Keleos withdrew into the hallway.

"He won't see another sunrise," Marta murmured.

"Why?" Keleos asked.

"Seled died of cardiac arrest despite the priory's best efforts. Loxias' body will also fail. The stress on his heart was just as extreme."

Gwenneth turned a stare filled with both dread and resignation on Keleos.

"Who was his last visitor?"

Before the latter could reply, Marta said, "Stearn. He's the only one able to do this."

When she noticed the abbess' stricken expression, Marta added, "But you already knew that."

Keleos nodded. "She's right. It was Stearn. How could he? Loxias treated him like a son."

They fell silent as the stretcher-bearers came through the office door with Loxias. The duty healer briefly met Gwenneth's eyes as she passed them and gave her an almost imperceptible head shake before hurrying off behind the orderlies.

"In hindsight, I suspect Stearn was a mental time bomb ticking away since the day I opened his third eye. A dark part of his soul has been struggling to come out ever since then. Something Loxias said or did set him off."

Gwenneth turned to where Landry waited at the foot of the stairs. "Find out where Stearn is. No one should approach him under any circumstances, save for me."

"And me," Marta said in a tone that brooked no dissension. "I enabled him. Loxias' condition is my fault, and I'm probably the only one who can stop him. If nothing else, after Seled, I know what to expect when evil lashes out in full fury."

"Agreed." Gwenneth gazed at Keleos. "Any idea of what they were discussing or doing?"

"No, but they were at loggerheads about something." Keleos paused as if embarrassed. "Truth is, Stearn has been exhibiting more and more erratic behavior of late. Not so most people would notice, you understand, but those of us who are close saw him suffer from momentary, and I mean for a few seconds only, loss of self-control. But it meant arguments with Loxias over the direction we should take."

"We meaning the Lindisfarne Brethren?"

Keleos stiffened. "With respect, Abbess, we meaning the Order. The Lindisfarne Brethren dissolved once we achieved our goal of having you declare Lyonesse the motherhouse."

"Then what do you call the Brethren who are politically active and seek to increase our Order's influence over the republic's affairs?"

Keleos visibly swallowed her reply and merely stared at Gwenneth with emotionless eyes.

"What did Loxias and Stearn disagree about the most?" Gwenneth asked in a testy voice. "Come now, it might tell us where he went. If he can erase what Loxias was, Stearn is a clear and present danger."

Keleos bit her lower lip.

"President Morane's warning he would declare martial law if plague ships reached Lyonesse orbit before the Navy could intercept them. Stearn held the belief Morane would either fake an incursion or use a real one to cancel the upcoming senate elections and stay president for life. That meant the Order would never get a chance of working with an administration more open to our taking on a greater role. Loxias, who believes Jonas Morane is an honorable man, wasn't having any of it. Their relationship was becoming rather testy." Keleos paused for a moment. "In truth, I and others are becoming a little scared of Stearn's mood swings."

A soft sigh escaped Marta's lips as a grimace of dismay twisted her usually smooth features.

"Wonderful. Stearn is developing symptoms of paranoid schizophrenia. This truly is the year we discover our limitations in awakening the mind's dormant abilities. My teachings unleashed an angry soul that should have remained behind his closed inner eye. If Stearn found a way of overcoming or skirting his conditioning, there's no telling what he might do to others."

Before Gwenneth could reply, three communicators, one per sister, chimed insistently. They retrieved them from inner pockets with eerily matching gestures and frowned at the small screens.

Keleos was the first to speak. "Good heavens. It's finally happened."

"And I know where Stearn is heading. Gwenneth, you and I must ignore the order to take shelter. The moment Stearn sees this message, he will head for Government House."

"Sisters." Landry reappeared in the corridor. "Stearn left the abbey alone in one of the ground cars an hour ago."

Gwenneth nodded. "Not long after the first warning, then. Meaning it probably was the trigger."

"There is no 'probably' about it." A stricken expression crossed Marta's face. "Because of his deluded state, he would interpret that notification as the first sign of Lyonesse's descent into tyranny."

"We need a car, Landry. I will drive. Then see if you can track the one Stearn is using."

The friar bowed his head.

"At once."

**

"We sent the message to every communicator on the planet, Mister President," Brigid DeCarde's hologram said, "and notices are going up in public spaces. The Republic of Lyonesse is now under martial law until the danger passes."

"Excellent. Thank you."

"Adrienne Barca has activated the emergency operations center. She and the senior command staff are on their way to Lannion Base. Will you join them?"

Morane shook his head.

"No. Lannion Base is the most secure place on the planet. Hiding there while the republic's citizens must make do with their dwellings or places of work as shelters, would send the wrong message. Besides, Adrienne doesn't want me breathing down her neck."

"That's what I thought you'd say. But by everything holy, if the Navy warns of debris headed for Government House, bug out, will you."

"James has the armored staff car on standby, but the chances of anything landing here are infinitesimally small. Don't worry, I'll finish my term and carry out an orderly handover with my successor, whoever that'll be. I'm sure the Navy will make a clean intercept well before that wolf pack crosses the outer moon's orbit, especially with our two newest warships leading the task force. And if the odd one gets through, *Myrtale* is more than capable of dealing with it." The elderly frigate now turned into a mobile orbiting battle station, carried the third heaviest broadside in the Lyonesse Navy, after *Vanquish* and *Savage*. "Fortunately, the Navy spotted them almost at once when they dropped out of FTL at the hyperlimit. It gave First and Second Squadrons the time they needed for an orderly deployment. Once this is over, I'd find out which sensor tech raised the alarm and see that his or her captain writes a citation."

"Will do, but still, we should take no chances."

Morane gave her a strange look. "You seem more worried than I am. What gives?"

"This is the largest wolf pack to date, boss. Twelve of the bastards. I know we outgun them on a one-to-one basis — except for the auxiliary sloops — but that's still a target-rich environment for a small Navy with a third of her strength guarding the wormhole termini. It just takes one chunk of wreckage shedding plague viruses impacting in or near a settlement…" She let her words trail off, then sighed. "On the other hand, I'm just a Marine. What do I know about naval combat in space? Probably way less than you've forgotten."

A crooked smile lit up Morane's craggy face.

"That's okay. I know little about ground combat, let alone Pathfinder operations. If ever you become president, make sure you hire a former naval officer as Defense Secretary. It's the only way you can cover everything."

"Me president? Perish the thought. Retirement and a casual gig as a Command and Staff College lecturer after the election sound surprisingly good right now."

"If Charis succeeds me, she'll keep you on."

"Unlike a nominee for the job of Void abbess, I can decline the honor, and I will. After working for you all these years, I don't think I'll take to her. Nothing personal. I just prefer working for someone with a military mind. It makes life easier. By the way, where is our vice president?"

"Charis is at her residence, suffering from the effects of a more common virus."

DeCarde nodded. The Sandino family owned an estate on the heights overlooking Lannion, close to Gerson Hecht's property.

"I thought she looked a little peaky at the last cabinet meeting. But it's good she's not in the office. The boss and his second in command can't ride out an attack at the same vulnerable location."

"The Government House war room, from where I will watch *Vanquish*'s live feed once First Squadron engages the wolf pack, isn't exactly a vulnerable location."

"Nor is it wreckage-proof, but fair enough."

"Unless you have better plans, join me so I can explain the finer points of naval tactics as the interception unfolds in real-time, say around fifteen hundred hours?"

— 46 —

"They're not powering shields or weapons," Lieutenant Stefan Norum said as he studied the bridge's tactical projection from his perch on the command chair. Lieutenant Commander Lisiecki had taken his battle stations post in the corvette's combat information center shortly after they broke out of orbit. "The bastards must see 1st Squadron in all its glory by now. We're boosting hard."

"Aye," Lisiecki's hologram, floating at Norum's right elbow, replied. "And *Vanquish* on her own will light up their threat boards, never mind the rest of us. They can't be that blind, not if they figured out we shoot intruders using the wormhole branch."

"Could be they're running on fumes after an extended FTL trip from Arietis through interstellar space." Norum frowned as an idea struck him. "Captain, has anyone pinged them for life signs?"

"You think they might be ghost ships?"

"We don't know how long infected people live before virus-induced mutations kill them. The plague could have reached the endgame in that wolf pack while they were in hyperspace."

"Excellent point. Link me with *Vanquish*. I'll suggest we and *Prevail* hammer the barbarians with our sensors on full power, seeing as how we're closest."

"Linking with *Vanquish*, aye."

The cruiser's captain, who doubled as 1st Squadron's commander, issued the order for intensive scans of the intruding ships within moments, and they found their answer less than ten minutes later.

"I'm not picking up life signs in ten of the twelve bogies," *Standfast*'s sensor chief reported, "and only faint ones in the remaining two."

Norum nodded. "Ghost ships."

A soft female voice sounded from the back of the CIC — Sister Hoshi, the corvette's counselor and chief medical officer.

"The ones still alive are dying in agony, Captain. They will not survive for long."

"Then our missiles will do them a favor. Signals, send our readings to *Vanquish*. Let's see if the intercept plan changes now that we determined at least ten out of twelve are under autopilot control at best."

**

"Ghost ships?"

Morane and DeCarde exchanged surprised looks at the announcement. They were ensconced in Government House's subterranean war room, a reinforced storage space converted during Elenia Yakin's first term at Morane's urging for just such an occasion.

He touched a control screen embedded in the conference table's wooden surface. A few seconds later, General Barca's face appeared on a side display.

"Yes, Mister President. What can I do for you?"

"If First Squadron can capture a ship with tractor beams and tow it to one of Lyonesse's Lagrangian points, it would give our researchers added study material. I think one and a half million kilometers from our atmosphere is a reasonable buffer, so long as we keep guns on it for the duration."

"Agreed, sir. A ship with or without life signs?"

"Without. Those with life signs carry live viruses and are primary targets for destruction."

"Understood, sir."

"Thank you, General. That's all I wanted. Morane, out."

He grimaced at DeCarde. "This might sound callous, but let's hope they died because of the virus and not because their environmental systems failed. It would give us a larger sample of victims to study and more importantly, victims not torn apart when their ships were destroyed, but killed by this thing."

"In an ugly way, if *Standfast's* mind-meddler is right."

"Be glad those mind-meddlers are aboard our starships. They're the only ones who can tell us about intangibles such as the agony those infected suffer near the end. Every bit of data on this damned plague is invaluable."

She gave him a grudging look.

"I'll concede the point. But I still don't like the increased interest a few of them show in matters beyond the abbey walls."

"I may have mentioned this before — the Brethren are full citizens of the republic with just as many rights and responsibilities as you and I. Even Gwenneth can't order them to stay away from secular affairs. The Void just isn't that sort of monastic order."

**

"I still can't believe it." Gwenneth dropped into the ground car's driver seat, waited for Marta to join her, then closed the side doors and fed power to the wheels. "Why would Stearn head for Government House? There are twelve presumptive plague ships inbound."

"In his dissociated state, he believes it's a sham cooked up by Jonas Morane to cancel the elections and make himself president for life under a state of interminable martial law."

"How does this even make sense?"

"It doesn't, in our world. But in his…" Marta glanced through the side window at the ripening fields surrounding the only home she'd known for more than a third of her life. "He stripped Loxias of everything but his last breath. Stearn is no longer someone we can understand by our own lights. I blame myself for not seeing his slow march toward the edge of the abyss."

"Self-blame is an indulgence none of us can afford at the best of times, as a wise person once said," Gwenneth replied in a dry tone. "Our friends in the Republic's Defense Force would say we fucked up, you and I."

Marta inclined her head respectfully.

"A fair assessment. Seled's destruction was mercifully quick. Stearn's might yet wreak havoc on everything we hold dear."

"And in a time of crisis."

The car's communication system came to life.

"Abbess, this is Landry. We traced Stearn's car to the residence of Vice President Sandino on the escarpment."

Gwenneth and Marta glanced at each other.

"Are you sure?"

"That's what the global tracking system says. It's still there."

Gwenneth nodded. "Take out the lawful successor who supports her president's policies, before removing the principal."

"Abbess." Landry's voice came over the communicator again. "The infirmary just called. Loxias died a few minutes ago."

"Damn." Marta struck her thigh with a clenched fist. "This is on me."

"On both of us. You know, if both Jonas and Charis die in office, Brigid DeCarde becomes president, and she's no great friend of the Order."

"Stearn isn't aware of that. Why should he?" Marta grimaced. "DeCarde keeps her feelings well hidden. You only know because of Jonas Morane and I because of you."

"It's worse. Brigid DeCarde is one of those rare people who can detect mind-meddling. I believe the ability has run in her family since before the birth of the empire. She somehow sensed Stearn brushing her mind several weeks ago. Jonas warned me."

"And you didn't think it might be a splendid idea if you mentioned this?"

"You were in the Windies."

Marta gave her superior a harsh glare. Gwenneth ignored it as she steered their car toward the escarpment, and Vice President Sandino's home. They encountered no checkpoints, nor did they see any police or military personnel as they skirted Lannion's northern edge.

Streets were eerily empty, though both sisters sensed human minds behind the polarized residence and office windows, many of them fearful. Everyone on Lyonesse understood the day would eventually come when desperate reivers with jury-rigged antimatter containment units bypassed the wormhole branch entirely to reach the last star system in the Coalsack Sector with a functioning high tech civilization.

Gwenneth always marveled at the sumptuous estates overlooking Lannion. They made Jonas Morane's comfortable home seem positively modest by comparison. To a mansion, they were metal-topped and clad in laser-cut granite blocks of various hues. Built so they could resist even the fiercest storm sweeping inland from the Middle Sea, they sat at the heart of park-like properties surrounded by fences that were both ornamental and provided security. Sandino's home was no exception, though hers was more securely guarded than the rest.

Both Sisters of the Void were therefore surprised when they found the front gate wide open with no sign of the police officers who protected the republic's vice president from what were mostly harmless citizens fixated on one issue or another. Sandino wasn't popular enough to attract more dangerous admirers or detractors.

The car used by Stearn sat abandoned in the curved driveway, across from the open front door, along with two prone, uniformed men who looked like they collapsed in mid-stride.

"Are they—" Gwenneth abruptly cut power to her car's wheels and opened both driver and passenger side doors.

Marta reached out with her mind. "They're unconscious but otherwise unharmed."

"Thank the Almighty for small mercies."

They climbed out of their seats, and while Gwenneth knelt beside the officers to check their vitals, Marta took the front steps two at a time with a surge of energy born from desperation. But she already knew her deepest fears would be confirmed. And they were.

She found Charis Sandino sprawled on her back across the marble-floored foyer, dead. A quick touch with her mind's tendrils confirmed the vice president's life essence was gone after being blasted to shreds by Stearn's unhinged assault. Though

Sandino's brain would show no physical damage, Marta saw nothing but ashes. Her former student had murdered another human being using the abilities she'd unleashed.

"Is she dead?"

Marta whirled around to face Gwenneth.

"Yes. Stearn murdered her, just as he murdered Loxias. Another death stemming from my actions."

"Where is Stearn?"

"Not here. He did the deed, abandoned the abbey car, and left, probably in the security detail's vehicle. He could be at Government House by now."

"So should we, though I daresay, he won't get in quite as easily."

As they hurried back to their car, Marta asked, "Should we call Jonas and warn him?"

"Of what? A demented friar who can kill with his thoughts? Either he'll ask how much gin we've been drinking or realize we are worse mind-meddlers than Brigid DeCarde imagines. I can live with the first outcome, which wouldn't help in this situation. The Order, on the other hand, can't live with the second one." As soon as they settled in and the doors closed, Gwenneth gunned the car's drive train. "Stopping that demented friar before he harms anyone else is our job, and ours alone. Let's pray we won't be too late, for everyone's sakes."

— 47 —

"Sir." Commander James Lutzow, Morane's naval aide, stuck his head into the war room. "There's a Friar Stearn at the main gate. He claims he carries a personal message for your ears only from Abbess Gwenneth, something she couldn't discuss over a comlink."

"Very well." Morane climbed to his feet, imitated by DeCarde. "There's no point in remaining here anyhow. Those ghost ships won't pass the outer moon's orbit. I'll lift martial law the moment I hear from the operations center that all save the one we're keeping for study are destroyed."

"If you don't mind, sir, I'll stay here and watch the intercept until it's over."

"Of course." He gestured at DeCarde's chair with an air of mock irritation. "And what did I tell you about standing just because I get up?"

"That there's a time and a place. Since it's just the two of us, this is neither the time nor the place," she replied with a sardonic grin.

"Why is it you know the lesson but never apply what you've learned?"

DeCarde shrugged. "Search me, Mister President."

He glowered at her. "Stubborn Pathfinder."

"Stubbornness is a professional requirement in my former branch of the service."

"I don't know that I'd call it stubbornness. Talk to you later, Brigid."

She watched Morane follow his aide out of the war room, then turned her attention back on the live feed from *Vanquish*'s CIC.

As Morane climbed the stairs, a vague unease came over him. Why would Gwenneth send a messenger now, during the long-feared intrusion? And why send Loxias' right-hand man instead of her own trusted assistant, Landry? There was something uncanny about Stearns and his mysterious history before *Dawn Hunter* rescued him on Yotai, not to mention his increasingly overt involvement in the current electoral race.

He stopped on the main floor landing.

"Jim, please take Friar Stearn to the waiting room and tell him I'll be along just as soon as I deal with a few urgent matters. Offer him a cup of tea or a glass of water. Something doesn't seem right about this, and I want to speak with Gwenneth before meeting him."

"Shall I alert the protective detail?"

"Yes. They should make sure Stearn stays put until I clear this with the abbey."

"Will do, sir."

Lutzow headed for the front hall while Morane entered his office. Once there, he called up the waiting room video feed, then opened a link with Gwenneth's office. To his surprise, a visibly stricken Landry answered.

"Mister President."

"Good afternoon, Landry. Is the abbess available?"

"No, sir. May I be of help?"

Morane was taken aback by Landry's strained tone.

"Perhaps. Friar Stearn just showed up at Government House claiming he carries a message for my eyes only from Gwenneth, something she can't discuss over a comlink."

Landry's eyes widened.

"Under no circumstances should you be in Stearn's presence, sir."

Morane glanced up at the video display and saw the friar enter Government House's waiting room under the steely gaze of two Pathfinder sergeants in civilian clothes that didn't quite hide their sidearms.

"Why?"

Landry hesitated for what seemed like an eternity while he mentally parsed possible answers. Finally, he said, "We suspect Friar Stearn assaulted Friar Loxias."

Morane frowned as he tilted his head to one side.

"What happened? Is Loxias okay?"

"He died in the abbey infirmary a few minutes ago. We don't know what happened or how. Gwenneth and Marta are out looking for Stearn."

"I won't even ask why they're disobeying a shelter in place order and violating martial law. How is it the Lannion Police aren't dealing with your wayward friar? If he killed Loxias, then it's murder and not something internal to the Order."

A pained expression spread across Landry's plain features.

"Sir, it would be best if you ask Gwenneth when she reaches Government House, which shouldn't be long now."

Suspicion reared its ugly head, and Morane's frown deepened.

"Why are Gwenneth and Marta usurping the role of the police during a lockdown, Landry? What is the Order hiding, and why is Stearn here?"

"I'm truly sorry, sir, but I can't answer your questions."

Morane knew the friar wouldn't speak without Gwenneth's permission, no matter what, so he dropped the matter, asking instead, "Should I ask my close protection people to detain Stearn until the abbess and Marta arrive? He's in the Government House waiting room right now. My aide told him I was dealing with several emergencies and would receive him the moment I'm free."

"No, sir. Please do nothing of the sort." The vehemence in Landry's voice surprised Morane. "He would react violently if faced with perceived threats. Lives could be lost. Keep up the pretense you're busy and contain him in the waiting room until Gwenneth arrives. And by everything holy, please stay away."

Gwenneth didn't surround herself with fools, and Landry was no exception. Though still young compared to most friars, many of whom came from other abbeys long ago during the empire's fall or had crewed the Void Ships before the Order turned them over to the Navy, he knew Gwenneth's mind better than anyone besides Morane. If Landry felt justified in telling the President of the Republic of Lyonesse he should treat Stearn as a walking piece of unexploded ordnance, then there were good reasons.

"I shall follow your advice and wait for Gwenneth, Friar. My close protection detail will make sure Stearn enjoys tea and scones in the waiting room."

"If I may offer a piece of advice, sir, withdraw your people from the room itself. Let them guard the doors from the outside. What Stearn cannot see, he cannot harm."

Morane gave Landry a tight nod, then touched the screen embedded in his desktop. "Jim, the protection detail will guard our visitor from outside the waiting room, and please warn the main gate that if Sisters Gwenneth and Marta show up, they should be brought in without delay."

Moments later, he heard, "Roger that, sir."

Shortly after that, both Pathfinders left the waiting room, each closing one of the two doors behind him. Stearn was now alone in a space reinforced so it would prevent anyone from penetrating deeper into Government House by sheer physical force. Of course, no one bearing weapons of any sort was allowed in, period.

A faint air of relief momentarily relaxed Landry's features.

"Thank you for listening, Mister President. I'll try to contact Gwenneth and find out where they are."

"You do that. Morane, out."

The president's eyes rested on the display showing Government House's waiting room once more. A visibly agitated Stearn paced back and forth, eyes never resting on a single spot for more than a heartbeat. The friar's demeanor seemed so utterly devoid of a normal Void Brethren's serenity that Morane felt a chill run up his spine. Something was utterly wrong.

Then, Stearn stopped in front of Morane's lifelike formal portrait hanging over the waiting room's fireplace. It depicted him wearing the commander-in-chief's dress uniform complete with the cuff stripes of a four-star admiral and a golden Vanger's Condor with crossed swords and anchor insignia adorning the sky blue beret on his head. Stearn's earlier agitation vanished so completely, Morane wondered whether he'd fallen into a trance while studying the painting. It was a good portrait, but one whose time in the waiting room was ending, along with Morane's second and final term as president. Once his replacement was sworn into office, it would join Elenia Yakin's in the main corridor bisecting Government House.

Without warning, a migraine unlike any other struck Morane, and he let out a grunt of pain as his eyes slammed shut. But rather than the pulsing agony he'd experienced many years earlier, this assault on his nervous system remained steady. Nausea a hundred times worse than that which accompanied the transition to and from hyperspace or the one associated with a wormhole transition, threatened to choke him, and he was barely conscious by the time he stabbed the call screen embedded in the presidential desktop.

When Commander Lutzow burst through the office door, alarmed by the voiceless signal, he found Morane slumped in his chair, unconscious.

**

"There's what looks suspiciously like an unmarked police car, just like the one Stearn took from Vice President Sandino's guard detail." Marta pointed at a dark, low-slung skimmer sitting on the curb a few meters from the main entrance to Government House.

A low groan escaped Gwenneth's throat.

"Let us pray we're not too late." The car's communicator buzzed at that moment. "What?"

"Landry here, Abbess. I just spoke with President Morane. Stearn is at Government House, claiming he carries a message from you. Fortunately, the president called to confirm. I told him Stearn assaulted Loxias, causing his death, and should be considered dangerous."

"You don't know the half of it," Marta said as Gwenneth pulled the car up to the closed gate where an armed soldier from the Lyonesse Rifle Regiment waited. "Stearn murdered Vice President Sandino and injured her close protection team."

"Good heavens! Fortunately, at my urging, President Morane is holding Stearn in the locked waiting room with guards outside each door, pending your arrival."

The soldier at the gate took one glance through the side window and gestured at an unseen comrade. The gate slid aside, and the man ushered them in with a wave of the hand, after which he snapped to attention and saluted.

"How close is the waiting room to Morane's office?" Marta asked.

Gwenneth, intent on reaching the front steps as fast as possible, kept her eyes on the driveway.

"Why?"

"I fear Stearn is one of those who can project over short distances, even without a direct line of sight. He merely needs a focus for his thoughts."

Gwenneth let out a soft moan.

"There's a life-sized portrait of Jonas in the waiting room, and it's a mere dozen meters from his office. What did we unleash?"

"The same thing we freed in our younger sisters with no ill effects, but we didn't know Stearn carried darkness deep within. He may not have known about it himself."

The car came to a jerky stop at the foot of the stairs, where, in better times, a pair of ceremonial guards stood, dressed in rifle green dress uniforms. Both sisters climbed out with alacrity when the driver and passenger doors opened. An alarm bell reached their ears the moment they entered Government House. The sergeant standing guard by the waiting room's entrance seemed to vibrate with repressed tension.

"What's happening?" Gwenneth asked.

"No idea, Sister, but it can't be good. That's the signal something happened to the president. Commander Lutzow should be with him."

Gwenneth turned to Marta and pointed at the corridor. "Find Jonas."

"But—"

"I'll deal with Stearn. Jonas needs your help."

After one last glance at the closed waiting room door, Marta nodded, then set off at a rapid pace. Gwenneth looked the Pathfinder straight in the eyes.

"I will enter now the waiting room now, Sergeant."

— 48 —

Gwenneth took a deep breath while the sergeant unlocked the door. It slid open, and she stepped through. Roget stood in front of Morane's official portrait, staring at it with disturbing intensity, unaware he was no longer alone.

"Stearn!" Her voice cracked across the room like the detonation of a long-dormant volcano blowing its top, but he didn't even twitch. "Stop it this instant."

After a second or two, he raised his left hand, palm facing outward, and aimed it at her. Gwenneth immediately felt an assault on her mind's shielding, a battering ram so strong she staggered. Malevolent, unrestrained power surrounded her inner being, seeking a way in. The pressure quickly became unbearable, and part of Gwenneth marveled at Stearn's raw mental strength.

She no longer doubted his guilt for the deaths of both Loxias and Charis Sandino. Her legs buckled, and she collapsed to the floor in a heap under the astonished eyes of the Pathfinder sergeant. But she remained conscious and collected her strength to create a shield that would reflect Stearn's energies back at him.

If she built a viable feedback loop, the mad friar would inevitably self-destruct.

A few rooms down, Marta knelt by Morane's chair, laid a hand on his forehead, and opened her third eye while a thoroughly puzzled Commander Lutzow spoke with the Lannion Hospital emergency services. The violence of Stearn's attack almost ejected her from Morane's mind, even though Marta was ready for the sort of onslaught she'd experienced with Seled. But she steadied herself and pushed back at the horrible darkness engulfing Morane's soul. At first, she felt no give. It was like wading up a raging torrent of waist-high water, knowing the slightest misstep could mean death. But at least she kept the onslaught from growing stronger.

Then, Marta felt Stearn's energy decline, as if something or someone was distracting him. Gwenneth? Marta pushed — hard. He recoiled enough to let her build a shield around Morane and protect it from further deadly blasting. But her strength was ebbing as well. That which fed Stearn's mind was beyond comprehension, something primal drawing its power from the very essence of the Infinite Void while Marta depended solely on her own resources.

With astonishing speed, Stearn's mental assault collapsed, leaving Marta gasping at Morane's side, searching for breath and her bearings. When she recovered, in a matter of mere seconds, Marta realized Commander Lutzow didn't notice anything amiss. He was still on a comlink with the hospital, waiting for notification that an emergency medical team was on the way. The battle to push Stearn away and save Jonas Morane was fought and won in the blink of an eye. But was she successful, or did Stearn destroy Morane as thoroughly as he destroyed Loxias and Sandino?

Marta gently reached into the president's mind, and at first, she found the same damage she'd seen before, starting with Seled. A wave of despair washed over her. But before she could probe any deeper, one of the sergeants from Morane's close protection team burst into the presidential office.

"Sister Marta. Something's happened. Both Sister Gwenneth and Friar Stearn collapsed."

She climbed unsteadily to her feet.

"Commander Lutzow, tell the emergency team they must place President Morane in a medically induced coma the moment he's on a stretcher. Otherwise, he might not survive."

"What happened?"

"I can't say, but I know an induced coma is his only chance. Make them do it at gunpoint if necessary. I must see what happened to Gwenneth and Stearn." Marta didn't wait for an acknowledgment — a Sister of the Void's medical opinion was almost sacrosanct on Lyonesse. She brushed by both Lutzow and the sergeant on her way out of Morane's office while trying not to stagger with fatigue. Marta feared what she would find in the waiting room. Stearn was stronger than Gwenneth, though not as experienced or cunning.

When she entered the room, one of Morane's close protection people was kneeling at the abbess' side, fingers pressed against her neck. He looked up at Marta and shook his head.

"I'm sorry, Sister. She's dead." The Pathfinder nodded at Stearn, lying on his back in front of Morane's portrait. "The friar still lives, but my gut tells me he's fading fast. It was the strangest thing. They both lost consciousness at the same moment. Well, he lost consciousness. She might already have been dead when she hit the floor. How's the president?"

"He was alive when I left his office just now, but he suffered a seizure."

"Him too?" The man gave Marta a hard look. "What's going on here, Sister?"

"I wish I knew." She leaned against the door frame before a wave of vertigo sent her spinning to the floor. "Vice President Sandino also suffered a seizure at her home. She's dead."

"What?" He climbed to his feet. "Why are so many important people getting seizures?"

Marta waved away the question.

"I can't answer that, Sergeant, but I suggest you send a security detail to the late vice president's estate."

He gave her a single, brusque nod and produced his communicator. She reached out with her mind, first to touch Gwenneth and repressed a sob when she found her soul was gone, leaving only an empty physical shell. Then, she probed Stearn, and he was still alive, but no more than a shadow of himself. Most of his mind was a blasted wasteland, and she understood Gwenneth set up a feedback loop with her last remaining strength. Marta pushed herself upright, crossed the room, and knelt beside him. She laid her hand on a forehead that already felt colder than it should. Stearn was indeed slipping away. He had minutes left if that. He woke at Marta's touch and stared at her without comprehension.

"Make your peace with the Almighty and tell me the truth." She gazed into the dying man's eyes, searching for what he once was. "Tell me about this inner darkness you've hidden from us?"

Stearn didn't answer right away. His lips moved silently while a shudder ran through his body. When he finally spoke, it was with a rasp.

"I claimed *Antelope* was a privateer, a salvager searching for advanced technology to bring home, but I lied. We were out-and-out pirates enriching ourselves by raiding the weak and vulnerable. I lost count of how many people we'd killed by the time *Antelope* crash-landed on Yotai. Early on, we tried to avoid casualties, you understand. None of us were born murderers. But people insisted on fighting back. It became easier if we simply opened fire without warning." Stearn's voice became fainter as his essence began merging with the Void. "The first time we deliberately murdered innocent people, most of us got sick to our stomachs, me included. But it was less nauseating with every raid, and with every starship we plundered until none of us thought of our victims as fellow humans."

"Is that how you got the Void beacon?"

"Yes. My story of finding it in the ruins of a spaceport on Montego was also a lie. We raided a Void priory on New Karelia. There were maybe thirty or forty Brethren. Mostly sisters. After killing them and taking their tech, I ripped it from the neck of the prioress. I can't explain why." A cough. "They weren't the only Brethren we murdered. I may not be a sociopath, but the rot in my soul does not differ from that in Seled's. Granted, I wasn't a moral man, to begin with. None of us were. Otherwise, we'd have stayed on Scotia helping our own people instead of cruising the wormhole network to pillage communities made vulnerable by the empire's collapse."

"Since none of that was noted in *Antelope*'s log or database, I gather someone tampered with both, correct?"

"I did. After the crash. In case someone found me." Another cough, this one weaker. "I really wanted a life here, but the lure of using my talent in ways I shouldn't was more than I could resist. If only I'd left well enough alone and not taken vows… I guess I'm a weaker man than I thought." His breathing became shallower and more labored, and Marta knew the end was near. "I won't ask for your forgiveness, because I don't deserve it."

She gave him a sad smile. "Yet, I forgive you nonetheless, and the Almighty will receive your soul, no matter how damaged."

One last rale and Stearn Roget was dead. Marta closed his eyes and climbed wearily to her feet. An entirely irrational craving for life as a hermit in Lyonesse's wilderness overcame her. And she needed sleep. Lots of it. Yet Marta knew the former was not her destiny, and the latter would be delayed. When she turned to the door, she found Brigid DeCarde and Commander Lutzow watching her silently. They might even have overheard some of Stearn's dying confession, but Marta found she didn't care.

"Emergency teams are on their way," Lutzow said.

"One team will suffice. Gwenneth and Stearn are now part of the Infinite Void. I'll call the abbey's infirmary. They'll remove the mortal remains. We will bury their ashes on abbey land."

"Will your people conduct autopsies to find out how they died?"

Marta shook her head.

"No need. They suffered cardiac arrest due to unbearable stress. I've seen it before. You'll find Vice President Sandino died of the same cause."

Neither DeCarde nor Lutzow spoke, though both watched her with undisguised suspicion.

"All Brethren, save those with hospital or clinic duties will return to the abbey as soon as possible and stay there until further notice while I investigate what happened."

"*You* will investigate?" DeCarde's face hardened. "Four people are dead; the president is in a coma, and you will investigate? I think not."

"Three of the four are Brethren, including the perpetrator, and until we hold a vote, I will assume the duties of the *Summus Abbatissa*. What happened today directly results from a breakdown within the Order, one which I must repair."

"We shall see. You probably know that since Jonas Morane is incapacitated and Charis Sandino is dead, I'm the republic's interim president until either Jonas recovers or the next senate elects a successor. We will have a heart-to-heart talk about the Order's future in the next twenty-four hours, Sister. I'm sorry — *Summus Abbatissa*."

DeCarde's tone took on a mocking edge that struck Marta like a physical blow.

"Because of his longstanding friendship with Gwenneth, our president knows more about the Order's inner dealings than he lets on. And he didn't share with me because of my opinion you people are dangerous mind-meddlers despite the good your healers and counselors do. It's time you come clean with me. I want answers about what happened here today so we can make sure it never happens again."

Marta inclined her head respectfully.

"Of course, Madame President."

— 49 —

DeCarde sat back in the presidential chair and studied Marta, her expression one of disbelief mixed with anger after the latter revealed some of the Order's most closely guarded secrets.

"So, the Ancestor was right. You *are* mind-meddlers."

"Only a small number of us, those with an open third eye, and only for healing purposes. Most of the sisters have only a highly developed sixth sense and can only read the emotions of those not shielding their minds."

"And Jonas Morane knew about this ability?"

Marta nodded.

"Yes. He understood the good we can do with our expanded senses. The friars have a heightened ability to read others because of a stronger sixth sense than most and their training. But the talent, as we call it, is almost purely a female phenomenon. Except for Stearn Roget. He was an unprecedented anomaly. Unfortunately, I didn't know until his deathbed confession, that he was also a cold-blooded killer, someone who murdered countless humans. Otherwise, I would never have taught him what I teach sisters with an open third eye. I suppose I was guilty of hubris."

"Without a doubt. You, Gwenneth, and the rest of the sisters are exploring things best left alone. Nemesis follows hubris just as surely as night follows day, and we saw plenty of nemesis in the last twenty-four hours."

Marta inclined her head.

"I cannot offer arguments to the contrary, Madame President. Without my teachings, Stearn would have lived a normal life in the community, and those he murdered would still be among the living."

"Until he opted for a little piracy on the side, and we found ourselves with a serial killer ravaging Lannion."

"Doubtful. By the time Stearn reached the stage at which I should have stopped his training, the darkness he carried within was safely bottled up where he couldn't feed off it. We successfully treated inmates with antisocial personality disorders and brought them to the same point."

The interim president gave her a hard stare. "Something you will cease doing until further notice."

"We already stopped weeks ago, when one of the inmates in question suffered from complications leading to cardiac arrest."

"Good."

"I've also decided we would ship our excess friars and sisters — those too interested in secular matters — south where they will set up a priory on Isolde's north coast. It can anchor the republic's first settlement on the continent and become its medical center. That will end the Lindisfarne Brethren's ability to meddle in politics."

Marta let out a heartfelt sigh.

"We played with fire and burned innocents. For that, I offer you my and the Order's deepest apologies. Nothing we can do or say will ever make up for what happened. You may also rest assured I will force through an amendment to the Rule which will forbid any involvement in secular politics."

"What about the mind-meddling?"

"We condition our sisters against doing so unless it's for medical purposes. Our version of the Hippocratic Oath makes specific mention of not violating someone's mind. And we do not train anyone to that level unless they take the oath and accept the conditioning. Unfortunately, it failed in Stearn, and I take full responsibility for that as well. He is proof the male mind differs from the female mind, at least where the talent is concerned. Procedures that work on sisters didn't work on him. Once his delusions led him into a spiral of self-destruction, there was no going back."

DeCarde looked away for a few seconds, jaw muscles working.

"Yes, let's talk about the delusion Jonas would use his emergency powers to suspend the legislature and make himself president for life. He was on the verge of ending the emergency when Stearn struck. We weren't facing an attack by plague-infested reivers. Ten out of the twelve were ghost ships, everyone aboard dead. The other two gave off life signs so faint, it was clear the last survivors weren't long for this universe. Lyonesse was never in any actual danger. Had Stearn waited a few minutes longer, he would have received the message it was over. He and Gwenneth would be alive, and Jonas wouldn't be in a coma."

"Perhaps, but by the time Stearn entered Government House, I think his last connection with reality was frayed beyond repair. Murdering Loxias, his friend and mentor, in such a horrible manner — stripping him of his very essence — was the act of an irretrievably damaged mind. The only way this could have ended otherwise is if someone had shot and killed Stearn before he reached the vice president's residence."

"You leave me in a quandary, you realize that, right? If the truth about what happened to Jonas and Charis gets out, you'll find citizens with torches and pitchforks swarming the abbey. Lyonesse will lose the backbone of its health system, and we won't just be burying a few of the Brethren. I cannot trust your lot and never will, yet for the greater good, I'll go along with whatever story you concoct and never tell another soul about your secrets. I cannot sever the symbiotic relationship between your Order and the republic without killing both."

Marta bowed her head again. "Thank you."

"But fending off the inevitable questions so far has been almost unbearable. A dead vice president and a president in a coma while the republic was under martial law? The more extreme conspiracy theorists are no doubt accusing me of engineering their removal, so I could seize power."

"Tell the truth or at least a version of it. Friar Stearn, the man *Dawn Hunter* rescued on Yotai and who later joined the Order of the Void, lost his mind for reasons we cannot yet explain. He went on a murderous rampage and used his privileged position to make his way past the vice president's security after killing the Order's chief administrator, who first realized Stearn posed a danger. He entered Government House intending to assassinate President Morane but was intercepted by Abbess Gwenneth, who gave her life to stop him."

"What about Jonas? Commander Lutzow and the close protection team know Stearn never got near him, yet he suffered a life-threatening seizure not long after your friar showed up."

Marta shrugged helplessly. "Some things cannot be rationally explained without revealing too much, so it's best we don't try. Let it be known I'm investigating what happened and direct any questions you can't answer to me."

DeCarde tapped the desktop with her fingertips while eying Marta.

"I suppose that'll have to do. What's the president's condition?"

"Jonas remains in a coma, but he's stable. I saw him this morning, and his mind is nowhere near as damaged as Loxias' or Sandino's. I reached his side in time to prevent Stearn from burning everything away. Since a good part of his essence or soul remains, he will recover with the right help. I've recalled Sister Amelia from the Windy Isles for that purpose. She was my most talented student and will sit with Jonas day and night so she can help rebuild his inner being. In a few weeks, the Almighty willing, we can wake him and heal his conscious mind. He'll never be quite the same as before, sadly, but then neither are those who suffer life-threatening physical injuries."

"I suppose I should thank you for saving Jonas." DeCarde gave Marta a grudging look.

"Gwenneth deserves your thanks more than I. She successfully shut Stearn down. Without her, I could not have saved the president."

"Should I lay on a state funeral for Gwenneth?"

Marta tilted her head to one side while examining DeCarde for any trace of mockery. When she saw none, she shook her head.

"Thank you, but no. Gwenneth wouldn't want anything more than a modest service in the abbey's chapter house, followed by the burial of her ashes in our cemetery, especially after what happened. We Brethren must pull back from secular practices and concerns."

"Yes, you do. I don't want to hear anything more about Lindisfarne Brethren or friars sticking their noses into politics. Gwenneth erred in tolerating them."

"She had little choice at the time. But after yesterday's events, I can do what's needed without opposition. The Brethren are in shock, and many fear you might unleash the sort of pogrom Admiral Zahar encouraged."

"I won't lie, Abbess. The avenger buried deep inside me likes the idea, so I'm glad your people are feeling a bit of fear. May it bring humility to those who forgot their purpose is serving the Almighty and the community instead of their ambitions."

"Breaking ground for the new Isolde Priory will do wonders to remind them."

"If they accept you as their leader."

"None dare challenge my assumption of power after what happened. I set the vote for next week, and it's a foregone conclusion. I will chart a new course for the Brethren, one that takes the Order back to its roots."

"Why do I sense a Furie of ancient myth stirring in you?"

A sardonic smile tugged at Marta's lips.

"Because in another life you would be one of us. The ability to read people will stand you in good stead as president. But that wasn't your question. Yes, there is a Furie in me, an Erinye which has remained silent since the rebels on Mykonos overthrew imperial rule and executed the father of my children. That Furie has been biding her time for a quarter-century. Gwenneth was a good abbess, but one wedded to the past. She couldn't envisage the changes needed, let alone force them through in the face of Brethren who forgot the Order's true purpose. I see that now, and it took Stearn's transgressions to open my eyes. I intend to reform the Order as atonement for my part in enabling Stearn and that will take my inner Furie's full strength."

"In that case, I wish you luck, Abbess."

"Thank you, but if it's the Almighty's will that I succeed, luck won't be necessary."

"And if your plans don't line up with the Almighty's?"

"Then, I will find another way. The Almighty does not close a door without opening a window. But I feel the path I'm contemplating is the right one. Lyonesse consciously rejected the spiritual and physical trappings of the empire so it could look toward the future. The Order must sever its connection with the past as well, or we will become worse than irrelevant."

"And what is worse than irrelevant? Or should I not ask?"

"We become a threat to the republic."

DeCarde smirked. "Finally, something we can agree on."

— 50 —

"You're looking well, sir." Brigid DeCarde smiled at Jonas Morane as she climbed out of the staff car that brought her from Government House to Vanquish Bay. She was traveling without a retinue, not even Commander Lutzow, and her close protection team had joined Morane's in watching over his estate the moment her aircar crossed its perimeter.

"Looks can be deceiving and don't call me sir. I think we presidents can use our first names in public as well as in private, protocol be damned. Congratulations, by the way. I remember you weren't keen to take the job, but the senate chose wisely."

She made a distinctly unpresidential face. "Thanks, I think."

Morane gestured at the gaping front door to his house, where Emma Reyes waited.

"Please come in. It's been too long."

"You missed a lot during your enforced timeout."

"Apparently." Morane and Reyes led her to the solarium, where a tray with drinks waited. "I'm still catching up. I understand your nomination to the presidency went unchallenged."

DeCarde sat in what was once Gwenneth's favorite chair and accepted a chilled glass of white wine.

"Viktor Arko couldn't drop his candidacy fast enough, seeing as how he was tainted by association with Stearn, the friar-assassin. And with Charis dead, that left the acting incumbent once most senate challengers financed by Hecht and his cronies either dropped out or lost their bids. Say what you like about Arko, he's a shrewd operator who knows when to fold his cards." She took an appreciative sip. "It seems that I am, in the opinion of certain political analysts, what is known as the steady hand on the tiller steering our ship of state."

"And those analysts aren't wrong. You'd have been my personal pick if it weren't for my conviction an outgoing president shouldn't put forward the name of his or her successor even indirectly, despite Elenia Yakin's discrete lobbying on my behalf. I'm not surprised Viktor backed away. He and I may not agree on much, but he has good instincts, the sort that keep him out of trouble both politically and personally. I may even go so far as crediting him with a personal sense of honor."

"Not me, but that's beside the point. I doubt he'll seek public office again. And how are you feeling?"

Morane took a sip from his glass and shrugged.

"Physically, I'm fine, though I need to rebuild my muscle mass after so long in a hospital bed. Emma's making sure I exercise religiously for at least two hours every day. She installed a gym in one of the empty bedrooms and asked the groundskeeping staff to cut a running path along the bay."

He fell silent, as if searching for words.

"But there's an emptiness inside me, a chunk of myself missing. I still have my memories and my emotions, and my thought patterns seem intact, yet I feel like a shadow of who I once was. Sister Amelia tells me that in time, the emptiness will fill up as I keep on living, and my soul finds renewed purpose. It won't be the same, but I'll no longer qualify as the hollow man. She's quite the mind-meddler herself, our Amelia. I doubt I'd have recovered this much without her help. We had long discussions about her part in the Stearn Roget saga, and she now sees matters the same way as Marta."

He gave DeCarde a crooked grin.

"Yes, I realize you trust them even less now that Marta revealed their innermost secrets, but keep in mind Stearn was an anomaly, one which will not repeat itself. The Order has been instrumental in helping us build a resilient Lyonesse in a galaxy gone mad. We mustn't let one deranged friar destroy everything."

"Oh, I understand that. We need them just as they need us. But no more picking up wild talents in ruined star systems and unleashing their pent-up abilities."

"That lesson will become part of the Order's Rule, believe me. Emma and I spent a few evenings here watching the sunset with Marta, discussing the future since my release from the hospital. She has a clear vision of what the Order should be and the will to make it happen. Mind you, we won't be leaving this branch of the wormhole network in our lifetimes or even our children's lifetimes, what with the Barbarian Plague ravaging humanity."

"I wouldn't be so sure. That ship full of undamaged bodies killed by the pathogen rather than our gunfire is giving the university's researchers, including some damn good Order of the Void virologists, undreamed of insight into the plague. They figure the virus is probably close to burning itself out if it hasn't already. Biowarfare agents by their very nature shouldn't be persistent, otherwise what's the use, right? Turns out, we've been overestimating the time the virus remains live. The various intrusions weren't from the same outbreak but different ones. That last bunch was infected long after the first one appeared at

Outer Picket. Besides, chances are good infected barbarians didn't spread the plague beyond the Coalsack. They only came to Lyonesse in such numbers because we're the last bastion of civilization for hundreds of light-years."

"What about an antiviral?"

"That's the wonderful news. They figure another two to three months, although there's no way of testing it on anything more than lab-grown human tissue. So even if it proves effective under those circumstances, we can't change our policy on incoming starships."

DeCarde sipped her wine, eyes on the shimmering waters of the bay.

"Now that you're officially an elder statesman, can I ask you for a few favors?"

"Of course. Anything."

"Since I don't trust the Order of the Void, will you be my intermediary with Abbess Marta?"

"Certainly, though since she's withdrawn the Order from the Estates-General and every other secular body not concerned with medicine, psychology, religious matters, or teaching, you won't see or speak with her much in any case. She plans on returning the Brethren to their monastic roots and undoing centuries of increasingly secular involvement in human affairs."

Morane paused for a few seconds.

"I don't think I ever told you, but long ago, when Marta first arrived on Lyonesse, Gwenneth told me she would play a big role in Lyonesse's future. That she might be charged with protecting the spark that saves humanity from eternal darkness. Maybe we're witnessing Gwenneth's prophecy come to life."

He shrugged again.

"I was never one for mysticism, but I must confess there's something about our new *Summus Abbatissa* that transcends what most of us consider normal. You said a few favors. What else?"

"The Lyonesse Defense Force Command and Staff College. Will you become its first chancellor?"

Morane gave her a surprised look.

"You're not putting a flag or general officer in charge?"

"I've decided I will reserve the position for retired flag or general officers. More stability, less internal politics. You'll be reporting to a board of governors named by the Defense Secretary and appointed by yours truly. The Chief of the Defense Staff has the final say on curriculum, the appointment of uniformed staff members, and the budget, but the chancellor can appeal decisions with which he disagrees."

"I accept, but you already figured I would."

"Jonas Morane spending his days gardening or playing the boulevardier in downtown Lannion simply doesn't compute. The first intake is in three months; the facilities are almost built; Defense Secretary Bryner has a list of proposed civilian and military staff waiting for your approval, and Adrienne Barca signed off on the curriculum you proposed last year."

"Reginus Bryner came out of retirement? I'm impressed by your powers of persuasion."

"Don't be. He wanted the job but wouldn't say anything while I had it."

"That's our Reginus." Morane raised his glass. "I can't believe I didn't do so yet, but I propose a toast to President Brigid DeCarde. The republic is in good hands."

"Hear, hear." Emma Reyes imitated him. "To our president."

They took a sip, then she said, "I'd like to propose the next toast to a friend whose absence leaves both of us feeling hollow. I know Jonas misses Gwenneth something fierce, though he won't admit it. We both do. She was a steadfast friend."

Morane nodded.

"Aye, from the moment she first boarded *Vanquish*."

DeCarde raised her glass.

"To Gwenneth. I'm sure the Almighty took good care of her soul."

"To Gwenneth."

Reyes and Morane raised their glasses as well, and DeCarde could have sworn she saw a bit of moisture in the corners of Morane's eyes.

"Finally, to the Republic of Lyonesse," he said. "Long may she shine as a beacon for humanity's rebirth."

Ashes of Empire continues with
Imperial Echoes

About the Author

Eric Thomson is the pen name of a retired Canadian soldier with thirty-one years of service, both in the Regular Army and the Army Reserve. He spent his Regular Army career in the Infantry and his Reserve service in the Armoured Corps. He worked as an information technology specialist for several years before retiring to become a full-time author.

Eric has been a voracious reader of science fiction, military fiction, and history all his life. Several years ago, he put fingers to keyboard and started writing his own military sci-fi, with a definite space opera slant, using many of his own experiences as a soldier for inspiration.

When he is not writing fiction, Eric indulges in his other passions: photography, hiking, and scuba diving, all of which he shares with his wife.

Join Eric Thomson at http://www.thomsonfiction.ca/

Where you will find news about upcoming books and more information about the universe in which his heroes fight for humanity's survival.

Read his blog at https://ericthomsonblog.wordpress.com

If you enjoyed this book, please consider leaving a review on Goodreads or with your favorite online retailer to help others discover it.

Also by Eric Thomson

Siobhan Dunmoore

No Honor in Death (Siobhan Dunmoore Book 1)
The Path of Duty (Siobhan Dunmoore Book 2)
Like Stars in Heaven (Siobhan Dunmoore Book 3)
Victory's Bright Dawn (Siobhan Dunmoore Book 4)
Without Mercy (Siobhan Dunmoore Book 5)
When the Guns Roar (Siobhan Dunmoore Book 6)

Decker's War

Death Comes But Once (Decker's War Book 1)
Cold Comfort (Decker's War Book 2)
Fatal Blade (Decker's War Book 3)
Howling Stars (Decker's War Book 4)
Black Sword (Decker's War Book 5)
No Remorse (Decker's War Book 6)
Hard Strike (Decker's War Book 7)

Commonwealth Constabulary Casefiles

The Warrior's Knife – Case #1

Ashes of Empire

Imperial Sunset (Ashes of Empire #1)
Imperial Twilight (Ashes of Empire #2)
Imperial Night (Ashes of Empire #3)

Ghost Squadron

We Dare (Ghost Squadron No. 1)

Manufactured by Amazon.ca
Bolton, ON

13229184R00221